The Gordon Place

The Gordon Place

ISAAC THORNE

Lost Hollow Books
Franklin, Tennessee

ISBN 978-1-938271-45-8 (Paperback Edition)
ISBN 978-1-938271-46-5 (eBook Edition)
ISBN 978-1-938271-47-2 (Hardcover Edition)

Library of Congress Control Number 2019934166

Cover design by Paula Rozelle Hanback
www.paulahanback.com

Published in the United States of America
First printing April 2019

Published by Lost Hollow Books
PO Box 1193
Franklin, TN 37065

www.isaacthorne.com
www.losthollowbooks.com

PRAISE FOR ISAAC THORNE

Isaac Thorne has written a collection of short horror
stories... with a large canvas and a colorful palette.
Different types of horror are explored fully, with a killer
style. (review of *Road Kills*)

—JIM UHLS
screenwriter of *Fight Club*

You'd be hard-pressed to find that much
entertainment for a dollar anywhere else.
(review of *Diggum*)

—DANGER SLATER
author of *I Will Rot Without You* and *Impossible James*

I'm convinced Isaac could be the next great
horror writer. (review of *Diggum*)

—DAVE KARNER
horror filmmaker and SCRM Radio contributor

Thorne has a nice writing style that "shows"
rather than "tells" and you'll feel and see every
bump under granny's wheels...
(review of *Decision Paralysis*)

—JOANIE CHEVALIER
author of *Heads Will Roll* and *Deadly Dating Games*

For the misunderstood kids,
even the ones
who have done bad things.

Prejudice is a burden that confuses the past, threatens the future, and renders the present inaccessible.

—Maya Angelou

In every conceivable manner, the family is link to our past, bridge to our future.

—Alex Haley

What is past is prologue.

—William Shakespeare

AUTHOR'S NOTE

The villain of this story is a man who is full of rage and hate. He is a product of a failure in American culture that, until recently, many of us thought was on the decline. It is important for you, the reader, to know that a significant portion of the following story takes place inside this hateful man's head. As a result, parts of this story contain scenes of physical abuse, racial slurs, homophobic rants, and misogynistic opinions. These scenes are intended to demonstrate the extent of this character's hate and ignorance and explain the choices he makes. They are in no way intended to be an endorsement of such behavior or thought patterns.

Hate is no path to a well-lived life.

Love each other.

CHAPTER ONE

"**N**o wonder they think it's haunted," he said to no one in particular. And he was right. It *was* no wonder the local young folks traded chilling tales about agonized screams echoing from behind the dilapidated old structure's walls in the dark of night. There was nothing about the old place that was not sinister.

The clouded dome on the lone security light that stood at the foot of the driveway hung askew on its hinge, providing no security and moaning creepy, creaking complaints at every cold autumn gust. Graham Gordon regarded the light for a moment, then stretched his left arm into the passenger window of his twenty-year-old Toyota Tacoma pickup and snagged his iPhone from its place on the seat. He dialed the town administrator's office. Empty or no, the old house was still private property. No light at the road was an open invitation for hoodlums and hobos to use it as a hangout, something Graham could not abide even if he weren't town constable. It was his place now, after all.

"Patsy," he said when the harried voice on the other end of the line finally answered the ring, "I'm out at the old house on Hollow Creek. Can we get the power company out here to fix the security light?"

There was a short pause. Graham could hear the shuffling of papers in the background. "I'm sorry, what did you say?" Patsy's voice came back to him some distance from the receiver. She had him on speakerphone so she could focus on something else.

Graham sighed. Her work hours for the week were waning fast, and Patsy had obviously already checked out for the weekend. He started over. "It's Graham Gordon," he said. "Your duly elected constable? I need you to call the power company and get someone out to Hollow Creek to fix the streetlight. It's broken."

The paper shuffling stopped. "Oh. The haunted house." She sounded closer now, and her last was followed by a click as she swapped the speakerphone feature for the normal hands-on mode.

Graham rolled his eyes. "It's not haunted. I own it."

"Doesn't mean it's not haunted, dear," Patsy replied musically. "It's almost Halloween, after all. I know where you are. I'll take care of it. Oh, speaking of which, I need to tell you about who I'm meeting tonight. I meant to ask you before you left today if it's ok for Channel—"

"Gotta go."

Graham tapped the End button, cutting her off. He tossed his iPhone through the passenger window of his pickup and onto the seat, glad to be rid of the encounter and especially delighted to be rid of the device. He caught sight of himself in the passenger-side mirror as he stepped away from the pickup. The man who looked back at him from his own hazel eyes was rounder than he usually thought of himself, with sandy hair that contained a hint of red. He looked tired. More tired than normal. There was a puffy dark circle under each eye. The scar his dad had made under the right one stood out against his flesh. Graham fingered it, watched it turn white under the pressure, and then released it. It filled and restored itself rapidly with the weight of his index finger gone.

Before the election, Graham had thought those circles were side-effects of spending too many work hours staring at computer screens while troubleshooting technical problems at the Media Place Smarty Desk way over in Hollow River. He fixed other people's computer problems for a living before he became constable. Now he'd made himself responsible for their real-life problems too. Mostly that terrified him. But in at least one way—the way that he and his counsellor had tried to convince him was the best way to frame it—he was fine with it. Being constable was at least different, maybe even a fresh start. He hated having the weight of the modern world's technology in his life as much as having that iPhone in his pocket. Returning to his roots on Hollow Creek Road in Lost Hollow felt like a reprieve from modernity. It was a psychological return to a time before cell phones and social media and twenty-four-seven cable news.

A small part of him regretted hanging up on Patsy, the town administrator and very nearly the only other Lost Hollow town employee, but it had sounded like she was about to try to dump a new to-do on him late on this Friday afternoon. It created anxiety in him the same way that, without fail, a problem customer walking up to the Smarty Desk at closing time on a Friday night created anxiety. Right now Graham wanted to concentrate only on the task ahead of him.

After a beat, he swallowed his regret and allowed himself to drink in the rest of the sight. The driveway was short and rose at a slight angle toward the house. The surface had long been washed away. The earth it had covered was rutted, battered by season upon season of torrential Southern thunderstorms. Graham could see a hint of the path that once upon a time was a hard-compacted trail of reddish-orange Tennessee chert. Peppered here and there along it were footprints and more than a few meandering pawprints, the former from the local teen nightlife and the latter left by the local Lost Hollow wildlife no doubt. A few more years of neglect and the driveway would end up entirely reclaimed by nature. It already bore patches of overgrown clumps of Kentucky fescue that had turned brown and bent over in the wake of autumn's arrival.

The quarter-acre plot of land surrounding the old home had once been a neatly kept Eden, at least in his childhood memories. The grass had been evenly trimmed under a mini-forest of enormous shade trees. Near the back of the lot had stood a swing set from which he'd spent many a summer afternoon pumping his legs until he'd climbed so high in the sky he thought he might just loop the loop. Thirty years on, the yard had become a pale greenish yellow field of grass and armpit-high cattails, many of them drooping or collapsed from the weight of their own overgrown heads. Some of the shade trees still loomed there, but they looked smaller now, dwarfed by the overgrowth. One of them was split in half by what must have been a lightning strike. The swing set was long gone. He had no idea what had happened to it. Probably stolen and carted off for scrap metal at some point over the years. Graham made a mental note to hire someone to bush-hog the place. He might also make next spring the one in which he bought a lawnmower.

The house itself put the final touches on the creepy vision before him. Straight out of *The Addams Family*, the two-story Victorian Gothic farmhouse towered over the surrounding landscape, its clapboard siding flecked and blotchy from years of unmaintained wear. The front door stood half open under the front porch gable, revealing a darkened interior that might as well have been a hole straight into the vacuum of space. Graham blinked and, for a second, thought he caught sight of a figure peering out at him from beyond the threshold. Then it was gone. *Tired*, he thought. *Just tired. That's all.*

Three of the four evenly spaced rectangular windows that lined the first floor bore spidery cracks and jagged holes, no doubt the work of some kid bored out of his mind by living along this stretch of barren country road. The fourth window had been gutted almost entirely. Only a single vicious looking spike jutted upward from its frame.

The second floor, by contrast, sported three cathedral-shaped windows, two symmetrically positioned on each side of the gable above the front porch and one directly in the center. Ghostly white linen sheers still hung in those windows, even after all these years of empty abandonment. Their tops were stretched across the width of each window.

The center window's drape flowed straight down, shutting out the view. One side of each sheer on the outside windows was tied all the way back at the vertical center of the window frame. The effect that it created was of a pair of jack o'lantern eyes cut to the left over the triangle nose of the gable and the gaping, ragged toothed maw formed by the windows and door on the first floor. Graham thought it was an appropriate look for the place given the season. The sheer in the right window fluttered and settled as he watched, as if something had brushed past it.

Indeed, he thought, the house looked like a screaming kind of place. No less so because it happened to be the abandoned childhood home of one Graham Gordon, the newly elected constable of a sleepy little Southern burg known as Lost Hollow. Graham hitched up the waistband of his town issue beige, braved the stroll through what remained of the old driveway, and placed a hand on the rough wood of the weather-beaten front door. The gable windows had not looked broken. He doubted the wind had moved that sheer. Maybe someone was inside after all.

"Hello?" He shoved the door all the way back against the wall so what remained of the afternoon light forced the inner darkness backward a pace. He jiggled the interior doorknob as he stepped inside. It would not turn. The bolt was lodged inside its housing in the door. There would be no means of locking the rapscallions out of it tonight. "Is anyone here?" His voice bounced off the walls of the empty hallways inside. "Constable!"

There was no answer, save for the scratching sounds of what might have been a family of rats scurrying around the aging supports in the walls. He stopped to listen. It sounded to him more like the clawing was coming from beneath the hardwood floor. There was also the crunch of broken glass under his boot when he stepped over the threshold. A quick look down revealed the shattered remnants of a Budweiser bottle, its label still valiantly clinging to the shards. More bottles, some whole and some broken, lay scattered about the interior. The golden late afternoon light glinted off them as it beamed through the door behind him, light that once upon a time would have been filtered through the front yard shade trees.

"Stupid kids."

That same light from the setting sun elongated his shadow across some of the broken glass and down the ancient oak floor of the entry hall. Ages of dust had settled there. There were dozens of impressions of footprints in the whitish blanket created by the fallout. Some of those prints were coated in a second, finer layer of dust. Others, larger ones that appeared to have been made by the thick rubber soles of someone's work boots, looked more recent. Within the tread marks of those prints, the floor was pristine. Graham glanced at his own feet. He braced himself against the hall wall and hoisted his right foot, which he supported around the ankle with his left hand. The newer footprints were perhaps a size larger than his own, but they could have been made by a pair of Wolverines, just like the ones on his own feet.

He slid his Maglite out of the holster at his hip. The weight of it was comforting in his hand. He gripped its shaft in his right fist and switched it on, steadying it at

shoulder height and shining the beam along the path of
dusty footprints. Several paces down the hall, the prints
veered off in all directions: some toward the kitchen, some
toward the formal dining area and the living room, others
toward the stairs that led to his old bedroom on the second
floor. It was difficult to tell which sets of prints had gone
where because whoever had been there had apparently
toured the entire house, leaving overlapping trails in the
dust as he (*or she?*) crisscrossed the hallway. Curiously, the
prints leading from the front door into the entry hall did
not overlap with a set of departing ones. It was as if whoever
had most recently trespassed on his abandoned childhood
estate had never left.

A final trail—one created by the larger pair of
Wolverines—petered out in front of a small plank door that
was inset into the same wall that formed the back of the
stairs to the upper floor. Graham remembered that door
well. It used to open onto a second, more rickety set of stairs
leading down and ending in a simple old-fashioned cellar. It
was a mostly underground cool spot where, in the old days,
it might have been convenient to store that autumn's potato
harvest or any other vegetable that needed to be guarded
against ruin by winter freezes or preserved from early rot
by the blistering heat and stifling humidity of late summer.

The cellar also made a damn near perfect place for a ten-
year-old boy to lay low while his enraged drunken father
paced the house, slapping his biggest leather belt against
his tree trunk thighs and threatening at the top of his voice
to "beat some sense into that lazy good for nothin' limp-
dick son of mine." His thundering footsteps boomed up

and down the entry hall. Each thud felt like it ricocheted against the walls of Graham's skull. If Graham were able to remain silent, the old man would eventually become either too drunk or too tired to care where he'd hidden. He'd settle down and go away. And forget.

Most of the time, he'd pass out on the couch, belt loosely gripped in one factory-chafed hand and an empty bottle of Budweiser dangling precariously from the other, long before he ever thought to look for the boy in the black dank of the cellar. On rarer occasions, a cough or a sneeze was enough to tip off the older Gordon to his young son's whereabouts. He'd tear open the door, stomp down those stairs, and drag the much younger version of Lost Hollow's new constable out by his hair, yanking some of it out of his head by the root.

"I told you never to come down here!" he'd roar. "You're gonna wish I never found you, boy!"

Then the belt would come down and lash him.

Across the right side of his face.

Across the left side of his face.

Across his ribs, butt, and thighs.

The *whip-crack* of the leather tore at his skin, sometimes ripping it open in thin slashes around his cheekbones. To this day, he bore that tiny grubworm-shaped scar under his right eye from one of those beatings. Graham again ran the tips of his fingers along its length. It felt larger than it looked these days. That one he got for forgetting to let Butch, his English bulldog, out to pee. The poor old thing had left a huge, sticky puddle just inside the front door, along with fresh scratch marks in the door's finish from where he'd been trying to alert someone of his urgency.

The elder Gordon had stepped in the yellowish ick upon arriving home that evening, a bottle of brew in hand and already drunk out of his mind. Graham had been lucky to not have lost the eye above that scar that night, not to mention his life.

He glanced at the open front door behind him. He couldn't see them from this angle, but the back of the old door probably still bore Butch's claw marks. The poor old fella had not been as lucky as his owner. Graham had found the dog's pummeled corpse laying on the front porch the next day. Butch's tongue protruded from his mouth and lay flat against the wood. Dried blood was caked on top of his head and had run in rivulets from various injuries in his face. It looked as if his skull and the bones of his face had been bashed in with some kind of blunt object. What muzzle the little guy had had was all but missing, revealing a large open cavity young Graham believed was a sinus. It might have been one of his dad's beer bottles that had done the damage. Broken fragments of one lay scattered about the body.

He'd buried the dog in the backyard that afternoon, fashioning a makeshift cross out of two fallen branches from a nearby walnut tree and a spare pair of shoelaces he'd found in his sock drawer. He'd never actually been to church. Sunday mornings were sleep-it-off time in the Gordon household. The cross was more of a warning for others to not disturb the remains than any kind of desperate hope that his friend might know a better existence on the other side of the dark curtain. The dog might still be buried at the back of the lot, alongside the edge where the clearing ended and the woods began. He would try to remember to look for the marker before he left, although he did not hold out much hope it would still be there.

The old man's attempts to relieve whatever shred of conscience he bore always dominated the next day's first meal (typically it was lunch because the elder Gordon sawed the logs of sobriety until at least 11 a.m. on weekends). No matter which way things had gone the night before, the excuses were as reliably forthcoming as the morning sun. "Your mother's gone, son. Run off with a nigger man." Graham always winced when his father said the *n*-word, even when it was only the memory of his father's voice. It was one of those words the elder Gordon spat at shout volume, even if he said it in the middle of an otherwise toneless sentence. He couldn't help himself. "I can't keep the place up all by myself. I have to count on you. And if I can't count on you, then I have to *make* you do what I tell you to do. I can tell you right now you don't ever want me to have to *make* you."

Thinking back on it, as he often did in the wee hours of an anxious, sleepless night, Graham sometimes wondered if his dear old dad wasn't more insane than alcoholic. No matter how many times he discovered Graham in that cellar, Lee Gordon would never think to look for him there the next time he tied one on. Graham also wondered why his teachers never said anything about the massive bruises and swollen shut eyes he often sported at school. Lee coached him to say that he'd fallen down the stairs, or got hit playing baseball in the backyard, or some other ridiculously unbelievable lie. But it turned out he'd never had to say any of those things, never had to explain how he'd managed to get the marks on his face. No one ever asked.

Graham shivered. That booming, angry voice of his father Lee, now twenty years in his grave, was still able to cow him, even when it was only inside his own head. He heard it most on the off days, those times when no amount of the prescription Xanax his counsellor prescribed seemed capable of warding off anxiety, the foreboding paranoia that some-one, everyone, wanted to hurt him. Everyone tried to bully him for his inadequacy, the sense of low self-esteem that always accompanies a man who has spent too much of his life trying to stay out of the way. He heard it on those long, desperate days when he wondered how he had ever managed to dupe the good people of Lost Hollow into electing him their constable.

He'd launched the whole campaign on a lark, in an unusual moment of supreme overconfidence following a first date with an online match from Hollow River who had turned out to have an over-the-top interest in commu-nity politics. Perhaps, then, it hadn't been overconfidence at all, but overcompensation for his *lack* of confidence. Not to mention his simple-minded and overtly masculine desire to impress the pretty girl. He had never intended to actu-ally serve as Lost Hollow's constable, especially after his match had sailed away mid-campaign in search of more exciting waters with a single attorney from her own town who was running for state senate. In his naivete, Graham had deactivated his online dating account when he thought things were serious between him and Katie. She apparently had not. Now here he was, unexpectedly elected and trying to fake it until he makes it in a law enforcement role he understood only regarding the description he'd read in a Wikipedia article.

Why did they pick me?

YOU WERE THE ONLY ONE WHO WANTED THE JOB, IDIOT, the voice of Lee Gordon chided in his head.

It was true. No one had run against Graham, ridiculous as it might have looked for someone in a help desk position at a major retail electronics chain to pursue a career in law enforcement. He didn't even own a gun. Didn't even know how to load one, much less aim and fire one. The city was paying for him to take a gun safety and training course, but the classes hadn't started yet. For now, at least, he was an *unarmed* and inexperienced law enforcement officer. How he was to go about enforcing laws without the protection of a piece (did they still call them *pieces?*), he didn't know. He could have simply quit, resigned the position as soon as he'd won it. But that would have made him look even more the wimp. He'd made this bed, albeit with help from Katie, and how he had to lie in it and pray he didn't shit it.

The only net gain for Graham, if it could be considered such, that had come out of the election so far was that he had been able to use the position to convince the town to turn his old homestead over to him for a song and a promise he'd clean up the blight. That had been another lark. In the same town board meeting that had seen him sworn in as constable there had appeared on the agenda a plan to demolish the old place as a means of curbing the juvenile delinquency it seemed to entice. The rumors being spread by the kids in town had reached the board's ears, and they had come to the same conclusion he had: the place was turning into an attraction for vagrants and ne'er-do-wells. Therefore, tear it down.

When the time came for public input on the matter, he'd suddenly found himself standing—without having previously planned to do so—and arguing that the place had sentimental value for him and that he'd like a shot at restoring it. He might even turn it into some kind of tourist spot, an idea he'd come to by way of town administrator Patsy Blankenship, she whom he'd hung up on moments ago. She had already renovated one old local homestead into a bed and breakfast that hosted the occasional guest or local event. The board had balked at his idea at first, but after he'd promised to either clean up the blight or hand the old Gordon place back to the town for demolition within a year, they'd relented. Now he owned the home: a shelter for rats, snakes, vagrants, and bored teenagers. He had no idea where to begin.

Graham pushed the thoughts away. This was no time to go second-guessing his life choices and cost himself what little nerve he had summoned to search for trespassers. He sidled up the hall. The back of his shirt created a loud scraping sound against the faded and peeling *fleur-de-lis* wallpaper covering the entry hall, a remnant of his mother's New Orleans roots. He left his own narrow trail of Wolverine sole prints in the dust on the floor, carefully avoiding stepping on the ones left by the previous visitor. The physical memories of life in the house came flooding back to him. The sound of his footsteps on the hardwood floor. The sound of his *father's* footsteps. Even the scrape of the wallpaper against the fabric of his shirt bubbled up memories of him dashing all over the house, running his hands and fingers over the walls as he did, just as any normal wild young boy might do.

The tiny hook and eye latch that had been meant to secure the cellar door was already undone when he got there. Graham didn't know whether his father had initially installed that latch, but he'd always thought it a silly and unnecessary addition. The door to the cellar was no more than three uneven slats of painted pine carelessly supported along their backs by two horizontal two-by-fours. Large gaps between each slat rendered useless any attempt to keep the cooler air of the cellar out of the entry hall by just shutting the door. Besides, it had always managed to swing shut and stay closed on its own—even unlatched—which was one more reason the cellar had made for such an excellent hiding place.

A small wooden cabinet knob was mounted a couple of inches below the hook. Graham grabbed it and pulled. The door swung open easily on its spring hinges and without much complaint about the new tension; surprising after so many years of disuse. The ray from his Maglite spilled into the opening and revealed three splintery and slowly disintegrating steps, approximately one-quarter of the familiar set of plank stairs leading from the mouth of the door before vanishing into the damp darkness below. Graham felt for the light switch just inside the cellar door and flipped it on, but it produced nothing. He'd had service activated so he could begin work on the place. Maybe the power company hadn't gotten around to it yet. That would certainly explain the state of the security light out front.

"Hello?" he shouted into the depths of darkness. "Lost Hollow Constable! Is anyone down there?"

There was no answer.

Graham stepped through the door. He'd covered only one tread before the sound of the creaking staircase started to get to him. There he paused, not allowing the door to swing shut behind him and not liking the soft and spongy feel of the tread on which he stood. It had much more give in it than he remembered from his youth.

From this position, the narrow beam of his Maglite enabled him to see the end of the staircase, but nothing beyond. The final step looked black and almost completely rotted away. The one above it didn't appear to be in much better shape. If he went forward, he risked breaking those steps, which would make climbing out of the cellar much more difficult. If he didn't go on, and someone was trapped down here, he might lose his job in disgrace. Worse, a real law enforcement officer, like a county sheriff's deputy, might end up investigating the "screams" and finding a dead body he'd missed out of fear, in which case he could at the very least be accused of neglecting his duties as an officer of the peace.

Maglite secured in his left hand, Graham pawed at his right hip, immediately taking comfort in the shape of the county issue radio clipped to his belt. He ran his fingers along the top of the device until they closed around the volume knob, which he turned to the right. A thin *click* and a spurt of white noise erupted through the tomb-like silence of the old house. It vanished just as quickly, leaving in its wake the distinct hum of radio silence. Even so, it was reassuring that he had not only remembered to carry his direct connection to the Hollow County Sheriff's Department inside with him but it also appeared to be in proper working order.

"Let's hear it for technology. Thank God."

From somewhere inside his head, he thought, the darkness replied: *GOD AIN'T GOT NOTHING TO DO WITH IT.*

The next thing he felt was the bone-crunching shock of something blunt and heavy striking the back of his head. He heard what sounded like the shattering of thick glass. He was able to stay upright just long enough to feel what might have been a trickle of blood oozing from his scalp to the nape of his neck. A pair of unseen hands at his back thrust him into the darkness of the cellar, launching him down the full length of the rickety staircase. He fell forward, plummeting face first into the densely compacted earth beneath the house. The bridge of his nose exploded in a bright starburst of pain. His upper teeth crashed down on his lower lip, ripping open the pliable flesh. He felt an immediate swelling there. A thin stream of hot blood ran tear-like down his chin from the wound. Dimly, he heard the *crack* of splintered wood as his shins came down last, disintegrating the deteriorated lower steps in a fireworks show of wood rot and ancient dust.

His radio went flying when he hit. He heard it shatter in a hiss of static somewhere off to his right. The base of his Maglite struck the ground at the same time. It flew from his hand and bounced off the earth once, twice, and rolled some distance over the ground before coming to rest against the farthest cinder block wall of the cellar. The lamp behind the flashlight's lens flickered madly, creating a nauseating strobe effect, a stop-motion version of Graham's shadow on the wall beside him as he at first struggled to regain his feet and then gave up, collapsing flat to the earth.

The lamp finally steadied itself at a low burn, illuminating almost nothing about the cellar but the corner in which it had landed. It had come to rest too far from the limit of Graham's reach. He stretched his left arm out for it anyway, hopeful that the darkness had merely created some sort of illusion of depth. His fingers clawed at the dirt for a second or two before they ultimately surrendered and lay still.

Graham Gordon lay broken and exhausted on the black earth at the bottom of the cellar stairs. In the fading last rays of his dying Maglite, he saw an eye: a disembodied, full white orb broken by jagged lightning-shaped lines of red capillaries. The iris in the center of the eyeball was a murky dark brown color, unshining and nearly black. Its pupil was but a pinprick in the beam from the flashlight.

It stared at him from just beyond the edge of the darkness, unblinking.

"Dad?"

The world went dark.

CHAPTER TWO

Joe "Staff" Stafford turned up his nose as the HOLLOW COUNTY sign grew large in the windshield. He rode in the passenger's side of the ugly white Chevy S-10 pickup Channel 6 had assigned them for the week. A similar white topper with a common locking mechanism had been installed over the bed of the pickup to ensure that all of the station's heavy, outdated video journalism equipment remained unmolested by any nefarious members of the general public during their stay in this small redneck town. Staff had always found these types of security efforts especially hilarious since there were glass windows on every side of the topper and the Channel 6 logo was emblazoned on the pickup's hood, both its doors, and its tailgate. He could imagine a would-be thief approaching: "Oh, look! It's Channel 6's truck with some expensive, out-dated camera equipment! Oh, wait. No. Nevermind. There's a lock on it."

Staff's partner in crime for the weekend (his supervisor for this particular outing, really), reporter Afia Afton sat behind the wheel. Her eyes were on the road, and her long fingers with glossy black polished nails were curled around ten and two. She didn't see him sneer as they blew by the rusty old sign full of buckshot holes and half-buried in Virginia-creeper, but he hoped she could hear the vexation in his voice.

"This? This is what we drove fifty miles on a Friday afternoon to see? I'm going to fucking kill Joanie."

Afia scoffed. "It's just the county line. We have a few minutes before we hit Lost Hollow proper. I used to live around here, you know. Back then, the town was pretty much all woods and farmland except for the church, the school, and the cemetery. Those who weren't farmers worked at the carbon plant way over in Hollow River. There was a tiny public square in the middle, but it was mostly used for town offices and a couple of small mom and pop places. If you wanted to get gas or mail a package or buy groceries or see a movie you had to drive to Hollow River."

"Where the carbon plant was." He might have sounded bored. He didn't intend it, but he felt it.

"Right. It might still be that way, but I can't imagine that the kids who grew up here wouldn't have made some progress by now. Well, if there *were* any kids who grew up here."

"What do you mean?"

"I mean that the Lost Hollow I remember was aptly named because it was kind of a lost place. It's where people lived or died or disappeared without anyone noticing much one way or the other. Fuck, I was only eight years old when my mom vanished. Twelve when my dad went. If his murder hadn't been all over the news in Hollow River and the other bigger cities back then, I don't know what would've happened to me. I got lucky, I guess. Got into the system just when it became fashionable for rich white folks to foster orphaned black kids."

She sighed. Staff shifted uncomfortably in his seat. He hadn't known that about her parents, and he wasn't sure how, or if, he should respond. But at least he wasn't bored anymore.

"Don't get me wrong," Afia continued, "my foster parents were good people, not like the horror stories you hear from a lot of kids who got handed to abusers or straight-up predators in those days. They never adopted me, but they did see me through high school and four years of college. I doubt I'd be here if it weren't for them."

Staff laughed. "You mean back in Lost Hollow?"

"I mean in the news business, asshole." She smirked at him. "But there has to have been some progress here since then. I know it. We're booked at a bed and breakfast right in the middle of it, aren't we? That certainly wasn't here when I was a kid."

"Yeah," Staff said, his voice distant. "A bed and breakfast that just happened to be completely vacant in a supposedly haunted small town in the middle of October. I'm sure. I hope you brought something with some DEET in it. I sure as hell don't want to go home with Lyme Disease."

Afia rolled her eyes.

"It's October, Staff, like you said. The risk of you getting a tick bite out here is about as good as us getting real ghost footage this weekend. I'm not happy about having to come back here, either, but this woman we're meeting has Joanie convinced that there's a story to tell. People love to hear about ghost shit this time of year. I just hope we can come back with *something* because I never heard so much as a single disembodied 'boo' the whole time I lived here."

Staff grunted. "All I'm saying is that you wouldn't see 'Channel 6's Own Dan Matthews' running around a dusty old house and leaping at shadows on the nightly news. He reports on real stuff like government shutdowns and disasters and robberies and murders and Republican corruption."

"Dan sits behind the anchor desk. He doesn't actually *do* the field work anymore. I'm not even sure he'd remember how. Like I said, I'm not happy about it either, but I try to remember that there will come a day when we won't be the ones they send to cover the puff entertainment shit. Channel 6 has viewers out here. Probably someone complained that we never cover them, so this piece is supposed to be their fluffy little make-good for the small town on the big city news. There's not going to be any leaping at shadows if I have anything to say about it, and I do have something to say about it. This is my story now. We're going to talk to some townsfolk and explore a house or a cemetery so we can tell their tales and give the viewers something to talk about. If the town is lucky, they'll get a few tourist dollars out of it for Halloween, but we're not fucking *Ghost Adventures*."

That settled him a little. Afia was on the same page, then.

"Yeah. We're not fucking *Ghost Adventures*. I just feel like we should've graduated from stuff like this by now. I paid my dues with groundbreakings and artsy-fartsy feature stories and make-good puff pieces when I was a newspaper photographer, for Christ's sake. You wouldn't know it to look at the credits, though. *The Review* never gave credit for in-house photography to anything but STAFF. Everything always said STAFF PHOTO at the lower left, even though I was the only photographer on the payroll. That's why I adopted the nickname. If they're going to credit STAFF for every photo, I might as well be Staff."

Afia laughed. "You've only told me that story a hundred times."

"Yeah. A hundred times. I guess I'm still bent about it. I honestly thought video journalism would be a better gig. What does a guy with a good eye have to do to earn a little respect, anyway? If I didn't know Joanie better, I'd think she had something against gay guys. She's sending us into what I know is going to be a redneck pocket hell of backward racist conservatives."

Afia took her eyes off the road for the first time and looked at him wide-eyed. "You're gay?"

"Yes," Staff replied with a deliberate lisp. "Can't you tell? And you're an African American woman. This is not news to anyone who has been half awake since we were both hired."

Afia examined her own hands, still responsibly wrapped around ten and two on the steering wheel. "I'm black?" she said in mock astonishment. "Oh my. Maybe we'd better forget the DEET and go buy ourselves some camouflage and a gun rack instead."

"Afia—"

"No, seriously, don't judge the place like that before you've seen it. Yeah, a bunch of racists lived here when I was a kid, but it wasn't the loud-mouthed redneck Trump resurgent racist types. At least, I never saw them around town back then. I never met racists in that balls-out throwing shit at you while you're just trying to go to school way. It was more subtle than that here, more patronizing, I guess. They wouldn't call you names, but they'd assume you couldn't speak as eloquently as the white folks, so you'd get the part with the fewest lines in the school plays. Most of the other kids assumed we were poor, too, even though my dad worked at the same carbon plant in Hollow River that theirs did. I guess they figured a single black father household wouldn't hold onto money the way a lily-white nuclear family would. I don't know. I never asked."

He looked away from her, focusing on the toes of his own sneaker-clad feet. They were crossed at the ankles and propped on the dashboard in front of him. "I'm sorry, Afia. I was just trying to be funny. You mean to tell me that in the whole time you lived in this white-bread small town in the deep South that no one ever once threatened you or called you the n-word? Not once?"

"Tennessee is not the 'deep' South," Afia reprimanded. She thought for a second. "Well, there was this *one* guy." Her upper lip twisted into an angry sneer. "His last name was Gordon, I think. I don't remember his first name. He had a kid my age that used to come to school beat up all the time. We had a lot of problems with him for a while, but I guess I was too young to remember too much about all that. I know he hated my dad's guts, and I know my dad had to call the sheriff about him trespassing at our place more than once. It wasn't long after my mother disappeared that all the trouble started, I think. Dad never told me what it was all about, though. Just said some crazy alcoholic white man thought dad had wronged him somehow."

She shuddered.

"I do remember one night when he woke us up, standing on our front porch with a beer in one hand and a shotgun in the other. Let me tell you, you've never heard anything scary until you're awakened from a dead sleep in a quiet country house by the sound of someone trying to bash in the front door. I don't think I've ever been more scared in my life, not before then and not since. He kept pounding on the front door with the butt of that shotgun, screaming for my dad to come out and face him. My dad called the sheriff on him then, too.

"I was afraid he was either going to break down the door or start shooting up the place before they got there, but he never did. He took off running when the deputy arrived with his strobes flashing. Nobody ran after him, though. I don't know why. He just ran off into the woods behind our house and disappeared. My dad went down to the station the next day to press charges, thinking they'd go arrest Gordon at his house. The sheriff told him that more than likely it wouldn't amount to anything in a court of law. His word against my father's and the judge was as likely to believe Gordon over my father as the other way around. My dad figured it was because we were black. Some part of the white folks believed we probably deserved whatever it was this dude was holding against us."

Staff grimaced. "Must have been awful."

"It was. I always wondered whether that man had something to do with my dad's murder. They found him, my dad, at the base of that bullshit obelisk the Daughters of the Confederacy placed in the middle of the town square back in the early Sixties. The town administrator showed up to open the office for the day, and there was my dad, propped up against it like a wino passed out in an alley. Only the red stuff running down his shirt wasn't wine. It was blood. Whoever attacked him had sliced him from ear to ear. Some kind of hunting knife, probably. That's what the sheriff's department said, anyway."

There was a hitch in her voice. Staff opened his mouth to tell her that she didn't need to relive this horrible chapter of her life for his sake, but she started up again before the words formed on his lips.

"Not that they were much of a sheriff's department. There were never any suspects, at least not that they publicly named. No apparent motive other than hate. My dad's wallet was still in his pockets. His car was parked in one of the slots in front of the administrator's office, keys in the ignition, and had apparently been wiped clean of fingerprints. The only blood in it was his own.

"The sheriff said he thought the murder had been committed somewhere else, and that the killer had driven my dad's car with him in it to the town administrator's office and placed his body against the obelisk as some kind of racist insult or something."

"They never even questioned this Gordon dude?"

Afia shook her head. "Not that I know of."

"So what happened to him?"

She shrugged. "Dead, probably. He was kind of old even back then. Quite a bit older than my dad, for sure, even though he had a kid my age. He was a heavy drinker, too, from what I heard. I can't imagine he's still kicking around."

"You've never looked him up?"

She did not reply. After a beat, Staff let it be.

"So, Joanie knows you're gay?" Afia asked when another few minutes of uncomfortable silence had passed.

Staff laughed. "Everyone at the station probably knows it. I actually prefer it that way because of the times we're living in right now. I thought things were getting better under Obama, but now...well, now you have to be much more careful about where you work because the company could see your homosexuality as a public relations liability depending on the demographic they want to serve."

Afia nodded.

"That's what it comes down to, anyway," Staff continued. "You won't see Nike backing down from a Colin Kaepernick campaign because racist conservatives aren't their demographic. It's the same thing with places like Chick-Fil-A. You won't see them cozying up with outspoken liberal celebrity spokespeople because their base demographic is conservative Christian with a capital K. Corporate America is starting to choose tribes just like the American people have chosen tribes. There's no middle ground anymore."

He sighed. "That's why I told Joanie up front during my interview that I was gay. I don't think she could legally ask me about it, but that hasn't stopped other companies from finding reasons to fire someone like me over it. Religious freedom is just the latest excuse to discriminate. Trump had just been sworn in when I was interviewing for this job, so I told Joanie straight up that if my being gay was going to be a problem for them, I didn't want to even bother with the rest of the interview."

Afia cocked an eyebrow and cut her eyes at him. "What did she say?"

"Well, obviously, I was hired. I think she went to some of the higher-ups before they agreed to hire me, though. It was like I was a felon or something. She kind of lost her poker face when I brought it up, you know? I don't think sexual orientation had ever come up in any of her interviews before."

"It's a pretty effective ice-breaker. That's for sure. Here we are, by the way. We just passed Lost Hollow's city limits. We'll be in the town square in just a few."

"So," Staff said after another short pause. "When did you tell Joanie you were a black woman?"

Before Afia could reply, Staff felt his body lurch forward against the seatbelt, His head thrust forward toward the S-10's windshield. His feet were still propped on the dashboard, and it now felt like his toes might punch through the glass. He threw his hands in front of himself, bracing against his own knees because his legs were in the way of the glove compartment. Afia, on the other hand, held onto the steering wheel at arm's length, forcing her back into the bucket seat and locking her elbows in place. She was practically standing on the brake pedal.

The S-10 came to rest one hundred-eighty degrees into the oncoming lane, straddling the double yellow line in the center of the Hollow County stretch of SR-501. Behind it lay two new semicircular skid marks along the ancient gray pavement. Had she been a teenage white boy in Lost Hollow on a Saturday night in the late Eighties, she would have no doubt been congratulated on the least impressive donut of the evening.

Staff, whose shoulders were already feeling stiff following his brace for impact, glared at her with wide eyes, his mouth hanging open. "What. The. Fuck?" he managed.

"I'm sorry," Afia said, her voice shaky and too loud. "Oh, God, I hope I didn't hit it. I hope I didn't hit it."

She fought with her seatbelt, popped open the driver's side door, and leaped out of the S-10. Staff watched her circle the vehicle, first examining the front tires, then the rear. She was frowning. Staff rolled down the window.

"Afia? What the fuck?"

"I...I'm not sure." She circled the S-10 once more and then climbed into the driver's seat. "Something ran out in front of us. Looked like a dog. Black. I was afraid I was going to hit it. I guess I didn't."

"We probably would've felt it if you had."

"Yeah, probably. It darted out from that road back there, just as we passed the city limits sign. It was just this little black coat of fur on four stumpy legs. I guess it was a dog. I'm not sure. Something was weird about its head, though. It didn't look like any other dog I've ever seen."

"Maybe it was a badger or a groundhog or something."

"Maybe. Are there black groundhogs that run on dog legs?"

Staff shrugged. "Well, at least we didn't hit whatever it was. We need to get the truck back into the right lane, though, don't you think? I'd hate for Channel 6 to have to shell out the big bucks for a new truck and new equipment because we were T-boned by a semi or something."

"Yeah." She shifted the S-10 into Reverse and straightened it into the correct lane. To their right lay a stretch of country lane that a faded green street sign identified as HOLLOW CREEK RD. A few notches below that sign was another, more faded yellow sign that merely read DEAD END. Staff jerked a thumb at them.

"Does every place in this county have the word 'hollow' in the name?"

"Probably. It has a creepy quaint ring to it that the locals like. Makes them feel Colonial or some shit, though I can't imagine the town dates back much further than the early nineteenth century. We can ask when we get to the town square. The administrator is supposed to meet us at the B&B and give us some ideas about the best places to visit. Her name is Patsy. Sounded like a real Southern Belle on the phone. Stretched out her o sounds and skipped the l in some words."

"Creepy looking little dead-end road, that's for sure."

Afia glanced at the sign. "Yeah. Let's get out of here. If I remember, that's where that Gordon dude lived when I was a kid. Our house was through the woods behind his place. Our driveway connected to another road a mile or so down."

"That close?"

"Yeah. I think I've had all the memories of those days that I can stand for one day."

"You don't want to see your old place, since we're driving by?"

Afia looked at him, resentment behind her tired eyes. "No."

She shifted the S-10 into Drive and hit the gas, allowing Lost Hollow's city limits and the dead-end Hollow Creek Road to diminish in her rearview mirror. From his side of the truck, Staff watched it as well. For a second, just as they rounded a curve to the right, he thought he might have seen the creature they'd nearly struck, dog or not, poke its head out of the weeds and scrub along the side of SR-501 that lay opposite the Hollow Creek Road dead end. Then it was gone. It had either withdrawn into the scrub or was obscured by distance and the black capital letters at the bottom of the mirror that read OBJECTS IN MIRROR ARE CLOSER THAN THEY APPEAR.

I hope not, he thought, as the pickup rounded another curve and obscured the scene entirely from his view. *It's just as well with me if objects keep their distance while we're fifty miles away from home.*

A few minutes later, Afia relaxed her grip on the steering wheel a little, stretching her fingers against the warming rays of the autumn sun as it began to set behind a cluster of buildings that loomed large in the windshield as they approached.

"Finally," she said. "We're here."

CHAPTER THREE

His face hurt. Graham's bottom lip throbbed, and his chin felt wet, coated by a layer of blood that had run from his injured mouth. He grimaced, then opened and shut his jaw to make sure everything still worked. It did, but it was all sore. Even flaring his nostrils produced a sensation in his cheeks, not unlike the soreness one experiences in major body muscles after an impact in a car accident or an intense gym workout to which one is unaccustomed. The same discomfort assaulted his shoulders when he attempted to push himself up to his knees against the cold earthen floor of the cellar.

On his knees, Graham gingerly placed a hand on the back of his head where he'd felt the blunt object come down on him, then pulled it away with a wince and a sharp hiss. That hurt like hell, worse than the soreness from the fall.

His eyes had fluttered open in a blanket of complete darkness. The cellar had no windows, no door other than the one he had entered, and now probably only half its staircase. The uppermost segment of the stairs might still be intact, hanging precariously by whatever nails had been used to secure the stringers to the joists and the bottom of the door frame eight feet above his head. But the lower half he knew he had destroyed on the way down. He felt it and, moreover, saw it before his Maglite had died. Now that it was gone, whatever light there might be from the first-floor hallway glimmering through the planks of the cellar door and into this dungeon was not enough to enable him to see anything around him.

He was trapped, but at least he was able to move. There was that. The next question was how to find his way out of the cellar. Stupidly, he'd tossed his iPhone into the passenger seat of his Tacoma before he'd walked inside. He'd lately made a habit of leaving the damned thing where he wouldn't have convenient access to it if something more critical needed his attention. The danger, of course, being that he'd stop paying attention to the critical task to check his Twitter feed or Instagram account, on which he could boast all of ten followers. Usually, he would have locked the phone in his glove compartment or placed it in a lower pocket of a pair of cargo pants, where he couldn't feel its presence as much. This time, he'd tossed it through the window of his pickup, onto the seat, in his frustration with Patsy. He'd assumed he would only be inside the old place for a few minutes and was unlikely to encounter anyone on this lonely stretch of dead-end who might nab the phone, or even his pickup, for themselves.

"*Thit!*" he exclaimed to the darkness. His swollen and bruised lip had given him the thick and labored vocalizations of a dental patient suffering from paresthesia as the numbing agent begins to wear off. "Thit! I can't believe I did that."

From somewhere else, his father's voice boomed: *YEAH! PRETTY FUCKING THUPIDT YOU SISSY SACK OF SHIT.* The sound rang inside his skull like a fire engine, making his eyes vibrate in their sockets. The old house dust and debris in his sinuses rattled like the ball bearing in an empty can of spray paint. Pain like railroad spikes ripped through the flesh of his scalp and sent him face-forward to the floor, elbows out. He clenched the palms of his hands tightly against his temples. Saliva flooded his mouth from somewhere in the back of his throat, where a lump had formed that was threatening to spill the partially digested cheeseburger and onion rings he'd had for lunch. He crouched in the darkness on the cellar floor until the sensations finally began to subside.

"Concuthion," he said. "Maybe I have a concuthion."

MAYBE, the voice boomed in his head again. *OR MAYBE YOU'RE JUST A STUPID SACK OF SHIT!*

Graham winced again, slapping his palms against his temples, and rolled over on his side. He wanted to scream, but the pain in his head was too much. Only a squeaky moan escaped his lips. Sometime later, the pain receded once more, and he was able to return to his knees. A concussion. Yes. That would explain the ringing in his ears. And the nausea. And the pressure against his skull. It was a concussion. He just needed to remain awake until he could escape the cellar or until rescue arrived. He couldn't call for help because his radio lay shattered somewhere on the floor of the cellar along with his Maglite, and he didn't have his phone. Patsy had probably already left for the day, assuming Graham would reach out to the sheriff's department if he needed any assistance out here. Law enforcement and investigating potential trespassers on his own personal property was his job, after all, not hers.

A concussion didn't explain his father's voice in his head, which was excruciatingly louder now than it had been before his tumble into the cellar. He'd always been able to hear his dad berating him. Probably a result of some psychological side effect of the abuse he'd suffered at the hands of the angry—now dead—man when he was a child. That's what his counsellor suggested anyway. He'd never been physically hurt by it before, though. Emotionally? Psychologically? Sure. Who wouldn't be injured in those ways by the chronic berating voice of a long-dead parent stuck in one's head, a voice that pointed in perpetuity at every misstep and error in judgment as a lack of intellect? Psychologists would call it a product of anxiety. He'd been told that before. Obsessive compulsive disorder, for example, had been known to create critical voices in one's own head that way. Graham didn't know for sure whether he was afflicted by OCD. His counsellor hadn't diagnosed him with that so far. He knew only that the voice was real, and that now it felt more real than it ever had before.

There was also the disembodied eye he'd seen as the light from his Maglite died out. Do concussions cause weird visions like that? Maybe. Since he'd awakened, he hadn't heard any movements other than his own in the darkness. He hadn't felt any hands reach out from the blackness and latch themselves onto his arms or legs. He was pretty sure that meant he was alone down here. Except for the voice of his dead father in his head, of course.

Ok, he thought. *No more talking out loud if that's just going to bring on my dad's insults. Have to find a way out of here. It isn't helping that I can't see anything.*

Time to locate the Maglite. Maybe it wasn't busted beyond use. Maybe it just needed a good shake to reestablish a connection between the bulb and the batteries. He should have upgraded to an LED model when he was elected constable. He knew that. His old incandescent bulb Maglite had been with him since he'd learned to drive. Usually, he stowed it with the first aid kit behind the driver's seat in case of roadside emergencies. Lately, it had hung from his hip in a loop on his constable's utility belt. But he hadn't upgraded it yet. Therefore it was what it was. In this case, it was one more drop of woulda, coulda, shoulda in a stream of the stuff. He told himself that there was no use crying about it right now, although he was sure the voice of his father would berate him about it later.

Ignoring the pain in his shoulders and his knees, Graham began to feel his way around the dirt floor. His first task was to try to find a corner. He remembered the cellar as a nearly perfect square. If he could locate a right angle, he could provide himself with a solid starting point and a straight line guide to the opposite corner. From there he could continue to feel around the perimeter, testing the floor immediately beside the walls for the metal cylinder indicating he had located his light source. He would need to keep track of the corners in his head, start at one and increment the number each time he encountered another one. When he reached number four, he'd know he was back where he started.

If he didn't find the Maglite in his crawl around the perimeter, the task would get tougher. He'd heard that people who walk blind typically end up walking in circles. The flashlight had rolled and come to rest against one of the cinder block walls surrounding him. If it didn't turn up there, he could try to expand his search inward from the walls of the cellar, but he risked losing his place in the dark as he searched. That could end in him repeatedly covering the same ground over and over. The more he searched in circles without finding the Maglite, the more panicked he was likely to become, and the easier it would be to allow his father's voice in his head to attack again. Alternatively, he could stop crawling around, wait for the next morning's light, and hope Patsy would realize she hadn't heard from him lately. That might cause her to call the sheriff's department and send them looking for him. Except it had been Friday when he'd plummeted from the top of the cellar stairs. He had no idea how long he'd been unconscious, or even whether it was still Friday outside the cellar. Assuming it was still Friday, Patsy would not return to her office until eight o'clock on Monday morning. The fact that he wasn't sure about the extent of his own injuries after the fall was also a good reason to nix that option. It was up to him to conduct the search and maintain hold of his sanity in the process. It was *all* up to him.

He crawled.

An agonizing amount of time later, Graham felt the tips of his fingers brush against the first of the cinder block cellar walls. A wave of relief washed over him, temporarily replacing the pain and soreness in his shoulders and his head with the endorphins and subsequent euphoria of a breakthrough. The block felt rough and cold against his fingers. It was not a corner. He still needed to locate one of those right angles to get his bearings. But it was a wall nonetheless. If he followed it far enough, he would eventually find his perimeter starting point.

With his right hand pressed against the newly discovered wall and his left planted firmly on the earth, Graham crawled onward, parallel to the wall, using it to guide him. Now and then he plucked his hand from the wall and cautiously groped the air in front of him, seeking the perpendicular wall that would indicate he'd found the corner. The last thing he wanted to do was accidentally head-butt solid block while conducting his search, especially if he might already have suffered a *concuthion*. The memory of his inability to pronounce the word gave him pause. He waited, wincing and bracing himself for the head-exploding volume of a smart-ass retort from his dead father, but none came. Instead, his mind called forth the image of Judd Nelson's thug character Bender crawling through the school ductwork in that scene from *The Breakfast Club*, the one where he's telling himself a joke about the naked blonde who walks into a bar. It was a joke that had no punchline because Bender falls through the ductwork before he completes the gag. It was a distraction technique, that joke. It was something to fill the space in Bender's mind while his body propelled him forward through a scary and unfamiliar environment.

Graham started forward again, struggling to remember a joke he could tell himself. Any joke would do. Even one of those stupid knock-knock jokes he heard over and over when he was a kid.

Knock-knock.
Who's there?
Banana.
Banana who?
Knock-knock.
Who's there?
Banana.
Banana who?
Knock-knock.
Who's there?
Orange.
Orange who?
Orange you glad I didn't say "banana" again?

It wasn't funny. Not anymore, anyway. But it did get Graham three more steps along his wall crawl. Hopeful, he stretched his right hand out in front of him and grabbed at the void as he'd done several times already. His fingertips brushed against a cinder block. Finally. He'd located the first corner. He crawled to it and crouched there for a time, cradling his knees under his chin as dungeon prisoners have done since times out of mind. Now that he'd located it, he felt a sense of safety within it, just as the cellar's farthest corners had once offered him protection from his father's violent drunken rages. He wondered how many times as a child he had crouched in this very corner, trembling at the thud of his father's Wolverines on the floor above him.

The memory created an equivalent thudding in his head and ears, the sound of his blood pressure escalating as the emotional recall washed over him. He hoped that was all it was, anyway: just the thud of his own racing heart in his head, not the stomp of work boots over it. He was aware of his hands trembling against his own legs.

You're panicking. Control it. Or else you really won't be able to get out of this corner.

He sighed, positioned his left palm on the ground and the other against the cinder block wall, and reminded himself of another joke from his childhood. *What's black and white and read all over? I don't know, what? An embarrassed zebra? No! A newspaper!* It was time to move. Gingerly, he felt along the wall with one hand and along the ground with the other as he made his way toward the second of the cellar's four corners.

After a few more advances, the fingers of his left hand brushed against something on the cellar floor that felt a lot like a piece of wood. One of the newly splintered cellar steps, maybe? He felt along its length until he bumped the side of his hand against an upright object attached to the wood. This object was narrow, cylindrical, but far too small to be his Maglite. He guessed it was a nail. Carefully, he pinched the cylinder between the thumb and forefinger of his left hand and ran those fingers up the shaft of whatever this was. Sure enough, there was a sharp point on the end of it. A broken tread had wrenched free of the staircase when he fell and had landed top-down, resulting in an upward-pointing nail that he could not see. Graham was suddenly glad he had so far had the patience to take his search slowly. The last thing he needed now was tetanus.

By the time he reached the second corner of the cellar, however, that patience had begun to show signs of wear. Graham had to repeatedly force himself to slow down, to thoroughly search the darkness in front of him for not only his Maglite but any other spikes that might be protruding from the cellar floor. Aside from the single tread, he found no others before he rounded the second corner and was on his way to the third. At one point, Graham's left palm landed on a small and smooth rectangular object that he eventually determined was a nine-volt battery. It had probably been dislodged from the antique police radio when it hit the ground. His Maglite required three D cells. The sheriff's department had bequeathed him the radio. Most likely, the *real* law enforcement officials in Hollow County had modern rechargeable radio equipment. His looked like it might have been from the Seventies.

He could feel no evidence that the remains of the device lay anywhere around where the battery had landed. He plucked the nine-volt from the ground and placed it in his shirt pocket anyway, just in case he found the radio mostly intact while he continued his search for the Maglite. If he found the receiver, and it was serviceable, and he was able to replace the battery, he might be able to call for help regardless of whether he was able to locate the flashlight.

That glimmer of hope rekindled his urgency, which he again forced himself to swallow before crawling forward along the cellar wall. After two more advances, the fingers of his left hand found another cylindrical metal object laying on the cellar floor and nestled in precisely the spot where the wall and floor met. This object was much too big to be a nail.

Graham sat on his haunches and gripped the cylinder in his right hand, hefting it from the cellar floor. It sure as hell felt like his Maglite. His left hand groped along the shaft of the object until it widened some and then ended with a flat surface. Yes. It was the Maglite. Fresh hope welled up from the middle of his chest and spread throughout his body, raising gooseflesh on the back of his neck. The flashlight had a simple pushbutton on the smooth part of its shaft, near the neck. Graham searched for it, found it, and pressed it. Nothing. He gripped the light in his left hand and twisted the battery compartment access clockwise to ensure that it was firmly closed. Then he rotated the beam focus mechanism on the head counter-clockwise to maximize the beam's width. He pressed the button again, and suddenly the lamp flooded the area in front of him with warm yellow light.

"Oh, thank God!"

From inside his head came the sound of ear-splitting laughter followed by the booming voice of his father: *GOD AIN'T HELPING YOU OUT OF THIS ONE, BOY!* He clapped his hands to the sides of his head, smacking himself painfully with the shaft of the Maglite in the process. He managed to hold onto it, however, and its light did not wane. Graham kept his position, eyes squeezed shut, and hands clamped at his temples until the railroad spike in his head withdrew again. When it did, he sat with his back to the cinder block wall where the Maglite had been resting and shone it around the room.

His radio, with its battery compartment exposed and its rectangular case entirely split open, lay a couple of feet farther to his right. It looked bad but appeared to have not been deprived of any of its electronic components upon impact. Graham snatched it from the floor. He fumbled the nine-volt from his shirt pocket and reconnected it. It was the kind with the lightning-shaped black cat leaping through the loop in the numeral nine for a logo, an Eveready.

Here's hoping you are.

There was a barely perceptible hiss from the radio's speaker as power serpentined its way through the device, but nothing else. Graham verified that the receiver was still tuned to one of the Hollow County emergency frequencies, then keyed the mic.

"Hello?" he managed. His tongue and lips still felt thick and uncooperative. "Constable Gordon here. I need help."

It occurred to him then that no one from the sheriff's department had bothered to train him on the proper use of a police radio, or ten-codes. It was one more indicator that his elected capacity really held no power or esteem at all among the population of Lost Hollow, much less the rest of Hollow County. If this was his fresh start, it so far felt like a start from the bottom rung of the ladder. He released the mic button and waited, but no reply came.

"Hello?" he said again after pressing the button. Then his dead father's voice was thundering in his ears once more. Graham started, dropping the radio so that he could grab hold of his head before the pressure within sent it soaring like a bottle rocket off his neck.

THE DAMNED THING IS BROKEN, FUCKWIT! CAN'T YOU SEE THAT? THEY'RE NOT COMING. A little quieter but still with that scythe-like malicious edge, the voice added, *YOU'RE STUCK WITH ME. GOTTA HAVE YOUR OLD DADDY BAIL YOU OUT AGAIN. YOU'RE NOT A MAN. YOU NEVER WERE. HELLO? HELLO? PUSSY FUCKWIT.*

Graham curled himself into a fetal position on the cellar floor, the still-glowing Maglite cradled against his chest. He lay there for some time, waiting for the railroad spike his dead father had buried in his brain to dematerialize. It didn't want to go. Before, the pain had lasted only a minute or two after the voice went silent. This time it lingered longer, an ice cream brain freeze that was more iceberg than spoonful, the throbbing in his head more thundering bass than heartbeat. As he writhed against the pain, an old familiar feeling arose in the back of his throat. He was going to be sick.

He heaved twice in the fetal position but brought nothing up. He rolled onto his knees, crouched on the cellar floor as he had been in the dark and heaved a third time. This one emptied his stomach of whatever had remained there from the day's (*Friday's?*) lunch. The foul liquid made a wet *smack* sound as it hit the hardened earth of the cellar. Some of it splashed from there onto the knees of his trousers and onto the cellar wall beside him. His throat felt raw and cut from the force of the expulsion, but at least it had eased the pain and throbbing in his head some.

When he was able to think again, Graham lifted the broken radio from the cellar floor and clipped it as best he could to his belt. It was useless now, but perhaps the sheriff's department would allow him to return it to them for an upgrade when he finally found his way out of here.

IF I find my way out of here, the unwanted thought arose. He attempted to replace it with another joke. *What are the three fastest forms of communication? Telephone, telegraph, and tell-a-girl.* Ouch. There's a funny that definitely wouldn't fly anymore. Not because the telegraph was long dead, but because of the apparent misogyny. For Graham, it served its purpose, however. His mind was off on a new tangent, and he could continue to investigate his predicament with some detachment.

He allowed the Maglite's beam to illuminate the corner of the cellar opposite his position. There was the half-splintered staircase, the last tread of its upper half hanging in space, connected to nothing at that end. The lower treads had all broken off. Most of them lay scattered directly below the cellar door. The single exception seemed to have been the one that could have impaled his hand while he was crawling through the dark. Both of the staircase's stringers were still attached to the cellar door frame. Graham thought he could shimmy up one of them and launch himself through the door at the top after he reached the unbroken treads. It might be worth a shot, as long as he didn't manage to bring the remaining section of the staircase down on his own head in the process.

He shone the flashlight around the remainder of the cellar, the parts he had explored on his hands and knees and the parts he hadn't. There was no sign of another person down here. No makeshift bed. No remnants of meals. No tools or playing cards. There was no evidence of his dead father or his eyeball, as he thought he'd seen just before the flashlight died and he'd lost consciousness.

Graham directed the Maglite's beam back to the stringers that ran from the cellar floor to the door frame. The cellar staircase had been a narrow one, less than the width of a man shoulder-to-shoulder, he figured. That meant he could probably straddle the open space between the stringers, using each one as both a hand-hold and a foot-hold for scaling until he reached the remaining treads that were secured between them. There were multiple obstacles to that end. Chief among them was maintaining his light source during the climb. He'd have to tuck the Maglite in his belt somehow so that it continued to shine a light on his path without the need for him to hold it in a hand as he tried to climb the stringers. Then there were his sore muscles, the not inconsiderable weight of him, and his general lack of dexterity to consider. Combine those problems with any yet untold damage he'd caused to the staircase on his way to the floor, and you have a potential recipe for a sequel to the disaster that landed him there.

Still, he had to try.

With the Maglite snug in his belt at his hip and pointed in a generally diagonal upward direction, Graham situated each of his hands firmly on the ridge of one stringer. He placed the toe of his right boot on the right-hand stringer, near the bottom but close enough to his right hand to allow him to shift his weight to his right. The leverage allowed him to raise his left boot from the cellar floor and plant it on the left stringer, slightly higher than the right. From there, he shifted his weight to his left, sliding his right hand farther up the right-side stringer while clenching his left hand on the ridge of the other. When he found new purchase with his right hand, he raised his right boot and planted it higher than the left.

It's working. Hot damn! It's working!

He was careful to not say it aloud. His dead father's outburst, if Graham were careless enough to vocalize his thoughts again, would startle him. It might cause him to fall. Or it might be more painful next time than it was when he yakked up his lunch, perhaps even painful enough to kill him this time. *Why did the boy bring a ladder on the bus?* he asked himself as he slid his left hand upward on its stringer and then followed it with his left boot. *Because he was going to high school!* Again he shifted his weight and slid his right hand upward, followed by his right boot. *Hey, what do you call a funny mountain? Hill-arious!*

In the swath of light emanating from his left hip, Graham discovered that he could see the edge of a tread, now just inches above his head and hands. He had to force himself to not rush toward it, lest he lose his balance and have to start all over again at the bottom of the cellar. *Have you ever been rock climbing? No, but I would if I were boulder.* Left. *Hey, what does a frog do for exercise? Jumping-jacks!* Right. *Knock knock. Who's there?* Left. *Dewey. Dewey who?* Right. *Dewey have to keep telling these stupid jokes?*

He could see the edge of the top tread at his eye level now, which meant that he was high enough along the stringers to try to put his weight on the lowest remaining one. His feet were still slightly below that tread, but he could raise one boot high enough to test the load it might take without losing his grip on the stringers. He chose his right foot for the task, placing it lightly against tread where it met the stringer, then shifting more weight onto it as it refused to give way.

The tread did not give at all. Good. Still gripping a stringer in each hand, Graham placed his left foot on the opposite edge of the same tread, balancing his weight on each side. He perceived no give. The tread held at the points where it fastened to each stringer. That meant it was time to stand up. Slowly. So as not to lose his balance and topple backward into the darkness. Graham steeled himself and let go first of the left stringer, then the right. He raised himself up into a position that was not quite standing erect and not quite the stoop of a fairy tale witch, but something in between, something to ensure that his top weight leaned toward the cellar door and not the compacted earth below him. A smile parted the puffy, blood-caked, and bruised remains of his lips.

I did it! A relieved sigh escaped from between his teeth. *I really did it!*

He tugged the Maglite free from its place in his belt and shone it on each of the three remaining treads that led up to the cellar door, to freedom. All three remained intact. He stepped a foot on each of them on his way to the top, careful again to neither hurry nor linger too long on them. The first thing he was going to do when he got back to his pickup was snatch up his phone and see what day it was. Next, he would call Patsy's cell phone and tell her what had happened, and that he was going to take a few days off to have his injuries

CHAPTER FOUR

L ost Hollow's only bed and breakfast turned out to be an old Queen Anne-style home with two floors and robin's egg blue fish scale siding Staff thought looked far too pristine to be original. It was out of place among the red brick and white clapboard siding that dotted the majority of the downtown landscape. He suspected the building's owners, with whom only Afia had spoken so far, were probably out-of-towners themselves, or they were in the beginning. It was also evident that the little province had no historic preservation society or homeowner's association looking out for its character because the public square through which they had driven on the way there was also an odd mishmash of old and new. An ancient bicycle shop with vintage signage painted in gold on its fragile picture window stood right beside a much more modern-looking vape shop that had erected a gaudy red, green, and blue glass tube sign in its own window. Diagonally across the square from these two businesses were a lawyer and the town administrator's office, both of which sported facades of stately red brick, had painted white wooden doors without windows, and advertised their contents by using small black wall-mounted wooden plaques at eye level beside the entrance.

What struck Staff most about the town center, though, was the full story-high obelisk that had been erected in the middle of it all. It was surrounded by a small concrete platform on which one might be able to stand and gaze at it but was otherwise not marked. No signs indicated its reason for being there. There was no historical marker anywhere in the square that reported an event of local significance that it might memorialize. It just stood there, a giant erect penis casting clock-hand shadows along the tiny one-way street that surrounded the square. He glanced sidelong at Afia—looking confident and professional in her crisp autumn-appropriate gold sweater over a white turtleneck, black pants, sensible flats—as she rang the bell at the door of the blue-gabled anachronism that was going to be their home for the weekend.

"Glad to see your time here didn't influence your taste," he said. "I've taken a lot of pictures of a lot of places in a lot of towns in my time. I haven't seen a mix of styles like this in...well, ever."

Afia grinned but maintained her focus on the door that still stood closed in front of them, her finger poised to ring the bell again. "You know that old saying, 'You can take the boy out of the country, but you can't take the country out of the boy?'"

"Yeah?"

"That's bullshit."

The door swung open. Within stood a squat older woman with silver hair, into which was tucked the temples of an enormous pair of eyeglasses with thick round black frames. The way the lenses of those glasses magnified the gray eyes behind them made Staff think she looked surprised. She probably always looked that way. He had to stifle a chuckle because the way she had suddenly thrown back the door to greet them only heightened the effect.

"You must be Afia Afton!" She stretched her hand over the threshold and grabbed Afia's right hand in a queenly way. She jiggled it lightly up and down before allowing the reporter to pull it back. "From Channel 6 News? You look just like you do on TV! Channel 6 is the only news I watch."

Afia smiled pleasantly. "That's me. And you are—"

"Patsy. Patsy Blankenship, town administrator, bed and breakfast owner, and soon-to-be Lost Hollow's first ghost tour guide. At your service."

Afia nodded and cocked a thumb at Staff. "This is my cameraman Joe Stafford."

"Everyone just calls me Staff." He stuck out his own hand, which Patsy pumped twice enthusiastically.

"Charmed." It came out with a decidedly Georgian lilt, confirming that not only was Patsy not from Lost Hollow, but she was also not a native Tennessean. Her accent was missing the nasal quality of a native. "Well. Let me help you get your stuff settled and then we can sit down and talk about ghosts! There's so much to tell you. I just know you're going to love our little town and all its mysteries. Come on in."

She swept her hand across the threshold and bowed as she bade them entry, the way a butler might do for an unwary traveler in an old monster movie. Afia entered first, followed by Staff, who tried to restrain himself from rubbing his eyes as they met a jarring mixture of decor. The space included modern furniture, colorful art deco paintings above a colonial fireplace in the common area, and a decorative butter churn in the entryway that looked as if it had been pilfered straight from the set of *Little House on the Prairie*. Beside the fireplace stood a short metal stand supporting a frame that contained a letter-size sign. Printed on the sign in oversized Comic Sans were the words NO SMOKING.

Staff cleared his throat. "How long have you been running this place?"

"Oh, probably about fifteen years now. It was in the most awful mess when I got here. So was the town, honestly. It was pretty much a lot of nothing but old empty buildings and farmland that had been overtaken by scrub bushes. But I'm an entrepreneur, Mr. Staff. Where others see a hopeless mess, I see an opportunity. So I bought this place with some family money I'd wanted to invest and pulled together a few locals to form a town committee. What you see in the square and my place here is only what we've done so far. With a little more money, some luck, and some elbow grease, we can turn this place into a real tourist attraction." She smiled at him. "That's why it's so good to have you here. You can make us look good for Halloween."

Staff glanced at Afia, whose brow furrowed. "Due respect, Ms. Blankenship, but I feel like I should point out that we're not creating an advertisement for Lost Hollow. We're doing a feature story. We'll be asking questions and following leads that we hope will generate a fun spooky Halloween segment for the news. But we won't be taking orders on what we are and are not allowed to cover. Of course, we'll let viewers know where they can find you, but we're not going to pimp you to them. If you want that, you'll need to reach out to our sales department and buy a local spot with viewership that matches your demographic." She knitted her fingers together in front of her hips. "I hope you understand."

Patsy's cheeks turned pink. "Oh, I know that! I'm just so excited about what's happening here in our little town. I don't see any way that you'll leave here without a wonderful story to tell." She spun on her heels and motioned them toward a set of stairs. "Off to your rooms we go, then."

"I'm sure you're right, Ms. Blankenship," Staff said. He glared at Afia after Patsy turned her back to them. She shrugged back at him. *What?* the gesture said. *I'm tired, and it's the truth.* Yes. It was the truth, but Afia had been in the news game long enough to understand how to handle with some diplomacy those types who do not understand the difference between news and advertising. Staff wondered how much the memory of her father's brutal murder might have had to do with her current mood, given that it had come up in their conversation over the drive and they had just come from the place in town where his body had been found. If it had been Staff's family, he wouldn't be particularly enthusiastic about giving the place free publicity either. "We're not here to rain on your parade or anything. It's just been a really long drive, and we're tired. No offense."

Patsy waved her hand in the air as she led them up a set of cherry stained stairs to the second floor. "Oh, none taken. I can imagine such a long drive after a full Friday of work can be exhausting. I do hope you didn't run into any problems along the way."

"Nothing more than a hungry stomach and restless legs. Unless you count that weird dog that ran out in front of us right when we got into town. I thought we were going to do a full three-sixty right off the shoulder and into the woods. Lucky for us Afia's such a superb driver, for a lady." She punched him in the bicep. "Ow!"

"Oh, that's terrible," Patsy replied. "Well, we do have more than our fair share of strays and wildlife out this way. Sometimes I think people bring their unwanted pets here, dump them, and leave. Then they go home and tell the kids that Fido ran away or Sheba probably just found another family she preferred to live with. Did you hit it with your car?"

"We managed to avoid it," Afia offered.

"Oh, good. Well, what kind of dog was it? Maybe I can print up some signs after dinner tonight. We can put them up as we tour the town tomorrow, just in case it's somebody's pet that ran off. Folks around here are pretty good about helping their neighbors find the odd lost pup now and then."

Staff winced behind her back. He imagined a stack of inkjet-printed LOST DOG signs featuring the headline in red Papyrus—probably bolded, italicized, and underlined with a drop shadow—and the critter's description along with a phone number printed below it in blue Comic Sans. "Honestly, I couldn't tell you what kind of dog it was. We didn't see that much of it. Afia saw it clearer than I did. To me, it was just a little black spot in the rearview mirror. Af?"

She shot him a look. "Don't call me 'Af.'"

"Sorry. Do you remember what kind of dog it was?"

"I don't know. Like you said, it was just kind of this black thing on four legs. It was a little dog, I think. Kind of stout looking. I might have been able to tell you the breed if I had been able to see any head details. It didn't even really look like a dog's head to me. It was just some creature going ninety miles an hour across SR-501. Maybe it wasn't even a dog."

Patsy scaled the final tread and then stepped off the cherry staircase. She turned back to look at them both. Afia and Staff paused mid-step and looked up at her. Her mouth was hanging open, and her gray owl-like eyes had grown even more impossibly wide. She glanced from Afia to Staff and back again, her expression transforming from one of surprise to awe and then to joy.

"You saw her!" she cried. "All these years and *finally* somebody sees her again! It would have to be someone from out of town, of course. Of *course* it would!"

Afia and Staff glanced at each other, then turned their attention back to Patsy. "Her who?" Afia said. "Who did we see?"

Patsy clasped her hands under her chin and bounced on the balls of her feet, her colossal owl eyes drifted toward the ceiling. For a moment, Staff feared she might topple down the stairs, taking him and Afia along with her on an injurious ride back to the first floor.

"Oh, my dear, I have so much to tell you. But not right now. We have to get you both settled first, and I need to finish dinner. I have a plump turkey that's been baking downstairs all day long. I need to go check on that. Then I'll whip up a few quick side dishes and bake some biscuits. We'll talk about it over dinner. Really. I'll tell you all about it."

She made a right turn at the top of the stairs and threw open a door. "This is your room, Ms. Afton. You'll find it provides you with a lovely view of the backyard. I planted a small orchard back there in the spring, and the leaves are at their most stunningly beautiful right now. There's a bathroom a little farther down the hall that you can have all to yourself. We have three full baths in this house, and two of them are up here."

Afia dragged her suitcase into her room. "Thank you. See you at dinner, then." She closed the door without looking back at either of them.

Patsy turned to Staff, her face positively glowing. "You, Mr. Staff, get the room in the opposite hallway. Mustn't allow the boys and girls to be too close to each other!" She led him across the top of the stairs to the west wing of the house and, not without some amount of drama, flung open the door. "You too have a view of the backyard, but you also get a lovely look at our developing public square. You can see the monument and some of the buildings from here, a nice sign of our progress."

"Thank you." Staff dragged his own suitcase into the room and turned to shut the door, only to find Patsy's face floating in the way.

"Oh, my," she said again. The euphoria in her voice was unmistakable, although she was whispering now, as if she were about to impart a secret that she didn't want anyone to overhear. "Oh, my dear, you're going to go back to Channel

6 with such a wonderful story. I can't wait to tell you all about the black bitch."

***

When the dinner bell rang, Staff washed up and then padded downstairs to the dining room to find Afia already seated there, looking exhausted and irritable. The table had been set with white china that sported a grandmotherly pink floral arrangement in its center. Beside each plate was a cloth napkin, a water glass, and a wine glass. Afia's water glass was full. Her wine glass, on the other hand, was only one-third full of the crimson liquid. Staff suspected this meant that she had already downed most of it. All of the other glassware on the table sat empty and dry.

"Oh, there you are," came Patsy's musical voice from behind him. "Hot dishes coming through!" She whisked by him with two serving platters, one full of thinly sliced turkey slices overlapping in a long accordion shape and one carrying a bowl of steaming mashed potatoes alongside a boat of thick brown gravy. "I'll be back with the rest of the sides in a moment. Why don't you go ahead and have a seat by Ms. Afton there? I'll fill up your water glass and pour you some wine so you two can relax while you wait."

Staff thanked her and pulled himself up beside Afia at the table. When Patsy disappeared into the kitchen again, he took up his wine glass and sipped from it. It was a semi-sweet, not bitter at all, and probably less than fifteen bucks a bottle at the local Grab 'n' Go. Just the way he liked it. He smacked his lips, grinning, and eyeballed the liquid with the satisfied expression of a man who has just settled into his favorite chair for the evening. Afia rolled her eyes.

"You would."

"I would, and I do. Although you don't seem averse to it, either, based on the contents of your own glass. Don't you know it's not polite to start drinking before the other guests arrive?"

"I guess I'm not in a manners mood."

Staff nodded. "Well, try to lighten up a little bit if you can. I'm not sure what I think about this place or this Patsy yet. She's very...odd, I guess is the right word for now. If she starts to go too far off the deep end, we should pick up and take ourselves to some other place for this story."

Afia chuckled. "You mean some other place where people who claim to have seen ghosts don't come off sounding like they're missing a few tools from the shed?"

"Here we go," Patsy sang as she bustled into the room balancing three more steaming dishes of food. Among them was a basket of dinner rolls wrapped in red-checked cloth, a bowl of Southern-style green beans (Staff could smell the aroma of freshly cooked bacon wafting off it), and a giant gelatinous glob of can-shaped cranberry sauce that had been carved into eight equal disk-shaped pieces. Staff unfolded his napkin and placed it in his lap, as did Afia almost simultaneously. "I hope you like it. I wanted to cook up a nice and filling autumn dinner so we can all get a good night's sleep before our busy day of ghost hunting tomorrow."

Staff smiled indulgently and cut his eyes at Afia, who met his glance. *Let's just play along, for now,* he tried to transmit to her.

"Now," Patsy said, wrinkling her nose above a preschool story time smile. "I was going to tell you all about the black bitch."

Afia set her fork against the edge of her plate. Her eyes narrowed. "The what?"

Patsy set down her own silverware and nudged her chair back from the table a smidge, making some room for what Staff figured was about to be a long-winded Lost Hollow history lesson.

"The black bitch. She's Lost Hollow's very own cryptid omen bearer. And you saw her! You saw her on your way into town. You said so!"

"What's a cryptid omen bearer?" Staff asked. He sounded the last three words out slowly, ensuring he enunciated them properly.

"Well, a cryptid is nothing more than a type of creature that some people believe exists but for which there is yet to be scientific evidence or proof. You know, like Bigfoot or the Loch Ness Monster. An omen is just something that signifies the approach of something life-changing, good or bad. It's a harbinger for something like a horrible accident or an untimely death."

"Oh," said Afia, not disguising her sarcasm. "Great."

Patsy ignored her.

"On the other side of the world, there's a supernatural omen bearer they call a black dog or a hellhound. It's usually a ghost dog, larger than most normal dogs, that has glowing eyes and most of the time portends death. You've read about them before if you've ever read Sir Arthur Conan Doyle's *The Hound of the Baskervilles*."

"I think I read that in middle school," Staff said. "Or maybe when I was a freshman."

"Most people think of the black dog as a European ghost or demon dog. In America, you don't hear much about them. Probably the most famous case of an American black dog was the one that John Bell saw just before all the poltergeist activity started at the Bell farm up in Adams, back in the 1800s. He said it looked like a large black dog with a rabbit's head. He took a shot at it, and it just vanished into thin air. Soon after, a poltergeist-style haunting began at the Bell farm. The whole thing eventually ended with John Bell's death. They say the spirit—who the family sometimes called Kate and who history tends to name The Bell Witch—quite literally laughed out loud as Bell's casket was being laid in the ground. Makes me shudder every time I think about it."

"And you think this is what I nearly ran over when we drove into town?" To Afia's credit, Staff thought, there was not a hint of skepticism or intrigue in her voice. "I should point out that we're miles and miles away from Adams. I've never even been there, and I've traveled pretty much all over this state covering the news."

Staff nodded. "Same. I'm not sure I even knew there was an Adams, Tennessee."

Patsy scoffed. "Pretty much anyone who studies American folklore knows the story of the Bell Witch in Adams, but not everyone studies American folklore. Surely you've seen that horribly inaccurate movie they made about it? *An American Haunting?*"

"I'm not really into modern horror movies," Staff replied.

"Oh. Well, in any event, I'm not saying that the black bitch is the same black dog that appeared to John Bell in Adams. I've never seen the black bitch, but I know a few people who claim to have and have lived to tell about it. Maybe I can introduce you to a couple of them tomorrow sometime for your story. The way they usually describe the black bitch is that she has the body of a small to medium-sized dog. She has completely black fur from head to toe and kind of a stocky build and a stubby tail, like some kind of bulldog."

"Sounds like a cute pupper," Staff said, grinning.

"Oh, you won't think so if you get a look at her face. Her face is where the similarities between her and a normal dog end. They say she has a human head on top of that bulldog body, and the face of a screaming woman on the front of that head. Every time someone reports seeing her, she's always screaming with an open mouth and wide human eyes. Some folks say she looks angry. Others say she looks anguished like she's sad or in pain. All I know is the two people I've met who saw her eventually suffered horrible tragedy in their personal lives. It was only about a month after old Mr. Kenner saw her that his house burned down and took his wife and cat with it. Now he's living by himself in a double-wide just outside the limits, crazy as a bat. The other one? Mr. Jepsen? He was a school bus driver for Hollow County. Flipped the bus traveling the speed limit over plain dry asphalt one day not two years after he saw the black bitch. Killed about half the kids on that bus."

"I remember that accident," Afia interjected. "Just a couple of years ago, wasn't it? We covered it on Channel 6.

The authorities at the time said it was most likely a medical emergency and that Jepsen wouldn't be charged with anything."

Patsy nodded. "Yeah, that's what they came up with on account of a brain scan they did on Mr. Jepsen afterward. Said he'd had a stroke while on his route. The thing is, Mr. Jepsen *did* have a stroke a few years before that. He says he didn't feel any warning signs before the accident, and that the place on the scan where they say he had a new stroke was the exact same place he'd had the old one. Now I'm no heart doctor, but I was under the impression that once you had a stroke the part of the brain that was affected is pretty much killed. If he'd had another stroke and it had caused him to roll a bus, you'd think it would have been in a living part of his brain. Needless to say, he's not driving the school bus anymore. He says he wants to move back to Canada but hasn't been able to come up with the money."

Staff leaned forward, hands clasped together in his lap. "What does he do now?"

"Oh, he still works for the school system. They won't let him drive anymore, but the school board didn't feel right about letting him go completely. He'd already devoted more than fifteen years of a bachelor life to hauling snot-nosed brats around to school and then back to their ungrateful parents. He was barely making a living doing that, to be honest. Now he's a custodian for the school here in Lost Hollow."

Afia's eyebrows shot upward. "He actually works in the school *with* the friends of the kids that were killed in the accident? I would think that would be kind of awkward for both him and the kids."

"I would have assumed a custodian makes more money than a bus driver, too," Staff added.

Patsy nodded. "You're right on both counts." She sat back in her chair and dabbed her fingertips on the napkin that lay draped over her lap. "He probably does make more than he did driving the bus, considering the job and the hours, but it's still not enough to both pay his bills and purchase his way back to Toronto. I also suspect he doesn't really make as much as most custodians do. The school board addressed your concern, Ms. Afton, by ensuring that Mr. Jepsen works late afternoons and evenings when most of the kids are long gone for the day. Custodians from the county's other schools rotate out the day job. It's not a perfect system, but for the most part, it keeps the kids out of Mr. Jepsen's sight and mind and him out of theirs."

"Do you think he might be willing to talk to us on camera?" Staff asked. "If the other guy, Kenner, has mental health problems that might make him come off as odd in an interview, Mr. Jepsen sounds like our only other option to discuss a 'black bitch' sighting." He formed air quotes when he spoke the creature's local nickname. "His story has a little less ring of truth to it, though, when you consider the stroke and the span of time between his sighting and the accident. Two years is a long time. Kind of smacks of the King Tut's tomb curse to me."

"He might talk about it. We could try to meet him at the school tomorrow evening and ask him if he's willing. I understand your skepticism, Mr. Staff, but you'll need to make sure you're sensitive to his story. Try not to ask him too many questions about the bus accident itself. He still carries so much guilt."

"I'm not sure the Jepsen bus story is a good piece for us," Afia said. "It will end up being less about the ghost dog and more about the dead kids and how horrible the bus driver feels about it. This is supposed to be a light story for Halloween, something that gives the viewers a little thrill of excitement without bringing them too close to the tragedy. We can interview *you* about the black bitch, Ms. Blankenship, as long as you can keep some of the gorier details vague, but I don't think we should try to force Mr. Jepsen to discuss it."

Staff, who now felt a little embarrassed about having suggested it, nodded. "She's right," he said. "This is supposed to be a feature story, so we should probably stick more to the mysterious and less to the psychologically damaging."

"I see. Well, I can give you the black bitch story myself, I guess. I've sort of become the unofficial curator of Lost Hollow history anyway, so it might as well come from me. I do have someone else in mind that I think you should meet, though. He's our newly elected constable. He just recently bought up his family's old place out on Hollow Creek Road, near the edge of town. The city had been planning to demolish it because it seems to have become a hangout for vagrants and truant teens who need a place to smoke and drink and God knows what else."

"What does that have to do with hauntings and Halloween in Lost Hollow?" Afia asked.

"Oh, that's the best part! Right after our new constable saved the old place, rumors started flying around town that some kids who were skipping school to drink beer had broken in and been nearly scared to death by some disembodied screams coming from somewhere inside the house. Later on, people started reporting seeing weird lights and hearing the most god-awful moaning sounds coming from inside." She laughed. "It doesn't seem to have stopped people from trespassing, but it's made our little town somewhat of an in-county tourist spot as the kids here have spread the story to other kids around Hollow County." She paused then, looking up and to the right, somewhere above Afia.

"Oh!" she said suddenly, and looked back at them. "I just made a connection there! At least one of those trespassing kids heard about my ghost tour idea and came forward recently. Jeremy was his name. Jeremy Beard. He said he'd been exploring the house and heard some frightful screams when he did. He gave me his number. Said he's going to major in history in college and thought helping me with ghost tours might be good experience. Maybe you could talk to him?"

Afia grinned. "An alleged eyewitness to a haunting who isn't burdened by a tragedy? That sounds more like a plan for a fun Halloween story to me."

Patsy was positively giddy. "Yay! You should see the place. Even if there's actually nothing there, it's got a great haunted house *look*, like something out of *The Munsters* or *The Addams Family*."

"Definitely sounds like a place we'd like to see," Staff said. "Is there any backstory to it? Any stories about someone who lived there that might shed some light on why it would be haunted? Some kind of incident, maybe?"

"I don't know of anything in particular that happened there. Our constable lived there when he was just a kid. I would love to have you meet him, though. Maybe he can give you some background that would be good for a chill or two besides the black bitch. The house is older than his family, so it's possible he conducted a little research into its history before deciding to save it. I can't imagine anyone buying that place for its sentimental value alone. Of course, the constable is a bit of an odd bird. But don't you dare tell him I said that!"

Afia assured her that they wouldn't. "So where can we find this new constable?"

"It's getting late. You two have had a long day, and I need to clean up our dinner mess here. How about I give him a call first thing in the morning and set up a meeting at the old place? I'm sure he'll be happy to show you around and tell you anything you want to know about it. I'll go out there with you if you don't mind. I'd love to know more about it myself. If the constable's not going to live in it, we might be able to turn it into something else: another B&B, maybe, or an events venue, or a little headquarters and museum for future ghost tours. I'll call Jeremy Beard for you, too. Maybe you can talk to him first.

"When we're done at the constable's place, I'll show you all around the other supposedly haunted sites in Lost Hollow. The obelisk in the square is said to have a bit of tragic civil rights history to it, as do some of the older buildings there."

From the corner of his eye, Staff thought he saw Afia flinch. "I'd like to steer clear of anything too racially charged if you don't mind," she said. "Those are important stories to tell, but I don't want to use them for entertainment."

"Oh, all right then. I also want to take you over to our cemetery on the other side of town. No one gets buried in it anymore because it's so old that all the spots were finally filled. The county keeps after the grounds now, but for a long time, we had a caretaker there who kept mostly to himself and had become quite insane by the time he died. There's a bit of mystery surrounding that whole thing. Some people say they see weird lights there when they drive past it at night, like little flames flickering among the graves."

"That's fine," Afia said. She sounded exhausted again. Staff wondered if he should talk with Patsy privately sometime before morning, let her know about Afia's past here. She didn't seem to recognize the reporter's name as having any local significance, unofficial historian or not. Telling her a bit about Afia's own history in Lost Hollow might help avoid some more awkwardness if the older woman knew what subjects and areas of town were best avoided.

"It sounds like you've got quite a few scary tales around here that we'll be able to tell," he said. He pushed himself back from the table, preparing to return to his room for the evening, at least until he was sure that Afia was secure in her own room. "We'll come away with something great. So what's the name of this constable we're going to meet tomorrow morning?"

Patsy smiled. "Mr. Gordon. His name is Graham Gordon. He seems a little shy at first, but I'm sure he'll open right up when we start talking about his little haunted place on the edge of town."

Staff paused in mid-repel from the dinner table. He glanced up at Patsy first, perhaps hoping she had misspoken and would correct herself. When she didn't, he turned to look at Afia. The reporter's hands were in her lap, the napkin beneath them clenched tightly in her palms, making the veins on the backs of her hands stand out. Her face had become stone except for a single throbbing spot on her right temple. Her eyes, narrow, were trained squarely on the squat older woman who sat across from her at the dining table.

Patsy looked at both her guests, one to the other, her smile fading. Her larger than life gray eyes were innocent behind her glasses.

"Did I say something wrong?"

CHAPTER FIVE

"You didn't actually say anything wrong," Staff said to Patsy. "It's just that Afia had quite a bit of her own childhood trauma from back when she lived around here. I didn't know anything about it myself until it came up on our way into town. Her father was murdered. They found his body propped up by that obelisk in the middle of town one morning. After that, Afia got shuffled into the foster system."

He had padded downstairs a half hour after dinner to find Patsy standing in her kitchen with a sink full of dirty dishes and a blank expression as if she wasn't sure where to begin the cleanup. Now he stood stooped over her kitchen sink, his arms clad in yellow rubber gloves that were in turn coated with a fine layer of bubbles courtesy of the liberal amount of apple blossom-scented Dawn Patsy had squeezed into the warm standing water. He was carefully scrubbing each of the serving plates from dinner with a sponge, rinsing them, and gingerly placing them in the nearby dish drying rack. Patsy, on the other hand, sat at the small circa-1970s kitchen table in the center of the room, her face cradled in the palms of her hands. Now and then the old chair beneath her squeaked and groaned as she fidgeted. Staff figured she was fighting an urge to leap up and take back the dishwashing task he had kindly offered to perform in exchange for a few words with her about Afia. Most likely, he thought, he wasn't washing them "right."

"Oh, my Lord," Patsy groaned. "I had no idea that the poor girl had ever lived here, much less that she lost her dad in such a brutal way. How horrible."

Staff deposited another dish in the drying rack. "Yes. The memory of it seems to have really done a number on her mood since we drove into town. She was fine on the drive until we started talking about it. She's been kind of sullen since then, like she hadn't realized how much she didn't want to relive any of that. She didn't say as much, but I kind of got the feeling that she hasn't been back here since those days."

"The worst part of it is that there's never been any justice. The case was just left unsolved. Afia thinks it's just because none of the local authorities were interested in pursuing the murder of a black man."

"Oh dear," Patsy said, shaking her head. "That might explain why I've never heard anything about it until now. This world. This awful, awful world."

"Then you mentioned that the constable's name is Gordon. That's kind of a double-whammy for Afia, I'm betting. She told me that there was this man with the last name of Gordon that her father had been into it with for years. There was bad blood between them, I guess, or maybe the other guy was just a straight-up racist. I don't know. Either way,

Afia always thought that this Gordon guy had something to do with her dad's murder."

"Well, it couldn't have been our constable." Staff thought he heard some defensiveness creep into her voice. "I very much doubt he's any older than Ms. Afton. How old did you say she was when all that happened?"

From somewhere behind the both of them, a yawning voice replied, "Twelve. I was twelve."

Staff whipped his head around from dish duty at the same time that Patsy scooted her chair backward and craned her neck to examine the newcomer. Afia stood in the doorway wearing what looked to Staff like an old-fashioned set of men's blue cotton pajamas covered by a white terrycloth bathrobe. She shuffled into the kitchen on slippered feet and drew up the chair to Patsy's right, making a short "uhff" sound when she slumped into it.

"That was the most horrible day of my life."

***

Twelve-year-old Afia Afton was startled awake by the rapid, repetitive thuds of someone pounding on her front door. She had fallen asleep while watching an episode of *Miami Vice*. Her dad didn't like her watching that show, but it was easy to sneak it in on nights that he worked extremely late. Most of the other girls in her class went all weak-kneed over Don Johnson with his linen jacket, dangling cigarette, and five o'clock shadow. Afia had a crush on Philip Michael Thomas, especially when he wore the black button-down shirt with the double-breasted jacket over it. Let the white girls swoon over Crockett if they wanted. Tubbs was the one who made her tingle.

The repetitive thuds came again, harder this time, rattling the doorknob on her side. Afia glanced at the clock on the wall opposite the television. It was seven o'clock in the morning. She had fallen asleep in front of the tube after the credits had rolled on *Miami Vice* and the real-life Barbie doll who reported the news on Channel 6 began reading her teleprompter. Why were the TV reporters always bubbly little bleach blondes with doe eyes, voluptuous lips, and large breasts? The way they constantly stumbled over their words and corrected themselves as they delivered the news made them sound illiterate. Well, maybe not illiterate, but they never sound as if they actually comprehend what they're reading. It was annoying.

"Dad?" she shouted. "Someone's at the door."

He must've found her asleep on the couch when he rolled in from work last night and not wanted to wake her. Usually he at least draped a throw over her if she'd allowed herself to drift to sleep out here. The fleece throw was still smartly folded in half over the back of the couch. She yawned and shivered, then grabbed the throw and draped it around her shoulders. Her father's bedroom was just outside the living room. She stood up and turned toward it. The door of her dad's room was wide open, which was also unusual after he'd worked the late shift.

"Dad? You in there?"

No answer.

There was a third round of pounding at the door, hard enough to rattle the decorative China set that still hung on the wall in the kitchen four years after her mother had disappeared. Afia heard them shaking against their hangers from the vibrations whoever was outside was creating. Why wouldn't he just take that stuff down? This round of aggressive knocking was followed by the booming, angry voice of a man who was not her father.

"Hollow County Sheriff's Department. Open up!"

Afia felt her skin crawl against the throw she'd draped over herself. She peeked into her father's bedroom as she passed by it on her way to the front door. The bed was still made. There was no sign of her father. No sign of the pair of boots he usually left sitting at the foot of the bed when he came home from work. He wasn't home, then. Was it possible that he hadn't made it home from work at all? Panic began to claw at her heart and creep its way into her throat. She was left at home alone often these days. It was just her and her father, after all. Sometimes she had to be home alone. But she could never remember a morning when she had awakened and not found her father either cooking bacon in a frying pan in the kitchen or sawing logs in bed that sounded like a growling grizzly bear.

"Dad?" she screamed. "Dad? Where are you?"

Another thud and the sound of splintering wood sent her running to her own bedroom. She slammed her door and searched frantically for something heavy that she could shove against it. The front door of the house she'd shared with her father since birth slammed against the interior wall. That was immediately followed by the *clomp clomp clomp* of an army of boots marching through her place. With nowhere to run, she peeked through her bedroom window.

There were two sheriff's department cars in the driveway, their strobes alternating red and blue. Behind them was parked an unmarked car. Inside that one sat a jowly white man in a tie and sport jacket. No sheriff's deputies were in sight around him. That must mean they were all in her house. If she opened the window and bolted, she doubted that the jowly man would be able to run fast enough to catch her. But where could she go?

"Afia Afton?" a baritone male voice called from the other side of her bedroom door. "My name is Abe Wickham. I'm a Hollow County sheriff's deputy. Are you in there, Afia? There's nothing to be afraid of. We just need to make sure you're all right."

The jowly man in the car caught sight of her then. She saw him snag a CB radio mic and start speaking into it before she ducked below the window casement. Her heart felt like it was going to burst right out of her chest. Her breath was ragged, shaky. Her hands trembled. Distantly from the other side of her bedroom door she heard another man's voice. He said something about a window. Then came the Wickham man's voice again: "10-4."

"Where's my dad?" Afia screamed. "What have you done to my dad?"

There was a long pause from the other side of the door followed by an exasperated sigh.

"Afia, we need to talk to you about your dad, but we need to do it face-to-face. I'm going to need you to open your door for me so we can talk. If you don't, I'm going to have to open it myself."

Another voice, male but not as baritone as Wickham's added, "Christ's sake. We don't have time for this." Someone else—Wickham maybe—shushed him.

"Nobody's going to hurt you, Afia," Wickham said. His voice was somehow closer now, as if he'd pressed his lips directly against the gap between the closed door and its frame. "We want to help you, but we need you to help us do that."

Afia glanced through her bedroom window again. The jowly man still sat in his car. He was staring off in the opposite direction now. Bored, maybe.

"Jesus, Abe, just open the door," said another man's voice.

Afia spoke up then. "Ok. I'm opening up. But if you try to hurt me I'm going to kick you all in the balls."

Laughter from behind the door.

"Ok, Afia," Wickham replied. "I'm stepping away from the door. Come on out when you're ready."

She opened the door to find four white men in uniforms with shiny gold badges pinned on their chests, shiny black boots on their feet, and shiny, intimidating handguns strapped to their hips. The tallest of them, a man with narrow eyes and what the other girls in her class referred to as a porn stache over his lip, wore a nametag with the same shininess of his badge just above it. On it was printed one word in all caps: WICKHAM. He went down on one knee as she approached him and removed his hat. Their eyes locked for a second. Afia thought he looked like an angry man who was trying to fake gentleness and sympathy. He wasn't good at it.

"Afia, I'm afraid I have some bad news," Wickham said. "We found your daddy this morning in the town square. He's passed away."

Afia's knees buckled. She collapsed to the floor in front of him. No one tried to catch her.

Minutes later, the newly orphaned Afia Afton found herself seated on her own front porch, tears streaming down her face while the deputies who had broken into her home with Wickham searched through all her dad's stuff and her own. They would not tell her what they were looking for. The jowly man that had remained in his car ambled his way toward her, a sympathetic twist on his lips, his tie blowing off his chest and over his shoulder as a sudden gust of wind embraced them.

"Miss Afton," the man said. "May I have a seat there beside you?"

Afia shrugged and indicated the spot on her left with a nod of her head.

"Thank you, ma'am. My name is Johnson. Inspector Johnson with the Hollow County sheriff. I investigate homicides."

She looked at him. "My dad was murdered?"

He nodded, focusing his own gaze on his car in the driveway. "Yeah, it looks that way. We're going to find who did this, but I need to ask you a few questions so we can figure out who it was. Do you feel like you can answer a few questions for me right now?"

Fresh hot tears streamed from the corners of her eyes. "What's going to happen to me?"

"We'll work all that out." He patted her left knee, still without looking at her. "Do you know if your daddy had any friends who came to visit him here? Anybody that you thought didn't look like a normal person?"

She glared at him. "What do you mean?"

"I mean did he ever have any buddies over who were drinking funny stuff? Or smoking anything that smelled weird to you? Ever see anyone with any funny white powder?"

Afia shook her head.

"What about strange women, then?" the Johnson man asked her. "Your daddy bring home any girlfriends since your mother went away? What did they look like? Did they dress funny? Wear clothes that you thought were a little too, uh, revealing?"

Afia's level of uncomfortable with this strange white man suddenly went to Red Alert. "My daddy was a good man," she said to him. "Only person he didn't like was that old drunk who lives through the woods there." She indicated the direction of the Lee Gordon house with an outstretched hand. She tried to meet his eyes, but he would not look at her. Instead, he patted her left knee again and stood up. He placed his hands on his lower back and stretched, yawning. Afia heard something pop. She thought it was probably a bone in his spine.

"Yep. Thank you for your time, Miss Afton," he said. He stepped off the porch and began the walk back toward his car, not looking back at her. "We'll catch the folks who did this, you betcha."

Deputy Wickham strolled out of her house just then, his entourage of three other deputies falling in behind him. He jogged to catch up with Johnson, who stopped his stroll and allowed Wickham to bend his ear. Their baritones made it easy for Afia to overhear what they were saying. Or maybe they just weren't bothering to hide it from her.

"No drugs or evidence of sex trafficking inside," Wickham said. "We did find a bunch of issues of *Ebony*. A lot of them look like they have stories about gangs in them. Think Afton might've been caught up in that stuff?"

Johnson nodded knowingly, his jowls jiggling as he did. "Oh, gangs are gonna be a problem for us," he said. "It's been all over the news. They're spreading out from the inner cities of the big towns, coming into small places like ours, trying to rob and kill the good people here. Reckon we'll just have to look out for their colors and symbols. We've got to get them before they have a chance to get us." He nudged Wickham in the ribs. "Maybe we just stock up on some white robes, huh? That'll keep them out." He brayed laughter. Wickham glanced uncomfortably at Afia behind them.

"What do we do with her?"

Johnson glanced back too, looking as if he'd forgotten she was there. "Oh, we've already called the state about her. DCS ought to be down here before too long. Just keep her fed and dry until they get here." He strolled back to his car then and, without another look back, drove away. Deputy Wickham took Johnson's former seat beside Afia.

"My dad wasn't in no gang," she said to him.

Wickham nodded. "Well, there's a lot of things grown-ups do that kids never know about." He produced a Winston from the right pocket of his uniform shirt and clamped it between his lips. "Them street gangs are some tough shit, but we're tougher. They don't know what they're in for if they think they're going to come down here and mess with a bunch of wild-eyed Southern boys."

Afia scoffed. He glared at her.

"You don't believe me? Well, that's all right, I guess. You don't have to. I just hope you don't grow up and turn out like your daddy did. You know, for your sake?"

She sneered at him. Her tears had dried on her cheeks. "And if my daddy really was killed by a gang, I hope you're going to spend every single night from now on in your car searching this town high and low for them until you find them.

"You know, for my sake?"

***

"Ugh," Afia said, cradling her forehead in her hand. "I don't think I ever saw those men again. Never heard another word about an investigation or gangs in Lost Hollow. I was just whisked away by the state and put into the foster program. Never even saw my dad's body. Don't even know if they had a funeral."

Staff felt a pang of remorse. It probably sounded to Afia like he and Patsy had been gossiping about her behind her back. He supposed it was an accurate appraisal, even if it wasn't intended to be mean-spirited. "Afia, I hope you're not offended. I was just trying to—"

She waved away the rest of his thought.

"No worries. I should've told Joanie to find someone else for this one, that's all. There must have been a part of me that thought it might help me to see the place again, how much it's changed. I guess I figured it might help me put the past in the past, you know? Especially if the place had grown up at all over the years. Then all those memories came flooding back while we were driving down here. Then we almost hit that...that...whatever it was."

"The black bitch," Patsy interrupted. "And then I brought up Mr. Gordon. I'm so sorry, dear. We can find someone else to talk to if it's going to be a problem. Like I said at dinner, there are dozens of old ghost stories around Lost Hollow."

Afia shook her head. "No, no. It's fine. The constable didn't murder my dad, even if his father might have. I actually kind of *want* to talk to Graham now. I have a few vague memories of him from school down here. Seemed like a quiet kid, but was always bruised up. I didn't interact with him a whole lot. I don't think he liked me very much. I remember there being some kind of tension between us, maybe because of our fathers. I don't know. I'm not sure what I think I'll discover that I don't already know about what happened, but I feel like maybe he can tell me something about what happened back then, give me some closure."

"You think that after all these years the constable might remember something that points to his father as the murderer?" Staff asked. "I don't know, Afia. Making an accusation like that when you meet what amounts to a total stranger after all this time seems dangerous, especially if that stranger works in law enforcement. You said yourself that you wanted to keep this story light-hearted."

"Maybe. But at the very least he should be able to tell me where his father is and what he's doing these days. He doesn't have to know that I suspect him. If I know where he is, I will at least know where the police can find him if I can ever find proof that he did it. That doesn't have anything to do with our story." She glared at Staff. "I am quite capable of keeping my personal and professional life separate."

Patsy winced. "Oh dear. You won't need to ask Constable Gordon that. I can tell you exactly where his father is these days. Lee Gordon is buried in a plot in our haunted cemetery that I mentioned earlier. He's been there since the mid-1990s, at least. I never met him, of course, but from what I understand he was widely regarded as the town drunk back then. They say he was mostly fueled by Budweiser and blind rage near the end, always taking it out on whoever happened to be nearby. Most of the time, his target seemed to be poor little Graham, uh, the constable."

"People knew Lee Gordon was beating his son. Somehow I think even those of us who were kids at the time knew it. But why the hell didn't anyone ever say anything?"

Patsy shrugged. "Small towns. All of them have secrets. Who knows? I mean, the whole town was run by baby boomers back in those days. Most of them grew up together around here, and those that had kids would have been physical disciplinarians. Bruised bottoms were the culture at the time. And since everybody knew everybody else, maybe Lee Gordon had as much on the rest of the town as they had on him. His sins were just so much more visible than everyone else's."

Afia folded her arms. "Well, that would certainly help explain their unwillingness to investigate my father's murder, wouldn't it?"

"I'm afraid so. But don't take my word as gospel on that. I don't know anything about what happened back then other than what I've picked up from the gossip of a few townsfolk over the last fifteen years. You know how gossip is. Most of the time there's only a grain of truth to it, and the rest is filled in by the gossiper's personal agenda. I'm sure there were plenty of people around here besides you and your father who didn't like Lee Gordon."

At the kitchen sink, Staff added the last of the dinner dishes to the drying rack and pulled off the rubber gloves. He dabbed up all the droplets of water that remained along the edges of the sink and then draped his dish towel over the neck of the faucet to drip-dry. He pulled up a chair of his own and joined Patsy and Afia at the table. "So, this Lee Gordon, how did he die?"

"Word around town is that he broke his neck falling down the stairs into his cellar. Drunk when it happened, most people think. Graham was already a young man in his twenties. He told the sheriff that his dad had been unwell for a long time, but refused to get treatment. He said that he had been bringing him food once a week after work. Then one day he showed up with a few bags of groceries and his dad was nowhere to be found even though his car was parked where it usually sat. So Graham goes to search the house when he notices that the cellar door is unlocked. He pulled the door open and flipped on the light, and there was his dad lying with his face smashed against the cellar floor and the lower half of his body sprawled on the steps at the bottom of the staircase. Graham says there was a broken bottle of Budweiser right beside him, so he must have been trying to negotiate that staircase while he was full of brew *and* sick to start."

"Dear God," Staff said. "And this man is constable now? That's pretty impressive. I doubt I could pass any kind of psychological evaluation for law enforcement after enduring all the abuse and then finding my dad like that."

Patsy laughed. "Constable isn't that much of a law enforcement position here in Lost Hollow. There's no psych exam. You won't see Graham tracking murderers or even stopping speeders. I don't think they've even approved him to carry a firearm yet. The sheriff's department has historically treated our constable role as a kind of Barney Fife to their Sheriff Andy Taylor. Most of Lost Hollow's constables have just tried to keep the peace between neighbors without having to call in the sheriff's deputies to take over. The guy before Mr. Gordon once had to break up a fight in the high school parking lot, but that was only because he happened to be passing by and saw these two young punks screaming at each other while a girl sat crying on the hood of a car. Young lust and some jealousy, I guess. He sent them all on their way home and followed the girl to her house, just to be extra safe, and that was the end of that.

"Besides, Mr. Gordon was the only person on the ballot for that position last month. The previous guy, Mr. Roberts, had been constable for pretty much his entire adult life.

Thirty-five years. He died back in the summer. Ticker. At first, the town council wasn't even going to bother replacing him, but then Graham threw his hat in the ring because he was trying to impress that girl, so they decided to have a special election to find out if anyone, uh, more qualified, wanted the job."

"Girl?" Afia asked.

Patsy smiled. "Yes. I asked him why in the world a quiet young man like him who does computer work for a living would want to take on a nothing elected position like Lost Hollow constable. He told me that he was talked into running for it by some woman he'd met online. Said she liked a man with some prestige and a uniform and figured she could help him get both. They dated for a little while, but then I guess she got bored with the lack of drama in this small town and left for greener pastures. Poor Graham. Just like a man, I think. Give him any reason to think he's going to bed a lady with big blonde hair and even bigger boobs, and he rushes in without thinking. Tries to make a big impression and then gets stuck in a situation he didn't want, and without the lady he wanted for it. They don't understand that they're not buying a girlfriend when they bend over backward to impress us." She glanced at Staff. "No offense intended, dear. I'm sure you're much smarter than the average bear where the ladies are concerned."

"None taken." Staff and Afia exchanged knowing grins. He wasn't a bear, but he did not plan on mentioning that fact to either Afia or Ms. Patsy just now. Nor did he expect the older woman to understand what the term meant to him.

"So, Ms. Afton," Patsy said, and stretched out her hand across the table to take Afia's. "I certainly didn't intend to dredge up any old horrors for you. I didn't know about all that stuff. If you don't mind my asking, though, where was your mother?"

"That's the other mystery. My dad told me he thought she just ran off, had had all of life in a racist small town like Lost Hollow that she could take. I was very small when she disappeared, so I only have a few vague memories of that time. It's kind of strange. There were only four years between my mother's disappearance and my father's murder, but for me, the span between them feels like it lasted a lifetime. There was some attempt to locate my mother when I went into the foster care system, but I don't really know the extent of it. I've always wondered how much of what my dad told me was a partial truth, him attempting to protect me from something else."

"Have you ever looked for her yourself?"

Afia rolled her eyes. "If she'd wanted me in her life she wouldn't have left dad and me in the first place. So, no. I haven't. The most I ever did was search local newspaper archives for obituaries or stories about missing black women from the time. Never found any that had anything to do with my dad or Lost Hollow, though. That always made me think he was telling me most of the truth, that she had run off on her own. Otherwise, you'd think someone would have gone looking for her. Well, you'd think that if it was any town other than Lost Hollow, I guess."

Patsy gave Afia's hand a squeeze and then let it go. "Oh, my dear. Well, just so you know, you're not the only one around here with a nose for news. If you ever want me to look into it, I can ask around and try to find out what happened. Someone somewhere in this town has to know *something* about what happened to your mother."

"Thank you, but that won't be necessary. In spite of everything we just talked about, I'm not in town to spend the weekend focusing on me. I'm just here to do a job, not stare at my navel. Right, Staff?"

He pounded the table lightly with a closed fist. "Right!"

Patsy yawned just then and blinked wearily from behind her Coke-bottle lenses. "I don't know about staring at navels," she said, "but I'm starting to feel the need to stare at the backs of my eyelids. Thank you, Mr. Staff, for all your help in the clean-up tonight. You don't know how much an old woman appreciates that. And you, Ms. Afton, get yourself a good night's sleep. You had a long drive after a long day's work and then relived some bad memories on top of it all. If you're someone who takes Xanax, I believe this is an evening that would call for one."

Afia laughed and put up a halting hand. "I try to keep my medicines as natural as I can. I have some melatonin with me. If I can't get back to sleep after this, I'll just take one of those. I'd also love a glass of water to go if you don't mind. I run my mouth so much for work that it tends to get extra dry during the night."

"I have some bottled water in the fridge. You can have one of those if you want."

The two women rose from the table simultaneously. Once Afia had her bottle of water in-hand, she bade the other two in the kitchen a good night and trudged upstairs.

"And good night to you, Mr. Stafford," Patsy said. "I always leave a light on here in the kitchen, so if you need any water or anything for yourself in the night, you can find it easily enough. My room is across the hall, near the base of the stairs, if you need me for anything."

"Thanks. And, please, just call me Staff, if you don't mind."

"I'll do that, Mr...uh, Staff. Feel free to call me Patsy. Good night!"

On his way up the stairs, Staff heard the older woman switch off the ceiling lights in the kitchen. They were shortly replaced by the bright white glow of what were probably under-cabinet LEDs. He found his way back to his room, switched off his own lights, and flung himself prone and fully clothed onto the still-made bed. He propped his head on one elbow and stared out the window into the darkness of the backyard beyond. Patsy was right. He could see a little bit of the town square from here, including the pyramidon segment of the phallic obelisk in its center, even in this darkness. He was glad that it was him in this room rather than Afia, and he hoped it was true that she would not be able to see the square at all from her place in the house. The trip was supposed to produce a fun little ghost story for the Channel 6 News. So far, it had instead resurrected some ancient demons for the station's hardest working field reporter and, as far as Staff knew, no one in the house or at the station was Catholic or had any idea where to get their hands on some blessed water. Well, maybe Patsy did. He couldn't know for sure. She claimed to not be the gossiping kind, but she had those substantial eyeballs and most likely some equally large ears under all that fluffy silver grandmotherly hair. He wondered, too, how much of Patsy's knowledge about hauntings and happenings in Lost Hollow was really knowledge, not her own imagination filling in holes where she thought they should be filled to turn a buck for her little adopted hometown. If the decor of her bed and breakfast was any indication, Patsy was adept at finding something, anything, to fill a void. It was true of her walls, and most probably true of her narratives.

He rolled onto his back and pried off each of his sneakers with the toes of the opposite foot. The air felt good on his sock feet. His mind continued to race for a time, trying to remember how much he might have seen of the "black bitch" Patsy believed they had seen. He tried to process what had happened to Afia so long ago and how it might affect the rest of their weekend in Lost Hollow, tried to remember whether he'd locked the topper on the S-10 before turning in for the night.

Just when he thought sleep was never going to claim him, it did.

CHAPTER SIX

Minutes, hours, or days? How long had he lain there in broken agony on the cellar floor? Graham's tongue felt thick and dry. His throat was sandpaper behind his cracked and blood-caked lips. It felt too narrow and lined by shards of broken glass whenever he attempted to swallow. In the darkness, with the Maglite switched off to preserve battery but attached to its loop in his belt so he could take comfort in the fact that it was still there, he had swum in and out of consciousness more than once. He wasn't sure how many times now. Even if he could figure out how often he'd drifted, there was no way that the count could reveal to him how much time had passed outside the cellar walls, so it was a pointless thing for him to worry about.

He was cold now, he knew that much. The air in the cellar around him felt cooler on what little of his skin was exposed to it. Conversely, his uniform felt tighter against him, even though he hadn't had a meal in...well, who knew? It felt like his clothes usually did when he'd spent too long outside in Southern summer humidity, which is to say that the dampness caused his clothes to cling uncomfortably to his skin. He wiped a palm across his brow. It came away clammy and wet. He probably had a fever, then, some kind of immune system reaction to everything his body had been through since he'd fallen down the stairs.

But I didn't fall, he remembered. *I was struck.* He dabbed at the back of his head with two fingers to verify. Yes, it was still tender, though not as wet as it had been when he'd last checked. The thinning hair back there felt sticky and matted to his scalp, a result of the blood having coagulated in it.

On a few of the occasions he had bobbed up from unconsciousness, he thought he had heard the sound of footsteps coming from somewhere upstairs. Heavy ones, like those made by his father's work boots back in the day, the days he was trying like mad to shove back into the recesses of his memory. Each time he heard that old familiar *clomp*, he was once again a frightened child, trembling against the darkness of the cellar in the hope that his raging father was too drunk and exhausted to remember to check for him there. Once, he thought he'd heard the cellar door swing open. He'd even thought he'd seen light from it spill down the broken cellar staircase and across the floor in front of him. In the middle of that light, there was a shadow, the silhouette of a man, maybe, staring down at him from above. Before he could summon enough courage to call out to whoever it was (his father was dead, after all, right?), the image faded, and he'd drifted back into the cottony folds of mindless blackness.

Completely awake now, the rational part of his mind— that part that knew that the darkness of the cellar that enveloped him was not eternal darkness, but merely a small box of it in the middle of a very much lighted world—could dismiss the image of the man in the cellar door. It was a product of the situation and his injuries, a fever dream perhaps. Along with that image, the rational Graham said, he could also dismiss the obnoxious voice of his dead father that he thought he'd heard in his head when he was searching for the Maglite. It had to be a product of panic, no doubt brought on by the total darkness and his own history in this environment. Whose mind wouldn't be playing fucked up games with them in this situation, right? Right? It had to be that.

"And the concuthion," he said aloud, automatically wincing as the sounds came out of his mouth. He waited, but his words were not answered by the abusive and sarcastic sonic boom of his father's voice in his head. "Good." *Good.*

There was the dog, too, the fearful part of him reminded, the dog with the strange human face that scared you and made you fall the second time. *Yes,* he thought. *There was the dog. But if the man in the cellar door and my father's voice were products of a fever, I'm betting the dog was too.*

He pushed the thoughts away, then grabbed the Maglite from his belt and switched it on. The beam immediately fell across the broken staircase and the splintered scrap that lay beneath it. He scanned the wall behind the staircase with the beam of the Maglite, crawling along it until it illuminated the closed cellar door above him. He was five foot nine, short for the line of males in his family. The cellar had a ten-foot ceiling. If he leaped for it and yanked with enough force, he could probably pull down the remainder of the staircase above him, which would open up the foot of the cellar door for use as a hand-hold. He wondered if he was strong enough to then grab hold of the transition, if he leaped for it, and hoist himself up through the door. Breaking down the stairs might use up what little remained of his energy. He also risked another fall, given how sore and broken he already was, and that might kill him. He supposed he was lucky to have survived the initial tumble after being struck on the back of the head *and* falling down the stairs. After all, the exact same thing had happened to his father. Everyone thought it had been an accident. And why not? Lee Gordon was a drunk, an abuser, and in the 1990s lived alone in a Victorian Gothic house on a dead-end road. Over time, in fact, Graham had even been able to convince some part of himself that it was an accident, never allowing the vise grip of guilt to clamp down on his heart. It's much more difficult to feel guilty over an accidental death than if you intentionally commit murder, or so he surmised.

But it had been murder, hadn't it?

Self-defense, Graham consoled himself, both then and now as the memories surged to the front of his mind. *It was self-defense. He was going to try to hurt me again. I know he was. I believe it.*

The old man had been drunk when Graham showed up at his door with two armfuls of groceries from the Kroger in Hollow River, enough food and supplies to get them through another week without having to see each other. Pale, coughing almost uncontrollably, hurling obsceni-ties between breaths, and waving a nearly empty bottle of

Budweiser in his face, Lee Gordon had laid the blame on his son for the pain and chronic sickness he now suffered. It was Graham's fault that his mother was gone. It was Graham's fault that he'd had to work so hard all his life to provide for them both. It was Graham who had driven him to drink. Graham who was responsible for the smoking that had damaged his lungs so severely. The ungrateful brat had never been any help to him. He had never been anything but a waste of space.

These were all things the younger man had heard before. When Lee Gordon went into a drunken rage, it was like a needle stuck in a groove on a vinyl record. He repeated the same insults and accusations, as loud as his ruined respiratory system would allow and for as long as his target would stand there and take it. Most of the time, Graham quietly walked out, locking the door behind him and allowing the old man to continue ranting at him from inside. On this night, as he stood in the open doorway of the house with two armloads of groceries, the anger boiling up from inside him had become too hot for him to back down.

"Where'd you get the beer, dad?" he had shouted at his father over the tirade, setting the grocery bags down just inside the door, the same spot where his dog Butch had once let go of his bladder and then lost his life for it. "Who is bringing you the fucking beer? You know you're not supposed to have it."

The old man either hadn't heard or pretended not to have heard him. He continued shouting at Graham instead, inching the bottle of suds in his hand ever closer to the bridge of the younger man's nose as he railed. Looking back, Graham now thought it might have been that act that had ultimately sent him over the edge, the closing in of his father's brutal hand: the hand that had punched him and pulled at him so many times over the years, the hand that he'd never had the strength to hit back at when it neared. Until now.

Suddenly furious, Graham snatched the brown glass bottle from his father's hand. Lee Gordon, perhaps to his credit, had enough presence of mind to appear momentarily shocked by it. The younger Gordon next grabbed the collar of his father's button-down work shirt and spun him toward the interior of the old house.

"Where is it?" he screamed in his father's alcohol-pinked ear. "Where are you hiding this shit? Show me. I'm gonna pour every bit of it down the drain, and then you're gonna tell me who's been bringing it to you. Then I'm gonna find them, and I'm gonna rip their throat out. Do you hear me? WHERE IS IT?"

He shoved his father, intending to force him to walk forward, but Lee instead plummeted to his hands and knees on the hardwood floor beneath them. Even through his own anger and hate, Graham could see that the sudden turn of events had badly scared his old man. His arms trembled at his shoulders as he clung to the floor, apparently unable to raise himself back to his feet on his own. Graham set down the beer, grabbed two fistfuls of work shirt at those shoulders, and hoisted his father back to his feet.

"Where is it?" he growled again. Then it dawned on him. The cellar. "You hide it in the fucking cellar, don't you? Of course, you do. Why wouldn't you? There's no reason for

anyone to go down there anymore, is there? You don't have any little kids left here to torment. So let's just go have ourselves a look in the cellar."

Graham stepped around his woozy father, who stood with his eyes half-lidded. The rest of him swayed in gentle circles at the ankle, trying to maintain his balance. The younger Gordon unlatched the cellar door and swung it open. He stretched his right arm into the door frame and flipped the light switch into the On position, bathing the dirt floor below with the loud white hum of tube fluorescents. He started to descend alone in search of Lee Gordon's stash but thought better of it when he remembered that his dad, though dazed by his son's pushback, was still very much in the throes of drunken rage. As such, Graham was likely to end up trapped down here if he allowed the old man to remain upstairs while he went down. It would be just like him to latch the door behind his nosy son and trap him down here for spite, at least until he felt the first signs of a hangover and needed someone to help him nurse it.

"All right, Dad." He leaned against the cellar door so that it remained open. "You first. I'm not leaving until you show me where you're hiding it."

The look on his father's face went from dazed drunk to exhaustion, to anger, and then to resigned resentment in the space of a second. The older man bent down, wobbling a little at half-mast, and plucked his beer bottle from the floor where Graham had left it. He had a little trouble returning to a standing position, but Graham did not leave his place against the cellar door to help him. After some waiting and more wobbling, Lee Gordon stood mostly erect again with the bottle of Budweiser gripped by the neck in his right hand.

"Fine." He shuffled to the cellar door while tipping the bottle and the remainder of its contents toward his open mouth. Graham snatched it from him again. He glared briefly at his son for his impertinence, but then went back to watching his own feet when Graham refused to avert his eyes.

Graham watched as his father descended the first step, then the second. The old man had become fat in that baggy, fleshy way an old drunk has. It was as if there was no muscle attached to his bones at all now, just mounds and mounds of blobby yellow fat creating pendulous bulges in odd places against crepe Hefty bag skin. His hair was still thick in most areas, although male pattern baldness had left a pear-shaped *cul-de-sac* of scalp on top from his hairline to his crown. Lee Gordon was no longer the frightening authoritarian strongman he had known for the majority of his life. He wasn't even strong in the mean sense of the word, the way that bullies see themselves as strong. He was petty and weak, no longer a man in his son's eyes. He was nothing more than a walking advertisement for the consequences of alcohol abuse. Some part of Graham felt sad for his father. Some part of him felt a little pity. Mostly, he felt rage. Rage that he had allowed a weak man like this to control him for most of his life. Rage that all he'd had to do to stop it when he was a child was to stand up to his father the way he had tonight. Rage that so many of his young years were lost to him now; years that could have been filled with the happiness of living elsewhere, away from the man who would rob him of a life well-lived, of pride, of courage, and of confidence. Rage. Graham's fist tightened around the neck of the Budweiser bottle in his right hand.

Lee Gordon teetered a little on the second step down, and again on the third. On any other night of his life, Graham's first instinct might have been to reach out and steady him. Not this time. Instead, Graham raised the bottle of Budweiser in his right hand by its neck over his head, dumping what little remained of its contents on the top step of the cellar in the process. He took two steps down the staircase behind his old man and brought the bottle down hard against Lee Gordon's baldness. What happened next probably lasted only seconds, but to Graham, it felt as if everything around him had been slowed down and stretched into minutes.

The crown of his father's head caved from the force of the blow, his skull crunching audibly beneath the *thunk* of the thick glass. The thin hot membrane of scalp covering the bone broke open as well, oozing thick red blood from the back of his head and into the hair below. The beer bottle did not break but remained clenched in Graham's right hand as he followed through. Lee Gordon pivoted on the third from the top step of the cellar staircase so that he faced his son. His half-lidded drunken eyes fluttered wide open, fearful, questioning "why?" His right foot became tangled against his left one as he turned and, just like that, he was pinwheeling his arms. Going down.

Graham heard a bone snap when his father's back struck the lower half of the staircase. The blow catapulted the old man's legs into the air and hurled him heels over head down the remainder of the stairs. When he crash landed against the cellar floor, he lay face down with his head pointed toward the stairs and his feet at the wall opposite them. His head was tilted at a weird angle, and the point of his spine appeared to now be visible through his shoulder, stretching it so that it looked very close to breaking through his skin.

But Lee Gordon was not dead yet. From his place on the stairs, Graham could hear labored moans of pain and suffering coming from the broken figure on the cellar floor. For a split second, he allowed his conscience to scream at him. *What have I done? Oh my God, what have I done?* He imagined himself calling for help, getting an ambulance, getting the sheriff's department. He imagined trying to explain his boiled over rage and support it by revealing all the abuses he'd suffered at the hands of his father that he'd never reported to anyone before now. He imagined trying to explain to a judge and jury that it was temporary insanity brought on by a long history of horrible physical, emotional, and psychological torture. Then he imagined himself in prison, wearing an orange jumpsuit, confined to the same small box hour after hour of every day. Forced to shower, eat, bathe, piss, and shit with other men. Men who were actual hardened criminals. Men with no empathy. Men who would rape him. Men who would tear him up and eat him for breakfast every day for the rest of his life because of the one second out of a whole lifetime of them when he had finally found the courage to stand up for himself.

He imagined all of that. Then he descended the rest of the staircase with the beer bottle. He smashed it against the back of his father's head again, listening intently for the new crunch of a broken skull beneath it. Then again. Again. And again. Until, finally, he realized that he was no longer bludgeoning a living and breathing human being, but a giant sack of bones, fat, and alcohol-withered muscles. Not a nerve twitched in the body that lay below him. Not a sound of breath flowed from its nostrils or from between its lips.

At last, Graham tossed the beer bottle from his hand, allowing it to smash into brown shards against the hard-packed earth of the cellar floor. He was grateful to it for having lasted as long as it had. Finally. Finally, Lee Gordon was dead.

I KNEW IT! Graham Gordon's dead father's voice reverberated through his skull, ringing his sinuses and rolling his broken body back to the cellar floor. The Maglite fell from his hand again but did not flicker this time. It went a short distance away from him and landed with its beam pointed where the staircase's stringers ended. *I KNEW IT! YOU MURDERED ME YOU UNGRATEFUL LITTLE SHIT. I BROUGHT YOU IN THIS WORLD. I BROUGHT YOU UP BY MYSELF, AND YOU FUCKING MURDERED ME FOR IT! I SHOULD'VE KILLED YOU FIRST WHEN I HAD THE CHANCE. I SHOULD'VE KILLED YOU WHERE YOU STOOD WHEN YOU WALKED IN MY HOUSE THAT NIGHT. YOU UNGRATEFUL LITTLE SHIT!*

Graham, in a semi-fetal position, rolled back and forth on his left hip and shoulder. He squeezed his eyes shut tight and clenched his hands mightily at his ears, trying to shut out the sound. The pain was worse now, not so much like a single railroad spike stuck in his brain, but more like the repeated stabbings of a pickaxe, as if his dead father were digging a deeper hole inside his head with every ferocious word. His father *must* be in his head after all. How else could he have known what Graham was remembering?

As the pain began to subside, Graham opened his eyes, intending to locate the Maglite and shut it off, conserve the battery. What he saw before him instead was the broken body of Lee Gordon as he'd last seen it in this place, lying on the cellar floor in the beam from the flashlight, eyes open, glaring back at him. His neck was still broken and twisted on his shoulders at an impossible angle. The fingers of each of his dead hands were dug into the cellar floor, his palms raised above them as if he'd been clawing his way across it. Dried blood and dirt were smeared over his gray and wrinkled face. His brown eyes had skimmed over with some kind of greenish-gray film. His mouth hung open, barely a tooth within, and thick black filth oozed from the corner that lay nearest the floor. As Graham watched, a glistening pink earthworm protruded from the slime, dislodged itself, and then went slinking along its way. Runners of pus crept from the corners of dead Lee Gordon's eyes and dripped on the floor beneath him.

"Noooot yeeeeet," the thing in the cellar with him groaned. It stretched one broken and twisted arm out toward Graham, impossibly digging the fingers of the attached hand into the compacted earth floor, and pulled itself forward, dragging its lifeless feet behind. "Iiiiii'mmmm noooot iiiinnnn yooouuurr heeeaad yeeeeet, buuuut IIIIiiii wiiiill beeeee soooon."

The remains of Lee Gordon stretched its other hideous hand forward, dug in its fingers, and pulled. The shoe on his left foot slid off as he did so, revealing gangrenous toes poking through threadbare socks. Graham could hear its toenails scraping against the cellar floor, gouging it, as it inched toward him, as if the gravity surrounding the animated corpse was pulling on him harder than it was pulling on Graham, trying to sweep this thing not of nature under the rug of the earth.

His dead father's rotting face loomed inches away from Graham's own. He blinked, hoping again that all this was just a product of the *concuthion*. He held his breath, thinking that maybe if he could no longer smell the presence of the thing it would somehow become less real to him. When he could hold it no longer, and dead Lee Gordon was close enough for his living son to see the rage undulating behind the putrid film over its eyes, he opened his mouth and tried to scream. But nothing came out.

The thing closed in.

CHAPTER SEVEN

Afia and Patsy Blankenship were already bathed, dressed, and drinking coffee at the breakfast table by the time Staff teetered down the stairs to the kitchen on Saturday morning. He glanced at his Fitbit, which informed him that it was only six-thirty, a ridiculously early hour for any sane individual to be up and ready to go on a weekend, work to do or no work to do. He supposed he shouldn't be surprised that Patsy was a morning person. After all, she was both older and an entrepreneur. Afia, on the other hand, typically worked the late morning-to-late afternoon shift at Channel 6. Perhaps her wine snooze following dinner the previous evening in addition to a good night's sleep had enabled her to get a head start this a.m.

"Good morning, sleepyhead," Patsy sang in that abysmally cheery and loud voice morning people save just for these moments. "There's fresh coffee in the carafe and some scrambled eggs, bacon, and sausage on the table. I made some biscuits and sausage gravy, too. Afia seemed to like them. There's some diced fruit in the fridge, if you would rather have that."

Staff groaned an appreciative affirmation. It was all he could manage. He poured the remainder of the carafe into a mug that had been placed upside-down beside it and pulled up a seat at the kitchen table next to Afia. No food yet. Mood fuel first. He held up a hand when Patsy pointed out the sugar bowl and the small silver pitcher of creamer she had placed on the table. Staff was a man who liked his coffee bitter and black, just like his soul before eight o'clock. After three long slurps from the steaming mug, he finally discovered his voice.

"You two are up bright and early." He managed to make it sound less like an accusation than it felt. "I haven't even had a shower yet. I hope you don't mind having to wait for me before we set sail."

"Not at all," Afia replied. She had definitely brightened since the previous night's onslaught of memories of injuries past. "Patsy and I have just been sitting here doing a little planning and waiting already. She texted the constable a few minutes ago about meeting us out at the Gordon place, but I don't think he's replied yet."

"He hasn't," Patsy said. "If I don't hear from him by seven, I'll call instead. Some people don't even bother to look at their phones unless they're ringing, believe it or not, even in this time when it seems like everyone has a screen permanently floating in front of their eyes. Mr. Gordon is one of those types. I don't think the constable cares much for being always in touch with the rest of the world."

"Don't blame him."

"Young Mr. Beard, on the other hand, is already on his way over."

Staff nearly spit out his coffee. "What?"

Afia was laughing. "She called him last night. He was excited about being interviewed. Said he'd be here by seven. We can talk to him while Patsy tries to contact the constable again."

The cameraman poured the remainder of his morning fuel down his throat and stood. "Guess I'd better get moving, then. I have to get showered and unload the equipment."

A blast of classical music from somewhere near the entryway interrupted him. Bach. Toccata and Fugue in D Minor. It was the doorbell. He hadn't noticed what it was playing when Afia had pressed it the day before. He'd been distracted then, though. Staff noted Patsy's broad grin as the pipe organ tones rang out.

"Like it? Young Mr. Beard taught me how to set it up for Halloween. I didn't even know you could change doorbell music. That's probably him now. He's a little early." Patsy pushed back from the kitchen table.

"Well, I guess I won't be getting that shower after all," Staff said to Afia. "I'll go get the equipment."

There wasn't much to Jeremy Beard. He was a slight fellow with dark hair and almond eyes. Today he was wearing a black T-shirt with the *Ghostbusters* logo on it over a pair of dark denims with a hole worn in the right knee. Staff surmised that the young man's wardrobe choices would be similar the next day, and the day after. He might change out *Ghostbusters* for the Batman insignia or Green Lantern, but that would be about as far as he was willing to branch out. Staff caught his eye and nodded at the shirt.

"What do you think about the remake?"

Jeremy rolled his eyes. "Never saw it. Heard it was awful, though. I don't think the fans appreciated it much. I would know. I'm in a cosplay group that does the Ghostbusters at conventions all over the state and it's pretty much still a sausagefest." He beamed. "I'm kind of the Ray Stantz of the group, I guess. I keep the ECTO-1 running."

"What's the ECTO-1?"

That provoked another eyeroll from Jeremy. "The Ghostbusters car," he replied. "I'm one of two of us who keep the car running. I drove it over here, as a matter of fact. After I'm done here I have to get it over to my friend John's place so we can take it to the comic shop in Uptown. They're doing an event today."

Staff smiled at him. "You're a budding historian *and* an auto-mechanic? That's quite a double-major you're headed for there."

The young man shrugged. "Yeah. I guess."

This exhausted Staff's supply of relatability to Jeremy. He muttered a "Yeah" in response and went about setting up the outdated Channel 6 camera and lighting equipment. After some discussion, Afia and Patsy eventually settled on the set of modern chairs in front of the fireplace for the interview, which would create a nice visual reference when they later interviewed Patsy herself in the same spot. Staff made a mental note to close in tight on his subjects so as to crop out the art deco piece hanging above them. Afia looked perfectly natural on camera as she seated herself on the edge of her chair, leaning in so that viewers could see how interested she was in Jeremy's story. Jeremy himself looked swallowed by his surroundings, like a toddler sitting in grandpa's recliner. Even so, his face came to life when Staff switched on the lights and indicated that they were rolling. He was eager to share what he knew.

Afia smiled at him. "So, Ms. Blankenship says you were hanging around in the Gordon house on Hollow Creek Road and that you heard something strange. Tell me about it."

"Jesus! We're just going to jump right in? I thought you'd ask for my vitals first, like Lois Lane did in *Superman*."

"We'll make sure we have your name right and everything afterward," Afia assured him. "Don't swear on camera, please. We can bleep you or cut it out when we edit everything together, but it creates more work for us."

The young man blushed a little. "Sorry."

"Now tell me about your experience in the Gordon house. Why did you go in there? Didn't you know you were trespassing on private property?"

Jeremy glanced at his hands. "Well, I guess I knew it was trespassing. We—I mean my buddies and I—weren't thinking about all that. We'd just heard the rumors and wanted to check them out for ourselves."

"What rumors?"

"About the screaming. There were some other kids at school who told us they were going to go in there to explore the place. One of them, Brandi Wakefield, is big into haunting shows. She was thinking she might try to start a new ghost investigation series, sell it to Travel Channel. Like *Ghost Adventures*, you know? Except with some girl power instead of somebody like Zak Bagans running around and shouting at dust. I asked her why she wouldn't do something new and original instead of gender-swapping a B.S. show like that. She called me a misogynist incel and said it was *her* business."

Afia chuckled. "Ok. What did they tell you about the screaming?"

"Only that they heard it." He shifted in his seat. "And that they didn't go in the place after that. Brandi said that they had parked her car on the street at the end of the driveway and were starting to unload when they heard this godawful screaming coming from somewhere inside the house. She said it was this horribly shrill and long shriek, some real ear-drum piercing kind of shi—uh, stuff. At first it startled them. Then they figured they must have been busted, so they hauled ass back to the car and drove off."

"Busted?"

"Yeah. They thought someone had told on them, alerted the owner or something. If I owned an abandoned house that's exactly the kind of thing I'd do to keep people away from it. Hide a set of high-power speakers where no one would think to look and setup a motion sensor trigger and bam! You got yourself a haunted house, talk of the town."

"Uh-huh. What was it about their story that made *you* want to check it out for yourself, then? I mean, your friends assumed they had been had. Weren't you afraid you'd get caught?"

Jeremy grinned. It was the sheepiest of sheepish grins Staff had ever seen. "I guess. But I think what I really wanted to do was debunk the screaming itself. Brandi *thought* it was probably the owner. I wanted to *prove* it. I mean, everyone knows that Constable Gordon owns the place. Before that he worked at the Media Place Smarty Bar. I mean, come

on! If you're a guy with some power and access to the right
equipment, why wouldn't you mess with people?"

Afia grimaced comically. "It would certainly keep *me*
away. So you went to the constable's house to see for yourself. You knew it was the constable's house and you weren't
afraid you'd get in trouble?"

"From him?" The grin on the kid's face would have
betrayed his lack of fear and respect for Lost Hollow's law
enforcement if the tone of his question had not. To her
credit, Staff thought, Afia chose to ignore that path.

"Tell me what happened then."

Jeremy leaned back in his chair. His right ankle was
propped on his left knee. He knitted his fingers together
in his lap, steepling the index fingers so that they pointed
at Afia.

"This is where things get weird."

***

There were no signs of another living human being at the
Gordon place when Jeremy arrived. Naturally, that didn't
mean anything if the constable, or even Jeremy's former
high school buddies, were hiding out somewhere on the
site, maybe preparing to leap out at him at the scariest possible moment. He pushed the front door inward, allowing
his iPhone's flashlight feature to cast its white light on the
interior before he stepped over the threshold. The moon
was full and bright. Not a supermoon this time, but it cast
enough light through the windows of the old place to help
illuminate the corners his iPhone did not. Within, there
was dust and footprints in dust.

So far, he didn't see a damned thing to be afraid of. Yes, it was an abandoned house of sorts. No one lived in it, even if Constable Gordon now owned the place. There were still signs of life. Whole and broken beer bottles lay scattered about the floor. The footprints were another dead giveaway. People had been here recently. That made Jeremy feel less like he was exploring a creepy haunted relic from the past and more like he was breaking and entering. Still, if the good constable didn't want anyone trespassing in this old house, why hadn't he bothered to put a lock on the place?

The old hardwood floor groaned when he stepped inside, but it wasn't menacing. Just a nail that had pried loose from a floor joist over time. It happened in every house. That's what his dad always said when Jeremy was little, anyway. Those strange squeaks and groans you hear in a house in the middle of the night—those footsteps of monsters, intruders, or ghosts in the imagination of childhood—were almost never anything more than the strained sounds of nails against bending wood, the sounds of a house settling. He glanced around the room with the ray of light from his iPhone and, satisfied that no one was going to jump out at him from behind the door, walked several paces through the interior.

To the left of him was a large room, something that looked like it might have once been a living area or family room. In front of him stretched a wallpapered hallway that ended with a window that probably looked out on the backyard. There also stood the mouth of a staircase that led to the second floor. In a wall beneath the back of that staircase, and closer to Jeremy's spot near the front of the place, was a small door with a hook-and-eye latch on it. It looked like it might close off a storage area or access to a basement. As the beam from his iPhone passed over the latch, he thought he heard something skitter behind that door. Rats? Maybe. Then again, a door like that might be a perfect place to bide your time if you had a friend who was exploring a supposedly haunted house and you wanted to scare the shit out of that friend when he did.

Jeremy grinned. "Ok, guys. I know you're here. Come on out." His words bounced off the walls and floors of the empty rooms and echoed back to him. There was no more response than that.

"Guys? I know you're in here."

Nothing. He was annoyed now. Pranks are funny, but they're best when you can share the laugh at yourself. There comes a point in a prank when it's more important that the joker knows it's time to stop or risk getting punched in the dick. Most of the time, that point is when the butt of the joke figures out he's the butt of the joke.

"I'm not playing around here. I'm giving you to the count of three to come out or I'm coming in after you. And you don't want me to have to come in after you. One."

Jeremy thought he saw the loose hook latch on the door jiggle a little in his light, as if the door to which it was attached had moved a hair's breadth and then become still.

"Two."

Nothing.

"Three!"

Silence.

He began to creep toward the door, trying to not cause the old floors beneath him to squeak and give away his position. "Ok," he called. "I guess there really is no one there. I suppose that means no one will mind if I just grab this little hook on the front of the door here and LATCH YOU IN!"

Jeremy threw open the plank door and held it against the wall with his right hand. In his left, the iPhone shone its beam into the blackness of the void he had just revealed. He had expected an old buddy or two, maybe even would-be Ghost Adventurer Brandi Wakefield, to fall out from behind the door when he yanked on it. Instead, all he saw was a flight of plank stairs leading down into...something. A faint odor followed the breeze the swinging door had created. It smelled musty and damp, like mildew or maybe a mouse that had been dead for a while but not yet decomposed enough to stop stinking.

"Hello?" he shouted down the stairs, although he couldn't imagine anyone would be stupid enough to try to navigate them in darkness like this and with a damp smell like that wafting over them. The decrepit old things would probably collapse under the weight of human feet. "If anyone's down there, say something."

From somewhere outside the void of the cellar there came a shriek so piercing that a startled Jeremy leapt backward from the darkness he had been peering into, dropping his iPhone to the hardwood floor in the process. The plank door, free of its restraint, swung closed on its spring hinge with a slam. He plugged his fingers in his ears and clenched his teeth against the sound. Goosebumps rose on his flesh and the prickles from them felt like they zig-zagged from the crack of his ass all the way up his spine and into his hair, forcing it to stand on end. The godawful sound was really some kind of combination of shriek and scream, as if a giant hawk had suddenly descended on an unsuspecting woman jogging at night and begun disemboweling her with its talons. It was a long shriek, without an overture, and ended as suddenly as it had begun. Whatever it was, there was no mistaking that it had come from somewhere *outside* the house, not within.

Jeremy's heart pounded inside his chest. His breaths came in short, shallow bursts. He hadn't been scared when he walked into the old house that evening. Now, though, he was beginning to fear walking out of it. He retrieved his iPhone. It was miraculously unbroken thanks to the Otterbox his mistrustful parents had insisted on when they bought the thing for him. He backed away from the plank door, pivoted toward the wide open front of the house, and shined the iPhone's flashlight into the darkness of the yard beyond. He could see only the shadows of the branches of trees cast by the backlight of the full moon. They stretched long across the dead grass, the shadowy fingers of Death clawing at the few fragile remnants of green summer grass. There were no signs of anything else: no animals, no pranksters, no ghosts. He launched the video app on his iPhone and tapped the large red Record button. It was probably too dark to see much of anything on camera, but when another shriek pierced the darkness, Jeremy would be ready for it.

He didn't wait long.

The second shriek was exactly like the first, except farther away. The first one was definitely outside. This one was both outside and somewhere behind him, as if whatever was making the sound was somewhere in the backyard. Jeremy plugged his ears and dashed to the window he'd noticed by the second-floor stairs at the back of the hall. There he plucked his left finger from his ear canal and shined the beam of his iPhone he held in that hand through the glass. He scanned the night for the source of the sound. It died away again as soon as his eyes adjusted to the lens of the window and some details began to emerge from the shadows. The backyard was small and edged by a long stretch of tall trees barren of leaves, and woods beyond that edge.

Jeremy crouched in front of the window and waited. He became aware that his back was to an open front door, that he was a sitting duck if someone or something from outside these walls wanted to come get him now that his attention was turned elsewhere. Even so, he felt safer inside the house than out just now, almost as if this place had once been his own. It felt familiar to him somehow, although he could not remember ever having set foot inside it before.

He's hiding in the cellar again, he thought randomly. *He's not supposed to be down there.*

Jeremy didn't know who "he" was and why "he" was not supposed to be in the cellar. The thought had simply formed in his mind. It surfaced there and popped open like a bubble from the bottom of a pot of water just beginning to boil. It was an apt simile, really, because Jeremy suddenly realized that he was angry. He wasn't sure about what. His left hand gripped the iPhone hard enough to turn his knuckles white. He only realized it when he heard the plastic beneath the rubber covering of the Otterbox case give and crack from the pressure. He made a conscious effort to relax his grip, tried to refocus his attention on his scan of the yard beyond the window. It was not easy. Anger, rage, and snippets of memories or old conversations that somehow seemed both familiar and entirely foreign to him raced through his mind.

There was a flash of a boy huddled over the body of a dead dog somewhere. Then it was gone. There was a woman. Several of them, actually. All of them hurt, screaming at him. Then they were gone, too. There was a brief memory of a man: a black man in blue work clothes with fire in his eyes. The man was angry, coming for him. Then there was a flash of the same man, either dead or sleeping, crimson liquid flowing down the front of his shirt.

Jeremy suddenly felt sick. His head swam with memories he did not recognize. They swirled in his head like water circling a drain. He lowered the iPhone from the window and bowed his head over his knees, duck and cover-style on the hardwood floor of the old Gordon place. He gagged and retched, but nothing came up. His left hand ached from where he had been gripping the iPhone. He also noticed for the first time a pins-and-needles feeling crawling throughout his right leg, all the way up to his testicles. The leg had gone to sleep on him at some point as he crouched by the window. He hadn't realized it until he'd changed position.

A third shriek cut through the silence of the backyard of the Gordon place, and it shocked him back to reality. The anger. The false memories. The sickness. All gone as suddenly as they had converged on him. Jeremy rose on his knees and peered out the window again, into the backyard. There, along the edge of the woods, he saw something. It looked like it might be a dog of some kind, but he couldn't tell for sure. He raised the iPhone to the glass, trying to get it on video, and it turned to look at him then. At least, he thought it did. As bright as the moon was that night, it was difficult to see the thing's head, even with the iPhone's flashlight beam pointed directly at it. It shrieked again and, as he plugged his ears for the third time that night like a toddler trying to avoid a scolding, he was sure that—whatever it was—it could not be canine. There wasn't a dog on Earth that could make that sound.

Then it was gone along with its shriek. He didn't know how. First it was there, then it was not. Silence engulfed the old Gordon house, and Jeremy's eyes suddenly felt like they were full of sand. He was exhausted. He wanted only to go home.

***

Patsy's gasp from somewhere to his left startled Staff. He whipped around to look at her, jiggling the news camera on its tripod when he did. She had padded her way to the interview area silently enough. Her iPhone, which she had been using all morning in her attempts to contact Constable Gordon, was still clutched in her right hand. Fortunately, Jeremy Beard had already presented Afia with the meat of his ghost story. The reporter was in the process of closing out the interview when Patsy exclaimed.

"Jeremy Beard! You never told me you saw the black bitch!"

Afia shot her a look, at which point the older woman appeared to realize she'd just interjected that thought aloud into the audio part of the interview. She grinned sheepishly, partially covering her lips with the fingers of the hand that was not holding the iPhone. "Oh my. Oh dear. I hope you can cut that out."

"We can," Staff said, "but you should go sit down while we wrap this up." He glanced at Afia, who provided him with the slightest of nods. "It won't be much longer."

Afia faced her interview subject but spoke to Staff. "Still rolling?"

"Rolling."

The scowl that had overcome her face following the interruption was immediately replaced with a warm and pleasant smile. "So, Mr. Beard, are you a believer in the paranormal after your experiences in the old Gordon place?"

The young man, who still seemed a bit distracted by Patsy Blankenship's outburst, shrugged. "I won't rule it out. I don't know anything about a, uh, black bitch, but I know I heard shrieks and saw something out in the backyard of that old place that night. Even more than that I *felt* something. I've never been in a fight in my life but that night, with all of those weird flashes of people in my head, I felt out of control of my own body. I wanted to punch someone. Or something. I'd swear there was a part of me that wanted to jump out that window and just start whaling on that animal, whatever it was. I think I blamed it for all those weird things in my head, maybe. I don't know. It's almost like someone else was in control of me just then, like I was being possessed."

Afia nodded sympathetically. "I think this is a good spot for us to end the interview. Thank you very much, Mr.

Beard. It was fascinating. Can I ask you: what would you think about joining us down at the Gordon place when we go to interview the constable? Do you think you could show us where some of these things you described happened? Maybe it will trigger something you'd like to add to what you've already told us."

Jeremy twisted his head toward Staff. "Is that thing still rolling?"

"Not now," Staff replied. He paused the recording.

"I don't think I'm ready to go back out there," Jeremy said to Afia. "Someday, maybe. But telling you all that just now...I don't know. It brought the whole thing back to me in a way I hadn't really thought about until now. I can tell you, Ms. Afton, I have never touched a drop of alcohol or used any drugs beyond vitamin supplements and the occasional Tylenol. I don't like feeling out of control of myself. That night? Alone in that house? I don't know what I would have done if that thing's shrieking hadn't broken whatever spell it was I was under. What I do know is I never want to feel that way again."

Staff stepped from behind the camera. "You said you were recording on your iPhone while all that was happening. Any chance we could use that video as part of the segment?"

Here the young man's mouth twisted down, his eyes sorrowful. "You *could*, if it showed anything. I got brave when I got home and played back what I had recorded. It doesn't show anything but the dark outside the window I was recording from."

"What about the sounds? The shrieks?"

Jeremy shook his head, morose. "They're not on there, either. I don't know why. I know I heard them. All the video I shot shows is my iPhone bouncing around the window while I'm trying to look out into the darkness. You can hear me shuffling around. That's all. Well, except for me dry heaving a few times. That audio made it on there."

"Do you have that phone on you? Can I see it?" Staff stretched out his hand. After a moment's hesitation, Jeremy produced the device, unlocked it, and handed it to him.

"It's the first one in the roll there. I haven't recorded anything since then."

Staff started playback. He watched as a full five minutes of black video unfolded. He could see the reflection of the iPhone's flashlight feature in the glass of the window through which the video was shot. He thought he could make out a little of Jeremy's own reflection there as well. The rest of the image was shrouded in darkness. Twice, the camera bounced around as Jeremy dry heaved beside it. The video stopped just as some shuffling sounds started. Probably the moment Jeremy had decided it was safe to leave and stopped recording.

"He's right," Staff announced. "You can't see anything. I won't say there's nothing there, but the backyard is way too dark to be able to see anything with the light from that flash bouncing off the window in front." He handed the iPhone back to Jeremy. "You might have had better luck if you had doused the iPhone light and just shot with the natural moonlight falling on the yard."

"Yeah. Thanks." He stood up and shook hands with Afia. "Hope I helped."

"Thank you so much, Jeremy!" Patsy called. "Let me know when you're ready to start hosting some ghost tours with me. I'm expecting I'll need some tour guide help right after Channel 6 airs this." She smiled sweetly at him.

"Will do," Jeremy said. He walked out the door of the bed and breakfast without looking back.

***

Forty-five minutes after Jeremy Beard left the bed and breakfast—and after Staff had finally had a chance to finish his coffee, take a shit, and take a shower—Patsy had yet to receive any acknowledgment from Constable Graham Gordon. She had texted him twice, attempted to call his cell phone three times, and called his landline once. Graham, Patsy explained to Staff and Afia, was like most residents of Lost Hollow in that he maintained a landline and still kept an up-to-date telephone directory within easy reach of it. These ancient technologies were in addition to his cell phone and internet service. "Just in case."

"It's not like him to not reply at all," she said when her final attempt to reach him by cell phone rang three times and then, just like the calls that preceded it, was finally redirected to voicemail. "I hope he's ok."

"He probably just left the house without his cell phone," Staff said. He tapped his own iPhone, which was clipped to the hip of the Army green cargo shorts he was wearing for their ghost hunt. "It happens to me all the time. I had to start hanging this on the doorknob with a shoestring so I'd find it when I leave in the morning."

Staff pushed back from the kitchen table and stood up, dusting his hands on his cargo shorts as he did. "Well, that's that. We can pick some other allegedly haunted place to do our story today, I think. I hate to give up on it after we spent all that time talking to the kid, though. Maybe if Mr. Gordon shows up before we're done for the day, we can go out to his place then. I'm going to go get the equipment and start loading—"

"I think we should still go out there," Afia interrupted him. She looked at Patsy. "I mean, Jeremy Beard did it. A lot of the kids have. You said yourself that the constable was out there just last night. Maybe he really did forget his phone and is out there working."

"Oh, yes. Yes, he did. He called to tell me he was out there just as I was leaving the office, as a matter of fact. That was the last I've heard from him. He said he was out there and that we needed to send someone out to fix the security light at the end of the driveway. I suppose it would be all right for us to go out there anyway. We can always try to call him again if he's not already there."

"Looks like I'm outnumbered, then," Staff said cheerily. "I'm going to go get all our stuff loaded up now so we can get moving."

Outside, with the topper door up and the tailgate of the pickup down, Staff began to load equipment. Just as he finished securing the last piece of hardware into the back of the pickup, Afia and Patsy emerged from the front door of the bed and breakfast. Afia was already striding toward him, jingling the second set of keys to the S-10 in her right hand, while Patsy appeared to be rummaging through a large black purse in search of her own. She located them and locked the front door of the house, then jogged a few paces down the sidewalk to catch up with Afia who was smiling brightly in spite of the previous day's disastrous effects on her mood.

"Any word on the constable?" Staff called out to them.

Patsy shook her head. "Not yet. I'll take my car. You two can follow me out there. I know exactly where it is."

So do we, Staff thought, although now probably wasn't the best time to remind everyone about their encounter with the black bitch from the day before. He climbed into the shotgun seat of the S-10. "All right, then, I'm ready if y'all are." Afia climbed into the driver's seat and started the engine, which idled smoothly in the driveway of the bed and breakfast after what sounded like a couple of rough knocks.

Patsy toddled to her own car, a silver Hyundai Sonata that had somehow maintained its showroom shine even after driving over the backwoods dusty roads and bridges of Hollow County, and climbed behind the wheel. She started it, revved the engine, and waved to the two journalists as she backed out of the driveway. She turned right, toward the square. Staff eyeballed Afia as the older woman pulled into a three car-length lead.

"We can still bail on the Gordon house if we need to, you know."

Afia smiled at him. "I'm fine," she said. Of course she was. Staff would have noticed it otherwise. After last night, he was quite sure of that. They rounded the comically out-of-place-for-this-small-of-a-town obelisk in the square (which Afia chose to carefully ignore) and followed

Patsy's Sonata down what would soon turn into SR-501 toward the city limits, toward Hollow Creek Road, where they had encountered the so-called black bitch. Toward the Gordon house.

***

Patsy Blankenship's relief was palpable when they pulled alongside Hollow Creek Road and parked in front of what Staff assumed was the Gordon house. He could see it in her body language even before she stepped out of her Sonata. The tension in her shoulders relaxed visibly, and she allowed one of her hands to release the steering wheel long enough to gently wipe at something along the back of her neck. She inched the car in behind a red Toyota Tacoma that was already parked at the edge of what looked like it might have once been a driveway, beside the overgrown front yard. Expertly, she left just enough room to be able to maneuver out of her chosen spot when it was time to go, a skill that Staff himself had never quite been able to master when it came to driving. Afia, on the other hand, eased the S-10 right up behind Patsy's Sonata perfectly.

Staff guessed that the red Tacoma must be the constable's truck. That made sense given Patsy's description of him. The constable was just enough of a Southern man to understand that he was expected to drive a pickup, but not quite testosterone-fueled enough to go for a full-size showboat like a Tundra, or a Dodge Ram 2500, or a Ford F-350. Most of the men Staff knew who drove beasts like that weren't even farmers or mechanics or other types that you might expect to need a heavy duty vehicle. They were mostly rednecks who were trying to impress other rednecks. Mr. Gordon had on some level understood the requirement that he drive a four wheel-capable pickup to fit in with the rest of the toxic masculinity of this small town, but didn't entirely understand all that that requirement entailed. He chose a safe and practical pickup over a showboat. Staff wondered whether the constable was aware of the distinction he was making for himself among his regional male peers. Those peers might not be aware either. For the average white Southern male who grew up in a small town, heavy-duty pickup ownership was mostly instinct.

Patsy had already leaped out of her car before Afia and Staff were able to release their seatbelts. She motioned for them to hurry up, mouthing the words "come on" as she did. Afia slid out of the driver's seat and walked the side of the road toward Patsy while Staff fussed with the camera that was stored in the back of the S-10. By the time he caught up to the two women, Patsy had decided to move inside and look for the constable while the Channel 6 news crew waited.

"I was thinking about it on the drive over," she explained. "Kids are one thing, but if I was Constable Gordon I would be a little off-put if someone just waltzed onto my property with a microphone and a camera unexpected." She started up the path to the front porch of the old Victorian Gothic house that loomed over Hollow Creek Road.

"Wow," Afia said, looking over the place. "I can certainly see why the kids think it's haunted."

"You were never over here as a young'un?"

Afia gaped at him. "Are you kidding? Old man Gordon would have *killed* me if he'd caught me anywhere near his property line. If he didn't, my father would have."

"Right. Stupid question. Even so, you knew the Gordon kid a little, right? What was he like back then, aside from the obvious long-term side effects of the beatings, I mean?"

Afia shrugged. "Quiet and shy, I guess. Like I was. Maybe we would've gotten along if our fathers weren't at war with each other. Most of the time, we were both just keeping our heads down, I think. He was probably trying to cope with being the drunk loser's kid who got his ass handed to him by his old man while I was trying to deal with being the only black kid in a school full of white trash. It didn't help that my single father worked with the majority of the other men who had kids in my same class. Every time those kids' parents came home with a story about 'what the nigger man said at work' it came back to haunt me at school the next day." She brushed a long strand of straightened black hair out of her eyes. "Let me tell you, you haven't been bullied until you're bullied by racist progenies for stuff your dad said or did that you had no control over and didn't even know about."

Staff's automatic response to her story would have ordinarily been "I can imagine," but he stifled it. He couldn't imagine, so he shouldn't pretend to. He had discovered his homosexuality early in his life and figured he had revealed it indirectly to his parents at some point because it felt to him like they always knew. He'd never even really had the unenviable chore of coming out to them. They had simply understood. As it blossomed within him at adolescence, they had coached him, warned him, to be discreet about it, even to deny it if the subject ever came up with anyone at school. Unlike some gay teens, he had been able to disguise his nature so convincingly that few of his classmates ever even teased him about the possibility that he was gay. How many girls' hearts had he broken in those days? Occasionally, he felt some resentment toward his parents for attempting to stifle who he was in spite of their own acceptance of it. So instead of telling Afia that he could imagine what she went through, he offered a simple "I'm sorry" and left it at that.

Patsy knocked three times on the wide-open door of the Gordon place before she swept across the threshold and stepped inside. Staff could hear her calling the constable's name as she did. "Hello? Graham? It's Patsy. Hello?" She left the door open behind her. They could hear the *thunk* of her footsteps echoing in the distance as she patrolled the interior. She'd worn heels, for some reason. They were wedges, so it's not like she was going to get them stuck between any loose floorboards, but still. The impracticality. It had to be difficult to walk in those things compared to something comfortable, like sneakers. Staff glanced at the bare dirt areas of the overgrown path that led to the house in front of them. Sure enough, the older woman had left some awkward indentations in her wake. Imprinted alongside them were the treads of a few sneakers and what were probably someone's work boots. The constable's, maybe. Who else would've been out here wearing work boots? There was also—

"Hey, Afia." He elbowed her in the ribs. "Look at this." He knelt at the edge of the driveway, right elbow propped on one knee, and pointed to the ground in front of them.

"What? The footprints? I saw that. They're Patsy's. The bigger ones are probably Constable Gordon's."

"Not those," Staff said. He leaned closer to the earth and indicated a much smaller set of prints that overlapped the sneakers and work boots in places. They were dark semi-circular blobs capped by four slightly less deep bean-shaped indentations. Each bean was also capped by a point, making the group of them look like two-part snowmen standing on top of a hill. Some of the beans pointed toward the old Victorian Gothic house. Others pointed away from it as if whatever left them there had come and gone.

"Pawprints," Afia said, kneeling down beside her cameraman.

CHAPTER EIGHT

Lee Gordon lay flat on his back on the cellar floor of his old house, grinning. He could feel the skin on his son Graham's face move and spread at his command. It didn't feel exactly like he remembered grinning as having felt, but it was close enough. Not that he had smiled that much when he was alive. He could not remember ever having much to smile about. Graham's lips and tongue felt strange to him, too. Sore, kind of. Throbbing. The kid must have busted them good when he hit the floor.

You know I did, came a small, barely perceptible reply from somewhere inside his head. *You know damn well I did. Did you push me, Dad? Did you hit me on the head and push me down here?*

He forced air from his son's diaphragm through his throat, attempting an out-loud chuckle. It came out more like a cough. *YOU KNOW I DID, SON. JUST REMEMBER THAT I DIDN'T DO ANYTHING TO YOU THAT YOU HADN'T ALREADY DONE TO ME THE NIGHT THEY FOUND MY BODY DOWN HERE, NOW DID I?*

There was no further comment on the subject from the wimpy little faggot inside his consciousness. Lee went back to probing the sensations he felt from within his son's shell. He reached out with tendrils from his mind, vine-like wisps of energy searching for nerve pathways from the boy's brain throughout the rest of his body. After a few minutes of searching, he found Graham's right hand and all five digits thereon. He flexed them, made them claw at the cellar earth beneath. Once he'd made the connection, it became rapidly familiar, and hopefully permanent. He could forget about the connection he'd just made and concentrate on reaching other limbs and organs. This process felt much easier than when he had tried to jump into the little dark-haired twerp that he'd caught trespassing a few nights ago. That was like trying to thread a sewing needle with a gigantic log of string cheese. The small piece of him that had been able to get through to the brat wasn't enough to take and keep control. The rest of his consciousness had just enveloped the boy's outer body and hovered there until the near-puking started. That was what had finally kicked him out.

Graham's body was blood kin. He was able to glide into that body like a hand into a glove. As a test, he ignored the digits on the hand he had just taken, focusing on his son's eyelids instead. He blinked three times and then focused again on the right hand. Yes. He was still able to move the fingers without any concentration or effort.

He sought the left limb next, finding the correct pathway after only a few seconds. Once he sent the signal, sensation flooded the entire arm immediately, but it was a minute before he could make it move. When he could move the fingers on the left hand, he tested his motor coordination. He raised both arms to the ceiling simultaneously, index fingers pointing upward. In turn, he touched his nose with first the index finger of his right hand and then the index finger of his left. It was a task he'd had to perform more than once for the local smokey bears when they'd caught him driving erratically down various and sundry Hollow County roads. A field sobriety test, they called it. Most of the time they gave him a pass, especially if he put in a call to his old compadre Abe Wickham. Abe had gone into law enforcement after high school, but they had remained friends. After time stole his youth and energy, Abe was kind enough to drop a six-pack by the house now and then. Lee had passed this self-imposed sobriety test, although he certainly wouldn't mind having a drink in this new body. It had been far too long.

The boy's legs proved a bit more challenging to control once he'd accessed them. He could feel them down there, sort of. The sensation was not the same as in the arms. There was an uncomfortableness, a soreness combined with the pins-and-needles of returning blood flow after having cut off the circulation. The legs were there for him, but the commands he sent them at first resulted in a series of jerky motions at the knee that ended with a single straight-leg spasm and release. That, or he'd find the foot on the end of each leg rubbing against the other one irritably, as if he was using one foot to scratch an itch on the other. Other attempts resulted in the legs waggling about against the floor. Each time these things occurred, Lee discovered that he'd lose the pathway to the leg he was feeling. He would have to conduct a fresh search for it from all the way back in the boy's brain. Maybe he was rushing it, he thought. He tried to lower the sense of urgency that had been building inside him since he'd taken control of the right hand, to take it slow.

Once the connection was reestablished with the right leg, he tried again to move it, first by wiggling Graham's toes at the end of his Wolverine work boot on the right foot. Next, he contracted Graham's calf muscle on the right side, then the thigh muscle. Finally, he was able to bend the right leg at the knee on command, without spasm, itching, or waggling, and without losing connectivity. The left leg was still being difficult. He reestablished his connection with it and then lost it when the entire leg spasmed, throwing itself into the air and then flopping around on the cellar floor like a fish that had been abandoned on shore by a summer flash flood.

Lee sighed. *YOU'RE FIGHTING ME, AREN'T YOU, BOY? I SUGGEST YOU STOP IT RIGHT NOW. I WAS STRONGER THAN YOU BACK THEN AND I'M STRONGER THAN YOU RIGHT NOW.*

Control of the left leg came more naturally after that. He located the path, and the sensation in that leg returned without the pins-and-needles feeling. He was able to wiggle the toes at the end of the left Wolverine, contract the calf, contract the thigh, and bend at the knee, just as he had with the right leg. For all practical purposes, Graham's body was now his. He controlled the eyes, though the boy obviously needed glasses. He commanded the mouth and tongue. He managed the arms and legs. He decided to leave some of the autonomic systems alone, thinking it might be better for the boy to retain automatic control of things like breathing and heartbeat, functions he was accustomed to not having to think about. At least for now, until he could figure out how to get rid of him. If it ain't broke, don't fix it, the old saying goes. Besides, none of those things were pathways to the arms, legs, or head, and those were the relevant muscles, the ones that gave the appearance of control.

With a final heave-ho, Lee Gordon forced his son's body to sit up. He gazed at his surroundings through slightly fuzzy but functional eyes. The Maglite that the kid had been tossing around like Luke Skywalker's lightsaber lay on the floor beside him, still shining its beam against the cinder block wall to his left. Lee rolled on his new body's butt until he was standing on his knees. He plucked the Maglite from the floor with the left hand, then placed the right hand on the floor and hoisted his new body to its feet. Pain from Graham's injuries thrummed through him like electricity. He sent commands to every nerve he'd accessed to dial it back. He couldn't filter it out entirely, not without losing all sensation and collapsing back to the floor, but he thought he could curb it enough to keep himself functional and the pain tolerable. He tested this by taking two steps toward the cinder block wall on which the Maglite was trained. The pain was still there, but felt like little more than a twitch now, an annoying muscle spasm that, with enough practice and a few glasses of water, could be easily ignored if not remedied.

Good. Very good.

Now to figure out what's next.

He shone the Maglite on the wall that stood behind the busted cellar staircase, past the stringers that led from the floor to the door and along the joints where the cinder block wall met the floor and the other cinder block wall that was perpendicular to it. He halted the beam of light after he had scanned three blocks along the bottom of the cinder block wall from its corner and then eight rows up. There, patterned among the neatly masoned joints, sat a set of blocks that appeared to contain no mortar: his secret door.

STILL THERE, he thought. *ALL THIS TIME AND IT'S STILL THERE. JUST LIKE I LEFT IT.*

Lee set the Maglite on the cellar floor with its beam pointed at the general area of the loose rectangle of cinder block. He approached it and slid a hand into the gaps on either side of the door and near the bottom. There was a part of him that feared his son's back wouldn't be up to this task, so he tried to leverage his new knees as much as possible when he yanked on the rectangle and plucked it from the toddler-sized hole in the wall that it was plugging. He slid about ninety pounds of cement and aggregate between himself and the wall in front of him, listening as the rough surfaces grated against each other. The door finally landed with a thud on the cellar floor just in front of the Wolverines his son was wearing. The work boot brand loyalty was apparently the only thing his boy had ever truly learned from him. He was glad the stack of blocks hadn't landed on his new toes, though. He might've been able to dial back the pain by sending it to his stupid son's weakling consciousness, but if he broke them, he wouldn't be able to walk even if he could ignore the pain.

He used both hands and his back to sturdy the door against the rear wall, then perched himself on top of it, so that he was seated beside the black hole it had revealed. Wet air crawled into the cellar from the outside, carrying with it a rotting odor. Lee thought it smelled like a mouse had died in the wall. Why did those things always manage to find a way in but then can't seem to find their way back out? There was a musty, mildewy smell layered just beneath the dead mouse odor.

HOUSE IS OLD. IT SURE AS HELL AIN'T HAD NO UPKEEP.

He stretched his right hand into the hole and patted down the opposite side of the wall. The row of blocks there was damp, and a bit slimy in places. Years of rushing water from rapid downpours had overpowered what he'd once believed was a watertight seal he'd added around the foundation of this old place. But it didn't matter. What he was seeking would not have been ruined by a mere stream of flood water. Or it shouldn't have been, anyway. Just when he was sure he would never find it, the fingernails of his right hand tapped against something hard, creating a thin *tink* sound from within the hole in the wall.

GOTCHA! Lee fingered the neck of the glass bottle he'd happened upon, then gripped it in his fist. He pulled it from the hole and examined it as carefully as his fuzzy vision would allow in the beam from the Maglite. That was his brand all right. The red and white Budweiser label shone as bright as new. The bottle appeared to be unbroken, not even a chip out of it, and the cap was still sealed down tight. He twisted it off. The *pssst* sound it made as the cellar air met the amber liquid within was weaker than he remembered. He held the mouth of the open bottle up to his nose and sniffed. Yes. It was, indeed, still beer. Budweiser beer. And Lee was a man who liked beer.

You did *have a stash down here!* a small voice echoed in his head. *I knew it! I knew you did!*

Lee chuckled. *YEAH. BUT YOU WERE TOO STUPID TO FIND IT EVEN AFTER YOU KILLED ME OVER IT. FAGGOT.*

He silently toasted the room around him and then turned the bottle up to drink. He expected the first taste to have some bitterness to it, creating a shiver that started at the back of the throat and ran all the way down his esophagus. Instead, it tasted flat and coppery, not like a Budweiser at all. But it was cool, and after that first taste, it flowed effortlessly down his gullet. In his living days, Lee Gordon would have downed the entire bottle before moving on to a second. His son, however, was likely to be a lightweight, so he chose to drink only enough to ignite that little spark of fearlessness and immortality that comes with the onset of a buzz. He'd nurse it a little, and then keep it burning at a low simmer. The better his buzz without going full-on drunk, the easier it would be to keep the kid inside him quiet, at least until he could find a way to get rid of him altogether.

You...can't have...my...life, bubbled to the surface from somewhere inside the boy's head, but Lee didn't answer him. Didn't need to. He took another swig from the Budweiser bottle in his right hand. Then another. Then the limp-dick little squirt of conscience inside him was silenced, submerged in a bubble of pleasant buzz-on in their shared stream of consciousness.

Lee set the Budweiser bottle between his legs on top of the cinder block door and peered through the blackness of the portal he'd opened in the wall. The beam from the Maglite on the floor didn't reveal much about the darkness therein. Lee thought he could make out a few mounds of packed earth and the corner of a stack of cinder blocks on which that section of his old house rested. There was only one access to this crawl space from the exterior of the old home, and he had blocked it up in a fashion similar to the cellar wall portal so that from the outside it looked like nothing more than a couple of layers of inaccessible foundation. If he climbed into the entrance with the Maglite and commando-crawled his way through the space between the earth and the floor above, he could probably find that old access and kick it down easily enough. If luck were with him, it wouldn't break into chunks. Then, once outside, he'd be able to place it back where it had been, at least until he figured out what he was going to do about the cellar staircase his idiot fatass son broke on his way down to this hell.

He searched the thin veil of memories he could sense from the buzzed but still conscious presence of Graham in this body. The boy had not only somehow convinced the Lost Hollow electorate to make him constable but had also persuaded the town council to allow him to repurchase the old place from the town, to save it from blight. So he had been planning to restore it, apparently, or turn it into something else. That meant Lee could actually rebuild the cellar stairs at some point without people asking too many questions, he supposed. For now, he'd probably just go down to the hardware store in Hollow River, assuming it was still there, and buy a ladder. That would at least allow him to climb down here and set the portal door back to right.

Lee downed the rest of the Budweiser and then set the bottle over the portal threshold from where he'd obtained it. It was a struggle, but he resisted the urge to celebrate his new-found life in a more than slightly used body by shattering the empty against the wall beside him. Instead, he leaped from the top of the makeshift cinder-block door, retrieved the Maglite, and shined it over the portal threshold and into the crawl space beyond. Cinder block pillars stood smattered throughout the cave-like void below his house. A few appeared to have cracks in them now. Lee supposed that decades of supporting the weight of a place like this had taken their toll. Still, none of them were crumbling. That meant that the floors above them were still stable. The house was unlikely to crash down on him while he sought his escape from its bowels.

He'd need to be careful where he was crawling, of course. Rib bones have sharp points. So do some human teeth. Lee Gordon didn't quite like the idea of getting stabbed or bitten by the remainders of any of the vindictive ladies he'd helped to disappear over the years. They were all still in there somewhere, undisturbed since the day he'd hauled each of their nasty high-falutin' corpses inside.

Graham's voice, incredulous and edged with panic, suddenly piped up in his head again. ...*What?... Dad?... What? My God! What did you do?*

Lee grinned.

*YOU REALLY WANNA KNOW, BOY? YOU SURE
YOUR LIMP ASS CAN HANDLE IT? THE FUNNY
THING ABOUT IT IS YOU NEVER KNEW. ALL THE
TIME YOU SPENT DOWN HERE HIDING FROM
ME, NOT ONE TIME DID YOU EVER NOTICE MY
LITTLE DOOR BEHIND THE STAIRS. NOT ONE
TIME DID YOU EVER NOTICE THE STINK. WHY
I WONDER? BECAUSE YOU'RE STUPID? OR WAS
IT JUST THAT YOU THOUGHT CELLARS WERE
SUPPOSED TO SMELL THAT WAY?*

He laid his son's head back against the cinder block and
shut his eyes, allowing all the memories to surge forward
at once.

***

Graham Gordon was living in a bubble. Literally. His
world had gone from physical to metaphysical in an instant
after his father had seized control of his corporeal being.
He could see the cellar through the eyes of his body, but
those eyes were distant from him. It was as if what had been
his body was now merely a camera that was broadcasting
images to a convex screen in front of his consciousness. He
couldn't look down at himself anymore. There was no body
there. He was inside his body, but his body was outside of
him and being controlled by someone else; someone who
had always hated him.

He watched his father Lee remove that secret door made
of concrete blocks from its home in the cellar wall. He felt
the coolness of the amber liquid from the Budweiser bottle
start to cloud his mind. On some level he must be still in

touch with physical reality. But just as his life had been as a child, it was his father who ultimately controlled that reality. Killing him all those years ago had not enabled Graham to finally escape him. Yet if the younger Gordon was really still in touch with his physical body, it might be possible for him to gain control of it again. Maybe he could test that.

Reaching out with his consciousness, exploring his new interior surroundings, Graham felt two thin tendrils of limbs forming. They protruded from the cloud that was currently his being, thickened, and became his metaphysical arms, hands, and fingers. He poked at the convex screen in front of him with the ends of those fingers, watched it ripple in response to his touch. The cellar world just beyond his reach stretched and contracted, wavering on the screen. Just as it began to settle, his father's voice in their shared head said something about killing high-falutin' women, and Graham had been unable to conceal his shock. He'd accidentally broadcast the feeling from within the bubble and out to his father, who would now most certainly kill him for it. Better that than allowing Graham to continue to exist along with the possibility that he might someday escape and reveal Lee's secrets to the world.

The image in front of Graham changed then, darkened and winked out like an old-fashioned television screen when the power is cut. Suddenly Graham felt himself yanked toward the bubble screen, into it. It wrapped itself around him like plastic cling wrap, squeezing him, forcing life out of him the way a proto-sociopath might torture a roach before ultimately juicing it with his thumb against a cold basement floor. He thought his father might have found a way to snuff him out, to finally solve his "problem" child.

Then that feeling was gone. Graham was somewhere else. No, not just somewhere else. He was *someone* else. He was Lee Gordon, fresh off a Friday at the carbon plant in Hollow River, nose hairs singed and clothes still reeking of burnt coal from stoking the fires. He sat in a plush square cube with an open front at Bombshell's, a strip joint. Standing over him, her legs forming a triangle with her ass at its apex and bent at his eye level, was an all of nineteen-year-old blonde. She was naked except for a white thong that glowed brilliantly in the house black lights that were used to indicate the beginning and end of a particular dancer's set on the center stage. She'd told him her name was Star, but it was probably really something more mundane like Jennifer or Kristy. The bass beat of the house music pulsed inside his skull, making his brain feel as if it were about to ooze through his ears. The young woman slapped her own butt cheek with the palm of her right hand in time to that beat. Lee took that to mean that it was time for him to tip her again. Graham could see the dollar in Lee's hand, rising up to meet the waistband of her thong, which she had helpfully stretched from her hip to receive it. She was gorgeous, Graham could hear himself thinking as Lee; a hell of a lot prettier than the woman he'd married and who had then begat him his sickly wimp of a son. She was watching him enjoy her beauty, smiling at him, making eye contact from behind the temptation of the mounds of jiggling flesh she was shaking in his face. Lee wanted her. She knew it. They didn't usually smile at him or make eye contact, those Bombshell's dancers. Maybe she wanted him too.

Suddenly the scene swam in front of him, dissipated and reformed into a new one. Graham was in an old Ford F-150 now, still looking and smelling like a much younger version of his dead father. Star was leaving the strip joint for the night. She was clothed modestly, effectively hiding most of the assets to which Graham and his father had been privy inside the club. She clutched with both hands the handle of the purse that dangled over her left shoulder. The bag was open. Her left hand was positioned where the handle was fastened to the bag as if she wanted to have quick and easy access to its contents. Pepper spray, no doubt. Or a handgun. And who could blame her? Lots of crazies probably hang out around strip club parking places at night.

And you'd deserve it, Graham thought at his father. *What are you doing?*

Graham as Lee climbed out of the cab of the F-150, unable to prevent himself from doing so. He was approaching Star or whoever she was. He called out to her, announcing himself while her back was to him so that he would not startle her. Graham heard himself proposition her, inviting her first to a late dinner, then to his F-150, or a motel room somewhere off the highway. He heard her reject him. He watched her laugh when she did. The heat of rage boiled up from the collar of Lee's work shirt. Graham felt it. Tried to reason it away, soothe it. But it was no use. Lee had thought he had connected with Star. He had thought she wanted him. But it turned out that she was just another cock tease working in another roadside bar, happy to take his money and allow him to masturbate over the memories, but not willing to get to know him outside of those bounds. Graham felt Lee's rage boil over into fury. Star saw it, too, apparently, because the next thing both Graham and Lee felt was hot, searing pain in his eyes. Tears streamed from them, tickling what felt like fresh sunburn around the sockets. His lungs were on fire as well, forcing him to cough up shit from within his sinuses that he hadn't even known was in there. Lee was hurt. Graham felt like he was dying. But he was glad. He was glad that his father was getting some comeuppance. The stripper, on the other hand, had made a run for it while he struggled. There was a pay phone on the wall outside the club. Would she call the cops? Probably. He sure as hell didn't think she was going to call an ambulance for him.

Graham wiped at Lee's eyes, feeling like that was only making things worse. Star had picked up the pay phone receiver. He could see that much. Mucus still running from his eyes, nose, and mouth, Graham saw himself as Lee lunging for her, knocking the pepper spray loose from her left hand, yanking her away from the pay phone by her purse. He tried to hold himself back, at the very least soften the blows his father was landing on this poor woman. But he was powerless because this was memory, not the real world. Graham felt Lee hitting her with a closed fist, a right against her temple and a left against the bridge of her nose. He saw her body collapse and go limp beneath him, saw himself pick up her body and throw it over his shoulder like Charles Laughton as Quasimodo in that old black-and-white movie he'd seen in late-night runs on television as a kid: *The Hunchback of Notre Dame*. He saw himself throwing this rag-doll version of Star the stripper into the shotgun side of his pickup, saw himself starting the engine and speeding off into the night.

The bubble squeezed him and the scene dissipated again, reforming. It was daylight outside. There was no strip club and no Star now. There was instead a black woman. Graham recognized her, he thought. She was standing in the hallway in front of the principal's office at his elementary school. He was standing there with her, still dressed in the carbon plant clothes. Lee had had to leave work early because something had happened at school, something involving Graham, something the black woman was angry about. She was screaming at Lee Gordon. Pointing at him. Accusing him of something. He watched her lips move but was unable to decipher (or remember) what she was saying. Graham felt his father's gaze drift downward, to the front of her blouse. Lee was thinking that it was possible that she was not wearing a bra. Graham tried to force his head and eyes up, but was again unable to change his father's memory. He saw the woman turn on her heels and storm away from him, leaving him standing there in front of the principal's office. He felt his father's arousal and predatory instincts as they eyed her figure from the back, her lovely hourglass shape and the sexy sway of her hips. Lee Gordon had never had a black woman before, and in life would never dare admit to anyone about having thought about it. Graham could not unsee his father's wonder about what it might be like to fuck her. She had fight in her. Would she fight a fuck? Star the stripper hadn't fought three years before, but she had been unconscious at the time.

Oh my God. Graham struggled to break free of these thoughts, squeezing his metaphysical eyes shut against them, trying in vain to place metaphysical hands over metaphysical ears. It was no use.

Star had also died unconscious because Lee couldn't risk having her identify him and thus destroy his life. The black woman wasn't carrying a purse and was unlikely to be packing heat anywhere else. He could try to take her on her way to the parking lot right now.

Except.

Except that she had gotten his stupid sissy brat of a kid in trouble with the school, which is why he'd had to leave work early and subtract several hours from his shift that day. And the dumbass kid had somehow made it his fault. Suddenly Graham's own recollections of this day came flooding back to him.

I remember that! Graham shrieked, although no words escaped the lips of this memory of Lee Gordon's he was living. *I remember that day. I was little. I told you that I thought a girl in my class was pretty. Her name was Afia. You said you knew her. You said black girls couldn't be beautiful because black girls had tails that were leftovers from their evolution. You made a fool out of me because I repeated what you said and the other kids laughed at me and goaded me into trying to pull the back of her pants down to check. I snuck up behind her at the see-saws and grabbed at the back of her pants. I didn't manage to pull them down, but that didn't matter. It was enough that I had grabbed at her waistband. She slapped me across the jaw and yelled at me for it, and she should have. I remember her screaming PURRRVUURRRRT at me on the playground, loud enough for the whole school to hear while the other kids just stood around the see-saw laughing at me. You fucking asshole. You miserable, hateful, murdering low-life son of a bitch asshole.*

From Graham's throat in the physical world, Lee Gordon laughed out loud. "Yeah. You always were a gullible little shit."

Grace Afton, mother to little eight-year-old Afia who did not have a tail, stalked away from Lee Gordon, the abusive husband of Anna Johnson Gordon and hateful father to Graham. Lee Gordon considered following her, getting what he wanted from her. But he did not follow her, at least not then. He liked a fight, but he didn't have the energy for it that day. Besides, he might accidentally get her pregnant and have to deal with that shit. Instead, he would take Graham home with a promise to the principal that he would apologize to Afia and never do anything like that again.

The scene fell apart and reformed. Graham as Lee Gordon was crouched among the shrubbery at the end of the semi-circle in front of Graham's elementary school, watching all the mothers and some of the fathers drop their kids off for the day. In his right hand he held what had once been his father's hunting knife. There was no crossing guard here, no blinking speed limit warning lights to draw attention to the fact that it was a school zone. It was just an ordinary school morning in a tiny town and, as luck would have it, little Miss Afia Afton was the last to arrive at school that day. Lee watched her climb out of the backseat of her mother's third generation Mercury Cougar. He watched her mom call out to her as she bolted for the doors, and then watched her turn back to blow the older woman a kiss. Grace Afton caught the smooch in her right hand and planted it on her cheek, then waggled her fingers in that "have a good day, sweetie" gesture that all mothers seem to become afflicted with once they've sent their first off to school. Graham thought it was sweet of them. But their happy, nonchalant expressions of unconditional love to each other in the face of what had happened the day before enraged Lee Gordon anew. What right did they have to carry on with their lives as if everything was normal?

After the school door had closed behind the little black girl, Grace Afton swung the Cougar through the rest of the semi-circle and brought it to a halt at the stop sign, looking right first, then left before attempting to turn. It was then that Lee Gordon leaped from the bushes beside the car, threw open the Cougar's passenger side door, and hopped in. Grace Afton screamed, let go of the steering wheel, and started trying to shove the burly man out of her car. Graham tried desperately to relax Lee's body, to allow her to push him out of the car so she could put the pedal to the metal and save herself. Instead, this memory version of Lee pushed the point of the hunting knife he was carrying into her ribs and demanded that she quiet down. He had seen Sylvester Stallone use that technique on a soldier when he'd taken Graham's mother to see *First Blood*. Lee informed the black woman that she was going to drive them somewhere so they could talk about what had occurred between them in front of the principal's office.

Another scene. Grace Afton was lying on the ground in the woods somewhere between her house and the Gordon place. They'd left the Cougar in her own driveway. She was bleeding from the slash across her throat, as well as from a more significant, more ragged wound on the left side of her skull. She did not move. She did not breathe. Graham watched himself as Lee picking up her body, dangling it lifeless in the crook of his elbows and across his forearms, and carrying it toward home.

From within his throat, Lee Gordon could feel a lump rising. He swallowed it down and smiled at the sorrow he could sense radiating from Graham's presence within his little prison of consciousness. *YEAH*, he said. *YEAH. I HAD TO KILL HER BECAUSE OF YOU, YOU LITTLE SHIT. I TOLD YOU TO LEAVE THE BLACK GIRLS ALONE, DIDN'T I? BUT THAT AIN'T ALL I DID. YOU AIN'T EVEN HEARD THE HALF OF IT YET, BOY. HAVEN'T YOU WONDERED ALL THESE YEARS WHAT HAPPENED TO YOUR MOTHER?*

No. Leave me alone.

YOU HAVE.

You told me she ran off with a black man.

Laughter. *YEAH. YEAH, I DID SAY THAT. WHAT I PROBABLY SHOULD HAVE SAID IS THAT I KILLED HER TOO BECAUSE OF WHAT YOU DID TO THE LITTLE BLACK GIRL.*

You. You what? You...

I KILLED YOUR MOTHER YOU LITTLE BRAT. I KILLED HER. I CUT HER. I CHOPPED HER AND THE OTHER WOMAN INTO PIECES AND SHOVED

BOTH OF THEM INTO THE CRAWL SPACE HERE. DO YOU GET IT NOW? I KILLED HER. I KILLED THEM BOTH.

But...why? Why? Why? Why?

Suddenly Graham was back in the cellar. He tried to look around himself and was briefly confused when his head didn't seem to work. Then he realized that the lights were on and the cellar was stacked floor to ceiling with dry goods and other items. He was still in his father's memories. Sweat ran from the top of his head and dripped off his nose as he tossed what looked like a black woman's arm into the portal in the cellar's cinder block wall that leads to the crawl space. Beside him sat an old ax that he had been using to chop the body of Grace Afton into smaller chunks. He hefted the ax over his head and brought it down on her remaining intact shoulder. It sliced most of the way through but became stuck in the last few cords of flesh. Lee Gordon was tired, low on energy, and the Afton woman had tight, tough muscles and tendons. He dropped the ax and grabbed the corpse's wrist, yanking it upward. He began to twist the arm on its remaining threads of flesh, intending to rip it off if he could not cut it. Then, from somewhere above all this, he heard the sound of the cellar door open followed by the thunk of sneakers coming down the stairs. Anna had come home early from wherever it was that she went during the days when he was at work (she didn't have a job, but she was indeed able to spend money like she had one). She had seen his pickup in the driveway. She was looking for him.

There was no time, Graham heard memory Lee thinking. No time to throw the rest of Grace Afton's mangled body into the crawl space and reset the portal door. No time to develop an excuse for the blood-soaked ax that sat propped against the cinder block wall beside him. No time to explain the sweat on his face and the crimson stains on his hands. There was only one thing he could do when his wife of ten years stepped onto the cellar floor, turned her head to look for him, and had time to register what was happening.

Mom! Graham tried to shout. *Don't come down! Don't come down here! Call the police! Run! Run! RUN!*

She could not hear him.

Lee Gordon snatched up his ax. Graham could feel the cords in his old man's neck standing out, could feel the muscles in his arms trembling with effort. He stood behind the staircase, between the back of it and the cinder block wall with the portal in it, out of sight of anyone descending. He held the tool in a batter's stance as if it were the bottom of the Ninth inning and Casey, Mighty Casey, was on the verge of striking out. When Anna Johnson Gordon strode off the last step of the staircase, he snuck up behind her and swung the ax with all the might he had left to muster from within his aching arms. The dripping blade connected with the back of Anna's neck and lodged there, just shy of severing her spinal cord. Her head lolled forward on her neck, then her body tumbled along with it, crashing onto the cellar floor in a fashion similar to the way her son Graham would land there years later.

Lee stamped one foot on his wife's back and yanked the blade free. In the present, the consciousness of Lee's son Graham wailed over the sight. Had he physical tears to shed, they would have been running down his face in torrents. Lee walked around her, noting that her head was tilted so that the left side of her face was visible to him. Her nose was pressed firmly against the ground, which forced the flesh at the tip of it upward in a way that reminded both men of Janet Leigh's death scene in Alfred Hitchcock's *Psycho*. Graham heard Lee thinking that he should have installed a drain down here to catch the blood. Like in the movie.

Again he heaved the ax above his head with both hands and brought it down against Anna's neck with every Newton of force he could summon from his arms, his shoulders, and his back, all of which were now screaming at the strain he demanded from them. This time, his wife's head came off clean, rolling on the tip of her nose so that it came to rest about a half inch away from the rest of her. Lee Gordon threw down the ax, exhausted.

No. No. No. No no no no no no.

The anguish that welled up inside his head from the brat Graham was powerful, probably more powerful than anything else he'd experienced after he had taken control of Graham's body. *SHUT UP, KID.*

No. No. No.

YES. YES. YES! I SAID SHUT UP!

***

Lee thrust open the eyes in his son's head, allowing the pool of illumination from the Maglite, the light of the present time, to fill his vision. He felt his son's sorrow swell and then recede again as Lee forced the body's other occupant down once more into the stream of consciousness they shared. It was like drowning an already dead rat in a bucket of water. There was no struggle. Graham simply went under. That was fine with Lee. He had better things to do now. Chief among them was getting his formerly dead redneck ass out of that cellar and into his brand new world, free of all the baggage he'd just relived from his previous life.

Then, from somewhere above the cellar, Lee Gordon thought he heard the sound of footsteps, tenuous double-clacking footsteps like the ones made by slick urban cowboy boots or women's shoes: heel, outsole, heel, outsole, *thik, thunk, thik, thunk.* Whoever was up there was moving cautiously throughout the living area. Seconds later, he heard a querulous voice with a lilting Georgian accent calling his son's name.

"Hellooo?" The call was muffled by the ceiling and walls above him, but it was most definitely coming from inside the house. Lee Gordon smiled at the mental horror movie reference he'd just made, something younger folks would never get, he thought. He'd have to be careful about things like that if he was going to live out the rest of his son's days for him. Maybe once this was all over, he'd go to that Blockbuster Video over in Hollow River and figure out what the kids were watching these days. It might help him fit in again. "Hello? Graham? It's Patsy. Hello?"

He had to hurry. If Patsy, whoever she was—Lee couldn't place her right now because he'd shoved his son's memories back down into that stream of consciousness along with him—happened to check the cellar, she'd first discover the broken staircase. If she didn't fall off it herself in the darkness, she might suspect that Graham had fallen and call for help. He could call for her help himself, as a matter of fact, let her know he was down here. Then she might be able to get someone with a ladder for him, and he'd have the convenient but entirely truthful excuse for why his face was so beaten up. That would also save him from having to kick out the escape door he'd built at the other side of the crawl space. It would ensure that all those bones he'd stowed away in there remained undisturbed.

Lee stood up from his place against the cinder block cellar wall, tossed the empty beer bottle back into the void from whence it came, and dusted off his hands. He crouched in front of the makeshift door, grabbed it at the bottom, and slid it upward against the wall with all the strength that was left in his legs. He pressed against the bottom of the structure with his knees until he'd reached a height above them. Just when the strain on his calves, thighs, arms, and back was becoming too much, he felt the edge of the door penetrate the air of the open portal. Above him, the *thik, thunk, thik, thunk* of Patsy's shoes sounded like it might be getting closer. He wondered if she had gone upstairs yet, to the second floor. If she hadn't, maybe she would before she thought to check the cellar. Maybe. Even with that thought for comfort, Lee felt the urgency to rush welling inside him.

He slid his hands along the sides of the doorway and tilted the structure into place until the entire thing came to rest atop the eighth row of cinder block that formed the lower frame of the portal. The sound of Patsy's footsteps approached the cellar door. "Hello? Graham? Are you here? It's Patsy."

Lee snapped up the Maglite from the floor, strode a couple of paces back from the wall, and scanned his handiwork. The door was in place, but it wasn't entirely flush with the wall surrounding it. In the old days, he could have taken his time with it, made sure it looked like part of the wall before climbing the stairs back to the living area. He'd gotten so good at it, that most times he didn't have to do more than give the door a good tap on each side to line everything up. The lip of the door protruding over the edge of the portal frame was much too obvious this time. He might need to try a few times to get it to line up. This Patsy lady and the pressure she was putting on him had screwed up his method, his mojo. If he overshot while trying to fix it, it would be her fault. He'd probably have to make her pay for it. Somehow. Especially if it meant losing his secret.

The cellar door creaked open, flooding what was left of the broken staircase with light from the hallway. From Lee Gordon's position beneath it, it looked like white light. Morning light.

"Hellooooo?" Patsy called from the top of the staircase. "Graham? Are you down th—"

There was a moment of indecision. Should he remain silent and wait for her to either leave or attempt to scale the broken staircase? Or should he call out to her and risk the discovery of his secret doorway? For a split-second, it looked like the nosey bitch was going to just close the cellar door and go on about her business. Then, as the light from above began to wane back into darkness, he felt a voice bubbling up from the stream of consciousness. It forced its way from the lungs in his son's body, up the windpipe, over the vocal cords, and out the mouth before Lee could do anything to stop it.

"Pathy!" he shouted. "Pathy! Down here! Help!"

Shit. Lee Gordon squeezed his son's eyes shut, retreating into the brain they shared. He shoved at Graham's consciousness, pressed on it, stifled it until once again he had it submerged in the stream. The dumbass faggoty little asshole had made his decision for him. Now he'd have to play it all by ear and hope that he'd have time alone to work on lining up the doorway to the edges of the portal while Patsy the nosey bitch went for help.

Lee shuffled Graham's body around to the foot of what used to be the cellar staircase, Maglite in hand. At the top of the stairs, silhouetted against the white light pouring in from behind, was the figure of an older woman. Patsy, no doubt. She of the lilting Georgian accent and *thik-thunk* shoes. He pointed the rays of the Maglite briefly at her, confirming her presence, and then shone it on his own (his son's) face from below.

"Hi, Pathy!" he said. "Uh, the stairs broke. I fell. I busthed myself up."

"Oh, dear! Oh, dear! I see that! We need to get you to a doctor. Your face is all beat up, and your mouth looks like it's about to split open. Let me call you an ambulance."

Lee tried to not clench his teeth. "Just get a ladder, Pathy. I just need a ladder for now." He watched the head of the silhouette tilt sideways a little. The old bat was having trouble understanding him because of his dumbass kid's busted fuck of a limp-dick mouth. He was about to try to repeat the demand when she finally processed it all.

"A ladder!" she shouted. "Of course, of course. I'll go find a ladder. But don't you think you need an ambulance or something? They should probably look you over before we get you out."

Fuck.

"No, Pathy. I'm fine. Get the ladder."

"Ok," she replied, sounding a little hurt. "I have a ladder at the B&B that I can go get." She started to walk away from the cellar door and then turned back. "Oh, I also have a crew outside from Channel 6 News. I tried to tell you about it last night, but you hung up on me. They want to check out some of the more famous haunted locations here in Lost Hollow. I told them that we might be able to get you to give them a tour of this place. You know, because it kind of got a reputation after all those kids started reporting screams coming from it? Since you're ok and everything, do you think you could show them the place? They only have this weekend."

Goddammit.

"Ok," he managed to keep the exasperation out of his voice. "Ok. We'll talk later. Just get the ladder, please?"

"Right, right, right," came the voice from above. Patsy's silhouette turned away from the cellar and allowed the door to slam shut behind her. Lee could hear her footsteps thunking away. From somewhere far more distant, he heard her call back to him, "Don't worry! We'll be right back!"

Right, then. He heaved a sigh. Back to work. Maybe his brat's little act of betrayal had worked in his favor after all. No sheriff's deputies or EMTs would hassle him today. If the newsies accosted him, he'd probably just tell the

Channel 6 team that he wasn't feeling well enough to give them their tour after all, much less an interview. His mouth was all busted up, and he was famished after having spent a full night, at least, trapped in the cellar. No one would want to be interviewed about a haunted house for a small town puff piece after a night like that, right? Right. He needed time to heal. They'd just have to come back some other day when he felt better, and after he'd gotten his bearings in... well, whatever year it was now.

Lee Gordon strode back to the portal and the too-much offset door within it. He placed the Maglite on the ground in front of it, making sure it shone at an angle that would not create a shadow of his body over his workspace. With both hands, he pressed hard on the lower left corner of the door, sliding it across its cinder block resting place and into alignment with the wall beside it. The friction made a grating noise, like the sound of a crypt opening in an old vampire or zombie movie. Carefully, he applied the pressure of both hands to the other corner, sliding it closer to alignment as well. It didn't quite get there. He'd have to try again. Just...carefully.

CHAPTER NINE

S taff's knees cracked like twin shotgun blasts when he raised himself from the ground where he and Afia had been crouched and examining the pawprints that led both into and out from the driveway. Afia stood up beside him, smiling. "Feeling some age creeping into the joints there, Staff?"

He stretched, placing his hands on each side of his lower back as he did. "Not a particularly comfy bed in my room at Patsy's. That's all. I believe I'm actually younger than you, thank you very much."

She chuckled at that. Staff bent and dusted away the dry ground that had clung to the fine hairs on his knees, eyeballing the prints again as he did.

"Are you thinking the black bitch made those?" Afia asked, noting his gaze.

"I think some kind of dog made them. Maybe even the one that ran out in front of us on our way into town yesterday. The intersection back there at Hollow Creek Road and SR-501 was exactly where we were when we saw it."

Afia followed his finger, nodding. "I guess it's too bad they finally paved this little dead-end road at some point. These tracks must be fresh, at least as far as I can tell. They're crystal clear. If it was still a dirt road, we might've been able to tell for sure if whatever it is had run off in that direction."

From inside the house, the distant sound of Patsy Blankenship shouting "Hello? Graham? It's Patsy!" found its way to their ears.

"How big do you think this place is?" Staff said. "You'd think he would have heard her by now if he's inside."

"You'd think."

He cut his eyes at her, smirking. "How much trouble do you think we'd get in if I just started shooting some B-roll of the exterior? If we're going to let Patsy and that Beard kid tell the whole mid-state about Lost Hollow's black bitch, we might as well get some shots of some alleged black bitch pawprints, shouldn't we?"

Afia looked doubtful. "I suppose if we just shoot from the road here, where we're technically not on anything but public property."

"I was actually thinking about following the pawprints. The ones that lead onto the property. See how far they go, if they lead anywhere."

"Staff—"

"It would only be for a few minutes, just while Patsy's inside looking for the constable. Besides, if anyone is going to be charged with trespassing, it'll be her. She just walked right in there like she owned the place, and now she's wandering around in it."

Afia laughed. "Yeah, she does act like she owns the whole town, doesn't she? All right. We'll just follow the pawprints for a bit until we hear yea or nay about the constable's whereabouts from inside. Just don't trample on any flowerbeds or anything like that."

"You're worried about flowerbeds here? Look at the yard. Ever see grass as tall as your ass in any place where the homeowner maintained a flowerbed?"

She scanned the front yard and grinned. "I guess you're right. Maybe you should just watch out for snakes then."

"Oh. Yeah." He hadn't considered that possibility. But it was autumn now. Snakes were a spring and summer thing, like ticks. At least, he thought they were. "You're not coming with me?"

"I think I'm just going to hang out by the truck while you get the shots. That way I can keep an eye out for Patsy. Let me know if you find anything interesting, though."

Staff heaved the weighty old school video camera he had retrieved from the back of the S-10 and mounted it on his right shoulder. There was a tripod in the truck as well. He briefly considered using it for additional support if he got tired and needed to put the thing down for a bit. In the end, he chose to leave it behind and rely solely on his own muscle and dexterity to get the shots he wanted.

"I guess I'm just lucky I don't have to crank it," he said to himself. "Damned thing almost dates back to that era."

He strode past Afia, crouched at the start of the set of pawprints by the edge of the driveway and pressed the Record button. Remarkably, the morning light shining down on the dead-end street was just right for the close-up he wanted. Through the viewfinder, he was able to close in tight on two staggered front paws pointing in the direction of the house. Once that was established, he rotated the viewfinder at a right angle, so that he could look down at it as he dragged the camera along the pawprint trail, inches above it. Stooped at the middle of his back, he held the device's handle in both hands, his arms stretched to their full length so that the landscape of pawprints disappeared into a vanishing point that was enshrouded in dry and overgrown clumps of Kentucky fescue.

Staff sidled carefully up the trail, trying to keep the camera steady, one eye on the direction the path was heading and one on the viewfinder. It would have been easier had he convinced Afia to follow the path ahead of him a little pace, so he didn't need to track it at the same time he was trying to get it on video. He hadn't thought of that before. Neither had Afia, apparently. And he was already recording. By the time he reached an apparent left turn in the trail's direction, which happened to occur at the base of the short stack of stairs leading up to the front porch, his forearms were screaming at him. Still cameras and recent video technology was so much lighter than this old thing. He'd need to have another budgetary word with Joanie when they got back to Channel 6. Staff set the bulky contraption down on the lowest tread of the front porch steps and called out to Afia.

"I'm sorry. I think I'm going to need some help. No sign of any snakes so far. Be careful where you step on your way over. Don't walk on any of the pawprints, just in case we have to do this again." From this spot outside the house, he thought he could hear Patsy Blankenship's wedge heels *thik-thunk*ing against the floors of the empty old house. Hopefully, she hadn't completed her search already.

"On my way," Afia called. In a few seconds she had skipped along the pawprint trail that had taken him nearly two minutes to shoot. She did not step on a single one.

"Thanks. See where the tracks take a left turn here at the porch steps? If you follow them out as far as they go, or at least until they make another turn, it'll be easier for me to shoot this length of the trail. I won't have to search for the trail if I can keep you in my periphery. I'll keep your feet out of the shot as best as I can."

"Interesting."

He looked up at her. "Well, it's the best idea I can come up with since I don't have a skater or a dolly in our little stash of equipment in the truck and Joanie won't buy me any modern equipment."

"No, not that. I mean it's interesting to me the way the pawprints go sideways after the porch steps. You haven't been this way yet. Look."

Staff left the camera where he'd set it on the bottom porch step and followed her line of sight. She was right. The pawprints at the edge of the house no longer formed a linear direction. Instead, at the base of the structure, there was a complete set of four pawprints pointing toward the house. They reappeared every few inches along the mortared stacks of cinder block that made up the exterior of the home's foundation. Between them were elongated tramplings and scratches, as if a dog had strafed alongside the outside edge of the house like a character in a first-person shooter video game instead of walking parallel to it. A few feet to the left of the front porch stairs, the trail turned a corner, out of view.

"What do you think it was up to?"

"She," Afia corrected him. "If we're going to use this for the black bitch story then 'it' needs to be 'she.'"

"Right. What do you think *she* was up to?"

"Well, every dog I've ever known likes to sniff things, especially when they're outside. It looks to me like she might have been sniffing along these blocks."

"Makes sense. Changes my shot a little, but makes sense." He snagged the camera from the front porch steps and aimed it toward the front of the house as if it were the dog's nose. Afia strode to the left wing corner and waited as Staff strafed alongside the wall, recording each set of pawprints up to the edge. He was about to stand upright again when Afia spoke.

"They continue the same way around this side." She followed the tracks ahead a few paces and stopped, crouching in front of an area of cinder block foundation that, from Staff's spot at the corner, looked a little bit more exposed below the backfill line than the rest of the place, like the root of a tooth that had appeared from behind a receding gum line. "Shoot the rest of the prints up to where I am and then come take a look at this."

"On it." He rushed a bit while tracking the last few prints that led up to Afia's position alongside the house. He might regret that later, but figured he had shot enough of the trail to be able to cut together some interesting visuals for the more boring exposition portions of the interviews they would conduct later that day. He shut off the recorder and set the unit down beside him as he crouched next to Afia in the overgrown grass. "What's up?"

"Take a look. I think our canine buddy might have decided that this was the best place to dig out whatever she'd been smelling. There's a little hollowed out spot of earth against the foundation here."

Staff snickered. "Maybe she was chasing a rabbit or something." Near the edge of the void, one corner of a bottom row cinder block appeared to be missing entirely. To Staff, the hole looked a bit like the archway holes Jerry Mouse made in the walls of Tom Cat's house in those old syndicated cartoons he'd watched as a kid. It was more ragged than Jerry's holes, of course, but it did kind of have that shape. He fingered the edge of it. "I'll bet a little rabbit managed to find an escape in there and our hound was trying to get it out."

"Probably right," Afia said, standing up again. "I wonder if this used to be some kind of storage area, though. The blocks don't have any mortar between them here...or here."

Staff hadn't noticed it before, but where the dog or whatever it was had apparently been digging stood a two-block-wide, two-block-high square of cinder blocks that were mortared together at both the horizontal and vertical axes. On every side of this structure except for the bottom, which rested directly atop the masonry below it, was a black void. As far as Staff could tell, it wasn't fastened at the bottom, either. It was just a cinder block rectangle that sat blocking an open hole in the foundation and attached to nothing.

Well, it was rectangular except for that mouse house-shaped hole in the lower right corner of it, anyway.

"Huh." He scratched his chin. "Some houses have crawl spaces. Maybe this used to be an entrance to one but someone doesn't want it to be the entrance anymore. Wonder why they didn't just put a crawl space door there with a lock on it?"

"Beats me. It's not like you can see it from the road or anything. Nothing faces this side of the house except rows and rows of trees. Looks like it continues around to the backyard as well."

"Yeah." Staff scanned the forest that lined the edge of the property behind them and led into the backyard. That must have been where the Beard kid saw whatever it was he saw through the window. He turned back to the cinder block and brightened. "Hey, Afia, what would you give me to stick my hand in this mouse hole and feel around a little? Who knows? Maybe we'll come up with some hidden treasure, or a dead body. Imagine how *that* would look on the news!"

She grinned at him. "Not unless Constable Gordon gives us the go-ahead on that, Geraldo. We're guests here, remember? It's not a fishing expedition."

He pouted theatrically, then stood up beside her. "Spoilsport. I'm sorry. I'm getting bored out here. There's only so much we can do while we're waiting on Patsy."

Then, as if on cue, they heard the older woman shouting from somewhere around the front porch. "Don't worry! We'll be right back!" There was urgency in her voice.

Staff and Afia's eyes met. "Uh oh," he said, then lifted the camera from the ground beside him and followed closely on

Afia's heels as she sprinted around the corner of the house to meet up with Patsy. The older woman was standing with her right hand against a column beside the front porch steps and her left clutching the center of her chest.

"Oh, dear," she said and looked up just in time to see Afia and Staff approaching. "Mr. Gordon seems to have taken a nasty tumble down a set of stairs. He's in the cellar. He's been there since last night. He wants us to bring him a ladder so he can climb out."

"He can't walk up the stairs?" Staff asked.

"Oh my, no. That old staircase pretty much just crumbled away beneath him. There's no way out of there now but by a rope or a ladder."

"Is he all right?" Afia asked. "Should we call an ambulance or something?"

"He says he's fine. He didn't want me to call anyone. He's having some trouble talking, though. It looks like he busted up his face pretty bad in the fall. Maybe I can just take him to a doctor when we get him out of there. Lost Hollow's health insurance for town government isn't the greatest. Residents don't want to have to pay extra taxes for it. An ambulance might be too expensive on his salary, especially if it has to take him all the way to the hospital over in Hollow River." She sighed and shook her head. "I have an extension ladder at the B&B that we can use to get him out of there. I just need a way to get it here. I don't think it'll fit in my car. We might be able to get it in the back of your truck if I could get a strapping young gentleman to drive me back to my place and help me lift it." She batted her enormous eyes at Staff in faux bashfulness. Staff thought but did not say, that she suddenly reminded him more than passingly of Robin Williams all dressed up in elderly nanny drag in *Mrs. Doubtfire*. Afia, meanwhile, faked an itchy nose, putting a hand over her own mouth to disguise her grin.

"Happy to help," Staff replied. "Just let me stow the camera." He eyed the pickup, noting the rails that had been installed along the roof of the topper. "I think we have some tie-downs in the back. We can probably just strap your ladder to the roof if it doesn't fit with our other stuff. The camera equipment is fragile so it might be safer that way."

"That works for me. We should get going, then. I told the constable we'd be right back to help him. I hate to leave him down there all alone while we're gone. I suppose I could text or call him, but that didn't work last night. I was so surprised by what happened that I didn't even think to ask him where his phone is."

Afia spoke up then. "I'll stay. It shouldn't take three of us to strap a ladder to the top of the truck. I can keep him company. Maybe I can ask him a few questions, too. Get the ball rolling for our feature."

Relief washed over Patsy's face. "Are you sure you don't mind?"

"Not at all."

"Good! Good, good, good. Well, let's get going, then." The trio strode the distance to the Channel 6 News S-10 together. "I'm sorry to take up so much time from your story with all this, but—"

"Shit happens," Staff finished for her as he opened the S-10's topper door and set the camera inside. He shut the door with a bang and twisted the handle to secure it.

Patsy blushed but laughed out loud. "Yes. Yes, it does! Shit does happen." She glanced at Graham's Tacoma. Its cab and the rails of its bed were dew-soaked and sparkling in the morning sun that dappled through the trees surrounding the old Gordon place. "Looks like the constable left his windows down when he went inside. I hope nothing's been stolen. There aren't many people out here, but kids like Jeremy Beard have been coming out here quite a bit lately."

Staff stepped over to the passenger side of Graham's pickup and peered inside. "Stereo and everything else looks intact." He reached inside and plucked a palm-fitting rectangular device from the seat in front of him. "I think I found his phone, though."

The iPhone's lock screen appeared when Staff turned it over in his hand so that he could see the face of it. The screen was a simple plain black background with white text that read PRESS HOME TO UNLOCK at the bottom. There was also a seemingly endless quantity of text and phone call notifications. Staff did not scroll through them, but he did notice that the most recent was a missed telephone call notification from one Patsy Blankenship earlier that morning. It was immediately preceded by a new voicemail notification.

"Yep. This is his phone all right." He handed it to Patsy, who gave it to Afia.

"You can take it to him when you go in. The cellar door is to the right toward the back of the entryway. It's a little slat door with a hook latch. You can't miss it. Don't try to go down there, though! The stairs are broken."

Afia accepted the device, depositing it into the side pocket of the wine-colored blazer she wore over a white cotton babydoll T-shirt. "Yeah," she said. "You told us."

"So I did. So I did." Patsy turned to Staff. "Are we ready, then?"

Staff nodded. "I think we're ready." He climbed into the driver's seat and buckled up while Afia helped boost Patsy into the shotgun seat. Had he indeed been a strapping young gentleman, he thought, he probably should have been the one to do that. Or maybe that would have been considered sexist since he was a man. Or perhaps not, since he was a gay man. Or maybe it all just depended on the woman who was being boosted. Whatever. When she was secure in the shotgun seat, and the door had been closed, Staff started the S-10 and shifted it into Reverse. He raised a two-finger wave to Afia as they pulled away. She waved back, and then turned toward the Gordon house, presumably to introduce herself to its currently incapacitated sole occupant.

"Quite a morning we've had so far, huh?" Staff said as he pivoted the wheel and made a reverse U-turn in the middle of Hollow Creek Road. When Patsy didn't answer him, he glanced at her. She had her head cocked to the right, cell phone pressed to her ear and was holding up a hand to shush him.

"Clara?" she said. "It's Patsy. Listen, I think Constable Gordon might be hurt. He was doing some work out at his old family place and left his phone in his truck. I'm on my way to the B&B to get a ladder. The cellar stairs broke on him and—don't laugh—he's stuck down there. No way out. Yes, I know. Anyway, do you think we can find some funds to send an ambulance out to the old Gordon place? Just in case he's hurt worse than he thinks? Uh-huh. Well, it doesn't seem to be an emergency right now. Just as soon as you can spare one, I think. Thank you. Will do. Bye.

"She didn't sound too happy," Patsy said to the windshield after she'd ended the call.

"Well, it was the right thing to do," Staff replied. "Don't feel bad about it. I mean, he might need the help, after all."

Staff swung a right onto SR-501 from Hollow Creek Road. He pointed through the windshield ahead of them. "Right there," he said. "That's where that dog or black bitch or whatever it was ran out in front of us yesterday. You can see the skid marks on the road where we nearly spun all the way around. We're probably lucky we didn't break any of the equipment in the process."

"Or your necks," Patsy offered.

"Yeah, or our necks."

Staff glanced in the driver's side rear view mirror to verify that he hadn't accidentally cut someone off. He couldn't remember whether he'd looked before making his turn. No one was there. He supposed they would have heard a horn blatting behind them if he'd hurt someone's ego. He was just about to divert his attention back to the drive ahead when he thought he saw a small black spot appear from the grassy shoulder of the road that was rapidly disappearing behind them. He blinked, and it was gone.

"*Deja vu*," he said.

"Hmmm?" Patsy was currently entranced by the glow of the screen from her cell phone.

"Oh, nothing, I guess. Just thought I saw something coming out of the grass behind us. Afia and I saw pawprints in the front yard at the Gordon place. We traced them to the front of the house and then around the corner. It looked like something had been digging at this little hole in the foundation."

Patsy dropped the phone to her lap and looked at him, large eyes wide. "Do you think it might have been the black bitch again?"

"I don't know. Do you want to go back and see for yourself?"

She appeared to think it over. "No. No, we really shouldn't. Poor Mr. Gordon's been trapped in that cellar for a long while now. Maybe when we get him out, we can go have another look at those pawprints. See if we can find some along the shoulder where you saw whatever it was." She grinned, stretched out her left hand and patted him twice on the knee. "This is exciting!"

"Yeah," Staff said. He supposed it probably was exciting for Patsy, but for him and Afia, the morning had grown far too long and unproductive already. Time was running out for them to get the Halloween feature they needed for Channel 6, and now they—a news team—were stuck helping a small town law enforcement official get out of a situation he shouldn't have been able to get himself into in the first place. Who leaves their phone in the car? He didn't think Channel 6 would fire them for not coming back with much more than an interview with some old lady and her cosplayer friend for the Halloween segment. It's not like they were dropping the ball on a hard news story like a murder or a car chase or a political sex scandal. But Joanie was a penny pincher. She might not reimburse them the cost of the trip.

"Yeah. Exciting."

CHAPTER TEN

The footsteps above him sounded different this time. Lee Gordon sat against the cinder block wall at the bottom of the staircase stringers, waiting. Just waiting. He had not expected to hear footfalls through his old house so soon after the woman named Patsy's departure. The flaky old bat was supposed to have gone somewhere to get a ladder so he could climb out of this spot. Unless that somewhere had been built somewhere on his land sometime in the years after his death, he didn't think she could have made it all the way back to him so quickly. Also, the footsteps sounded softer and more deliberate, like someone walking through a place where they knew they had no business being.

When the cellar door creaked open, Lee switched on the Maglite he had been toying with in his right hand and shone it up at the figure that appeared in the frame just above the demolished staircase. For a single horrifying instant, he thought he saw a face he recognized peering down at him from the main floor of his own house. It was the face of Grace Afton, that black bastard Darek's wife, whom he'd long ago slaughtered, and whose body he had stowed in the crawl space along with the dead stripper and, unfortunately, his own wife after she'd caught up to what he'd been doing.

He blinked, and the illusion vanished. It wasn't the black woman. This woman was black all right, but skinnier than the Afton bitch. She had the same slightly almond-shaped eyes and full lips, but she was missing the curves around her hips, at least as far as Lee Gordon could see from his vantage point at the bottom of the cellar. She was dressed a little funny for a black woman, too, he thought. She sported a blazer that made her look like she might be some kind of professional; a real estate agent, maybe. Or a teacher. She must have been new in town. He doubted that she had grown up anywhere near Lost Hollow, or even Hollow County.

"How-do?" he called, tipping the brim of an invisible hat to her. "Don't thwy to come down. Stairs are broken." The stupid lisp created by his kid's swollen tongue and busted face was starting to irritate him. It hurt his throat to shout up at her, but he also wasn't keen on having another black woman end up dead down here if she fell. Not after he'd won his corporeal life back from his fuck-up of a son. Even an accidental death might bring the sheriff's department, and they might want to look around the cellar this time. Plus, Lee needed time to get his bearings in a new era as well as figure out how to get the brat out of his head. He was successful at pushing him down in the stream of consciousness for now, but it didn't seem to be drowning him.

"Oh, I know," the woman said and smiled at him. "Don't worry. Patsy warned me about the stairs. I'm just here to keep you company while she goes back to the B&B to get an extension ladder. I guess by the look on your face that you don't remember me, huh? My name is Afia. Afia Afton. We went to elementary school together."

Fuck.

Fuck. Fuck. Fuck.

Well, at least now he knew why his dumbass son's eyes had fooled him at first glance. She was Grace Afton's daughter. The daughter resembled her uppity mother in the face, if nowhere else. Of all people to think they're coming to his boy's rescue, there could have been none worse. Lee Gordon looked down at his hands, forced a smile to spread over his son's face, and then looked up again at the woman standing over him.

"Athia," he said. "Of course. I remember you."

She chuckled. Was she laughing at him? "It sounds like you've done a number on yourself. I won't make you talk too much while we wait. Patsy just didn't want to leave you here all by yourself while she went to get the ladder. They should be back pretty soon."

"They?"

"Oh, yeah. My cameraman went with her. I'm a reporter for Channel 6 News now. Staff—my cameraman, Joe Stafford—and I are staying at Patsy's this weekend. We're trying to get some good Lost Hollow ghost stories for a Halloween feature segment we're doing this year."

"Halloween," Lee Gordon repeated, mostly to himself.

"Right. Patsy was trying to call you this morning to ask if you would give us a tour of this old place you have here, but you didn't have your cell phone with you. We found it in your truck just now." She plucked a rectangular object from the pocket of her blazer and held it up so that he could see. The front of it illuminated when she held it up, sort of like the light from a black screen on a television. There was some kind of blue rectangles on the black screen, but he couldn't make out anything about them from this distance. "If we're careful, I can probably toss it down to you. Looks like you've got a nice Otterbox case on it, so it should survive an impact if you miss the catch. It might give you something else to do while we wait."

Lee shrugged. He placed the Maglite on the cellar floor so that its beam shined straight up at the ceiling, and stood up. He stretched out his hands, cupping them for the catch. "Ok. Toth it."

With both hands cradling the device, Afia tossed it at a slight arc just above the cellar door. The phone dropped straight down into the cellar. Lee had to take one step forward, but it was enough. The thing came to rest against the palms of both his hands. He grabbed it with his left and held it at arm's length, hoping that he looked as if he knew what he was doing.

The screen illuminated again when he raised the device to a vertical position in front of his face. He could see the blue rectangles on it close up now. One of them said something about a missed call. Across the bottom was a message that read PRESS HOME TO UNLOCK. Lee had no idea what that meant. Before he could try anything, the screen dimmed to black again. He was tempted to shake the thing to...what?...wake it up again? Then he thought it might look to the black woman above him like he didn't know what he was doing.

BOY! he shouted into the stream of consciousness he now shared with his son. *BOY! WHAT DO I DO WITH THIS THING? I DON'T KNOW WHO TO CALL ON IT NOR EVEN HOW TO MAKE IT WORK IF I DID!*

There was no answer from his son. Lee Gordon relaxed his psychic grip on the boy. He could feel him down there, somewhere under the waves and ripples in the stream. Graham was still alive. He knew that. Maybe he really was unconscious right now. Or maybe he was just petulant, as useless to his old man now as he had been as a child. Lee shoved the device into the front pocket of Graham's uniform pants, then bent and retrieved the flashlight from the floor. He shined it in Afia's direction but made sure to prevent the beam from illuminating her face too much.

"I'll look at it later."

"Suit yourself." She crouched at the mouth of the cellar, planting her feet against the door frame, and hugged her knees to her chest. "I don't know how long it will take them to get the ladder and get back out here, but I'm sure they'll be as quick as they can about it. Staff's become pretty good at loading and unloading heavy equipment."

Lee nodded. "Uh-huh."

"Is there anything I can get for you? Do you have any food or water or anything out in your truck? I could text Staff and ask him to bring you back something if not."

"Un-uh. Not hungry."

"Ok, then. Let me know if you change your mind."

Lee heard her yawn. He could also hear and see her tapping the soles of her shoes against the cellar door frame. She was bored with him, maybe. Good. Maybe she would go back outside. The sound of those tapping feet was maddening.

"So Patsy says you're planning to do some restoration work on this old place," Afia said after a while. "Any ideas yet what you're going to do with it? She thinks it might make a good haunted tour attraction. Based on what I've seen so far, I'd have to say I agree with her."

Lee scoffed. He hadn't known for sure that the boy was planning to do anything to the house, but he certainly did not approve of turning it into some kind of small-town tourist trap like the ones that used to litter Route 66 back in the day. Nice places to visit. Wouldn't want to live in one.

"I don't know yet," he managed.

"Well, I'll give you my card so you can give me a call if you're going to turn it into a business or a museum. Maybe we can do a separate story on that sometime."

"Yeah. Maybe."

Afia swiped her palms against her knees and stood up. "Well, if you don't need anything, I think I'm going to step outside and text Staff, see how long he thinks they'll be." She reached into her blazer pocket and removed what looked like a business card. She tossed it into the cellar. It fluttered to the floor before Lee could catch it. "My cell number is on the card there. If you need me for anything before they get here, just call or text. I'll be right outside."

Lee bent and plucked the card from the floor. He shoved it into the pocket of Graham's uniform pants along with the "phone" device that looked to him more like a tiny television. He did not bother to look at the card. "Ok," he said. "But I'm fine. I just need a ladder."

"I know you've had a problem with kids drinking in here," the woman added. "There are some old beer bottles scattered along the floor. I might be able to use one to prop this cellar door open for you. That will at least let a little bit of light in from up here. You won't have to rely so much on that flashlight you have there."

He nodded at her. "Ok. Soundth good." Now just go away already.

The cellar door slammed shut when she stepped back from it. Lee could hear the clacking of her feet above him. It was not a straight march to the door, more like a few steps with pauses in-between. *She must be gathering those beer bottles*, he thought. He was about to fling himself on the floor against the cinder block wall again while he waited when his head suddenly exploded with pain. The sound of crashing waves inside his ears drowned out everything else, including Afia's footsteps from above. He plugged his ears with his index fingers and rooted around inside the canals, trying to physically locate the source. Lee had let down his guard for too long, and Graham had taken the opportunity to surface from their shared stream of consciousness. He thought he could feel the boy's presence, clawing its way down the brain stem, out through the nerves, toward the vocal organs and the hands.

***

Why did the chicken cross the road?
To prove to the opossum that it could be done.

Graham Gordon could hardly believe his own body's eyes when he had seen Afia Afton's face standing over him. She was all grown up now, and said that she's a reporter for Channel 6 news. In her face he could see the Afia that he'd known as a child, the girl he had liked. The girl his father had dismissed along with her entire race as being a freak of evolution. The girl whose pants he had tried to pull down at the see-saw on the playground because he'd told the other boys what his dad had said and they had goaded him about it, demanded that he prove it. It was an act Graham had nearly forgotten until his father's memories had brought it surging forward again. Like most childhood mistakes, he had once been able to chalk it up to youthful stupidity. Now he truly felt bad about it. He had been manipulated by a racist, had allowed himself to be manipulated by a racist father steeped in the racist culture of a racist small town. Now he knew better. He had evolved. But that couldn't fix what he had done before. Nothing could.

She had found his iPhone, had tossed it into the cellar for him. He saw and thought he might even have felt his hands capture it on its descent. His father's voice boomed at him through the Ether shortly after: *BOY! BOY! WHAT DO I DO WITH THIS THING? I DON'T KNOW WHO TO CALL ON IT NOR EVEN HOW TO MAKE IT WORK IF I DID!*

Graham made no effort to respond. He shrank back against his bubble cell, in fact, curled in on himself until he was radiating as little of his thought and presence as he could. He'd spent most of his young life finding ways to hide from his father in the physical world by simply curling up and remaining quiet. Maybe he could do the same thing in the metaphysical realm. Seconds later, he felt his father's attention drift away from him and back to the woman above. Graham unfurled himself and stretched the tendrils of his proto-hands toward the lens of the bubble. His father had jammed his iPhone into the right pocket of his pants. That was followed by Afia Afton's business card. This was as good a time as any to try out the idea that was forming.

What has four wheels and flies?

A garbage truck!

One of his tendrils pierced the wall of the bubble and stretched outward, seeking the nerves that controlled his body's right hand. The bubble in which he was imprisoned wavered and wobbled, making strange sounds as it did. To Graham, they sounded like he imagined the roar of crashing waves must sound, although he'd never been to a beach. Another tendril followed the first one, piercing the skin of the bubble. That one snaked upward along the spine. The sound of the bubble reacting to Graham's actions was hurting his father. The old man had plugged his ears, trying to drown out the sound.

Graham seized control of the right hand, freed it from his right ear, and jammed it into his pocket. He grabbed hold of the iPhone, loving that he could sense its weight and form through the skin of the hand he now controlled.

Next, he closed his metaphysical eyes and concentrated on his connection with the device, pressing the home button to unlock it and then opening the Messages app with a tap of his body's index finger. In contact with the device and surrounding its electromagnetic field with his own, he was somehow able to "see" what he was doing without actually laying eyes on it, although not entirely. It was a fuzzy image, like old TV shows broadcast from distant areas in the days before cable television grabbed a foothold and lightyears before internet streaming.

His father Lee was aware of his lost control. He could sense that. He needed a distraction. The left tendril, the one that was not controlling the hand, continued to wend its way up Graham's body's spinal column, eventually reaching his throat. There it grabbed control of his vocal cords and mouth while his index finger continued to tap buttons on the iPhone in his pants pocket.

***

Lee fought back. He was able to maintain control of the left hand. The right hand had suddenly unplugged from his ear and jammed itself into the right front pocket of Graham's uniform pants, where Lee had stowed the "phone" device and the black woman's business card. Lee was aware of its presence there but was unable to feel any movement of the hand or its attached fingers. His son's will was weak and always had been. Overpowering him was easier when he was just a kid. Now he was a grown man with a job, and maybe he was still a pushover in many ways, but the physical occupation of his body was apparently not one of them.

As if to underscore this thought, Lee suddenly felt a bulge of air from his son's diaphragm force its way up his windpipe and over the vocal cords. He clapped the left hand he still controlled over the boy's mouth, attempting to stop what was coming next, but it was no use. Graham had located enough strength of will from somewhere down in their consciousness to scream the words so that Afia was sure to hear even from behind the closed cellar door.

"Athia!" Lee heard the voice from within the body he occupied shout. "ATHIA! I'm thorry! I'M THORRY!"

Then, just as suddenly as he had broken the surface of the stream of consciousness, he was submerged again. Lee Gordon regained control of the mouth, lungs, and diaphragm. Pins and needles flooded the right hand that had been thrust in the front right pocket of Graham's uniform pants. It was under Lee's control. He removed it from the pocket and examined it for any signs of damage. There were none. He was able to wiggle each of the fingers individually, to close the fist and reopen it, all without issue. He balled up his left hand and smacked the knuckles into the palm of the right as hard as he could. There was no pushback, and he was able to feel the hot tingling sensation the punch from the left created in the right palm. Good.

The cellar door swung open again. In its frame stood Afia—or her silhouette, anyway—holding what appeared to be three beer bottles by their throats between the fingers of her right hand. She propped the door open with her right foot while she determined the best placement for the bottles to help the door resist the call of its springs.

"Sorry for what?" she asked.

Lee blanked for a beat, unsure at first as to the meaning of what she was asking him, and then remembered what his son had screamed during his attempted coup. "Oh! Thorry!" he said through Graham's broken mouth. "I'm thorry for..." His mind raced. "...the thee-thaw! I'm thorry, Athia. I'm thorry for what happened at the thee-thaw when we were little. I was...misthinformed I guess."

Silence from above him. Lee began to think that it must have been some other black girl his boy had tried to molest on the playground all those years ago, but then she spoke again.

"That was you?" she said, and actually chuckled a little at the memory. "Oh my God, I had completely forgotten about that until just now. It *was* you, wasn't it? I was so mad at you that day. What made you think you could just walk up and try to pull down a girl's pants right in the middle of the playground? Or anywhere, for that matter?"

"I... I was misthinformed," Lee repeated in what he hoped was a good imitation of his idiot son's ridiculously over-wrought conscience. Not that the bitch in his house right now would know the difference, he supposed. Still, if he was going to be Graham now, there was no better time to practice the limp-dick facade. "My dad told me that black girlth have tails. I wanted to see for mythelf, I guess."

Afia's shoulders slumped, the beer bottles in her right hand bounced against the side of her leg. "And you believed your dad? Seriously? Had you ever in your life seen a person with a tail?" She raised her voice a tad. Not angry, more incredulous. "And even if you did believe him you could have just asked me, not tried to pull down my pants in front of God and everybody. Jesus, Graham!"

"I'm thorry," Lee tried again. "I was just a thupid kid. I didn't see anything. I promise."

She sighed. "All right. Well, I guess there was no harm done, was there? Except for my pride and your behind when the principal got hold of you. Honestly, Graham, I don't remember a whole lot about all that. Maybe I blocked it out. Or maybe it's just that we were very young at the time. But I do remember my mother getting really pissed off about it. How old were we?"

"I don't know. Theven or eight?"

"Eight. It must have been eight. I think I remember telling on you to Mrs. Batey. She was out there on the playground with us at recess. So we were probably eight. That's how old I was when my mother disappeared. The same year, I guess. So I think in the grand scheme that this incident seems to have weighed on you a whole lot more than it affected me, don't you think?"

Oh, if you only knew, Lee thought.

"Anyway, it was years ago and, like you said, we were just stupid kids. Kids do stupid things. Although I will say that your father was a racist for telling you things like that. And, I'm sorry to say, that's not the only reason I think about him that way. He and my dad didn't get along, either. Did you know that? I don't know why, but there was some nasty blood between them. I never got the full story out of my dad before he was murdered."

Lee stifled a smile as that memory arose from the depths. What his dumbass son had done to her on the playground was infinitesimal when compared to what Lee himself had done to Afia's family. Not only had he killed this woman's bitch of a mother. He'd also murdered her father when the dude had gotten a little too close for comfort that night after work. But, hell, it was the man's own fault for not controlling his bitch of a wife in the first place. Plus, Darek— and what kind of name was that anyway—had threatened his job at the carbon plant. That left him with no choice.

***

Inside the bubble, the holes that Graham had made in his prison sealed themselves when he withdrew the tendrils. He'd hoped that would not happen. He had hoped he could bide his time, gather some strength after his excursions and then use that strength to stretch out those punctures he'd made. If he could make the hole big enough for his entire consciousness to step through, maybe he could force his father into the stream instead, imprison him there until he could find a way to rid himself of this thing. Would he need a doctor or an exorcist? He didn't know, but he'd also *never* know if he didn't find a way out.

He allowed the cloud of his consciousness to absorb the tendrils he'd formed from it and then curled in on himself, wanting to rest until he could find the strength to pierce the bubble again. He could feel himself drifting. Could he dream when he was only his consciousness and not directly attached to his physical body? His father was thinking about something else now, something that felt to Graham like a dream. From somewhere outside, he distinctly heard Afia say her father was murdered. Then that feeling from before enveloped him. His father was reliving another memory.

The bubble closed in on Graham, squeezing him, forcing him into yet another past wherein he had no power.

***

They'd always hated each other, at least as far as Lee could remember. It started when the carbon plant gave the Afton man a locker right next to Lee's own, where Lee had to smell his sweat and look at his nasty parts every goddamn day of the week after their shift was over. He kept having to tell the faggot to stay on his own side of the locker doors, quit trying to rub up against him while he was changing out of his work clothes, but it never did take. It was enough to drive a man to drink. If that is, the man wasn't already a drinker. It was that stuff that had nearly gotten him fired. So-called Darek had apparently one time caught sight of the flask Lee stowed in the bottom of his locker, usually under a spare pair of coveralls. He'd told on him, just like his bitch of a daughter had told on Graham on the playground about four years prior. Their supervisor had searched his locker, found the flask, and poured it out. No drinking on the job, he'd said. There were safety concerns on account of the furnaces and heavy equipment. He'd only get one more chance. If they caught him with alcohol on the job again, he'd be fired and escorted off the grounds immediately.

In his defense, Lee had held off butchering the black man as long as he could stand it. He had genuinely tried to clean up his act. His livelihood was at stake, after all. He left the beer at home for a while, content to make up for lost time once he'd crossed the threshold into his own castle every evening. Then came the blackouts. Drinking over six hours what he usually drank over eighteen was too much to metabolize. Often, he awoke the next morning with a monster hangover and mud caked to the bottom of his Wolverines, with no idea of where he had gone or what he had done the night before. For all he knew, he had been out killing young whores again. It was the next best thing to fucking them when all the beer makes your ding dong dangle instead of coming to attention. There might have been a few flashes of memory of standing in front of the black man's house, bottle in hand, screaming at him to come out of there, to show himself and be a man about all the trouble he'd caused. He remembered someone—maybe the black woman's little daughter—gawking at him from behind the corner of a shade in one of the windows, but not much more than that.

The worst of the icepick headaches and throwing up were the days he had to call in sick. Those missing hours had caused the bank account to dwindle. Bills were getting harder to pay and his will to roll out of bed in the morning had all but vanished. So if he couldn't maintenance drink after his shift, and the black man was preventing him from maintenance drinking at work, maybe the best thing he could do for himself would be to rid himself and the carbon plant of the black man: the root of the problem, the snitch, the tattletale. Hell, Lee and the supervisor were perfect pals at work most of the time. He'd probably forgotten all about the flask incident by now. So maybe it was time to get rid of Darek, get his work life back to normal once and for all.

It was old hat for him by then. He'd followed Darek Afton out of the carbon plant after the end of the shift that evening. It was a clear night. The sodium security lights that lined the employee parking had buzzed to life hours ago, but there was enough shadow to protect him. Hidden in the folds of the spare pair of coveralls he carried under his arm—those that were once used to protect his drinking at work and since then had served no purpose—was his dad's old hunting knife, a long fixed blade that his father had intended for him to use for Boy Scouts. Except there were no troops in Lost Hollow and Lee Gordon's father had been much too lazy to drive him to Hollow River to locate one. He'd held onto it anyway, thinking that someday he might put it to good use and learn to hunt. Back then he thought he might be hunting deer or rabbit or squirrel. Turns out that humans made for better practice.

Except Darek Afton was younger than him, not a drinker, and fast. Lee Gordon at that time in his life was thick around the waist and probably had heart disease from all his years of alcoholism. Darek had climbed into his car and driven off before Lee was even close enough to call out to him. Fine, then. He'd follow him. Lee leaped behind the wheel of his F-150 and sped off in pursuit. At some point, Darek had noticed that he was being followed. He'd swung the Cougar, the car his now deceased wife used to drive every day, into a slot in the parking area next to the side-walk around the town square. It was a violent act. Lee could hear the squall of the Cougar's tires and the squeal of badly worn brakes as the other man made the turn and dragged the old boat to a halt. Lee glided his own pickup into the slot on the passenger's side of the Cougar, using Darek's car to provide cover as he snatched the hunting knife from the pile of the spare coveralls on the seat beside him, and slid out from behind the wheel of his F-150. Darek, meanwhile, had to walk around the Cougar to confront Lee face-to-face. He chose to walk around back, which suited Lee just fine.

"What the fuck do you want?" Darek shouted at him. The black man's fists were clenched and his eyes ablaze in the light that shone from the full moon hanging over the town square. It was bright enough to cast shadows, including a long clock hand-like shadow from the obelisk that appeared to be pointing directly at them.

"Just this." Lee dashed toward the other man, hunting knife clenched in his right hand and tilted at an upward forty-five-degree angle from his hip. He brought it up to Darek's face as he closed the distance and, before the black man could completely process what was happening, dragged the blade that was explicitly honed for the cutting of flesh from the lobe of the right ear and across his throat. He finished with a flourish at the flap of the left ear while Darek, eyes wide, clamped his hands over the fresh wound, trying in vain to stop the lava-like flow of precious blood from his throat. It had already begun to pool at the crew-neck of the T-shirt he wore, and seeped from there into the thinner fabric below.

Darek stumbled backward, his fear-filled eyes bulging from their sockets and his mouth gaping for either air or words. He fell into the middle of the street that encircled the town square, crawling crab-like on his elbows in a panicked last-ditch effort to escape. He was still alive, then, but not for very much longer.

Lee strode back to his F-150. He gathered some McDonald's napkins that had littered the passenger side floor mat for ages, bundling them into a single dry rag that he used to wipe down his weapon. The blood smeared over the blade. He would need to clean it again later, but that could wait until he got home. After this chore was finished, he'd clean it again and then drop it in the crawl space with everything else he'd ever had to hide. He placed the knife, with his dry rag wrapped around the bloody blade, back into the folds of the spare pair of coveralls on the seat. Then he turned his attention to the dying black man.

Four years before this, Lee Gordon had managed to carry that dead bitch Grace Afton through the woods from her house to his, get her inside, drag her down the cellar stairs, and shove her into the crawl space to rot. Now, after nearly half a decade of downing Bud after Bud and chain-smoking Winstons, he began to wonder whether he would be able to handle a man twice the dead woman's size and who had at least ten pounds on him in a similar fashion, especially after a long day at work and a goddamn street fight. He supposed he could drag the body back to the F-150. If he got Darek around the shoulders, he might be able to haul him up over the tailgate and shove him inside. But that was bound to leave a shitload of blood both on the tailgate and in the bed of the truck. That was a hell of a lot to clean up when your brain is foggy with a hangover.

There was also the fact that the black man's wife was already down there in the crawl space. Lee Gordon wasn't exactly superstitious, but there was a part of him that remembered tales his father used to tell him about the black

people and the voodoo they practiced. He wasn't sure it
was a good idea to put the man's murdered body in such
close quarters with his bitch of a dead wife. What if black
folks around here were into voodoo and devil worship and
bullshit like that? What if bringing them together somehow
triggered something? What if it left some kind of mark or
curse on his house? No, he thought. It wasn't ideal, but it
would save Lee some strength, some clean-up effort, and
possibly some lousy juju if he merely left Darek Afton in
the square. His body would be discovered, unfortunately.
Lee struggled with the calculations, but couldn't think of an
obvious way the man's death might be traced back to him.
There was no one out in Lost Hollow's town square at this
time of the evening. He doubted that there ever were on
nights like that one. Most folks were home digesting dinner
or dozing in front of the idiot box by now, and no stores
were open here past five o'clock on a weeknight.

On the street before him, the last bubbles of life strained
through the open wound on Darek Afton's neck. They surfaced like translucent red boils along the edges of the cut,
burst, and were then no more. Lee Gordon sighed, wiped
his hands on his pants, and heaved the still-warm corpse
by its armpits. He dragged Darek Afton out of the street,
where he would most likely have been used as some groggy
driver's speed bump the next morning. After some effort,
Lee propped him against the obelisk, allowing the man's
head to roll forward on his neck as if he were sleeping and
the blood that spread across his shirt was nothing more
than red wine he'd vomited all over himself in the night. It
was a fitting end for the black man who had caused him so

much trouble, he thought: bled to death in the shadow of the Daughters of the Confederacy monument in the middle of lily-white Lost Hollow's town square. Finally, he had been put in his place.

***

You bastard! Graham's diminished voice shouted from somewhere in the stream. Lee ignored it. He forced what he hoped was a sympathetic look on his son's face and nodded in the beam from the Maglite. "I'm thorry about your dad, too," he said to Afia. "You've been through a lot."

"Yeah. Yeah, I have. I won't lie to you, Graham. This hasn't been an easy trip for me. When Patsy told me that she wanted us to talk to you for this Halloween story we're doing, I had a bit of a panic attack. There was bad blood between your father and my father and—please don't be offended—I always wondered whether your father had something to do with my father's murder. I mean, it was more than bad blood, really. They hated each other."

She paused, perhaps waiting for him to reply. Lee said nothing.

"I mean, your father stood outside our house, drunk and shouting threats at us, more than once. The police wouldn't help us. When I was little, it felt like this horrible vicious cycle that was just going to go on forever. There were nights of peace and quiet, nights when my dad and I could talk about normal things like my day at school or what we wanted for dinner. Then there were those other nights, the nights when I was terrorized by the possibility that your father in his drunken rage was going to break down our door and murder us both." She shivered visibly, then chuckled. "Did you know that I told Patsy and Staff that we—you and I—probably would have been friends way back in elementary school if it hadn't been for our family circumstances. We were both outcasts in a way. You with your bruises and shyness, me being the only black girl in the class, and both of us missing our mothers."

Lee Gordon remained quiet. In his heart, he seethed. Seriously? This black woman was seriously suggesting that Lee Gordon's son would ever befriend a nigger girl?

Yes, came Graham's voice from somewhere within him. *I would have. Maybe if things had been different I would have even asked her out when we got to high school. How do you like that? Does that bother you?*

Lee scoffed. The boy was getting too big for his britches.

After a time, the bitch standing over him seemed to give up on her attempt to drag him into this particular set of navel-gazing exercises. She bent and placed against the open cellar door the three beer bottles that she'd held by their necks in her right hand. Next, she carefully stepped back from it, testing her system. When the door stuck, she applauded her own efforts and smiled down at him.

"*Voila!*" she said. "Let there be light!"

"Thankth," Lee intoned. It was the most he felt that he could muster under the circumstances.

"All right, then," Afia replied. "I suppose if you don't need me I'll take another walk around outside. If you don't mind, of course. Staff and I discovered some pawprints out there earlier that look like they lead to a little blocked off area, maybe something that used to be a crawl space access. It looks like the dog or whatever made those prints was trying to dig out the blocks. Do you have any idea what might be under there?"

"Ain't nothing under there as far as I know." He hoped he wasn't showing on Graham's face the alarm he felt at her inquiry. "Place has been blocked off for years. The only thing under there should be insulation and plumbing."

"Staff thought maybe it was chasing a rabbit or some other kind of critter that ran in there to escape."

He nodded. "Yes. Thath's probably right. I'd prefer if you didn't go pulling and prodding at that old set of blocks, though. I don't know what condition things are in over there. You could get hurt."

"Oh, sure. I won't disturb anything. I promise. It's just that Staff and I are here to try to get some Halloween stories and Patsy was telling us about the local legend of the black bitch, which is supposed to be some kind of dog with a human face. She says it's an omen of some kind."

Lee shrugged his son's shoulders for show. "I wouldn't know."

Except that he did know. He had seen the creature prowling around the perimeter of his house for years, once or twice while he was still alive, he thought. He had heard her lonesome screams in the night, sounding like what older folks might think was a banshee. Before his own son had shoved him to the bottom of the cellar, he thought she might have just been a product of his semi-guilty conscience, some kind of memory of his encounter with an enraged Grace Afton as she nosed her way into his life, trying to cause trouble. But then he'd seen her again—sensed her, really—countless times throughout the years he had paced the floors above in his Ethereal form. Now and then she'd come by, sniffing, sensing, seeking. Occasionally she would scratch at the front door, clawing at it as if trying to pry it open. That scratching would continue down the front porch and across the front of the house, around the corner, toward the old crawl space access. And she would scream, sometimes right there on his front porch. She would scream loud enough to wake the dead, and always it ended with a low, mournful canine howl. Ghost or not, it was that scream that had chilled him most. Often he told himself that it was probably just some form of wildlife that was somehow able to mimic a human voice. Maybe a hawk. He couldn't really have seen a human face on it in those few glimpses he'd gotten over the years. Could he?

I saw her, too, Graham's voice chimed in from somewhere among the waves in their shared stream of consciousness. There was a taunting quality to it, a courage he'd never heard from his brat in life. *I saw her just last night, Dad. Up there in the cellar doorway. Just before you happened to me. She was inside the house, Dad. She was finally in the house. You must have opened the door for her in all your bullshit bravado. I'll bet she's finally coming for you.*

SHUT UP, BOY! Lee screamed inside his head. *YOU DON'T KNOW WHAT YOU'RE TALKING ABOUT!*

He shook his head to clear it and then realized that Afia Afton was still standing over him. She looked concerned, but also mildly amused.

"Can I ask you one more question, Graham?"

He cleared his throat. "Thure."

"Why do you want to restore this old place? Your dad beat the hell out of you here, from what I understand. Didn't he also die here? What possible good for you can come out of bringing this place back from blight?"

He shrugged on the surface. Inside, Lee felt burned by her accusation that he was somehow not a good father. Was he strict? Sometimes mean? Sure. But he was raising his son the same way his daddy had raised him, and he'd turned out all right. "Good question, I guess," he replied. "I don't know."

"Ok, then. Well, I'm going to go back outside. Just call or text if you need me. We'll be hearing back from Staff and Patsy pretty soon. I'll call and check in with them if we don't."

"Ok."

She started to turn away again, unblocking the white light from the hallway that spread through the cellar door frame.

As she walked away, Lee felt a wicked grin spread across his son's lips. "Oh!" he shouted up at her. "Oh, and Athia?"

"Yes?" She paused in her steps but did not turn back to look at him.

"Your *mother* is a black bitch," he shouted.

He switched off the Maglite and flopped onto the cellar floor, leaning his back against the cinder block wall for support.

CHAPTER ELEVEN

Afia Afton sat in silence on the decrepit front porch steps of the old Gordon place, her forehead cradled in the palm of her right hand, her elbows propped on her knees. She cursed herself for allowing Joanie to talk her into this assignment. A slightly more ashamed part of her also cursed Staff and Patsy Blankenship for their catalysis of the memories of the bad history Lost Hollow held for her. There was an old adage she'd heard growing up, heard frequently after she was placed in the state foster system: you can't go home again. What no one ever bothered to tell her is it's best if you never try.

There was another old adage that Afia had often heard. She supposed she had been naïve to dismiss the one about the apple not falling far from the tree. Graham Gordon had grown up in a backwoods racist home with a backward racist father. The man had never even moved outside the city limits. He had never experienced life outside a small Southern town full of white people who tried to absolve themselves of their racism by clinging to the myth that the American Civil War was all about state sovereignty, not slavery. These were people who flew Confederate flags beneath the Stars and Stripes in their front yards and assuaged any twinges of guilt they might feel over it by claiming they did it all in the name of preserving history and heritage. The problem with that excuse, of course, is that knocking down racist symbols does not actually erase history. Preserving history is for museums, history books, and documentaries. Flagpoles and town squares dedicated to the heroes of lost causes do not preserve history so much as they lionize oppressors. Everything about Lost Hollow that had influenced Graham in his childhood still held sway over his world view and, apparently, that included his dead father's irrational fear of and hatred for black people.

She should just walk away, Afia thought. There was no story here. At least, there was no story that she wanted any part of broadcasting. Graham Gordon's father had endlessly harassed her family when she was little. His son, now trapped in the cellar of his father's old house, had tried to pull down her pants on the playground when they were eight years old. He'd been stupid enough to believe his father's racist myths, and at least racist enough himself at that age to think he had the right to put his hands on her in order to validate that myth. Afia had practically forgotten the incident from all those years ago. Now that Graham turned it all up fresh in the soil of her memories, she seethed over it. What right did he think he had to put his hands on her? And what right did he have to call her mother a bitch? She was the woman who had loved Afia enough to risk a confrontation with a white male principal in a redneck school district. She was the woman who had dared to stand up to Afia's assailant and demand an apology. She was a brave woman. A strong woman. But a bitch? If she was a bitch, it was only in the most empowering feminist connotation of the word.

He had no right, the distant voice of Afia's mother Grace Afton said inside her head. It was a voice she barely remembered, not a voice she heard often. Until this moment, Grace Afton had been a giant question mark in Afia's history. She was unfinished business. Afia had spent most of her life angry with her mother for having disappeared. Now, thinking back on the incident at the school playground, she felt the sting of guilt over that anger.

The fury, the outrage, that had overcome Grace Afton's face when Afia told her what had happened had been frightening at the time. On some level, Afia supposed the child version of her had been afraid that her mother was angry with her. As an adult, she could see that Grace wasn't angry *with* her daughter. She was angry *for* her daughter. Now her daughter was angry too. And sad. She'd never told her mother how much that love and support meant to her that day. Now she might never get the chance.

The hooting of a nearby screech owl broke her out of her reverie. She hoped it was an owl anyway. There was something oddly human in that trilly sound. It wasn't repetitive like a hoot owl or the caw of a crow. It ranged in pitch and varied in frequency and, at least twice, she thought she heard it say her name: *A-fee-aaa. A-fee-aaa.*

A cool autumn breeze caressed her just then, making her shiver, raising gooseflesh. Afia looked up from her hands and shaded her eyes against the morning sun. She glanced

at the cars parked along the side of the road near the front
yard, scanning beyond them, searching for the source of
the call. There was nothing there that she could see. Only
a few tall brown cattails swaying hypnotically in the breeze.
She started a little when a loud *thump* sound came from
somewhere inside the house. Graham getting restless, she
assumed. And that was fine. Let him be restless. His cavalry would get here by and by. Until then, he was no more
of her concern. She and Staff should just be on their way
once he and Patsy returned with the ladder. It was not her
responsibility to save the man.

No. You won't save him, the voice of her mother said in her
head. *You can't save him. What's done in the dark is brought
to the light, sweetheart. What man sows he reaps, and the sins
of the fathers shall be visited upon the sons.* Where had she
heard that line before? It sounded biblical. Afia had never
had much use for the patriarchal strictures of the Christian
church. She was certain she'd never heard her mother quot-
ing scripture. Even so, the words made sense. The only
person who could truly save Graham Gordon was Graham
Gordon. Yes, he might need someone to bring him a ladder
to get out of that cellar, but getting out of that cellar didn't
absolve him of anything.

There was the screech again. *A-fee-aaa. A-fee-aaa.* She
wondered then if the local kids had been hearing an owl
out here at night instead of the screams they'd been reporting. The vaguely human sound of the screech owl certainly
gave her the creeps. That didn't explain what Jeremy Beard
had said he'd seen out the rear window of the place, but
she could understand how the owl's vocalizations, wherever

they were coming from, could easily be mistaken for the mournful wail of a human woman.

She heard something skitter by on the pavement at the road. It sounded the way a dog's claws or a deer's hooves sound when they panic and bolt for elsewhere, when they just can't seem to get their legs under them as they attempt to flee. In the shadow between the back end of Graham Gordon's Tacoma and the front end of Patsy Blankenship's Sonata, something moved. It might have been a leaf being dragged along the pavement by the autumn breeze, although at that moment Afia hadn't noticed any pickup of wind. She supposed it could have also been a squirrel or some other rodent scampering away with some spoils that had recently fallen from the already near-barren branches on the trees that surrounded the Gordon place. Whatever it had been, it was gone in an instant and probably not important.

Afia's thoughts drifted back to the Halloween puff piece that she and Staff had been assigned to obtain for Channel 6 News. They had the Beard interview. They could still get Patsy on camera to describe other scary legends of Lost Hollow. But she would be damned if she would now allow Graham Gordon to sully her airwaves.

CHAPTER TWELVE

Staff and Patsy Blankenship had just finished securing the extension ladder they'd hauled from Patsy's
garage to the luggage rails atop the Channel
6 News pickup's topper when the familiar sound of an
iPhone's default Note text message alert caused them both
to prick up their ears. Staff automatically grabbed at his
hip, where the holster on which he hung his iPhone was
clipped, even though it should have been evident to him
that the sound was not coming from there because he'd felt
no accompanying vibration. He glanced at the screen as he
lifted the device, then clipped it back into place.

"Not me. Must be yours."

Patsy stretched her arms through the open passenger side
window of the S-10 and lifted her purse from the seat. She
rummaged around inside it for a minute, reminding Staff
of his grandmother searching for a pack of chewing gum
when he was a kid, and mumbled something about why bag
manufacturers always use black as an interior lining. She
located the phone and stared at the screen, her enormous
eyes looked confused behind her Coke-bottle lenses.

"Well, I guess this means Afia gave Graham his phone back, but he must have hit his head harder than we thought," she said. "Either that or Afia's using it to text us random nonsense."

She held the iPhone up so that Staff could see the message on the screen. Just beneath all of her attempts to text Graham earlier that morning appeared a single balloon with the reply, "Knock knock. Who's there? Cotton. Cotton Who? Cotton a trap." Just as Staff was about to ask Patsy what she thought he meant by that, another balloon appeared. "Why shouldn't you tell secrets in a cornfield? Because it has too many ears."

"He's texting you kids' jokes?"

Patsy examined the new text and shrugged. "I guess so, although I can't imagine why." Another text arrived just then. Patsy read it aloud. "Why are the zombies unhappy with their roadmap? It only leads to dead ends."

Staff actually laughed out loud at that one. "He's delirious. I guess if I had been trapped in a dark cellar for a day I might be randomly texting some groaners, too. There's nothing like a bad dad joke to take the focus off your own physical pain and put it on someone else's funny bone."

"Yeah," Patsy said distantly. She sounded out the words as she tapped a reply on her iPhone's keyboard. "Are you ok?"

Another text arrived on Patsy's iPhone then. She turned the screen so that Staff could read the response after she'd processed it herself. It was one word. "NO!"

"I see," Staff said. "Maybe we'd better get back there, then. I haven't heard a peep out of Afia since we left. We haven't even been gone thirty minutes. What could've gone wrong?"

Staff unclipped his own iPhone from his hip and verified again that he'd received no messages. He briefly considered calling Afia, just to confirm that everything was still on the up-and-up out there, but then thought about the possible effects on his own coping skills if she didn't answer. He still needed to drive himself and Patsy back to the scene, after all, and that would be much more difficult to do in a panicked state. Besides, there was no real reason to panic just yet. No news is good news, as the old saying went.

He yanked one final time on each of the straps they'd used to tie the ladder to the topper, ensuring that they were tight and secure, then piled behind the wheel of the S-10. "Let's go." He motioned to Patsy, who was now staring at the screen of her iPhone as if she had been hypnotized by it. He tooted the horn, a short burst that broke her spell. Then she climbed into the pickup's passenger seat.

"I do hope everything's all right," she said after stowing the iPhone in her purse. She struggled a bit with the seat belt. The shoulder harness kept locking on her as she tried to drag it across her mid-section to meet the buckle."

"Let's just get back there as fast as we can. The sooner we get him out of that hole, the sooner Afia and I can get on with our work here. You might want to give that Clara woman a call back, tell her it might be more of an emergency than we thought."

"Good idea."

Staff shifted the S-10 into Drive and made a right turn onto the street from the bed and breakfast. Over top of them, he heard the extension ladder rattle against the luggage rails when the pickup's right rear tire hit the curb. He'd cut it too close. He checked the rearview mirrors and saw no sign of the ladder having tumbled off the roof. Satisfied, he mashed the accelerator and pushed the speedometer up to forty-five, ten miles over the speed limit for this part of town, and twenty miles over the limit for the section of it that encircled the town square. But it was a Saturday morning in this smallest of small towns and Staff just happened to know that the town constable was otherwise occupied at the moment. He occasionally glanced at his passenger who, after having updated her apparent dispatcher friend Clara on the situation, remained glued to the view in front of her, her eyes enormous even in profile and her hands clenched tightly at the seam of the seat into which she sank. He was scaring her. Probably badly. He hated that, but there was an undeniable urgency building within him to get back to Afia—to know that nothing terrible had happened to her—and, less urgently, to the trapped town constable Graham Gordon.

There was no sign of the black bitch as they approached the old Gordon place. Staff only glanced at the shoulders of the road along the way, just enough to maintain a watch for any wildlife that might leap out at them and cause a delay. None did. He slowed the S-10 to a stop in the same location that it had previously rested behind Patsy's Sonata. There was a part of him that wanted to go just a little farther than that, maybe "accidentally" push the car ahead of him into the shiny red truck that had today become somewhat of a landmark in their visit to Lost Hollow. Not only did the Tacoma, which shone a blazing Confederate red in the sun now that the dew had evaporated from it, represent that small town white man's desire to remain part of his redneck pack while holding onto something of an individual identity, but it also served as a barrier to both Staff and Afia. They were here only to do their jobs and get paid for doing those jobs, not to rescue straight middle-aged white men from their own failings. And it was this Constable Gordon's own failings that had gotten him into this mess, wasn't it? Who in their right mind goes poking around a rotting and abandoned old house without a cell phone in hand? Staff reached for the key to switch off the S-10 and felt relief wash over the muscles in his right hand. He'd apparently been clenching the steering wheel. The knuckles on the hand that was still wrapped around it were bone white.

Patsy had already exited the S-10 and was trundling her way up the overgrown driveway toward Afia, who as it happened was seated on the top step of the front porch, her elbows on her knees and her chin resting on her fists. She was watching her own feet. Staff was relieved to see her there. He climbed out of the pickup, dropped the keys into the right front pocket of his cargo shorts, and raised the door on the topper. From within, he removed the camera he'd earlier used to record the pawprints that he and Afia had found outside the house. With his other hand, he grabbed the tripod for that camera. He attached the tripod expertly to the port at the bottom of the camera and carried the entire assembly with him as he made his way toward the mouth of the old Gordon place.

"Shouldn't we get the ladder?" Patsy asked him when he was within earshot. She was kneeling behind Afia on the front porch, gliding a comforting hand across the other woman's shoulders. Afia looked up at him when she said that. Staff could see that her cheeks were wet. She had been crying. He set the tripod down and glared at Patsy Blankenship.

"What for? We have an ambulance on the way. They'll probably want to see to him before we try to move him." He nodded at Afia. "What did he do to her?" The two women only looked at him. "Tell me."

"He's just another redneck from a small town," Afia said finally. She waved a hand in the air as if batting away an insect. "There are a lot of old ghosts here for me. I guess being here and talking to him got to me. That's all."

Staff eyed her skeptically. "Afia, if he said anything to you about what went on between your dad and his dad, anything at all, we need to drop the ladder here and let Patsy deal with him. We can go find our ghost stories somewhere else. I'll tell Joanie that there was nothing of interest here for us." *Maybe she'll be in a generous mood and not dock our pay*, he thought about adding but didn't.

Afia shook her head. "No. It's not that. Look, he said some shit that pissed me off and now there's too much personal history between us. We're not doing his interview. We have Jeremy Beard and Patsy, but I'm not going to talk to Graham anymore."

Staff sighed. "Fine, but I'm at least going to get his rescue on video when the ambulance arrives. We've wasted most of the morning on this guy already and have absolutely nothing to show for it. I'll be damned if I'm going to go away from here without *something* to report on."

He hefted the camera onto his shoulder, grasping the tripod around its middle, and brushed past the two women. Inside the house, he saw both whole and broken beer bottles scattered about. Three whole but empty ones had been placed directly in front of a smallish door made out of three wooden slats. Only darkness emanated from within the door's frame. That must be the cellar. Staff did not approach it. Instead, he spread the tripod's legs out and stood the camera up on the creaky hardwood floor. He pointed the lens at the darkness in the center of the door frame but allowed enough width so that the door frame itself and some of the wall into which it had been set were visible in the viewfinder. Then he pressed the button to begin recording. This way, the good constable's rescuers could conduct their work in full view of the entire world. They'd at least have *something* to take back to Joanie that she could air on Channel 6 News. It might not be a special Halloween segment, but it would give viewers someone to laugh at and talk about the next day at work. It was probably the least they could do for Graham Gordon and Patsy Blankenship in return for what was looking more and more to Staff like a complete waste of a weekend.

His view in place, Staff returned to the S-10 and retrieved two lithium-ion battery-powered LED light kits from the bed. These were the only relatively new tools the station had allowed him to carry along for this trip, and he'd had to use the production director's ancient sign-in/sign-out sheet method to procure them. The LEDs provided lighting that was less warm than the traditional lamps, but they also spread the light more evenly throughout the frame, making the shot look less like it was lit by a manually adjusted spotlight, more natural. He placed the lights at a wide distance from each side of the camera and trained them toward the cellar door. Then he switched them on and returned to the camera to check the shot through the viewfinder. A little adjustment on the right side was required to smooth the scene's lighting, but not much. He tapped the top of the right-side lamp with his finger, nudging the angle down a smidge. He rechecked the viewfinder and was satisfied that this was the light that would cast the fewest shadows on the good constable when he emerged through the cellar door. He pivoted on his heels, about to return to the S-10 and retrieve the extension ladder that he and Patsy had brought from the bed and breakfast so that it would be available for the first responders when they arrived. Then a broken, lisping voice rose up from the cellar below.

"Hello?" the voice called. "Ith someone up there?"

"Channel 6 News," Staff grunted. "I'm setting up some equipment. Some people will be here with the ladder soon to get you out." He peeked through the cellar door then. Below him stood a pumpkin spice muffin of a man: doughy in the middle, sandy brown on top, and sweet on its face. The man's mouth, lit from below by the incandescent bulb of a flashlight, looked bulbous and blistered from Staff's angle. His eyes were large and innocent, reminding Staff of the pitiful eyes that the Musketeering cat in the *Shrek* movies used to use as a manipulation superpower. They were effective. He felt a twinge of guilt about turning this stranger's obviously embarrassing predicament into weekend news fodder. Then again, the man was technically a public figure after having been elected to law enforcement. Small town or not, if your local law enforcer falls down the stairs and gets trapped in a cellar somewhere, it's newsworthy.

"I don't want thith on the newth."

"Sorry, Mr. Gordon. Just doing my job here."

He strode back outside and was about to step down from the front porch when Patsy stopped him. She was still seated by Afia on the top step of the front porch, her arm around the other woman's shoulders. "Staff, I really don't think this is a good idea. Mr. Gordon is not himself right now. He said some *very* ungentlemanly things to Ms. Afton while we were gone. I've assured her that what he said does not sound like the Graham Gordon I know. I don't think it will be good for the people of Lost Hollow or anyone else nearby to see our constable in this, uhm, *vulnerable* state."

"What did he say?" Staff demanded.

Afia looked up at him. "He called my mother a black bitch," she said matter-of-factly. "Up to that point, we had only talked about the old days, when we were both kids in school here. He apologized for something that had happened on the playground a long, long time ago, something I had almost completely forgotten about. He'd tried to pull down my pants on the playground because his racist father had told him that black girls have tails. The school wasn't going to do anything about it, but then my mother got wind of it, and Graham got called to the principal's office. I'm guessing he probably got a pretty good beating from his father over that, too.

"Maybe he got upset with me for calling his dad a racist. I didn't make any bones about what a monster I thought he was, and I brought up the bad blood between my dad and his. Maybe he wanted to poke me back for that."

"I'm positive he didn't mean it, dear," Patsy interjected. She turned to Staff. "You saw the crazy text messages he sent me. I'm sure I can't tell you how to do your job, but I just want to go on the record as not approving of this. Would you want all your missteps laid out all over the news for all the world to see?"

"Probably not, but I'm not the town constable."

"Staff, we're not doing that story." Afia was looking at him solemnly.

He threw up his hands. "Fine, but if Joanie chews on my ass for not coming back with enough footage for her goddamned Halloween special, I'm going to refer her to you." He stormed off toward the S-10 and then turned back, eyeing Patsy. "You coming? They're going to need this ladder if they're going to get him out of that cellar."

Black bitch. It was about the billionth time he'd heard the phrase since the previous night. He didn't know Graham Gordon the way Patsy Blankenship did. Hell, he didn't even know Graham Gordon the way Afia, who hadn't seen him in thirty-some-odd years, knew him. The fact that he'd chosen those words after not having seen Afia since they were kids—not to mention his pumpkin spice muffin look and his red Tacoma—was enough for Staff to feel confident about his first assessment of the man. He was just another small town straight white-boy racist and probably didn't even deserve the attention that Staff's video of his rescue

would have given him. Fine, then. Fine. They'd do their
good Samaritan bit, and be on their way. Fuck Lost Hollow
and its administrator's desire to make it a tourist destination. Fuck the weird dad jokes the deranged occupant of the
Gordon cellar was sending to her. Fuck the black dog that
had run out in front of them and nearly rolled their pickup
as a result. It wasn't worth another ounce of their energy.

Staff pulled the release levers on each of the tie-down
ratchets, creating enough slack in the straps to unhook them
from the topper's luggage rack. With Patsy's assistance, he
slid the aluminum extension ladder from where they had
secured it and then heaved it into his arms, refusing Patsy's
offer to assist him with carrying it inside. He and the older
woman had nearly made their way all the way back to the
front porch when Afia, who had remained seated there
waiting for them, suddenly stood up. Her eyes grew large,
and her mouth fell open. She pointed past them, at something that had apparently emerged behind them.

"Oh my God!" she shouted. "Look!"

Staff and Patsy simultaneously turned their heads and
looked in the direction that Afia was indicating. What they
saw there caused Staff to let loose of the ladder. It slammed
into the ground in front of him, barely missing his sneaker-clad toes. It landed first on its side and was then pulled
over on its face by gravity. Standing in the shadow that
lay between Patsy's Sonata and the grill of the Channel 6
News S-10 was a squat and not quite dog-like creature. It
stood on four stumpy legs. The front two were longer than
the back, but bowed, creating a horseshoe shape about the
thing's breast. Staff thought it looked like a medium sized

dog, an English bulldog, perhaps, except for its roundish head. Alas, the silhouette in front of them revealed precious little detail about that, at least at first.

Instinctively, Staff stepped over the fallen extension ladder and then knelt on one knee in a spot of bare earth among the overgrown clumps of dead Kentucky fescue in what had once been the Gordon place's driveway. He stretched out his right hand, palm up, and rubbed his thumb against the pads of his middle and index fingers on that hand as if he were offering the creature an invisible Milkbone. He made a repetitive kissing sound with his mouth as he did so, the intuitive "come here, I'm safe" sounds and gestures any human makes when confronted with a frightened small animal that might run away from an approach.

"Staff!" Patsy admonished in a stage whisper through clenched lips. He shushed her with a sidelong glance and then turned his attention back to the thing that stood between the vehicles in front of them.

He saw no sign of a wagging tail, but that could just be because the thing had a stub, like an English bulldog, or just about any other breed of bulldog he'd ever seen. There was also no apparent dangling tongue in that silhouette. Staff was about to give up and stand again when the thing took a single wary step forward, enough so that its face became partially lit by the late morning sun over the old Gordon place. Whatever it was, it could not have been an English bulldog. Its face was more of an oval shape. And although its body appeared to be covered in short black fur, the fur that hung from the head was longer and more hair-like, parted in the center of the head and falling down its sides in twin waterfalls. There were no visible ears, which meant that the thing either didn't have ears or they were not canine ears and were covered by hair. The eyes, nose, and mouth were the most terrifying attributes of the thing that now stood before them. Cupid's bow lips perched above a rounded chin curved upward toward a broad and destroyed human skull-like nose, all of which was covered in patchy black hair that allowed telling glimpses of the features that lay beneath it. Most astonishing were the creature's eyes, though. They were warm, sentient eyes with brown irises and small black dots for pupils, all floating in the center of white orbs.

They were sad eyes.

They were human eyes.

They were the eyes of a woman, perhaps even a mother.

"It's..." Patsy began.

"The black bitch?" Afia finished for her.

CHAPTER THIRTEEN

S taff rose to his feet, but slowly, remaining bent at the waist in a fashion he hoped the creature in front of him would interpret as non-threatening. He backed up a few paces to join Afia and Patsy. Both of the women had produced their iPhones and were apparently recording video of the encounter as they gaped unbelieving at the thing that had emerged from the shadows between the two vehicles. To his left, Patsy's outstretched iPhone hand was quivering slightly. Was she panicking or merely excited that she'd finally laid eyes on the local legend of the black bitch? He glanced at her face and judged that it was probably excitement, which was better than panic but not as good as calm. Afia, on the other hand, appeared to be calm in that interested but professionally detached way television reporters have perfected. Staff felt soothed some by his coworker's demeanor. The flight response that had been thrumming in his calves and thighs settled, allowing him to take a few hot breaths.

"Let's all stay cool," he said, mostly to himself. "It's not growling or snarling at us. If it wanted to attack us, it probably would have done that by now."

On his left, softly but with some quiver in her voice, came Patsy's reply: "I'm texting the constable. Going to let him know we're waiting for some help."

"Good. Send him the video you just recorded. It would be nice to have some law enforcement backup witnesses for this if anything happens to us. God, I wish I had my camera."

"I'm getting some good shots of it on my phone," Afia said. "Video and stills. As long as it doesn't run off or run at us, we'll have plenty of evidence of what we're seeing."

Staff nodded. "Ok, good. I'd like to get some footage with the Channel 6 camera, too. Just in case. If you two can keep it busy, I can back into the house and get the camera. It has a better zoom on it. I can get some close-ups of the face. Oh my God, that face!"

"Go. Patsy and I will close the gap between us, keep her distracted."

Staff slid his left foot backward. "Ok. Here I go."

He'd taken only two steps backward when the creature in front of them reacted. As Afia and Patsy attempted to close the gap he'd left between them, the black bitch opened its human mouth. Its eyes changed, too. The humanity inside them vanished, was replaced by solid black orbs of insentience, or maybe it was insanity. Its human-like mouth elongated and became more muzzle-like. Its teeth transformed from rows of tombstones into fields of spikes. Staff attempted one more backward step, and then the thing took its own step forward, toward the women. Patsy screamed. She tried to retreat but managed to trip over her own wedge heels as she did, tumbling backward into the overgrown clumps of grass that lined the driveway. Her iPhone flew out of her hand. It went straight up into the air, made a short arc, and then plummeted back to earth where it smacked her on the forehead. There was a wet *thunk* sound when it hit her. She yelped in pain, then grabbed the iPhone and started trying to scramble to her feet.

The thing lunged forward from between the two vehicles without a sound: no growling, no snarling, no shrieking or screaming. Afia lowered her phone and dove on top of Patsy then. Staff figured she must have been afraid that the creature was going to take advantage of her fall and pounce. Staff, prompted by her, fell on top of both of the women and shielded them as best he could by stretching out his arms. He partially buried his face in Afia's hip, attempting to protect himself from losing it to the thing's jaws. When the black bitch didn't land on them, he allowed himself one peek to see if it had vanished.

It had not vanished. Instead, it had crouched outside the shadows in the middle of the driveway, eyeing the pile of humanity before it. Its now distinctly dog-shaped head was close to the ground, sniffing at it through its destroyed nasal orifice in a distinctly non-human way. After poking around the area immediately in front of it, the thing crawled forward again, toward Staff, Afia, and Patsy. It paused halfway between the vehicles and the huddle of frightened people to sniff again in what appeared to be one of Staff's own footprints in the dust of the driveway.

"Just lie still," Staff whispered into Afia's hip. "Maybe it doesn't want to hurt us. Maybe it's just curious. Afia, do you still have your iPhone out?"

"Yes," came her whispered reply. "It's in my right hand."

"Give it to me. It's getting closer to us. I'm going to try to get a close-up of its face when it does." His eyes trained on the black bitch, he stretched out his hand toward the point in space he thought Afia's right hand most likely occupied and soon felt her press the iPhone into his palm. He transferred the device to his left hand, where he could aim the rear-facing camera more directly at the thing in front of them, and held the screen up to his face. Either Afia had never stopped recording, or she had restarted the video camera for him before handing him the iPhone because the recorder appeared to be already running. Staff grimaced. He might need to edit out their panicked tumble later on.

Its examination of his sneaker's print in the dust completed, the creature on the iPhone screen crept closer to him. Its face appeared to change again as it did. The canine teeth shrank and reformed into tombstones. The elongated muzzle with the destroyed nose on the end retracted some, although the wound did not heal. The mouth took on a more human shape. Not Cupid's bow lips this time. It was more of a masculine mouth and chin. Above them, angry brown eyes stared back at the device in Staff's hand. For a few seconds, anyway. The creature didn't settle on that face. Each step closer to the pile of human beings on the ground seemed to change the beast's appearance, at least around its head. The darkened skin that was partially visible beneath the black fur on the thing's face lightened next, becoming pinkish. The angry brown eyes became angry hazel eyes with elongated lashes above them: feminine eyes. Its mouth and tongue changed again, too. The human-like lips pinkened along with the flesh around them and took back some of the feminine quality he'd noticed when the thing first emerged. The fur on its face lightened somewhat as well. It had taken on something of that pumpkin spice muffin flavor that Staff had noticed atop Constable Graham's head.

One step forward. Two steps more. Until finally it was within inches of their pile. Staff kept the camera trained on its face, which continued to transform into something more human the closer it came. No, not just human. It looked more *familiar*, the face of someone he knew but could not quite place in his memory. Its fur darkened again and the skin beneath along with it. The hazel eyes remained, but their shape was different now, more almond-shaped than the round orbs it had had a few seconds ago. The thing was close enough now that the iPhone was having difficulty maintaining its focus on its subject. Now and then a yellow frame appeared around the creature's face as if the device had recognized it as a person. Then it would disappear again as the thing nosed around them, sniffing the ground, sniffing the iPhone in his hand, sniffing at their clothes. On one approach it had come so close to his face that Staff could feel its fur or hair or whatever it was tickling his cheek. It had an odor, too. It wasn't the smell of dog, or wet dog, or even human body odor. It was a stink of rotting flesh, the stench of the grave.

The creature moved out of frame then, too far for Staff to twist the camera without startling it, not to mention Afia and Patsy. He could no longer see it, but he could hear it sniffing, hear the pads of its feet as it patrolled the perimeter of the heap of humanity that lay before it. It smelled around back of Staff, no doubt gathering the scents of Afia and Patsy below him. From somewhere inside the mound of flesh they had created, he felt someone twitch. Probably Patsy trying not to panic again. Then, from his periphery, he saw the thing come around the opposite side of their pile, nudging in close to Afia, whose face was buried in between Patsy's shoulder blades, the straightened black hair on the back of her head in plain view. Staff risked turning his head a little, angling for a better look, just in time to see the thing nuzzle its human skull-like nose into the folds of Afia's hair and inhale a good long sniff. It backed away then, exhaling audibly and, Staff would swear it, uttered something in what sounded to him like plain English. He couldn't make it out exactly, but it was two syllables, the last of which ended with a hard *arr* sound. Immediately following that, he heard—and felt— Afia gasp.

The black bitch padded away from them then, toward the front porch. Staff craned his neck to follow its path, watched as its head continued to transform shape while it marched up the driveway and beyond his range of vision. He rotated his head in the other direction and located the beast, which was now sporting the pumpkin-spice flavored fur on its face again. It had planted itself in front of the porch steps and sat there, staring at them from that distance, its head slightly cocked to one side, its amorphous facial features becoming clear in his sight and then unfocused again as they ceaselessly transformed.

"Everybody," Staff whispered. "I think we can move now. It's just sitting in front of the porch steps. I'm going to slide off Afia and stand up. If it stays put, Afia can stand up next and then Patsy. All in?"

There was simultaneous acknowledgment that they were. Staff rolled to his left instead of sliding off the top of the pile and landed, as quietly as he could, on his bare knees. The black bitch did not move. She only sat there, watching, transfiguring as she did. It was difficult to tell from this distance, but Staff thought her black orb eyes might have returned and then rapidly changed back into the soft, sad brown ones he'd first noticed. When she made no moves toward him, Staff stood up. He pointed Afia's iPhone at the creature, stepping only close enough to get Afia and Patsy out of the shot at the bottom of the frame.

"Safe?" Afia called.

"Oh, right. Yes. She hasn't moved."

Afia stood up more quickly than Staff had. So suddenly, in fact, that Staff winced, fearing that she might provoke the thing at the steps to charge them. It remained there, however, unprovoked, as if waiting for the trio of strange beings it was watching to finally be done with their outdoor and mat-free game of Twister. Patsy arose last. Her iPhone had left a reddening slash mark across her forehead that Staff figured would probably be a lovely shade of purple by sundown. Her Coke bottle glasses sat askew on her face. She adjusted them automatically before dusting the earth from her rear end with her left hand. Her own iPhone was still clutched in her right. She seemed to suddenly realize that she had her back to the black bitch and spun on her heels, nearly taking a second tumble in the process. Staff stretched out a steadying hand to prevent it.

"She didn't hurt us," Patsy exclaimed. "I think she sniffed my hair, but that was it. She didn't hurt us. Her face, though! Look at how her face keeps changing!"

Staff studied Afia's expression, which was calm still, but perplexed. He sidled up to her, close enough so that he could speak to her without Patsy overhearing. The iPhone video camera was still rolling, and its mic would no doubt pick up what they said, but he could edit the sound from it later if he needed to. As if she understood his intent, Afia combed her hair out of the way of her left ear with her fingers, revealing a single gold stud earring in the lobe, the glamorous without being gaudy mark of a female television field personality. "I saw it stick its nose into your hair," Staff whispered to her. "It sniffed me, too, and it sounds like it sniffed Patsy. I think it was especially interested in you, though. I also thought I heard it say something to you. Did you hear it say anything?"

Afia nodded. "*Her*," she corrected. "I heard *her* say something."

"Point taken. But don't keep me in suspense. What did *she* say to you?"

Afia shook her head but was not looking at him. Staff wondered whether that meant she was trying to remember what the creature had said or to understand it.

"It was just one word if I heard it right. I think it was 'daughter.' She said, 'daughter.'"

Together, they faced the—what? Dog-woman? She-dog? Spirit? Omen? Staff was suddenly uncomfortable referring to the creature as "the black bitch" anymore, or even "the creature" or "it." It was an entity, a being of some kind that had the body of an English bulldog and was able to somehow shape-shift its face, so that it alternately looked canine and human. More than one human, in fact. And the voice. It—*she*—had a voice and had spoken the English word "daughter" practically in the ear of an entirely human woman as she lay on the ground in fear of an attack.

Patsy glided over to them then, her large eyes endlessly trained on the creature that sat on its haunches at the foot of the porch steps, as if hypnotized by it. It stared back at her, at them, waiting for them to connect the dots. "I think she wants us to follow her," Patsy said. "I don't know why I think that. It's just a guess. Maybe it's intuition. Either way, I feel like she wants us to follow her somewhere."

Afia nodded. "I'm getting the same thing."

Staff, who would have called himself an "empath" if he were more New-Agey, felt no message, intuitive or otherwise, emanating from the beast. He nonetheless agreed. There was no reason for it—*her*—to just sit there staring at them. If she was just a dog with a weird face, she might have already been distracted by something else by now or might beg one of them for a treat or a belly rub. Instead, the creature simply stared at the trio from her sad, constantly changing eyes, patiently waiting and simultaneously insistent upon it. "Well. I guess there's no time like the present. Would it be too callously journalist of me to ask that we all record it on our phones like you two were doing before? I can edit the footage together later. Since I can't get to my camera equipment right now, using our phones is the next best thing."

"I don't think it's callous," Afia replied. "But let's not let our cameras do our thinking for us. If she leads us into some kind of risk to life or limb, we stop recording and back out. This ain't *The Blair Witch Project*. Right?"

"Right," Patsy said, "but I never saw *The Blair Witch Project*." Staff followed that with "Got it."

When they each had their iPhones aimed with cameras rolling, Staff took the first step toward the creature. For a moment, he felt ridiculously like Dorothy in *The Wonderful Wizard of Oz*, following the dusty overgrown driveway toward the mysterious oracle with Afia on one side of him and Patsy on the other and a Toto with an endlessly transforming face leading the way, seeking answers to questions that had not yet themselves become fully formed in their minds. He allowed the image to present itself to him and then brushed it aside so he could focus on the task. He glanced at the hands of the women on either side of him. Each of them held their iPhones in landscape mode, obtaining a television-friendly full-width shot of the creature and its surroundings as they approached. Staff chose to shoot his video vertically. Not to be different or contrary, but just so he could obtain an additional perspective. The portrait-oriented video allowed him to close in tighter on the creature itself—*her*self—without zooming, and that would be valuable for presenting detail to viewers when everything was eventually all cut together. He wasn't sure whether the morphing face would look as electrifying on-screen as it looked through the iPhone lens, but he was hopeful.

As they closed in on the creature, Staff saw her eyes transition again from those soft brown irises against white eyeballs into matte black orbs. He hadn't noticed the matte appearance of the blackened eyes the first time he'd seen them, but it was there. There was no shine. It was as if they had been drained of all moisture or had had their natural lenses removed. There was no light reflected in them. He stopped short the forward momentum of the group when he saw the transition occur, and waited. The face had stopped changing. The features hardened, becoming clear and real against the backdrop of the physical world. For now, the thing had its canine face on. The beast drove her missing nose into the ground in front of her and began to sniff. Her inhales were short but loud, like the sound of a bloodhound tracking an escaped prison inmate through a field. She turned her back to the news crew and Lost Hollow town administrator, sniffing at the lowest step to the porch, and then veered to the right around it, sniffing against the exterior wall of the Gordon house as she strafed along its length.

Afia leaned into Staff. "She's following the exact path of those pawprints we found," she whispered.

Staff nodded and whispered back, "She's not only following them, she's leaving them." He indicated the fresh pawprints that the creature was creating as she moved in the dust between the clumps of overgrown grass that sprouted alongside the house. "I've always heard that some ghosts are mostly just residual after-images, sort of sometimes visible external memories of some event that happened in the past. I wonder how many times she's followed this exact path around the house?"

"No idea. I wonder if we're the first ones to have ever tagged along with her like this?"

When the creature was far enough away from the porch steps and not quite to the corner of the house, Staff stepped

out from the middle of the two women and positioned himself at her right flank. Afia, taking the cue, placed herself at
the creature's left flank, which forced her to step backward
as the creature strafed along the wall to keep her in the
frame of the iPhone's camera. Patsy, apparently unsure what
to do at this point, remained behind the creature, following
along with its strafe. When Afia reached the corner of the
house, she went ahead and turned it, focusing the iPhone
on the edge itself so that she could capture the creature as
she rounded it. Staff had no doubt that she would. She was
so far perfectly following the original trail that he and Afia
had discovered earlier that day.

By the time Staff, the last in the line of the creature's
videographers rounded the corner of the Gordon place, she
had already sniffed her way up to the square of cinder blocks
that served as a barrier to what at one time had apparently
been a crawl space access. The creature was pawing at the
ground there in front of it, wiping away dust and small
clumps of grass that had sprouted there since the last time
she had scraped it away. Most of her pawing and clawing
was focused on the small mouse hole-looking damaged
section of the barrier. It was the same spot where Staff had
earlier surmised that a rabbit might have squeezed through
to escape this...well, she wasn't exactly a *dog* now as far as
he was concerned, but he couldn't seem to think up another
name for her species.

Staff crept closer to her, crowding the frame of his
iPhone's camera with the black fur of the creature while
Afia and Patsy both stood back a few paces, obtaining their
wider-angle views. He wanted to get as close as possible to

the action, the spot where she was digging, perhaps even get a peek through the hole in the wall by shining the iPhone's LED bulb into it. Too close, and he might scare her away or—worse—make her angry enough to finally lash out at him the way they had all feared she would when she was sniffing at them before. Then, just as if she had heard his thoughts, the creature stopped pawing at the ground and stood before the cinder block barrier with her head erect and cocked at that "processing" angle dogs use when they're attempting to understand something. From his position, Staff saw her eyes change from the matte black eyes—what he was beginning to think of as its "dead dog" eyes—to the sad brown human eyes, then the angry brown human eyes, then the angry hazel human eyes, and back. Its transformations had churned up again. She jerked backward a step, as if the wall had unexpectedly tried to grab her or as if she'd heard something behind it that didn't quite ring true. Then she bolted, running away from the house and toward the wooded area behind it, away from the shadows of the pickups and the dead-end street. She leaped into the woods through a massive tangle of scrub and blackberry shoots. At the apex of her leap, she disappeared into thin air without disturbing any of the growth beneath her.

That's where the Beard kid saw her through the window, Staff thought. *I knew it!* He chased after her, video still rolling, but stopped short at the edge of the scrub bushes. He peeled the growth back a little with his hands, revealing two small broken-off branches of a tree that had been tied together in a cross pattern. The graying old thread that held them looked like it might be shoestrings from someone's sneakers.

He figured that it must be the remains of an old grave marker, or the makeshift mast of some kid's old cardboard box pirate ship. Perhaps, he thought, this is where someone's dog had been buried once upon a time.

"What the hell happened?" Patsy asked the air in front of them while Staff strained to see if he could make out any sign of the creature through the dense thicket of dead grass, bushes, and autumn foliage that remained on the trees. "Did you two see what I think I saw?"

"She just disappeared," Afia acknowledged, "right into thin air." She looked earnestly at Staff as he strode back to them. "What do you think spooked her?"

"Has to be something about the crawl space. That's the obvious guess. Maybe it's time we had ourselves a look-see?" He glanced at Patsy. She shrugged back at him, then nodded.

"Sure, whatever. What's one more little act of trespass in a day full of it?"

Staff tapped the little lightning bolt symbol in the upper left corner of his screen and then tapped the word ON. He waved his hand in front of the camera and verified that the device's LED bulb was lit. Then he knelt in front of the spot where the creature had been so furiously pawing at the ground and bent, ass in the air, to have a look inside the "mouse hole."

"While you do that, I'm going to go back inside and tell Graham what's going on," Patsy said. "I need to make sure he's all right, anyway. I'm sure he probably thinks we've forgotten all about him. Honestly, I thought we would've seen that ambulance pull up by now. Wonder what's keeping them?"

"Yeah," Staff agreed from his spot on the ground. "You go ahead and do that. We'll be along right behind you. I don't see much in this crawl space except for some mounds of dirt, a few stacks of cinder blocks, some plumbing, and—"

That was when he started to scream.

CHAPTER FOURTEEN

Well. Most likely, that was a fuck-up. Maybe he'd been dead too long. He'd forgotten how sensitive the black folks could be about being called out like that. He wondered if the anger he felt wafting off the kid with the lights and the camera and the embarrassment of news media work ethic just then was because he'd called the girl's mother a black bitch. Just doing his job, he'd said. The problem is that his job involved butting in where he's not wanted and trespassing on private property. Besides, the Afton bitch had deserved it. What right did she have to criticize the way he'd raised his own son? Spare the rod, spoil the child was the rule he'd grown up with, and there was no good reason he shouldn't have applied it to his own boy. Sure, maybe he'd conditioned Graham to be afraid of him, but it was for his own good. Maybe he hadn't turned out perfect, but look at him now! Town constable!

You said I only got the job because no one else wanted it, said the voice of the other inside his head. *I thought that was my thought and I had just heard it in your voice, but it wasn't, was it? It was you all along.*

Lee Gordon spread a malicious grin across the face he was wearing. *OH I'VE BEEN TALKING TO YOU EVER SINCE YOU KILLED ME, SON. I WAS JUST NEVER CLOSE ENOUGH OR STRONG ENOUGH TO GET INSIDE BEFORE. NOW THAT BOTH YOU AND THE BLACK MAN'S KID ARE IN TOWN, WELL, I GUESS I FINALLY HAVE A REASON TO EXIST AGAIN.*

In response there came a low rumbling sound from somewhere in their shared consciousness. Lee Gordon paused, then shouted *WHAT DID YOU JUST SAY TO ME, BOY?*

The low voice returned, a little stronger, audible this time. *I said, not if I have anything to say about it.*

Lee Gordon felt a tug at the nerves and muscles in his right arm just then, signals emanating from somewhere in the stream and spidering their way from the brain stem, down the shoulder, toward the fingers. He clenched both his fists in response and squeezed his eyes shut, fighting the takeover. It was a drain on precious energy that he needed. He shouldn't have turned down the black woman's offer of food or water. If he didn't get fuel soon, some kind of hot meal to nourish these cells and provide a few extra calories to burn, he risked losing his hold entirely. Lee wasn't sure how he knew these things. Maybe it was instinct, like how you intuitively know how to suckle against your mother's tit as a newborn. Either way, he could feel the energy drain away from him as he fought his son's advance, pushing him back toward the stream. Lee's will was stronger than Graham's. For now, at least.

As his own consciousness swam the length of the nervous system and back to the fore of Graham's body, Lee suddenly became aware of some kind of buzzing in his right front pocket. At first, he thought his leg was being shocked by something he must have touched while he was involved in the struggle with his son. Then he realized that it wasn't a shock, but a vibration, and it was accompanied by the loudest, most annoying chiming sound he'd ever heard, as if someone were hammering the high notes on a kid's xylophone that had been plugged into a PA system mounted right beside his ear. It was coming from that goddamned phone device the black woman had given him, the thing that looked like a tiny television screen except flatter and rounded at the corners and with no receiver antenna that he could see.

He plucked the thing from the right front pocket of his son's uniform trousers and nearly dropped it when it vibrated again in his hand. As it buzzed and sounded its annoying chime, the screen of the thing lit up. He held it up so that he could see it. On the display was a blue comic strip balloon looking thing that contained black text. The headline of it was merely the word PATSY. This was followed by the message: "BRT. Dealing with something. Sending pic."

Lee examined the message for a few seconds, uncomprehending. Then the screen faded to black, and the text was gone from his sight. "What the fuck does BRT mean?" he mused aloud. "And who is Pic?" He thought about yanking Graham back from the stream to ask him but decided that it wasn't worth the risk. The message was not meant for him to reply. At least he didn't think it was. There were no question marks, nothing to indicate that the old woman wanted any information from him. The blackness of the screen against the new bright white light that was falling into the cellar from the door above him revealed a reflection of his son Graham's busted up face and what looked like smudges of fingerprints against the glass screen of the phone device. Lee raised a finger to wipe at one of the prints when the thing buzzed and chimed again in his hand.

The screen lit up immediately, and Lee was presented with another blue balloon that was labeled PATSY. There was no text within it this time, but there was something that looked like a small photograph with a translucent white triangle in the middle of it. The triangle obscured the center of the tiny photo, but he could see at its edges were the front and rear bumpers of what looked to him like a couple of cars. One of the fingerprint smudges on the glass was also visible atop the image. Lee used a thumb to try to wipe it away, and that's when the picture in front of him enlarged and started moving.

What had been a small still photo in a blue balloon in the center of the phone device expanded to fill the entire display he held in his right hand. The translucent white triangle in the middle of it vanished and was replaced by the image of something that looked quite a lot like Graham's stupid old English bulldog Brutus. Or was it Butch? He couldn't remember. Whatever its name was, it looked like the dog he'd bashed to death for pissing on the floor when his son hadn't put him out all those years ago. There was no way that dog had survived the beating. Even if it had, there was no way it would have lived an additional thirty-some-odd years following that. It had to be a different dog or...or, not a dog at all. Something was wrong about its head. Off, somehow. The thing took two steps closer to the screen he was watching, and then the image was still again. It shrank back to its original tiny size in the center of the blue balloon on the screen. Lee mashed on it with his thumb, as he had when he was trying to rid the display of that fingerprint smudge, and the photo sprang back to life again, starting over from where it had begun before as if someone had rewound the tape for him.

This time he ignored the dog-like qualities of the thing in the frame and tried to focus entirely on its head, its face, which looked to him like a human head on top of the canine body. Not just human, but familiar. He thought that the face of the dog creature reminded him of someone he knows or used to know when he was alive. It was something in the shape of the mouth and the sad brown eyes. Then the thing on the screen opened its mouth, and the sad brown eyes turned downward in what looked like anger. Suddenly it clicked. The face he saw in the head of the dog thing was the enraged face of a thirty-something and very much alive Grace Afton. It was Darek's wife that he'd slaughtered all those years ago, the one he had chopped into pieces and thrown into the crawl space beneath this old house along with the Bombshell's whore and the mother of his son.

The video ended again, just as it looked like the face of Grace Afton was changing, transforming somehow into something else. The features he thought he'd recognized in the face had gone fuzzy. Now he wasn't sure he'd seen the face at all. Lee Gordon stared at the reduced still image with the translucent triangle on it, hovering his thumb above it, for as long as it remained on the screen. He mashed down on it again just as everything began to fade to black, but he was too late. It was gone for now, and he had no idea how to get it back. He shoved the device into the front right pocket of his son's trousers, ensuring that the back of the phone rested against his thigh instead of the screen. That was foolish and superstitious, of course, but it had become apparent to Lee that he knew very little about how the technology of whatever age this was really worked. Who is to say that the black bitch in the phone device's movie wouldn't somehow be able to transport its way from there to here like they used to do in that old *Star Trek* television series. If that was true, Graham probably could have simply transported out of the cellar in spite of the broken stairs. Except, of course, that he hadn't had his phone with him.

Still. After all these years, everything had finally clicked into place. Grace Afton, the wife of Darek, mother of Afia, and a thorn in his side, was not only a black bitch. She was *the* black bitch, the thing that had been screaming and howling and scratching outside his old house for what now felt like an eternity. Lee felt a shiver travel up the center of his back, culminating in a warm prickly sensation at the back of his neck. Fear? Excitement? Maybe it was a little bit of both. The black bitch that had been sniffing around his house all this time was Grace Afton—or at least some part of her was Grace Afton—and she might finally be leading her own daughter to the door of the crawl space where he'd tossed her like so much yesterday's garbage decades before. Carefully, the elder Gordon prodded the stream of consciousness he shared with the sentience of his offspring. *BOY?* he called. *YOU AWAKE DOWN THERE?*

There was no reply. And that was good. Because now
Lee figured that he was going to have some pretty stren-
uous work to do, and it was going to require almost all of
his remaining energy if he meant to do it right. Lee raised
his palms to his occupied son's face and spit directly in the
middle of them. He rubbed them together lightly, spreading
the saliva across his palms and onto his fingers. He glanced
up at the cellar door and, satisfied that Patsy, the skinny
kid, and the black girl were all otherwise occupied, strode
to the rear cellar wall, the one that stood directly beneath
the stringers of the broken staircase. He crammed his son's
fingers into the mortarless joints that formed the frame of
the false wall and heaved it, allowing it to slide down the
wall and come to rest on the floor in front of him. Next,
he retrieved the Maglite from the cellar floor, ensured it
was switched on, and crawled through the portal and into
the dark void beneath the old house. The black bitch was
outside, and might right this moment be leading her uppity
daughter to where her earthly remains had been scattered.

There was no more time left for him to wait on a rescue.
If the black bitch intended to take him down by trapping
him and then exposing his little gravesite work to the news
people, she had another thing coming. And coming soon.
Lee Gordon shone the beam from the Maglite around the
narrow height crawl space that stretched out before him.
He'd not seen it with human eyes for more than twenty
years now. The crawl space had to have been more than
twenty-five square feet given the size of the rooms above
him that it supported, but from his angle—akin to a World
War I infantryman crawling on his belly under a barbed

wire fence—the expanse of it appeared vast. A wave of panic and uncertainty washed over him. What if he was wrong about the nature of the black bitch? What if he slithered his way to the other end of the crawl space only to find that he'd revealed his own long-buried secrets to a group of busybodies because of some dumb disfigured animal that just needed to be put out of its misery?

He considered reaching for the phone device in his pocket so that he could try to figure out how to rewatch the little movie Patsy had sent him. Maybe he could try to reach out to Graham again, search the boy's memories and knowledge to determine how to operate the thing. Then again, by the time he figured it out, it might be too late to stop the black bitch from revealing his criminal past to the entire world on the nightly news. So he slid forward on his belly instead, dragging himself on his knees and elbows along the dirt inside the crawl space. The mound of earth under him was so high on his first slide that he felt the floor joists above him scrape against Graham's fat back. The stupid kid never did know how to eat right. Not that either of them had done much eating right after he'd chopped up the boy's mother and tossed her bits into this little hidey hole that he was passing through.

That memory spooked him a little. His nosey bitch of a wife was in there with him somewhere, probably little more than scattered yellow calcified bones by now. But she wasn't alone, was she? There was the whore from Bombshell's, too, who was no longer able to shake her curvy little ass in his face or jiggle her naked titties at him while she gazed on him with her lying-ass come-hither eyes and her fire engine red lips parted by her teasing tongue. The old human remains of the black bitch were also strewn around somewhere. At least, they should have been. It was creepy, though, crawling through this wet vegetation smelling patch of ground under the house, able to see only what lay directly in front of the Maglite's beam, and continually thinking he saw movement in the shadows at the edges. Each time he trained the light on a darkened area of the crawl space where he thought he'd detected movement, whatever he thought he had seen there either vanished in the light or was never there to begin with.

Twice, Lee noticed yellowish white protrusions sticking up from the coating of dust that lay atop the compacted earth below him. Bones, probably. The first one lay directly in his path from the cellar portal to the makeshift cinder block access "door" that would serve as his escape hatch from the house. The second one he'd noticed after shining the beam of the flashlight to his left, where he thought he'd seen something move. That turned out to be a small gray field mouse. It stood on its rear haunches, white belly exposed to him, watching his progress from its beady black eyes. Beside it lay what looked like it once might have been a part of a finger or a toe.

Half-way across the crawl space, and after crawling over a second tight squeeze that resulted in an itchy scratching sensation that traveled down his son's fat-ass back, Lee saw what he thought was probably daylight shining through a small arch-shaped hole in the cinder block of an exterior wall. Above it, a much thinner line of sunlight shone through, indicating that the joint formed by the blocks at that location was not mortared. He'd found the old access door.

***

Through the bubble lens, Graham Gordon watched his own body crawling, without any effort or concentration from him, through the dank mess that was the crawl space under the house. Hatred welled up in him. He hated his father for the things he had done to Graham as a child. He hated him for the things he had done to his mother, to Grace Afton, to Darek Afton, to the stripper with the fake name. But for the first time, he also felt a glimmer of hope. Had he known about the crawl space, he might have been able to escape the cellar before his father had grabbed hold of him. He might have avoided all this. Then again, he might've only delayed it because he had been planning to renovate the place, which meant he would have been spending much more time here than he already had. Now, he thought he could feel his father losing some of the initial strength he'd found to imprison Graham. He hadn't eaten or had any hydration for a long period of time now and that fact was beginning to take a toll.

The membrane in front of Graham's metaphysical eyes seemed thinner now. The world beyond it just a little more defined than it had looked only a short time ago. Was the durability of the bubble somehow tied to his father's energy? If so, maybe it would get even thinner, easier to puncture the more the old man exerted himself. Meanwhile, Graham would have to store up his own energy, keep himself strong and at the ready for a moment when he could force his father into a bubble prison of his own. Without so much as a thought radiating outside the bubble for his father to overhear, Graham Gordon curled his consciousness into the smallest cloud he could summon. He had seen the little video that Patsy Blankenship had sent to his phone. He had heard his father call out for help in using the device, but he had not answered. If what his father thought he saw in the video was true, maybe the odds of taking back his body were improving.

Graham Gordon hid inside his bubble prison.

And waited.

***

From there, things got easier. There were no close-quartered mounds of earth left in front of Lee to scrape his back as he slithered toward his destination. There were no more bones of dead women poking up from the dust as he collected it on the elbows, knees, and belly of his son's bullshit constable uniform. The sparks of a new plan were kindled in his mind as he crawled.

It was possible that the black bitch knew about him. It was likely, even, given all the years she'd spent sniffing around the edges of his house. And, yes, she might be able to lead the nosey old woman and Grace Afton's daughter to the access. But it was just as likely that the creature did not know that he had taken over the body of his kid. If he crawled his way to the access before they found their way into it, and was able to slide it open, he could tell them that he'd found the crawl space entirely by accident. He could say that the light from his flashlight had hit upon the cracks in the cinder block wall, and he'd suddenly noticed that they were uniform cracks, on-purpose cracks that formed a square. He'd crawled in and tried to find his own way out because his rescuers seemed to be taking their own sweet time about it.

He hadn't decided yet, but maybe he would even tell them about the mouse standing on the bones within the crawl space. He could say that he'd heard the mouse scuffling about the crawl space and shined his flashlight at it to try to frighten it away. When he did, he discovered what looked like human bones. He could tell them that he needed to contact the sheriff's department to investigate. When they put the pieces together, they might even discover the identities of the three dead women, although Lee suspected that that was unlikely, not unless that DNA testing process they were talking about on the news back before his son murdered him had come a very long way. Those bones had been down here maybe decades now. What would be left to test?

Even if they were somehow able to identify the bodies, it was not the end of the world for Lee Gordon because no one except his boy Graham knew that he was Lee Gordon. As far as the world was concerned, Lee had fallen down the stairs of his cellar and died in the 1990s. As angry as he was with Graham for murdering him in the first place, Lee could continue to protect that little piece of information from prying eyes. If no one knew he was Lee, not Graham, then he had still gotten away with murder even if he was eventually identified as the murderer of Anna Gordon, of Darek Afton, of Grace Afton, and of that big-titted whore from Bombshell's. Graham's only crime other than shoving his father to his death down the stairs was being a pushover who accidentally got himself elected town constable. That was something Lee himself could fix in his new life, provided it was him and him alone in charge of his son's body from now on. The truth it was to be, then. To a point. The truth would set him free, at least as far as the bodies he'd stowed in the crawl space.

Just as he reached the exterior access door, Lee Gordon's thoughts were interrupted by the breaking of the light that shone through the mortarless joints. The space went dark, and then was lit, then dark again, as if someone was walking around on the other side of the wall, casting shadows. Lee pulled himself up close to the cinder block barrier and pressed his shoulder against it, ensuring that none of his son's overly broad body lay in the light from the gaps. If something or someone attempted to peek through the open joints or the mouse door-shaped hole in the corner of the access, they'd most likely see only dirt.

"What the hell happened?" Lee heard the older woman— Patsy—say. "Did you two see what I think I saw?"

All three of the busybodies were there, then, blocking his way out of the access. Had they peeked in while he was crawling around? He supposed it was too late to matter now. He was already there, and so were they. Should he go ahead and shove the access door out, reveal himself to them? Or should he wait and see if they try to get in? Pretend that he had arrived at it just as they discovered it? Which would be most likely to appear to them as if he'd been fumbling his way around the crawl space for some time instead of making a direct beeline for the exit when he'd departed the cellar?

"She just disappeared," he heard the black bitch's daughter say, "right into thin air. What do you think spooked her?"

What were they talking about? The old bat with the big eyes had sent him a picture of the dog creature. Was it gone now? If so, then good. What he was about to reveal to them—the secret exit and a crawl space full of human bones—was bound to distract them from pursuing the dog thing any longer. And it might even prevent the dog thing from coming back period, if all it wanted was for the world to know what had happened, what he as Lee Gordon in the 1990s had done, then all its problems were about to be solved.

Another voice, this one male, spoke up from outside the crawl space. "Has to be something about the crawl space is the obvious guess. Maybe it's time we had ourselves a look-see?"

This was it, then. It was time. Lee heard movement on the ground just outside his custom access barrier. There was the scraping of fabric against the rough surface of the cinder block. The skinny man with the lights and camera was probably on his knees, perhaps about to peek into the mouse hole. That little feature hadn't been there when he'd first made the door. He wondered if the little rodent who'd spooked him along the crawl toward the access was to blame for it.

"While you do that, I'm going to go back inside and tell Graham what's going on," he heard Patsy say. "I need to make sure he's all right, anyway. I'm sure he probably thinks we've forgotten all about him. Honestly, I thought we would've seen that ambulance pull up by now. Wonder what's keeping them?"

They'd called a fucking ambulance?

A new, larger swath of white light appeared through the mouse hole in the block, just in front of Lee Gordon's face. The skinny man spoke up again. It sounded as if he was speaking right into Lee's ear now.

"Yeah, you go ahead and do that. We'll be along right behind you. I don't see much in this crawl space except for some mounds of dirt, a few stacks of cinder blocks, some plumbing, and—"

Lee Gordon shoved his left hand through the mouse hole. He grabbed what felt like the skinny man's wrist and squeezed. The skinny man screamed. Lee thought it sounded like the scream of a little girl who'd just seen a spider. He heard the thunk of something solid hitting the ground. Then he smashed his right shoulder into the access barrier with all his might and grinned broadly when he felt it give against him.

CHAPTER FIFTEEN

Staff was still screaming as he tore his wrist away from the filthy, crimson-streaked hand that had latched onto him when it emerged from within the Gordon house's crawl space. It left a smear of wet dirt and grime across the flesh of his arm when he broke loose from its grip, but a quick check of himself revealed no open wounds or flowing blood of his own. He bounced off his knees and landed on his feet in front of the mouse hole, keeping enough distance to prevent his ankles from falling within the hand's grasp. One second of courage and a desire to protect his property enabled him to swing his right foot briefly into the hand's range and kick his iPhone away. He chased it, snatched it from the ground, and aimed it toward the hole just as the entire square of cinder block that was not mortared to the house's foundation thudded face-first to the ground, raising a cloud of brown dust in its wake.

At his periphery, Staff heard the *clomp* of Patsy's wedge heels approaching from the corner of the house. "What happened?"

Afia was in sight on his right side, her own iPhone intently aimed at the action. From inside the crawl space access, the arm that was attached to the hand that had grabbed him emerged up to its elbow. It was followed by a second hand—the right one this time—that was just as blood-caked and filthy but held against its palm what looked like an old school heavy duty flashlight, the kind that Staff and his parents had taken on camping trips when he was a lad. As the trio watched, the two hands positioned themselves on top of the fallen cinder block, allowing the flashlight to roll away and drop to the ground beside the structure. Then, with a single push-up, the rest of the arms, a head, and a torso emerged from the newly revealed hole in the wall. The body collapsed on top of the fallen block, eyes closed and damaged mouth hanging open.

"Graham!" Patsy shouted from Staff's left. "Oh my God! Graham!" She ran up to him and went down on her knees. Placing a comforting hand on his back, the older woman leaned into his face. "Just hold still. Some help is on the way. Hold still." Without a glance at either Staff or Afia, she leaped to her feet and ran around the corner of the Gordon house. To check up on the progress of the ambulance, Staff assumed, although she could have done that from where she'd knelt.

***

Somewhere along SR-501, between Lost Hollow's square and the mouth of Hollow Creek Road, Brandi Wakefield's older brother Jake was standing on the front bumper of the one ambulance Hollow County Medical Center kept

stationed in Lost Hollow. His baby blue shirt sleeves were
rolled up past his elbows. His thick fingers, wrists, and forearms were covered in engine grime as he pressed on hoses
and checked all the connections under the hood. Sweat
rolled from his forehead and down his face in spite of the
coolness of this particular Saturday in October. He wiped
his brow with his right forearm, smearing a swath of grease
and dirt across it as he did.

"Try it now."

Inside the ambulance, Jake's co-worker Alan Potts turned
the key in the ignition of the circa-1995 Type II ambulance
to the On position. The indicator lights in the dash lit up,
but barely. He completed the turn to start the engine. There
was a click. The lights in the dashboard dimmed. Then
nothing. Whatever juice was left in the wagon's battery
might be enough to squeeze some light out of the dash, but
it wasn't enough to turn the engine over.

"No go," Alan shouted out the driver's side window.

"I know," Jake shouted back. "I'm under the hood. I'm
sure I'd be aware of it if it the engine had started." He
hopped off the bumper, released the hood prop and snapped
it back into its clip, then allowed gravity to bring the hood
down on its latch. "Try the radio again."

Alan keyed the mic. "Hollow Medical, this is HC-LH-1.
We're 10-14 on SR-501 en-route to a Code 1. We're gonna
need a 10-26 because this rusty piece of crap quit on us,
which means we're currently SOL."

Jake had stepped around to the driver's window as Alan
made the call and was now glaring at him.

"What?" Alan said innocently. "They can't hear me. It still ain't working. I told you that alternator was probably going. Ain't no coming back from that. We'll have to get a tow to get her back to the station. Bet she'll be out of commission until the bean counters get back on Monday and approve a repair."

He tossed Jake a bottle of hand sanitizer and a shop rag from inside the cab. Jake applied a liberal amount of the stuff to his hands and forearms, wiping as much of the grime off himself as he could without soap and water.

"Any service on your cell yet?"

Alan checked. "Nope. No bars."

"What about mine?"

Alan grabbed Jake's cell phone from the shotgun seat. He tapped the screen, waited, and tapped it again. "Yours is dead, bro. No batt."

"Well, that's just fucking great, huh? We're stranded out here with a busted wagon, no radio, and no bars. Guess it's a good thing you swerved to miss that old dog or whatever it was that ran out in front of us, right? Maybe if you'd just run over it we wouldn't have had to stop and the engine wouldn't have died."

Alan scoffed. "If stopping for that dog killed the wagon, what do you think would've happened when we got to the scene and had to put the brakes on there? Hope whatever it is doesn't turn out to be an emergency. We ain't going nowhere."

Jake did not answer. He was angry, and anger made you say stupid things sometimes. But he didn't want to admit that to Alan. Instead, he looked down at the shoulder of

SR-501 and kicked a loose piece of gravel in the direction they'd seen the weird little black dog run. *Jesus*, he thought. *It's like that thing just sucked all the juice out of everything as it ran by.*

"Probably just chasing a damn rabbit or something," he mumbled. "Stupid mutt." For a second, he thought he saw a furry face staring at him from the spot where his rock had tumbled from the pavement and into the overgrown dead grass along at the edge of it.

Then it was gone.

***

Afia and Staff glanced at each other. She shrugged and, iPhone still aimed at the fallen fellow before them, knelt down in front of him. Staff kept his distance. His heart was racing from being grabbed by a hand from the darkness of the crawl space, even though he now knew that the hand was attached to the man they'd been there to rescue in the first place. He'd ended up saving himself, which meant that Afia and Staff could now consider themselves no longer a direct part of the story they'd be reporting for Channel 6 News that night. So much the better.

The man lying prone on the cinder blocks by the house raised his head from them only a little, just enough to scrape the tip of his nose against their rough surface as he turned to look at the two figures who stood over him. The seeping gash on the back of his head glistened in the autumn sunlight. To Staff, the injuries to the man's face and head from his apparent fall into the cellar looked even more ghastly in the light of day than they had in the glow

THE GORDON PLACE   253

from the flashlight and broadcast LEDs in the house. There were substantial purplish-green bags under each of his eyes, though it was difficult to tell whether they were from exhaustion, dehydration, or the fall. One of them sported a small grub worm-like scar. It did not look recent. Staff thought maybe it was a souvenir from the man's youth, the days when he was living with his abusive father. More evident was the bruised and broken mouth below them. Graham Gordon's bottom lip was swollen several times the size of the upper and showed a rather significant crease in it where the swelling had surrounded, but not inflamed, a small cut he had there. The whole thing looked a little like those long balloons that kid's entertainers use to make animal shapes when they were first twisted in the middle. Although he was pretty beaten up from his time in the cellar, Staff found the expression on the man's face a positive indicator of his mood. Graham Gordon looked both haunted and angry.

"I was trapped," he shouted. Saliva sprayed from his mouth when he did, spattering the back of Afia's iPhone. Staff watched her swap the device to her left hand, then wipe the knuckles of her right against her hip. He had a travel size container of hand sanitizer in the console of the Channel 6 News S-10. He'd have to remember to offer it to her the next time they climbed in. The professional journalist's detached expression on her face never wavered.

"Mr. Gordon, why did you call my mother a black bitch?"

The constable sighed, frustrated.

"For fuckth sake leave me alone! Where's Pathy?"

"Right here," the older woman said, rounding the corner of the house. Her iPhone was still pressed to her ear. "An ambulance was on its way. Clara is kind of surprised that it hasn't gotten here yet. She's sending some sheriff's deputies out to check on it. They haven't heard anything from the EMTs since they left. I guess I should have called them sooner."

"You were just suppothed to bring a ladder!" he shouted at her. "That's all I wanted was a ladder!"

Staff had begun to feel annoyed by the man who was lying on the cinder blocks in front of them. He'd made no moves to climb back to his feet after his apparent crawl through the belly of the Gordon house and displayed no gratitude for Patsy Blankenship's attempts to help him. He looked like a giant forty-something toddler who was throwing a tantrum after being told by his mom and dad that they wouldn't be going for ice cream on the way home after all. Yet he'd been elected town constable. With that attitude, maybe he'd one day be president.

"Well," Staff said, unable to disguise the sarcasm in his voice, "in our defense, we actually did bring you a ladder. Then you started texting a bunch of stupid kid's jokes to Patsy and you called Afia's missing mother a black bitch. So, you know, we thought you might need some medical attention."

Patsy shot him a look, then her eyes flew open wide behind her Coke-bottle lenses, making her look owlish and surprised. "Oh, dear, Graham!" she said. "Did you see the video clip I sent you? I texted it to you. We finally saw her! All three of us! We actually honest-to-God-in-his-holy-temple have a video-documented *sighting* of the black bitch! That's what was taking us so long. We recorded her. I sent you the video clip so you could see what was happening and, I guess, so you'd know we hadn't forgotten about you."

"I don't know what you're talking about," the constable replied, although Staff thought he saw some kind of recognition in the man's bloated and sleep-deprived eyes.

Graham Gordon crawled up on his knees and knuckles on the fallen cinder block. He still looked angry, Staff thought, and he shot daggers at the iPhone that Afia was holding. She was holding the device much too close to his face to get a decent clear shot. From this angle, it looked antagonistic, provocative. He could suddenly understand why celebrities get angry and throw punches at the amateur videographers who grab paparazzo-style footage for TMZ. But in his mind, that did not excuse what happened next. The man on the ground batted the device from her hand, and stood to his full height, his busted chin thrust out in front of him, and his work boots planted firmly on top of the fallen wall like a soldier who had just conquered a particularly valuable hilltop. "Get that outta my face," he shouted. Afia, who was very obviously taken by surprise, recoiled at first. She glared back at him and then bent to retrieve her iPhone from the ground. Staff stepped forward, meaning to either yell at the constable or fatten the other side of his lip, but Patsy beat him to it.

"Here, now!" she shouted. "I know you're hurt, Mr. Gordon, but that's no way to behave. These people are here to do stories about us for the nightly news. They're not trying to hurt you." She paused, then added. "And they're not trying to embarrass you, either, if that's what you're thinking. You're a nice man, Graham, but you're still a man. So I feel like I need to tell you that this is not about your ego."

Staff grinned in spite of the circumstances. He understood why the older woman had added that last bit. The expression on the constable's face was an all too familiar one. There was rage in the man's eyes. If he had been a cartoon, his pupils would have turned into little TNT symbols as red crept up from his collar to the top of his head like an old-fashioned mercury thermometer that was about to explode. Staff himself had grown up a little angry, mostly as a result of coming of age gay in a smallish Southern town, he thought. He resented having to hide who he was as his parents had advised him to do. He was still angry on some level but had become capable of managing it. He had learned—some through counseling and some on his own—that rage in men was often rooted in untreated anxiety, depression, and childhood shaming or humiliation. No doubt the constable felt humiliated by this turn of events. These days, Staff's own anger was most evident when he feared missing a deadline or getting into some other kind of trouble at work that might cost him a paycheck, or his job. Even on those occasions, he had learned to breathe, to confront the feelings rather than bury them and deal with any problems or misunderstandings head-on. Graham Gordon had not yet learned these lessons.

Patsy, like most women, seemed to understand the source of male anger as well, which is why she added her "ego" speech, Staff thought. Unfortunately, it was precisely the wrong thing to do. Women think you deal with male anger by attempting to shame and suppress it. It was that sort of misunderstanding on the part of women and the inability to communicate feelings on the part of men that led to so many centuries of mistrust and bad feelings between the sexes. Well, that was his opinion, anyway. Maybe even an uninformed one. But Staff was able to see that what the older woman thought would douse the constable's rage was actually going to stoke it if Staff himself didn't intervene, and quickly.

"Hey, bro," he said and stepped between Patsy and the constable. To his left and at a safer distance now, Afia continued to shoot video with her iPhone. Thankfully, the angry fellow hadn't broken it when he'd knocked it out of her hands. He went down on one knee and peered into the crawl space access behind the Gordon man. "How the hell did you get out through that tiny crawl space? Must've been hard. I don't think I could've done it. That's pretty badass."

The constable's jaw remained clenched, but a shift in his body language—fists unclenched, shoulders relaxed, slight counterpoise at the hips and legs—indicated to Staff that he'd affected a change, thrown a little water on the fire, perhaps. There was that, and then there were his eyes. Suddenly they weren't pinched in the middle of his brow anymore, but sad and hazel and sporting oddly feminine lashes, like the hazel eyes of the black bitch during one of her transitions.

"Knock, knock," Graham said. His sad eyes were open, but unfocused, not looking at any of the three other people surrounding him. Staff glanced at Patsy, who shrugged at him, and Afia, who was still intent on her recording, then turned back to Graham.

"Who's—"

"Who'th there?" Graham interrupted, continuing the joke on his own. "Europe. Europe who? No, *you're* a poo!"

Staff grinned, not because the joke was funny, but because he was surprised by it. This was the type of joke Graham had been texting to Patsy a little while before, when she and Staff had gone to get the ladder. Beside him, Staff heard Afia snort as she attempted to stifle a chuckle. Patsy was less amused. "Graham," she said. "I really don't think this is the type of thing the news crew came here to tell stories about."

"Knock, knock."

"Oh for God's sake."

"Who'th there?"

"Graham, please stop."

"Police. Police who? Police open the door, it'th cold out here."

Patsy sighed and pinched the bridge of her nose between her enormous Coke bottle glasses. "This isn't helpful. Why are you doing this?"

At his hips, Graham's hands began to tremble, curling themselves into fists. His sad eyes had transitioned to something that Staff thought resembled fear or worry. His teeth chattered in his skull as he spoke again, the words of the joke coming rapid fire from between his busted and blood-encrusted lips.

"Knock, knock? Who'th there? Pathy. Pathy who? Pathy my father was a murderer and he killed my mom and Grace

Athton and Darek Athton and now he'th controlling my body *pleath help me!*"

Staff looked at Afia. He'd wondered why she was choosing to record this encounter with Graham after telling him that there would be no interview. Maybe she'd changed her mind. If so, he was glad she had. She still held the iPhone aimed at the freakshow in front of them, but she'd cut her eyes toward him with alarm. She'd always assumed that Graham Gordon's father Lee had had something to do with the death of her father Darek, but it had apparently never occurred to her that he'd also had something to do with her mother's mysterious disappearance four years before that. She was still processing it, but some part of her was already connecting dots. Staff could see it in her eyes. The lower rims of them had reddened and welled up a little. The professional journalist inside her would be trying to prevent her from showing she'd been hurt, at least until she was safely enclosed in her own room at the end of any given long day, when the lights and cameras had been shut down, and the demons were allowed to come out and play with her head.

When he was sure she wasn't going to freak out on him, Staff returned his attention to Graham Gordon, but the Graham in Graham Gordon was gone. The eyes in his skull flickered alive with rage and hate, they were thrust open and pinched at the bridge of his nose. His nostrils flared wide, and his twisted mouth bore what looked to Staff like it would have been a snarl under normal circumstances, when it wasn't obscured by the swelling of what were probably significant skull fractures as a result of his fall.

"GET BACK IN THERE YOU FAGGOTY-ASTH LITTLE SHIT!" the furious man in front of them screamed. He squeezed his eyes shut as he did so, and then raised his head wolf-like on the chubby roll at the back of his neck and bellowed into the late morning autumn air. "GET BACK I SAID! I'LL FUCKING KILL YOU!" Staff felt Afia's hand on his shoulder then. He turned to look at her and saw questions in her eyes that mirrored what he was thinking. What the fuck was wrong with her elementary school peer Graham Gordon and how the fuck did he know her coworker Staff was homosexual?

Suddenly he remembered their interview with Jeremy Beard that morning. *I've never been in a fight in my life but that night, with all of those weird flashes of people in my head, I felt out of control of my own body,* the kid had told them. *It's almost like someone else was in control of me just then, like I was being possessed.*

Staff patted Afia's hand reassuringly. "I don't think he's talking to me," he said. "Remember what Jeremy Beard said about what he experienced here? If what he told us is true, and based on what the constable here just said, this man might not actually be Graham Gordon."

"Staff," Afia said. "I'll be honest. I'm scared, and I don't know what to do right now. Should I keep recording this... this...whatever it is?"

"If you can, do. We might need it later."

Cords and bulging veins stood out on Graham's neck and forearms now. His teeth were clenched tightly together behind the open grimace of his mouth. To Staff, he looked like he was constipated and straining mightily in a frustrated

effort to evacuate his bowels. He stamped his right foot on
the cinder block on which he stood: once, twice. Then he
bellowed again, loud enough to scare off a wake of vultures
that had taken up residence on the remains of a gigantic
walnut tree at the edge of the woods behind the house. As
the vultures took flight, the weight and angle of their take-
off was enough to cause the tree's rotted trunk to buckle
under them. The dead giant groaned loudly and crashed into
the overgrown backyard of the Gordon place. Staff, Afia,
and Patsy all winced when it landed, but Graham, caught
up in the throes of whatever had hold of him, was either
unaware of what had just happened or simply unaffected
by it.

At long last, he appeared to compose himself, although
his eyes were still alight with hate. He stepped off the fallen
cinder block wall and lunged at Afia, possibly intending to
grab the iPhone out of her hands. She stepped backward
instinctively while both Staff and Patsy raced toward him,
trying to block. This only angered him more. He grabbed
for Staff, balling up the neck of the video journalist's T-shirt
in his left hand and landing a claw-shaped right hand
against his throat. Then he squeezed. Hard. Staff clutched
and batted at the other man's arms but to no avail. He could
feel the life draining out of him as he gasped for breath. His
chest hurt, and his vision was going dark around the periphery as his cells were depleted of oxygen. He felt his body
going limp against the constable's grip when, suddenly, he
was turned loose. He collapsed to the ground on his hands
and knees, finally able to draw breath again. He glanced
up to see the constable writhing in pain on the ground in

front of him, his hands cupping his balls. Next, an older feminine hand came into view, offering Staff assistance in getting back to his feet.

"What," Staff started, but was interrupted by a coughing fit. His throat felt scratchy, and the cool air of autumn stung it as it fed his body with fresh oxygen. When he was able to control himself, he started again. "What the hell just happened?"

"Crazy men have testicles, too, dear," Patsy replied. "He was squeezing the life out of you, so I thought I'd give him a taste of his own medicine."

"And I got it on video," Afia said and laughed.

"I guess they do," Staff said to Patsy. "I guess they do. But maybe we should go around front before he's able to stand up again, huh? We could go inside and lock the door if it locks, or we could just lock ourselves in the pickup until the ambulance and sheriff's deputies arrive. If he's still acting like that when they get here, they'll have to sedate him or take him into custody or...something. I don't know. I'm having trouble thinking clearly right now. Need to sit down for a minute and get my breath back."

"Let's go to the truck, then," Patsy offered. "Even if this old place does have a lock on it, I'm not sure it works." She wrapped an arm around Staff's waist. Afia pulled up on his other side and allowed him to put an arm around her shoulder. Together, the two women supported him as they made their way from the side of the Gordon place back to the vehicles at the end of the driveway.

"I don't know what's gotten into him," Patsy added. She glanced back at the writhing constable to make sure he was not giving chase. "Graham's always been such a nice boy.

I know he's been through a lot over the past day or so, but he's acting like a man possessed."

Knock, knock? Who'th there? Pathy. Pathy who? Pathy my father was a murderer and he killed my mom and Grace Athton and Darek Athton and now he's controlling my body pleath help me!

Staff nodded and met Afia's eyes. "Yeah. A man possessed."

CHAPTER SIXTEEN

*T*HAT CUNT! THAT GODDAMN PIECE OF SHIT CUNT!

Lee Gordon rolled to and fro on the ground beside his crumbling house, both hands clutching his injured and throbbing balls. He wanted to shout the words he was thinking at the old bat who had laid such a bitch move on him while he was trying to take care of a little business. Only old bats and bitches go for the balls, after all. Men, especially men of strength and honor, avoid hitting below the belt. It's a sign of weakness. Cowardice. Only women and limp-dick little boys ever go there. He probably should have guessed it would happen, though. The skinny man with the camera was the black bitch daughter's lackey, apparently trying to suck up to her enough to make a move on that brown sugar pussy. The old bat, on the other hand, needed both the little black girl and her sissy-boy to paint the pretty picture she wanted to paint of this piece of shit small town in which he'd lived most of his previous life and had become stuck in throughout his afterlife.

When the pain in his nuts finally began to subside, Lee swiveled his head and scanned the area around him, seeking out the trio who had just become his number one reason to retain his grip on his son's body. He was just in time to catch sight of them as they disappeared around the corner, toward the front of the house. He'd heard the skinny cuckold say something about going inside the house, but the old bat had dissuaded him, telling him that she didn't know whether the locks worked. That meant they were probably trying to get away, heading for someone's car, maybe.

I HAD A CHANCE TO LIVE A NORMAL LIFE AGAIN, Lee shouted at his only son's consciousness, which he currently held at bay under their shared stream. *NOW I HAVE TO KILL AGAIN, YOU LITTLE SHIT. YOU FUCKED THIS UP, JUST LIKE YOU ALWAYS FUCKED UP EVERYTHING. YOU DID IT. YOU SHOULD HAVE KEPT YOUR GODDAMN NOSE OUT OF IT AND LET ME GET ON WITH GETTIN' ON. KEEP THAT IN MIND. IF THIS BODY ENDS UP IN PRISON, I'LL BE GIVING IT BACK TO YOU. I'D RATHER BE DEAD THAN SOME PRISON RAPIST'S BITCH BOY. I'M ONLY ALLOWING YOU TO STAY ALIVE INSIDE HERE UNTIL I KNOW FOR SURE HOW THIS ALL TURNS OUT, YOU OBNOXIOUS PISSANT LITTLE PIECE OF SHIT. SOON AS I FIX EVERYTHING YOU JUST FUCKED UP, YOU'RE DEAD.*

***

Graham was laughing inside his bubble-walled prison. The vibrations from his giddiness rippled the membrane, making the world beyond it look like a reflection in a pond he'd just skipped a rock across. He'd been right. His dead father's grip on his consciousness was in jeopardy. The longer the old man kept control of Graham's physical body—which was probably going on twenty-four hours now without food or water and was suffering from a not insignificant amount of physical pain—the faster he exhausted himself and the less control he could exert on his internal fight with his son.

The jokes helped. They took his mind off the strain of breaking through, much the way they had when he had been trying to scale the stringers in the cellar. Moreover, they seemed to irritate his father. That was a bonus.

His brief emergence to the forefront of his own body had exhausted Graham himself. Coming forward like that, breaking the membrane and seizing control of everything at once, must be what being born feels like. For an instant, he'd felt a gentle autumn breeze fluffing his short hair, felt the kiss of the October sun on his skin. Then the pain set in, taking his breath and his clear head with it. He'd had to hurry. Had to get the words out of his mouth before his father was able to wrestle control of his physical body back.

Now his dad was screaming at him again. Shouting that it was somehow Graham's fault that his father didn't have a second chance at living a life. Shouting at him that it was his fault that his dad was a murdering asshole in his previous life and in this one. The flood of rage might have overwhelmed and cowed him as recently as a few hours ago. Now, he was too exhausted from his breakthrough to care.

Graham Gordon curled himself into his metaphysical ball, his resting state, and smiled. Had it been visible to anyone, the little cloud that was Graham Gordon's consciousness would have looked like it was glowing.

Knock knock, he thought.

***

From the stream, there was only this response to Lee Gordon's tirade: *Knock knock*. Lee chose to ignore it for now. The brat had taken him by surprise when he'd emerged into the sunlight. He'd been able to retake control of his body, however briefly, and spilled his guts about the little war that he was waging from inside his own skull. Would the trio of troublemakers believe him? It probably didn't matter at this point. In his rage, he'd lashed out at them, physically attacked them. They were scared of him now, and that was enough of a mistake to ruin everything he'd worked for up to this point. Now that Graham had found a path to the surface from under the stream, it was imperative that Lee shut them all down, silence them so that it wouldn't happen again—*couldn't* happen again. He'd see to that.

He rolled onto his knees and sat up on his haunches, breaths coming in ragged gasps as the movement squeezed at the sensitive coils in the tops of his testicles. The old bitch must have damaged something. He'd been dead a long time, but he still remembered how it hurt to get kicked in the nuts. It was usually a temporary breath-stealing pain that, when it finally started to subside, dampened down to a throb. This was new pain apart from the pulsation caused by the initial attack. He considered trying to shove the pain downward, into the stream, allowing Graham to have to deal with that like he'd done in the cellar, but he feared that

it might create additional pathways to the surface. Better
to suck it up himself than potentially lose control over the
entire body, even if it did feel like someone tied an anvil to
the neck of his scrotum and was allowing it to dangle there
in mid-air.

Carefully, Lee climbed to his feet again. He stood bow-
legged, allowing his balls to hang free of restriction from
this body's thick thighs. He patted down the front pockets
of his pants. In his right was his son's devil phone device
that the Afton girl had returned to him in the cellar. In
his left, he felt a clump of hardness in the familiar shape of
keys on a keyring. He shoved his left hand into that pocket,
mindful of his aching testicles, and retrieved the set. In
addition to the four shiny metal keys that occupied the ring
was a round black piece of plastic. On one side of the plastic
was what looked like a red button. On the other side were
two buttons that were labeled with tiny pictures: an open
padlock and a closed padlock. Below the buttons were the
new-fangled Toyota logo, the three-circle doohickey that
Lee always thought someone had probably just doodled on a
notepad while on a boring phone conversation. His dumbass
kid must still be driving a car from the 1990s. There's no
way they would've held on to a logo like that for more than
a few years. It didn't even have the company name in it anywhere. Well, at least Lee could now narrow down which car
was his, provided the Japanese hadn't taken over America
in his absence and were demanding that everyone drive a
Toyota now.

Following a few cautious steps to test his pain threshold,
Lee rounded the corner of the house. The skinny cuckold

and his little black girl were in a white pickup that had a topper on it. It sported some butt-ugly Channel 6 News decals. The skinny man was on the passenger side, cradling his forehead in a hand that was propped on an elbow against the window. His brown sugar sat in the driver's seat. Figures. She had her head turned away from him, craning her neck out the driver's side window so that she could see to back up. Were they trying to get away? The little old bat who'd violated him was nowhere to be seen. Either they'd tucked her in the back of that pickup, or she'd already bailed on them under her own power.

In front of the white Channel 6 News pickup sat a shiny maroon double-cab truck with what Lee thought were somewhat feminine curves on its front end and over its fender wells. The words Toyota Tacoma were clearly visible on the passenger's side door facing him. It sat on thin-tread street tires and silver star-pattern wheels that no respectable Southern man would be caught dead installing on his ride. He glanced down at the fob in his left hand and noted the Toyota logo again. It was his son's pickup, sitting there overnight with the windows down. Of course it was. Figured.

Neither of the Channel 6 assholes had noticed him yet. Lee hobbled forward, searching the key ring for the pickup's key. He found one with the Toyota logo on its black rubber bow and held it apart from the rest of the ring. The Channel 6 pickup was already reversing its way down Hollow Creek Road. He would not have time (or the pain threshold) to chase after them on foot. A car chase it was, then. He no longer had access to his hunting knife—God knew what his stupid kid had done with it after murdering him—but he'd make sure this one ended in some way similar to the way his last car chase did: with the pursued dead and their pursuer off scot-free. Not an easy task, for sure, but he was now the duly elected constable of Lost Hollow, was he not? He at least *looked* the part. If cops around here were anything now like they had been when he was alive, they'd believe him over the rantings of the lying news media any day of the week and twice on Sunday. If they survived long enough to tell their side of the story, he could just claim temporary insanity from spending the night in the cellar and their failure to rescue him. Isn't that how people were always getting away with shit on television? The insanity defense? Was it still a thing? The old bat who might have escaped him on her own was another matter, but one he'd have to deal with in due course. The little black girl and her cuckold were within his reach right now and had to come first.

He had taken only a few more hobbling steps toward his son's girly ride when the skinny man looked up from his palm and noticed him. Shit. Lee tried to hurry, but the friction of his legs against his sack shot a fresh bolt of electricity through his balls. The world swam in front of him and, the next thing he knew, the Channel 6 News pickup was closing the distance between him and its front end. It screeched to a halt just shy of his knees and shut off. Before he'd had time to process that he wasn't going to be run down, stars exploded in his vision. The black girl and her skinny cuckold had leaped simultaneously from the pickup and launched themselves at him. He felt Graham's bottom lip rip open anew in the spot that he'd busted in his fall from the cellar stairs. He went down fast and hard, striking the back of his head on the ground. That pain combined with a new lightning strike from his scrotum caused a wave of nausea. He felt the acid emptiness of Graham's stomach rise in his esophagus and choked it back down in a single large gulp.

"You're not going anywhere," a voice from somewhere above him said. Most likely the black girl. "Pin his arm. Like this."

Lee felt weight crash down on top of his right forearm, pinning it to the ground. He tried to resist it, to raise the arm, but it was no use. His son Graham's bicep was too stretched out and was of no use as leverage against the black girl's knees. Following her lead, her cuckold crashed down on his left forearm, causing that hand to thrust open. The Toyota keyring fell from his palm. The late morning sun was blinding from this supine position, but he could make out the shapes of the skinny man and the black woman who knelt on top of him against the unseasonably blue Southern sky above them.

"Get off me," he managed. Blood from the reopened bottom lip trickled into his mouth as he spoke.

"No can do, buddy-roo," the cuckold said. "The ambulance and the sheriff's department are on their way here. Patsy's waiting for them at the mouth of the road over there. We can't have you wandering off after we just now found you, can we? Especially after you attacked us."

Lee's eyes rolled back in his head. He could feel Graham struggling to free himself from the stream again. With his arms pinned this way and pain firing shots at his consciousness from both ends of his body, it was getting harder to hold the little son of a bitch under. He felt the boy sending words to his mouth, tried to clamp down against them, but it was too late. He heard himself say "Athia!" The girl heard it, too, because she responded.

"What, Graham?"

"He'th trying to kill you."

"Who is trying to kill me?"

"My father."

"Your father is dead, Graham. Just like mine. Did your father have something to do with my dad's murder?"

"I told you. Yeth. He killed your father. He killed your mother. He killed my mother. He killed a stripper. Now he wants to kill you too."

Lee Gordon yanked on his son's consciousness then, pulling on him, trying to drag him back down into the stream. It had been a pleasant few seconds, even a restorative few seconds, to be away from the excruciating pain in his son's testicles for a little while, but the more he let the little asshole ramble to the black girl, the more likely it was that they'd start to believe his ramblings and try to help him. On the surface, Graham Gordon's body began to twitch and jerk beneath the weight of Staff and Afia. The boy was fighting hard to stay out front. Lee countered his efforts by letting him go. At first.

He felt his boy's body relax almost immediately after he released his grip on his consciousness. Lee could even feel the cords in the forearms deflate a little against the pressure being applied by the black girl on one side of him and the skinny man on the other. He held himself back for a time, pressing his own consciousness into the folds of an elastic bed at the bottom of their shared stream. He stepped back into those folds, stretching the bed beneath him, pulling it taut. So taut was the strain that the fabric of the stream had begun to pull together around him, nearly closing him inside a bubble.

"Your father can't kill me, Graham," he heard the black girl saying. "Your father's dead. Patsy told us. He's buried in a cemetery on the other side of town."

"No," he heard his son's voice insist. "He'th inside me. He'th possething me. Controlling..."

Lee Gordon loosed his hold on the bed of the stream, allowing the tension he'd created against it to catapult him forward, distorting the bubble that had been forming and turning his own consciousness into a missile, a projectile that he could use to smash through Graham's takeover and regain control of the physical body. With luck, the force of the blow and the element of surprise might be enough to cause the boy's body to tense up again, perhaps catch his captors by surprise, finally throw them off him.

He was not wrong.

He smashed headlong into the consciousness of his son, or what he perceived as headlong anyway, and wrapped his phantom arms around him, choking him, yanking backward on him. The forward thrust shocked Graham's body in a way akin to that machine in the doctor shows on television, the ones with the paddles that the operator always screams for everyone to stand clear from. Graham's torso lurched upward, pulling his shoulders and arms along with it. On the right side, his forearm slipped from beneath her knees and out of the black girl's loose grip. Her conversation with Graham and the relaxing of his muscles beneath her had had the unintended consequence of relaxing her too. She rolled off him and onto the ground.

With the right arm loose, Lee Gordon was able to turn the forward momentum of his son's torso into a one hundred eighty-degree arc that ended with him wrapping both arms around the waist of the skinny man. He heaved the little asshole who had reopened his son's busted lip off his feet and then threw him to the ground. He crashed to earth on his right side and curled into a fetal position there. Lee thought he'd probably landed on his elbow, thereby punching himself in the gut and knocking his own breath out of his lungs. Good.

The black girl was off the ground and running at him from his left. He swung his left arm outward from the center of his body and caught her across the cheek with the hammer of his fist. There was a time in his life when he would have considered pulling that punch, or not even striking out in the first place. His dad—Graham's grandfather—had always told him that a real man never hits a woman, that men are naturally stronger than women and hitting one made you look like a cuckolded fool who'd been emotionally overpowered by the weak. But Lee's dad had apparently never encountered that bitch Grace Afton or her uppity daughter Afia. In these cases, Lee thought, he was acting in self-defense. Besides, they were both black women. They might have the right to vote or own land, but no one gave them the right to interfere in his life.

There was an audible crack of flesh against flesh, and the woman cried out in both pain and surprise: pain because of the hit itself, and surprise because she'd probably been thinking she was somehow above being punched in the face. The blow stopped her in her tracks. Her hands went to her face, dabbing at it, checking for blood as tears streamed from the corners of her eyes. Lee didn't see any evidence of bleeding, and that was too bad. He was sorry that he hadn't broken the skin, but she was at least very likely to have a swollen cheek before the end of the day, a perfect look for her face on the nightly news, he thought.

On the ground, the skinny man had begun to stir again. Lee gave him a swift kick to the back of his head with his son's steel-toed Wolverines. Again he felt that fatherly surge of pride that he'd at least managed to teach his boy one thing throughout his miserable life: loyalty to a man's brand. Maybe if Graham had followed his lead with Budweisers and Winstons as well as work boots, their relationship would've been a hell of a lot closer. It was too late now, though. If Graham survived this, Lee would not. If Lee survived, Graham would be gone. No two people could occupy the same physical body without one eventually over-powering and destroying the other.

The skinny man howled in pain and tried to roll away from him. Lee took the opportunity to kick him again, this time connecting with his chin. He realized a second too late that he'd turned his back on the black girl in the process. She leaped on him from behind and landed on his back like a squirrel skipping from tree to tree. She wrapped her legs around his waist and tied her arms around his neck, hug-ging his windpipe, cutting off his air. Pain and hot blood exploded from his left earlobe as she leaned into him and bit down on it. Lee screamed, although it came out as more of a groan because of his empty lungs, and tried to shake her off him, clutching at her taut and wiry arms around his throat as he did. He spun her in circles and thrashed against her with his elbows, but she would not budge.

From their spot in front of his house, Lee could see the window into the living room that his trusty old Sylvania television used to occupy, where he'd spent so many Saturday nights drinking Buds and watching Hulk Hogan and Rowdy Roddy Piper go at each other on the WWF's *World Championship Wrestling* show. He remembered how so many WWF wrestlers released themselves from choke holds in the ring. Lee sprung backward on the heels of his son's boots and fell flat on his back, crushing the black woman beneath him. He heard her breath leave her with an "uhhhff" when she hit. Her hold on his throat was loosened, and he rolled free, landing in a crouch on his hands and knees and gasping for the return of his own air.

He couldn't afford to wait for it. As soon as the world slowed its rotation in front of his eyes, Lee scrambled to his feet. He teetered, nearly collapsing when he was hit with a fresh wave of nausea that caused him to hang his head in expectation of a regurgitative blast, but managed to steady himself and swallow it down instead. He blinked away the tears that had welled behind his eyelids after that wave and caught a glint of sunlight off the Tacoma's key that lay where he had dropped it when the girl and her cuckold had taken him down. He stumbled over to the keyring and snatched it from the ground. He had no weapons. The Maglite lay on the other side of the house near the crawl space access and his dumbass son had apparently accepted the constable position without demanding access to a handgun. The girl and her boy were both still lying in the overgrown clumps of grass in front of his house, each of them nursing their wounds and trying to recover their strength. The bitch was already starting to make motions as if she was trying to pick herself up. If he was going to end this, it had to be now. Fuck the consequences. They knew he was not Graham—even if they didn't yet realize they knew—and like the fruit of the Tree of Knowledge in the Garden of Eden, that knowledge was going to cost them. Instead of their eyes being opened, Lee Gordon meant to close them forever.

The key with the Toyota logo on it was a long one. It created a perfect pocket knife-length dagger when squeezed between the second and third knuckles of his right hand. After he used it to gouge out the black girl's eyes, he'd turn it on her cuckold and do the same. Blinded, they had no advantage over him. Neither of them would be able to fight him. Neither of them would be able to see death coming for them if they even survived the gouging. Was the key long enough to allow him to stab their brains when he went in through the eye socket? Part of him hoped it was. Lee didn't know much about anatomy beyond what he'd learned by experimenting with his own son's nervous system earlier that day, but he knew he had grown tired of these two and their need to obstruct his access to his new life above the ground.

He straddled the black girl, ignoring his own mind's warnings that this could be a mistake. She was not yet in any condition to assault his testicles the way the old bat had done. Just in case, he planted his knees in her ribs, squeezing them the way a rider kicks a horse to make it move, forcing whatever air she'd managed to retrieve in her downtime out of her lungs. He gripped her throat with his left hand, using the leverage of his fingers to straighten her chin so that it pointed up at him. Her eyes were closed, squeezed shut against the pain she was in, he thought, but it shouldn't matter. If he jabbed hard enough, the key should penetrate her eyelids as well as the softer organs beneath them. With a grimace, he raised his right arm into the air, cocked at the elbow so that the dagger he'd fashioned from the Tacoma key pointed down from his knuckles, toward her face. He needed a single accurate punch, just hit the nail on the head. A good steady inhale and an exhale with the thrust and—

That was when he heard the low growl coming from somewhere in front of them. He missed his mark and plunged the length of the Tacoma key into the ground beside Afia Afton's right ear instead of into her eye. He cussed the distraction and swiveled his head around to confront it.

Then he felt the teeth.

CHAPTER SEVENTEEN

Staff's pain subsided. He was breathing easy again. He sat up just in time to see the animal with the continuously transforming face leap over his legs and lunge with bared teeth at Graham Gordon, or what everyone had previously believed was Graham Gordon. The man, whoever he was now, yelped in pain and surprise when the creature sank her (human) teeth into his right thigh. He'd been squatting on top of Afia, planning God knew what. The forward momentum of the creature bowled him over and sent him rolling across what used to be a driveway and into what used to be the front yard. The beast remained with him, snarling and biting as opportunities presented themselves, while the man jabbed at her with something that he was holding between the knuckles of his right hand. Staff thought it might be the key to Graham's Tacoma.

When the two combatants had rolled far enough away from her, Staff crawled to Afia, who was lying motionless on her back. He scrubbed the palms of his hands on his cargo shorts to clean off the dirt and then leaned over her, gently cradling her face. Her eyes were open, and she cut them to look at him. He saw her fear there. She gasped for air. Staff crouched behind her head and raised her to a sitting position, supporting her back with his hands and forearms. It wasn't an easy thing to do. Her muscles were tight as drums and uncooperative.

"Relax. Try to relax your neck and your shoulders, at least." He felt her loosen a little. Good. She was responding and, even better, trusting him to help. "The wind's been knocked out of you. I want you to close your mouth and inhale through your nose, ok? I'm going to count to two. I want you to inhale as long as I'm counting. Let the air fill your whole belly, just like when we were kids and tried to make ourselves look fat. Understand?"

She nodded.

"Ok. One," Staff said. Afia shut her mouth and began to inhale. It sounded a little ragged to him, but he could see her back straightening and feel it broadening as she sucked in the air, which was good. Her lungs were filling. "And two." He realized as soon as he'd reached the count that he'd forgotten to tell her to pucker her lips when she exhaled. She did it on her own anyway.

"Again. This time, when you exhale through your mouth, let me count to four before you try to inhale."

She nodded again. When her second exhalation was complete, her autonomic systems took over. A painful-looking bruise was swelling on her right cheek, and large dark bags had appeared under her usually perfect television reporter eyes, but she was breathing again. He helped her to her feet and then jerked a finger at the creature and the man who claimed to be Graham Gordon as they rolled and fought on the overgrown dead grass in front of them.

"What should we do?"

Afia shrugged. "I guess we should help her."

"You get the arms, and I get the legs?"

"Sounds good to me."

The pair dashed forward, Afia stumbling a little as she struggled to regain her strength. The man who should have been Graham Gordon was thrashing on the ground. He was on his back. The creature was on top of him, biting at his throat as the man tried to hold her back with one hand and stabbed at her brown, hazel, brown, hazel eyes with whatever it was he clutched in the other. Staff straddled the man's legs and shoved them together. He sat on them at the knees, hoping that would prevent him from obtaining any leverage against the ground.

Meanwhile, Afia was attempting to grab at his wrists, but to no avail. The struggle between man and beast was too fast and furious for her to keep up. As soon as she grabbed for a wrist, it was gone from where it had been, and all she could snatch at was air.

"Can't get him," she shouted to Staff. "They're moving too fast!" Somewhere underneath Afia's call and the grunts, groans, and growls of the battle in front of him, Staff thought he could hear another voice. He couldn't make out what it was saying, but he *could* hear it. Afia called to him again, "Staff! What do I do?" He shushed her then, listening. There it was: a low, murmuring voice. It was coming from the man on the ground. He was saying words, but his voice was too low for Staff to make them out.

"He's saying something," he shouted to Afia. "Can you make out what he's saying?"

She bent to listen.

"Careful!" Staff admonished. "Don't get too close."

She waved a hand at him, simultaneously indicating to him that she understood and that he needed to shut up so she could hear. From between flying fur and flailing arms, Staff saw her grimace, roll her eyes, and then sit back on her heels again.

"He said, 'Why didn't the mummy go to the party?'" she shouted. "'Because he was all tied up.' Jokes. He's telling stupid kid jokes again."

A thrum of excitement ran up Staff's spine. Stupid kid jokes, like the ones Graham was texting to Patsy when she'd gone with him to pick up the extension ladder. Like the knock-knock jokes he'd been telling when they'd discovered that he'd found a way out of the cellar through the crawl space of the old house, right before he said to them that he was "pothethed" by the spirit of his dead father. Stupid kid jokes, familiar and repetitive, like a mantra or some kind of incantation, a way to focus concentration and shut out distraction from a particularly difficult task.

Graham Gordon was "pothethed" by the spirit of his dead father, and the stupid kid jokes were his way of breaking through the other man's hold on his body. It had to be. Whenever he wasn't spouting jokes and grimacing like he needed to take a shit and all the toilets were occupied, he was assaulting Afia and Staff.

Those were the two Grahams: the need-to-shitter and the enraged fight-picker.

"Holy shit," Staff shouted. He leaped off the man's legs and ran over to where Afia had pretty much given up trying to restrain the man's arms. "It's Graham. It's Graham trying to break through, Afia! He's Graham now! He's Graham. Call off the dog thing!"

She looked at him incredulously. "Why would *I* be able to call her off?"

"Just do it. I'll tell you after he's safe."

But Afia hadn't needed to call her off after all. The beast had either heard and understood their conversation or had on her own determined that he was no longer a threat. It seated itself to Graham's side and remained there, watching Afia. The thing's continually transforming face had more-or-less settled now on the sad brown eyes and Cupid's bow lips. This was the face Staff had hoped Afia would see. The creature and she gazed at each other, and Staff heard Afia say, "daughter?" It was the same word that the creature had said to her when they'd both been piled on top of Patsy, trying to protect her.

The creature stood up again and sauntered the distance between herself and Afia, seating herself face-to-face with Staff's coworker. Afia stretched out her hands and attempted to part the fur, or hair, away from the beast's features. A tear crept from the corner of her right eye and ran over the swelling bruise on her cheek as she for the first time examined its face in detail. Then, suddenly, she threw her arms around the creature's neck and pressed her face into the soft fur there.

"Mom?" she cried. "Oh my God, Mom? Is that really you in there?"

A sudden blast of cool energy threw Afia backward then. The creature in front of her became enshrouded in a white mist. It was a thin membrane of cloud at first, but soon thickened into a pillar that obscured the creature behind it. As Afia and Staff watched in amazement, the cloud began to dissipate, and the figure standing in front of them was no longer a composite of canine and human, but the full-height figure of a woman: a smiling woman who Staff thought looked a hell of a lot like Afia herself. It was a relieved and radiant human smile that warmed her sad eyes.

"Daughter," she said. "Afia. My daughter."

Afia raised herself from the ground in front of the figure and approached her, tears silently streaming down her face. "It *is* you. What happened to you? I don't understand what's happening right now."

Grace Afton stretched out her hands, cradling Afia's right one in both of hers. "I can't hold this form for very long," she said. "This...thing...I can become is made up of all the energy and rage of those who have suffered and died at the hands of Lee Gordon." She glanced to her left and indicated the form of Graham lying in the dead grass. "*His* father. *Your* father is in here with me. So is the Gordon boy's mother. There are faint wisps of another woman, a white woman with long blonde hair, along with the jumbled thoughts of a dog that I think once belonged to the Gordons."

Beside them, in a half-asleep voice, Graham said, "Butch."

"Butch it is, then. Right now, I'm the strongest of these entities. The others have allowed me to come forward so I can talk to you. I knew one day you'd come back here, just as I somehow sensed that one day Lee Gordon would try to leave this house and return to the living world."

She shook her head, looking down at the ground in front of her. "I don't have any memories after Lee Gordon murdered me. The next thing I knew, I had been sucked into this...thing, whatever it is. This other entity. We don't know who brought us together, but we do know why. We, the victims of Lee Gordon when he was living, are here to prevent him from hurting anyone else." She sighed. "Until we're rid of him, your father, Graham's mother, the dog, the other woman, and I are stuck here together. Occasionally we exhaust ourselves, and then we must separate in order to regain our strength. Those occasions do not last for very long. Then we're thrust back together, forever patrolling the perimeter of the Gordon place."

Afia furrowed her brow. The spirit of Grace Afton allowed her daughter's hand to slip out of her own. "But we saw you," Afia said. "As the creature, you ran out in front of our truck yesterday afternoon while we were on our way into town."

Grace nodded, smiling. "We have found that we are not entirely tied to this spot in Lost Hollow. We can move outside of this plot of land, but we start to pull apart if we stray too far. We have gone almost as far as the square, but never farther than that without losing our cohesion. Sometimes, we can borrow energy from other things to hold our form for a little longer. Electronic devices, things that use batteries for power, can boost us. We try not to use them often, though, because doing so can tether us to the living.

"Yesterday, I sensed you when you and this one were near." She cocked her head at Staff. "I had to find you. Lee Gordon was never punished for all those he murdered, and I knew that he wasn't done. We could smell him waiting somewhere inside that old house. Well, Butch could smell him, and that meant that the rest of us could, too. I didn't know what he was waiting for, but then Graham showed up and started poking around the old house. I watched him from just outside the door, and I saw the hateful ghost of his own father smash him over the head with a phantom beer bottle. I saw Graham fall, heard the stairs collapse beneath him. We didn't know what to do then." She smiled again. "And then I sensed you."

"So you tried to stop us when we got close to the house," Staff said. He was smiling. Fuck Channel 6 News and their Halloween special. The events of the past twenty-four hours were starting to make sense, and that was more satisfying at that moment than any potential paycheck or reimbursement. Grace nodded, but she did not look at him. Her eyes remained fixed on her living daughter.

"I don't have long now," she said. "We were elsewhere only moments ago. We borrowed from some batteries to build ourselves up for this fight, but we've used up too much of ourselves. I have to allow us to separate, recover our strength so we can form again when we need to."

Afia looked troubled. "Patsy—Patsy Blankenship, the town administrator—told us that the black bitch is a death omen. She said anyone who encountered you was bound to suffer horrible consequences. The other places you've been seen had to have been farther away than the square."

Now it was Grace Afton's turn to look troubled. "They were not us," she said. "Over decades we have come to realize that the fabric between the living and dead is thin in Lost Hollow. Too thin. Whatever brought us together to fight Lee Gordon seems to be benevolent, on the side of peace and justice. But there are others. I don't know if they're the spirits of other dead people. They might be demons. Hell hounds from another plane." She fixed her eyes on Afia, her mouth turned down in a grimace. "Don't pursue them, Afia. You and this gentleman here. Stay away from them. If they latch onto you, tether to you, you're cursed."

Fresh tears formed along the rims of Afia's eyelids. "All right," she said. "Is there no peace, then? Is there no rest after this life is over?"

"There can be," Grace replied softly. "We can rest. We have been commanded not to for as long as Lee Gordon remains earthbound. When he is gone, and there is no more danger of his return, your father and I will rest together while we wait for your time to come."

"What can we do to stop him?"

Afia's mother shook her head.

"I'm afraid I don't know the answer to that, sweetheart. If I did, he would be gone already." She looked at her own hands. "We're starting to fade. That fight drained us more quickly than usual. I can feel us losing cohesion. We'll be back when our strength returns again, be sure of that. While we're gone, try to find a way to help Graham stay in control of his body. Do not let the other one through. He cannot win.

"I have to go," she said then, and turned to face the shadow between the Channel 6 pickup and Graham's Tacoma. She walked toward it, but stopped when Afia called out to her. "Mom?"

"Yes, sweetheart?"

"I love you. Both of you. You and dad."

Grace Afton smiled at her. "I love you, too. Good-bye for now." She took three long strides, the last one into the shadows between the pickup trucks, and vanished.

On the ground, Graham—Staff hoped he was still Graham, anyway—rolled onto his hands and knees and was struggling to stand up. Staff thumped Afia twice on the shoulder and pointed to him. "What do we do?" was what he intended to convey. A shrug was her response to him. Staff nodded and then motioned her back, toward the shadows where her mother's spirit had vanished a moment before.

"Graham?" Staff said, taking a single step in the groaning man's direction. He had risen to one knee and was resting his forearms on it. He looked exhausted. "Graham, is that you?"

The kneeling man sighed heavily and nodded without looking at the two journalists who had been trying to restrain him only moments before. "Yes," he said. "It'th me."

"How do we know that?"

He shrugged. "I don't know," he replied. Staff sensed defeat in his voice. It was evident even with the lisp. It might have even been funny under other circumstances—if this were a movie, for instance—and had not become a matter of life and death. "I don't know. But I'm sick of it.

I justh want it to be over now. My dad is suppothed to be dead. I killed him. Pushed him down the cellar stairs a long time ago." He paused for a beat, appearing surprised at his own admission of guilt. "I should've done it when I was a kid. Maybe my mother and Athia's parents would still be alive then."

Staff couldn't be one hundred percent certain he was talking to Graham, but something about the admission that Lee Gordon hadn't merely fallen down the cellar stairs on his own made him think he probably was talking to the son. There was regret in his words, as if he was the hero of a story who had done the right thing, but too late for that thing to have been of any benefit. As shocking as it was, it wasn't the admission of having committed murder that convinced Staff, but that he regretted not having done so sooner.

Staff strode the rest of the distance to where Graham knelt and extended a hand, assisting him to his feet. Graham wobbled a bit but was able to steady himself after a few seconds. He looked from Staff to Afia and back again, his expression sorrowful beneath the blood and grime that were smeared and caked all over his face.

"He'th fighting me," he said. "I can't hold him back forever. He'll take over again soon, and I won't be able to stop him." He teetered again, almost went down, but Staff caught him under his shoulders.

"Let's get you over to the porch steps so you can sit down. It's got to be harder to keep fighting him if you have to fight yourself just to stand up."

Graham nodded and allowed Staff to lead him to the front porch steps. Afia followed, aiding them by taking

Graham's other arm as he eased his bottom down onto the second of the three porch steps, his Wolverine-clad feet situated on the ground in front of him. He exhaled a long, pained sigh as his muscles relaxed against the steps.

"Thank you. I don't know how much longer I can last. He'th coming back now." Graham gulped audibly. "The keyth are still in the yard."

"I'll get them." Afia ran for the spot where Graham's body had toppled while Lee was still in control. Staff watched her long enough to verify that she'd found the Tacoma keyring among the clumps of overgrown grass. She held them high so that he could see.

"Pocket them! If we have to run, he'll still be able to get away, but he won't get as far on foot as he would in the truck." Afia nodded and shoved the keyring into the front pocket of her jeans, then hustled back to the porch steps.

"He can't get them now."

Graham looked at her from tired, lidded eyes. "He'll try. He'th coming. You should probably run."

"Hold on just a little longer," Staff said. "The police and ambulance are on their way here. If you can hold him back, we can get you strapped onto a stretcher or something, get you restrained so that when he does come back, he won't be able to do anything. Maybe then we can figure out how to get him out of you."

Graham scoffed. It looked like he was trying to smile, but couldn't quite make his face muscles work. Something was happening in those exhausted eyes, too. Staff could see them changing, transitioning similar to the way Grace Afton's eyes had transitioned to that lifeless matte black when she had become more dog than woman and gone sniffing around the edges of the house. Graham's eyes didn't go matte black, but transformed from what Staff assumed were his ordinary hazel to a much darker, almost black color, a walnut maybe. The lids widened around them, and Staff, who had placed a hand on each of Graham's shoulders while they were chatting, felt the muscles beneath his palms tense against them.

"He'th coming," Graham said again. He sounded as if he was speaking from somewhere inside a deep state of hypnosis. "There'th only one way to escape him. Downstairs. Hide. He doesn't alwayth look in the cellar."

Staff had a flash of memory of an old episode of the CBS television show *The Incredible Hulk* that he'd watched in syndication when he was a kid. It was the episode in which Bill Bixby's David Banner had to land a plane mid-way through a Hulk-out and was trying to somehow stay in control of the transformation long enough to do so. He did it by focusing on the task and by listening to the air traffic controller constantly repeating the phrase "stay in control," like an incantation, or a mantra. A mantra. Suddenly, Staff had an idea.

"Knock knock," he said, maintaining his grip on Graham's shoulders.

From behind him, Afia snickered, "Staff, what the hell are you—"

He shushed her. "Graham. Listen to me. Knock knock."

The smile that Graham had tried to form earlier finally began to surface on his malformed lips. "Who'th there," came the robotic voice from somewhere deep inside him.

There was a beat as Staff attempted to remember a knock-knock joke, any knock-knock joke, from his childhood. Then it came to him. "Orange!"

Distantly, Graham chuckled. "I've used that one already."

Staff tried to resist shaking him. "Orange!"

"Orange who?"

"Orange you glad it's almost Halloween?"

Behind him, Afia groaned.

"They don't have to be funny," he shot back at her. "They just have to be something he can concentrate on while he's fighting." He allowed himself to glance at his surroundings, looking for anything that might prompt a memory of another joke. Behind Graham, the front door of the old house stood slightly open.

"Hey, Graham," he said brightly. "When is a door not a door?"

Graham's mouth twisted into something that vaguely resembled a smile again. "When it'th ajar!" he replied.

Mounted to the right of the door frame was a doorbell button, the kind that should glow when power is applied to it. This one was utterly dark.

"Knock knock," Graham said.

"Who'th there?"

"Figs."

"Figth who?"

"Figs your doorbell, would ya? It's broken!"

That one got another chuckle out of the body of the Lost Hollow constable. Staff hoped that meant that somewhere inside that body, Graham was winning his fight to stay in control.

"Knock knock."

"Who'th there?"

"Wanda."

"Wanda who?"

"I Wanda when that ambulance is going to get here?"

Graham frowned. Not good. Might be best to stick to jokes that didn't necessarily directly apply to the situation at hand. Afia, who saw that he was struggling, crouched beside him then.

"Hey, Graham," she said. "Remember when we used to sing songs in school? You know, songs like 'Pop Goes The Weasel' and 'The Hokey Pokey?' Remember those? Can you sing one of those songs with me? I'll start:

"You put your right foot in, you take your right foot out..."

"You put your right foot in," Graham sang. "And you thake it all about."

"You do the hokey pokey, and you turn yourself around—"

Something had gone wrong. Staff felt the muscles in Graham's shoulder tense. His eyelids had narrowed over those walnut irises. His brow furrowed in the middle, creating an arc in his eyebrows that made him look angry. The smile on his lips had faded and transformed into something that—if his lips hadn't been busted wide open—would have looked like an angry sneer. His nostrils flared dramatically with each breath he took. Staff wondered whether Afia's participation in their little game might be upsetting to Graham. She'd reminded him of their school years together, and it was during those years that Graham had tried to pull down her pants on the playground. His idiot father had told him that black girls have tails. If that memory crept in, Graham's guilty feelings about it might have broken his concentration on fighting his father's possession.

Staff put up a hand to try to stop Afia's song. He'd go back to telling knock-knock jokes or making silly puns, or even dirty jokes if he had to, anything besides Afia's song.

"Knock knock," Staff said. He could hear the panic in his own voice and hated himself a little for it. His mind raced to come up with a new response for whenever Graham spoke the next line. But it was too late. Graham's hands, which had been resting atop his knees, clenched into fists and began to tremble. His face screwed up with strain, the cords standing out on his neck as blood rushed to the surface of his skin and colored him red from the neck to the top of his head. Staff again was reminded of those old episodes of *The Incredible Hulk*, when David Banner would inevitably get hit or hurt, become angry, and then Hulk out. Except that the Hulk was a gigantic green hero, not a red bully who had murdered at least three people and maybe four.

That's when Lee Gordon thrust himself forward again, shoving Staff backward onto his butt and leaping to his son's two feet.

"THAT'TH WHAT IT'TH ALL A-FUCKING-BOUT!" he roared.

CHAPTER EIGHTEEN

G raham Gordon watched in horror from the stream of consciousness in which the spirit of his dead father was trying to drown him. It was quite literally like watching events unfold from just behind a full glass of water. Images fish-eyed in front of him, growing larger in his vision as they approached the center of his window into the real world, and shrinking as they departed to the left, right, or down. The sounds from the outside world were audible to him but muffled and distant as if he was hearing them from another room while his ears were stuffed with cotton balls.

His reemergence into his own body had not lasted as long as he had hoped. He'd been able to use his father's distraction, the fight with the creature that had turned out to be an amalgam of Lee Gordon's murder victims, to his advantage. While his father was busy with that, Graham had used his knock-knock joke technique and the tendrils he'd been able to fashion from his consciousness to peel apart the thin bubble membrane and surge forward again. What he hadn't anticipated was how unaccustomed he had already become to physical pain. It had pricked and stung him like a swarm of angry bees at first. Then it had drained his strength once Afia and the young man she was with had pulled the spirit off him. Holding on to his body had taken every ounce of energy he could spare, but it turned out he hadn't had much in the way of extra.

Graham watched his own hands reach out and grab for Afia Afton, who had no injured testicles, hadn't been thrown down a flight of stairs the day before, hadn't been attacked by a supernatural creature, and wasn't fighting another entity for control of her own body. She quickly dodged his grasp. He watched her run from him, relieved in a way that his physical body had been so horribly battered. He wasn't in shape. It's possible that she could have outrun him anyway, but the less strength and agility he had right now, the better for his father's would-be victims. A smidgeon of envy for her ease of escape from the man who had made his entire life a living hell crept into his heart. Not only that, but she had made something of herself. She was on television every night, being a professional and reporting the news. She had made opportunities for herself in spite of having lost both of her parents to his angry, hateful father, in spite of having the handicap of growing up the only black kid in an otherwise all-white, rural elementary school full of the children of Southern carbon plant employees. Meanwhile, Graham had squandered his own opportunities by trying to fit in, trying to be *one of* those typical redneck offspring of Southern industrial workers. His accidental election as constable had been scary, but part of him had secretly hoped it would mean a fresh start for him, a path forward to all the generosity of the universe that he had previously squandered. Instead, his father was trying to take that from him, too.

He watched Afia's young cameraman—Staff, was it?— leap into the middle of the chase and manage to turn the weight of Graham's own body against his father with a simple grab and twist of his shoulders, the way a defender brings down a runner on any given Sunday in the NFL. He was lithe in his movement, like a dancer or an illusionist. He was a Bugs Bunny-style bullfighter, dodging and annoying the brute as it charged him. Graham felt another stab of jealousy at that. He'd always been fascinated by the world of entertainment but had never had the opportunity to pursue it. Dance was for girls and magic was for fags, at least that's how it was perceived in Lost Hollow. This Staff person was a young white male who had traces of a Southern accent. Maybe he hadn't had the barriers to entry and prejudices that Afia would have experienced, but he also hadn't been held down by a need to be a part of the group. He was an individual who had pursued a career behind a camera, something a simple redneck son of a carbon plant worker who spent his days just dreaming about one day being able to afford the things his father was able to provide would have never even considered pursuing. Staff and Afia had seen and done the things that he'd always been afraid to see and do because of the way he might be perceived for seeing them and doing them.

Dully, Graham felt the flash and then the throb of pain in his nose and mouth as his father toppled to the ground and smashed his face into the hard dead earth there. Blindness and rage were wafting from his father's consciousness, filtering their way through the stream. Graham could feel it but was able to remain distant from it, an observer of the outer world from within his own head. Lee Gordon was no longer following a plan, even if he'd had one when he threw his son into the cellar and subsequently assumed his identity. He was operating on pure adrenaline and animal instinct. If the response to a threat was fight or flight, Graham's father seemed to have all of the former and none of the latter, and Graham now believed he knew why.

Lee Gordon's father had taught him the same fictions that Lee had tried to teach Graham: that the feminine and the dark-skinned were weaker, less moral, and less intelligent. It was virtually impossible to lose to them unless you had become weak, stupid, and loose morally. It was what his counsellor had once referred to as "toxic masculinity," this line of thought and lesson. It was an eternal fire, always combusting and fueling itself on generation after generation of hate and fear of the "other" that exists only to threaten its dominance. It was the fire that had consumed his father's father, his father, and Graham himself in a way. Why else would he have stayed in Lost Hollow? Why else would he be driving a pickup and running for town constable just to impress a girl? He was living the life that Lost Hollow's culture of toxic masculinity had demanded from him, not the one he had wanted for himself. Had he been allowed to continue to live his quiet life in his own skin, he supposed he would have eventually sought a wife (as much to quell the rumors among the population of Lost Hollow that he was a gay man as to actually obtain a partner). That wife might have even produced some offspring with him, to whom he would have undoubtedly passed the toxic flame so that they could suffer the same lack of identity, the same lack of individuality, that he had experienced. Then his offspring could pass the toxic flame along to the generation after them in an endless stoking of the fires of manhood's own crematorium.

Through the bubble in the stream, he watched the landscape come into view again as his father stood up, wiped the dirt from his eyes, and then scanned the area for his prey. The duo had split up. Afia stood at the corner of the house, peering around it at him, ready to bolt if he ran for her again. Staff, on the other hand, was standing in front of Graham's Tacoma, watching him from there. He supposed they planned to gang up on him. Whoever he went for, the other would leap onto his back. Lee could not fight them simultaneously, but neither could they do anything to free Graham's body from his father's hold over it. It was a stalemate, and Graham felt great disappointment from that. He'd given them the answer, after all. He needed them to lead his father back to the cellar stairs, fight him inside, get him to fall into the cellar again. The physical damage his body had thus far suffered meant that another fall like that, especially if he went down head-first, would probably kill him. Kill the body, and the spirit leaves. Of course, that meant that Graham himself would die as well, but at least his death would have some meaning. He would be free of the prison of his father's toxic masculinity, and he would be freeing history of the mystery of what had really happened to Anna Gordon, to Grace Afton, to Darek Afton, and maybe even to that Bombshell's stripper, who might have had a family somehow, somewhere along the way who missed her.

But that's not what was happening. Instead of being slammed head-first into the compacted earth of the cellar, Graham's body was playing a game of chicken with the Channel 6 News reporters. He supposed if he waited long enough, the sheriff's deputies and the ambulance would eventually arrive and do...something. Shoot him, maybe? Only if his father remained insanely enraged enough to act out around them when they got here. Even then, the great blue shroud of police camaraderie might spare him a death in the field, which would give his father time to regroup and rethink, to strengthen his hold over Graham's abused and fatigued shell. He had no guarantee that Staff and Afia could continue to remain free of his father's clutches long enough for the cavalry to arrive anyway. Besides, what right did he, Graham, have to ask them to lead him to his death? A Lost Hollow town constable dead at the hands of two members of the news media, one of them a black woman, would most definitely prick the ire of the conservative majority of Hollow County and fellow members of law enforcement, whether they respected him and his job or not. When it came down to us versus them, harm to even the least of "us" was enough to rain down hell on "them."

So it would have to be Graham who led his father to the cellar door, who shoved him over the edge of it and forced him to fall as Graham himself had done only yesterday and as Lee Gordon had some twenty years or so before. The flames of toxic masculinity were a binding fire, tethering father to son throughout the ages, flinging their ashes heavenward only to have them discarded and broken apart on the cold ground outside the radius of the fire's warmth. He'd found the strength to shove his father back into the stream before, to temporarily take over his own body to get his story out there, to fight back. If he could summon that strength one last time, he might be able to walk under his own power to the mouth of the cellar and cast himself in this time, headlong into the abyss, something he'd never dared to achieve before.

The answer was simple, really. It was as simple as the humor in a knock-knock joke. As a kid, he had loved those old jokes, had sometimes even dreamed about writing jokes and telling them for a living. If he'd had the artistic chops, maybe he'd also draw a comic strip for the daily newspaper. He'd never been the class clown, the guy that everyone always assumed was going to have a career on television or doing stand-up. But maybe if he'd been brave enough, maybe if he'd had the guts to defy the toxic masculinity of Lost Hollow one time and step out of the radius of its warmth and comfort, he could have at least tried. Maybe he would have failed at it, and possibly failing wasn't a very masculine thing to do, but did it really matter if he failed at it as long as he had once upon a time had the drive and the ambition to follow his own path in the world? He felt anger begin to boil beneath the surface of his consciousness, making the bubble of water through which he was viewing the world burst into smaller bubbles around him. He was angry with himself for not seeing the truth about his world before it was too late to do anything about it. He was angry with his father for seeing fit to strap him into a going nowhere culture and lifestyle like this one. He was angry with his mother for not being strong enough to stop his father from abusing him when he was little. He was angry with his city, his county, his state, his country, his entire world for putting him in this box from which he had never been able to escape. Now that there was a crack in that box through which he was finally able to see light, Graham Gordon decided that it was time, finally, to grab hold of his one shot at redemption.

Knock knock, he thought.

CHAPTER NINETEEN

Jake Wakefield rubbed his eyes and then shaded them from Lost Hollow's balmy October sun. To the oncoming car, whatever the hell it was, it probably looked like he was saluting. Jake and his partner EMT Alan Potts had figured it would be only a matter of time before someone came looking for them. He just hadn't expected that someone would be driving something that looked like a hearse that had been painted white and converted into something almost, but not quite, resembling an ambulance. As the strange vehicle with the *Ghostbusters* movie logo on its passenger side door pulled up alongside them near the shoulder of SR-501, Jake thought he recognized the fellow behind the wheel.

"Hey," Jeremy Beard said after he'd rolled down the passenger side window. "Something happen here?"

"Ambulance broke down," Alan shouted from his spot in the driver's seat. Jake motioned for him to shut the fuck up.

"I think our alternator's bad," he told the kid who had only a year or so before asked his younger sister Brandi to the prom. Brandi had rejected him, and that hadn't gone over well. He'd developed some kind of obsession with her. Their parents had had to talk to this kid's parents about how creepy and stalkerish he was acting. Shortly after that, he'd backed off. At least, Jake was under the impression that he had. "How's it hanging, Jeremy?" He hesitated, not wanting to scare the kid off but also not wanting to encourage contact. "You still keeping away from my sister?"

Jeremy Beard looked at his hands. "I talk to her every now and then if we happen to see each other. But it's not like that anymore." He grinned. "I was just a kid back then. No hard feelings. Anything I can do to help?"

Jake looked at Alan, who shrugged and rolled his eyes. "At least there's room to load some kits in there," he said. "We can attend to the patient on-scene even if we can't transport him."

"The siren and flashers work on this thing?" Jake asked Jeremy.

"Oh, yeah. I've spent days getting her ready for this event we're doing at the comic store. Everything works. Well, except the traps and proton packs, of course. They're just special effects."

Jake slapped the roof of the ECTO-1 with his right hand and turned to Alan again. "Grab the kits. Looks like we've got ourselves a ride."

Jeremy looked confused. "I'm supposed to—"

"You're supposed to be somewhere, I know. But the way I see it, you owe me for stalking my sister last year."

Alan tossed two medical kits in the backseat of the ECTO-1 and then climbed in. Jake sat down in the shotgun seat, slammed the door, and pointed through the windshield ahead of them.

"Move. I'll tell you where we're going on the way."

***

Patsy Blankenship sat at the mouth of Hollow Creek Road, her iPhone pressed to her right ear, and nervously tapped the index finger of her left hand on the steering wheel of her Sonata. The Hollow County dispatcher's hold music wasn't music at all, but dead silence. Patsy kept pulling the phone away from her ear so she could check the screen and make sure that the call was still connected. Clara had put her on hold only a minute ago, but to Patsy that minute seemed like it had stretched into five. She felt the tension in her shoulders release when she heard the *click* on the other end of the connection that meant Clara had returned.

"They'll be there in just a few more minutes," the voice in her iPhone said. "Abe said they were rounding the square as we speak. That means they're getting close. Apparently they had to come from all the way out at the Hollow River Mall. They were doing some kind of crisis training simulation or something out there."

Patsy made a mental note to bring up this incident at the next town council meeting. Not that the town could tell the county sheriff how to do his job, but it didn't make sense to Patsy that they'd take everyone out of the field at the same time for a training exercise. Someone had to patrol the streets.

"Ok, thank you Clara," she said. "I'll just keep looking for them, then. What about the ambulance? Any word?"

"They're *still* not there?"

"No. No sign of them."

"Hold please." *Click.*

Patsy sighed. Knowing the sheriff's department was on the way was nice, but Graham was hurt and, in her opinion, needed to be seen by trained medical professionals. Hollow County Sheriff Abraham Wickham was more likely to rough Graham and stuff him than offer him so much as a band-aid, constable or not. Personally, Patsy abhorred angry men. They were intimidating and all too often showed poor judgment in sensitive situations, typically escalating them when they should be stopping them. And ambulances don't just vanish into thin air. They had to be somewhere.

Click. "I can't raise them on the radio," Clara reported. "I have no idea why. Do you want me to send another unit? They'll have to come all the way from Medical, so it'll be a while."

Just then, a long white hearse-like car with flashing lights on top and a broadly grinning Jeremy Beard behind the wheel made a left onto Hollow Creek Road from SR-501. Patsy rolled down her window and flagged him down. Beside him sat another man who had dirt on his forehead but was otherwise dressed in what looked like a medical uniform. Someone else who appeared to be in a similar uniform occupied the space behind and between them. Jeremy rolled down his own window, his eyes gleaming.

"Back off, man," he said. "We're the EMTs."

Patsy gaped at him. "What are you doing here? I thought you wanted nothing to do with this place now?"

Jeremy jerked a thumb at Jake. "These guys were having car trouble. Ambulance crapped out on them. I'm not staying if I can help it."

"You might want to stick around." Patsy showed him her most knowing smile. "I've seen some things out here today that might interest you. But what happened to the ambulance?"

Jeremy started to answer, but Jake cut him off. "Sitting on the shoulder of SR-501 a few miles back. We think it's the alternator. Hopefully, we have everything we need but we'll have to get another ambulance out here if we have to transport anyone."

In her right ear, Patsy heard what she thought was the sound of fingernails tapping against the keys on a computer keyboard. "Clara?" she said.

"I heard," came the response from her iPhone. "I'm letting Abe know now and I'll have another wagon on the way shortly."

CHAPTER TWENTY

"Who'th there?"

Shit. The boy was back. The words had come out of his mouth before Lee Gordon had even realized that his son's consciousness was emerging from the stream they shared. It was again becoming a challenge to keep him down. He'd had a little time to rest, it seems, to gather his energy in the same fashion Lee himself had used when Graham had had his brief control over the body a minute ago. But this body was weak, and the energy Lee now had to expend on fighting its aches, pains, and demands for food was taking a toll on his ability to fight his son.

Graham hadn't been under nearly as long as Lee had, and that meant he might still be weak enough to reign in. At least, he would be if Lee could get rid of the black girl and her cuckold first. The distraction from fighting them and that goddamned she-dog were what had allowed his son to come to the surface before. The dog was nowhere to be seen now, but that didn't mean that keeping his son in his place while he murdered the two nosey news people was going to be any easier. What he needed was a weapon.

"Weapon," he said out loud. "Weapon who?"

Goddammit.

Lee forced himself to ignore the black girl and her cuckold for a moment. He had to deal with his son first. It wasn't wise to switch gears in the middle of his standoff, but he did it anyway. He turned inward where his boy was trying to break free from the stream. If that happened, the fight with the two newsies wouldn't amount to anything anyway. *WILL YOU SHUT UP YOUR FAGGOTY ASS ALREADY? YOU'RE NOT GETTING OUT AGAIN, AND I HAVE ENOUGH TO DEAL WITH UP HERE RIGHT NOW. SHUT. THE FUCK. UP.*

"Weapon we'll find a way out of this mess?" he heard Graham's voice say from the mouth that Lee thought he had been controlling.

WHAT ARE YOU, IN FUCKING KINDERGARTEN? THAT'S NOT EVEN FUNNY! he shouted into the depths. What floated back to him was most definitely his son's voice, except that it didn't sound fearful anymore. If Lee Gordon had known the word obsequious, he would have said that his boy no longer sounded obsequious and unsure of himself when he spoke to his father. Graham's thought beacons were calm and collected, even serene.

It doesn't have to be funny, he said. *It just has to be for me.*

"Knock knock," Lee heard his son's voice say from outside his own head. He turned outward again, examined his surroundings with Graham's body's eyes. The black girl and the

skinny man had drawn closer to him while he was inside.
They had seen that it was happening again. They had crept
up on him while he was occupied, trying to surround him
and knock him down. What then? Their she-dog had not
returned, and neither of them appeared to have weapons
on them other than those stupid little phone devices. He
had one, too, in fact. If only he knew how to use it. Instead
of trying to figure that out, Lee took two lumbering steps
backward, putting some distance between him and his
would-be captors.

"Who'th there?"

It was like having the fucking hiccups. Uncontrollable
now. Just when you thought you were over them, up another
one bubbled and out it came before you had time to stifle
it. Lee took another step backward. The heel of Graham's
right Wolverine bumped against the riser of the lowest level
in front of the porch. Lee raised the right foot and stepped
up onto it. If the skinny man and the black girl insisted on
confronting him, it would have to be inside the house, the
place where he'd lived almost his entire life, the place where
he'd died, the power supply for all his residual energy on
this plane.

"Graham."

Lee sighed. There were also weapons inside the house,
at least of a sort. They might not be guns or swords or
knives, but he could convert a beer bottle into a cutting
tool lickety-split, just like in all those old westerns he used
to watch on television. There were plenty of bottles strewn
about the main living area, including three easily accessible
ones that the black girl herself had used to prop open the

cellar door when she claimed that she was keeping him company while her cuckold and the old bat had gone to get a ladder to rescue him. Then they'd gotten nosey, and the she-dog had shown up. Things had suddenly changed for everyone. If they'd only gotten him out of the cellar like they'd promised, everything would have been fine. Well, not for Graham, but Graham didn't really matter. He was a lazy pussy good for nothing who wouldn't have been able to handle the responsibility of being town constable for more than a month. At most.

"Graham who?"

Fuck it, then. Fuck it. Lee Gordon decided that he was tired of playing this game. He climbed the rest of the way up the front porch steps, backward, eyes on the two others who were closing in on him more rapidly now. Not running at him, at least, but not taking their time, either. The front door was ajar (*ha-ha*). He would not need to turn from them to enter it. If they did run at him, he'd have to face front to run inside, but that was a mere spin on the balls of Graham's feet. Lee Gordon was still in absolute control of those. For now.

"Graham my favorite color!"

The skinny man groaned audibly from the front yard. The black girl glared at him and then shushed him. He shrugged back at her. They were distracted by each other. This was Lee's chance. He spun around and bolted for the front door. If he was fast enough, he might even be able to close and block it somehow before the skinny man and the black girl were able to shove their way across the threshold. He was able to get as far as that threshold before he suddenly stopped moving, as if he'd struck an invisible barrier of some kind in the doorway. He tried to push the legs under him, but couldn't. He couldn't feel them at all anymore. He sent runners from the brain to the spine and out from there to the leg paths he'd learned in the cellar, but something had gone wrong with those connections. They'd been severed or had moved. It was as if he was standing in superglue or quicksand. He couldn't pull up the Wolverines.

"Knock knock," he said again.

Graham's body turned on its own, against Lee Gordon's will, to face the skinny man and the black girl, both of whom had managed to climb onto the front porch behind him and looked braced for an attack.

"Who'th there?"

In front of him, the skinny man began to smile. The black girl maintained what was probably her poker face if she was smart enough to play cards.

"Legth."

Lee groaned. The sound came from somewhere deep inside Graham's body, though. Lee was still in charge of his eyes, possibly even his ears, and his nostrils, but Graham seemed to be reclaiming everything else. He felt the sensation in his hands fading away to a tingle, and then nothing. He had previously been able to feel the sweat trickling down Graham's cheek from the top of his head. That sensation was gone now, too.

"Legth who?"

The body Lee was beginning to feel imprisoned in took two more involuntary steps backward, into the entryway of the old Victorian Gothic home that he and the boy had

shared for much of three decades. Lee fought, flailing
against his son's sudden surge of strength with all he had
left, and tried to regain control of the boy's motor functions,
but he was not letting up. Lee felt Graham's teeth clench
together in his mouth. Then that sensation was gone.

"Legth get this over with, shall we?"

His vision changed. The world in front of him suddenly went from clarity to something that lay just beyond
his vision, as if he was looking at everything through a
bubble or a glass of water. He'd been dunked into their
shared stream of consciousness, where he'd been holding
his son throughout this ordeal. He pounded against the
"glass" with phantom fists but succeeded only in rippling
the surface of the bubble-like enclosure in front of him,
making the images there appear to waver outward from the
center. When they steadied, he could see that the skinny
man and the black girl had crossed the threshold and were
standing only feet away from him. He tried to stretch out
Graham's arms, to make fists and strike at them, but nothing happened.

Someone—Graham, he thought—was speaking now. It
was distant and muffled from where Lee was confined, and
his flailing was drowning out some of it by his disturbing of the psychic solution in which he was suspended. He
stopped fighting, allowed the stuff to settle around him,
and listened.

***

At the mouth of Hollow Creek Road, Patsy Blankenship
had just turned her car around so that she could follow

Jeremy Beard's ECTO-1 back to the Graham place. Jeremy, Jake, and Alan sat in the painted hearse and waited for her to complete the maneuver. It ended up being a five-point turn. Just as she was straightening the wheel of her Sonata, a new set of flashing lights arrived behind her. Sheriff Abraham Wickham and another car that contained at least three deputies had arrived.

**

"It'th the only way," Graham said. The skinny man was nodding. The black girl was only gawking at him, open-mouthed and with sorrowful eyes. "If I destroy the body, he has no vessel to posseth anymore."

"What would keep him from just leaping into one of us?" That was from the black girl.

"I don't think he can," his son replied. "He'th tied to this house. To my blood. I think the only reason he was able to posseth me is because I am his kin. And to some degree, he'th alwayth been able to control me."

"Graham, there has to be some other way, some way to get rid of him and allow you to live."

"I don't see how. He'th so hard to fight. I don't think I can keep going thith way."

So they were planning to kill him: father, son, and body. Destroy the vessel, and neither consciousness had anything to fight for anymore. He'd float into the Ether again, trapped in this old house with only occasional glimpses into the real world when the spirit dogs come sniffing around the perimeter. And Graham? Well, who knew? Maybe they'd be trapped here together. Maybe Graham would go on to some other place. Hell, possibly. That would be nice. Lee hoped Graham would go to Hell. Of course, that was only the outcome if Lee permitted it, and he would be damned if he was going to resign himself to that when he'd come so far already.

Lee cocked an Ethereal arm inside the stream and threw his hardest punch. His fist slammed into the wall of the bubble in front of him, which wavered as it had before, but did not give. Before the visage in front of him had time to settle, he threw a second punch, and then a third. The film made a warbling noise with each hit, and that noise rippled outward from the center along with the concentric circles that he could see warping his view of the real world outside of Graham's body. Were the sounds real? Was the bubble itself? Lee didn't know for sure and, at this point, he no longer cared. Even if they were only symbols that his and Graham's minds were able to conjure to represent each of their psychic imprisonments by the other, they were reactive to the punches he perceived he was throwing at them. That meant that he might be able to regain some control before his idiot son did something that permanently damaged one or both of them, before he could commit suicide for both of them.

He threw punches until his psychic arms were screaming at him to stop, and then allowed the bubble to settle so that he could check for damage. There was none. There were no signs that he'd been punching it, no rips or tears, not even a knuckle-print on its surface. Beyond the film, he could see the black girl and her cuckold walking toward Graham with slow and careful steps, as if they were approaching a sleeping dragon. Their faces were contorted by the shape of the bubble, but Lee could see that they expressed concern, caution, pleading. They were trying to stop Graham from doing whatever it was he was planning to do, and that was good. Lee would take help now from wherever it came. Each time the dynamic duo in front of him stepped forward, he felt (and could see) Graham step backward. At each side of the bubble, he could see his son's hands, raised in front of him and palms out in a warding off gesture. Distantly, he heard the black girl saying something about getting in touch with a church, finding an exorcist or a Reiki master to somehow channel the evil spirit out of him. Evil spirit? Lee couldn't help but be amused by that label. He'd performed much more evil when he was alive than he'd ever done as a ghost. As a spirit, all he'd wanted was his second chance to walk the Earth in a physical body. Was taking over his son's life really so evil? Mainly since it was his son who robbed him of his? For Lee, it felt justified, more like a reckoning than a crime. A crime might have been when he used his hunting knife to slice open Darek Afton's throat. Even then, he wasn't sure he would have been held to account for that in Lost Hollow, even if they'd ever bothered to find out who did it.

His hunting knife.

It hadn't occurred to him before, but if the physical sensations he was experiencing as a consciousness trapped in a bubble in a stream in his son's body were really only his own creations—his twisting of the energy that remained of him into physical signals in order to comprehend them— then maybe throwing punches at the bubble wasn't his only means of bursting it. His idiot son had been successfully using some kind of hippie guru-style mind games that involved horrible knock-knock jokes in breaking free of this little Ethereal force field. Surely he could do better than that. If Lee Gordon could manifest a visible form in the cellar where he possessed his son's body, why wouldn't he now be able to manifest his hunting knife and merely slice through this thin fabric of a prison that was keeping him from controlling that body?

Lee closed the eyes of his consciousness for a moment, shutting out the distorted visions of the real world beyond the bubble, and curled his phantom right hand into a shape that approximated a fist. He left a little space between the tips of his fingers and the palm of his hand, what he thought was probably about the width of the handle of his trusty old hunting knife. He squeezed the fingers and the palm lightly, imagining the feel of the wood pressing into his palm as he applied the pressure, forcing himself to feel the weight of the weapon there.

With the fingers of his non-corporeal left hand, he glided along the spine of the blade. He pinched it in several places, calculating its width as it formed between his fingers. He tapped the tip of it with his forefinger, felt its steel fang-like point, and then gently slid all four fingertips of his left hand along the blade's tip and down its edge. It was sharp, razor-like. If he had put even a fraction of an ounce more downward pressure on it, he would have sliced open his own fingers. Lee smiled broadly and opened his eyes.

The distant, muffled sound of police sirens wailed their way through the fabric of the bubble and to Lee's ears. It was perhaps the only time he'd ever thought of them as music. They were the distraction he needed. On the other side of the bubble, the black girl and the cuckold craned their heads simultaneously, peering out the open front door of the old house, searching for the arrival of their cavalry. At first, he was surprised that the sheriff's department would come up on a scene like this one with all guns blazing. They didn't know what they were getting into. Why would they telegraph their presence?

He felt a surge of panic wend its way from his son's brain to his nervous system. The boy's heart went into overdrive, pounding against the chest wall and making rapid, irritating *bump-bump-squish* noises in Lee's ears as blood raced through Graham's body in an attempt to feed it what it needed for a fight. It was now or never, then. He hoped he hadn't waited too long. That panic meant that the boy's judgment was impaired and his defenses were up, which just made Lee's job that much more difficult.

Knife in his hand with its edge up, Lee knelt in front of the bubble. He jammed the weapon point-first into the bottom center of the lens, pressing it into the flesh of the bubble with all the strength he could muster. It resisted the force, stretching outward behind the point of the knife and further distorting the images that were playing out in front of him. His shoulder was strained, and his hand began to quiver, his palm growing wet with the effort. Just as he began to fear that the non-corporeal blade was going to slip from his fingers, the point punctured the bubble. He felt the tip of the knife make its first cut into the film in front of him. The stretched area of the bubble settled back onto the blade, returning to its normal form, except now with Lee Gordon's hunting knife stuck through it.

Lee glanced at the image in the bubble now. Therein, he saw that Graham had taken another step or two backward from the camera and the lights. In front of him, the black girl was staring wide-eyed with the fingers of both hands covering her mouth. The cuckold was on one knee, a hand stretched out in Graham's direction as if he was proposing marriage. He was mouthing things that Lee couldn't quite hear over the physical roar of his son's panic, but it certainly looked like he was pleading. Lee shoved the tip of the knife into the cut it had made in the bubble and dragged upward on the handle, using the blade's edge to open his escape route the way a camper might unzip the doors of a tent when it was time to brew the coffee.

The thought occurred to him that he might literally be damaging the stream beyond repair, that he might no longer be able to shove his son's consciousness in here and keep him at bay until he found a way to destroy him. In that case, he might need to only allow the boy's body to collapse to the floor or do whatever it did when no one was really in charge. With or without his physical body, he was stronger than his son. And now that he knew he could just think a weapon into existence and slice open his prison, what would prevent him from cutting his boy's consciousness into tiny pieces that he could then just sweep into the stream, where they might float and drown forever?

When he'd formed a slit in the bubble that he thought was large enough for him to slip through, Lee Gordon unimagined his hunting knife and felt it fall from his grasp.

He would try to recall it later—if there was a later—when he might have more time to experiment while his son's body lay in a hospital bed or a jail cell. He shoved both of his hands into the slit and parted the middle of the bubble like a curtain. The image that had been distorted and wavering behind it at once became crystal clear in his non-corporeal eyes. He could see the cuckold still on his knees, the black girl still cupping her mouth and...was that a tear running down her cheek? He could also see regular splashes of red and blue light against the interior walls of the old house. They seemed to be coming from outside the open front door. The cops were finally here. The ambulance too, probably. They'd take him into custody first and maybe take him to the Emergency Room for a once-over before throwing his flabby ass behind bars. All that was only if he could yank control of the body away from Graham before the boy could finish whatever the hell it was he was about to do.

Lee Gordon shoved the walls of the bubble out of his way and stepped first his right Wolverine-clad boot into the physical body of his son—into the real world—and then the left. The walls of the bubble prison in what was about to be Lee Gordon's exclusive stream of consciousness closed behind him.

CHAPTER TWENTY-ONE

raham Gordon was slipping away. Or maybe he was hallucinating, perhaps a result of low blood sugar and dehydration over the past twenty-four hours. It had to have been at least that long since he'd had a drink of water, and even longer since he'd had a meal. The world in front of him swam out of focus and back. Well, it swam "back" in terms of the sharpness of the images before him anyway. Although (*the skinny man*) Staff and (*the black girl*) Afia were clear in his field of vision, he could see two of each of them. (*Skinny*) stood beside Staff and (*the black girl*) stood beside Afia. Between them were two video cameras, each mounted on its own tripod. On the two (*Staffs'*) skinnys' left there were two giant poles with bright lights mounted on them. On the two (*Afias'*) black girls' right was an identical pair. The illusion was brief. When Lee Gordon stepped forward to regain control of his son's body, the identical twins of everything began to merge again into single bodies and objects. Graham felt pressure on his chest as if an invisible hand was shoving him backward, forcing him out of the driver's seat.

Not now, Graham thought. *Please dear God, not now.*

OF COURSE, NOW, his dead father's consciousness shot back at him. YOU'RE TRYING TO KILL US. NOW IS THE BEST TIME.

In front of him, both Afia and Staff were pleading with the man they still thought was Graham to step away from the steep drop at the open mouth of the cellar. Stupidly, he had allowed them to distract him. There was, after all, a big part of him that would rather continue to live than sacrifice himself to destroy the evil spirit now residing within him. Staff and Afia's voices had become distant, their words indistinct in his ears. The flashes of red and blue light from outside the house continued to pulse through the open front door behind them. Soon, Sheriff Abraham Wickham, a man who had dismissed him to his face as not cut out for law enforcement at his own swearing in ceremony, would stroll in and demand to know what was happening. Graham might lose his shot at ending his father's reign of terror over his body if that happened, but right now that was less of a risk than losing control over his own decisions and movement again.

While he still could, Graham opened his mouth and shouted: "Knock knock!" He was immediately silenced by searing hot pain. It slashed in a ribbon across his mouth. It wasn't from a punch or an impact, not like what he'd felt when his mouth hit the cellar floor yesterday afternoon. It felt more like a cut, like someone had sliced a Joker-smile across his face from dimple to dimple. He could feel the hot trickle of blood running down from there. His right hand—the physical one—went up to his face and patted it, checking for wetness and damage, but came away clean.

What are you doing to me, Dad?

From somewhere inside him, there was the sardonic sound of laughter.

I LEARNED SOMETHING NEW WHILE I WAS IN OUR LITTLE BUBBLE PRISON, BOY. NEAT, HUH? DON'T YOU WORRY ABOUT HOW OUR FACE LOOKS, NOW. I'M ONLY CUTTING UP THE INSIDE YOU. GONNA LEAVE THE OUTSIDE PRISTINE...WELL, NO LESS PRISTINE THAN IT IS NOW, ANYWAY. OUR BODY WILL BE WALKING AWAY FROM THIS MESS, BUT YOU WON'T. THE OLD SHERIFF AND THE REST OF THEM WON'T EVEN KNOW YOU'RE GONE. I'LL JUST BE YOU, LIKE I'D PLANNED, AND NOBODY WILL BE ABLE TO TELL THE DIFFERENCE.

Graham tried to open his body's mouth again, to start another knock-knock joke, try to regain control, but it was no use. His exertion and the stress of choosing to end his own life while he'd been in control of his body had sapped him. The words would not come, and now the pain he felt wasn't restricted to only when he was in control of his physical self. His consciousness hurt, too. It was getting hard for him to remember any more jokes, or even focus on ones he'd already used, because of the hot pain in his metaphysical mouth.

There was another slash. He heard the swipe of a blade through air that was not there. Fresh pain burst from his phantom belly, just below the navel, and ripped upward from his pelvis all the way to his chest. If his consciousness had had intestines, they most likely would have spilled out through the opening. Graham screamed, and the full opening of his mouth stung his wounds there. But it was a scream no one could hear. No one could hear it except for the spirit of his dead father, anyway. At the bottom of his thorax, the invisible blade made a left turn and cut open what should have been the flesh just below his rib cage. Then it twisted a hundred and eighty degrees inside the open wound and slashed in the opposite direction, flaying the belly of Graham's consciousness open wide in two triangular flaps.

Please, he thought. *Please. I only wanted to live my life. Why wouldn't you ever allow me to live my life?*

The blade stopped moving. An answer exploded in Graham's ears as if his father were screaming into a megaphone that he'd jammed against his head. *DID YOU ALLOW ME TO LIVE MY OWN LIFE, YOU LITTLE SHIT? YOU CAME WARBLING INTO THIS WORLD BECAUSE YOUR PIECE OF SHIT MOTHER WANTED YOU, NOT ME. I DIDN'T EVEN KNOW SHE WAS FUCKING PREGNANT. IF IT WEREN'T FOR YOUR FACE AND YOUR CHOICE IN BOOTS I WOULDN'T EVEN THINK YOU WERE MINE. WHERE WERE YOU WHEN I WAS BREAKING MY BACK IN THE CARBON PLANT? WHERE WERE YOU WHEN I WAS TRYING TO PUT FOOD ON THE TABLE? ALL I EVER WANTED WAS THE RESPECT I DESERVED FOR THE HARD WORK I DID. A LITTLE FUCKING APPRECIATION. BUT ALL YOU AND YOUR MOM COULD DO WAS SUCK UP THE MONEY AND BITCH ABOUT THERE NOT BEING ENOUGH OF IT.*

There was a *thunk* sound just then. Graham perceived one, anyway. A bright new bolt of pain struck him on top of his head, puncturing it, and sheathed itself into what, if he were a physical being just now, would have been his skull. It pierced his brain, too, he thought and hammered the base of his skull where it was attached to his spine. Whatever the knife was that his father had dreamed up from their shared stream of consciousness—probably a hunting knife like the one Graham had auctioned on eBay after his death—it was a long one.

Whatever remained of Graham in his cerebrum was fading fast. With the first two cuts, his father had meant only to injure him, he supposed, to prevent him from retaking control of the physical body they had been sharing. He'd saved the most destructive blow for last. Flashes of memories from his life paraded before the eyes of Graham's consciousness. There was the elementary school playground, with little Afia Afton standing beside the see-saw, about to climb onto it. He could see his little boy hands stretched out in front of him, sneaking up on her, preparing to try to get a look at the tail his father had told him that black girls had. There was Butch, his English bulldog, quivering beside a pool of his own urine at the front door of the old house, that shamed expression in his eyes as Lee Gordon stomped and shouted and screamed at them both. There was his mother, Anna, seated on the edge of his bed at night and stroking his hair, telling him that dad didn't really mean all the horrible things he did and said, that dad was just a hard worker who was under a tremendous amount of pressure to do a good job and provide for his family. There he was crouched in the cellar, abandoned by his mother—who was long gone from the house to God knew where—and rocking back and forth on his butt with his hands cradling his knees, tears streaming down his face. Above him, the sound of his father's Wolverines on the hardwood floor created thunder. There he was winning his campaign for town constable, and asking the town council to allow him to purchase his old family home back from them, to restore it. Finally, there he was at the bottom of the destroyed cellar stairs, broken and bloody, and wondering why he had ever bothered to survive his atrocious, abusive upbringing in the first place.

The pain receded. He was losing the physical sensations he had clung to in his abstract form. So much the better. At least he would not die hurting. His vision began to fade at the periphery, closing down toward the center like the iris fades in one of those old black-and-white monster movies from the thirties. He'd never enjoy one of those again. That fade created a tunnel effect in front of him, and from the center of that tunnel, he could see a bright white light. In the center of the light was a small dark figure. Not human, exactly, but a figure nonetheless. Graham felt gravity take him. He fell forward, toward the light and toward the figure, which then grew more substantial in his vision as a result. It was definitely not a person. It might be a dog, sitting on its haunches and staring at him.

The brilliant white light surrounding the figure began to dissipate then, and Graham could see that it actually was a dog. It was an English bulldog. It was Butch! Butch had come to greet him and welcome him into the afterlife. Graham tried to force the muscles in his face to smile at the dog, but couldn't tell for sure whether he was successful. He tried to stretch out a hand to him, to rub the tips of his fingers together, calling the dog toward him so that he could pet him again, feel his soft fur and cold, wet button of a nose against his skin one more time. To his relief, the gesture seemed to have worked. The dog started forward, blocking out some more of the white light that was radiating out from behind it.

As it drew closer, Graham began to think that it might not be Butch after all. Its body resembled Butch, but its face...its face was a human face. It was Afia's face. No, wait. Not Afia. It was Afia's mother's face. It was the face of the creature that had looked in on him as he lay broken on the cellar floor, the beast that had fought his father down to the ground in the front yard when Graham had been unable to regain control. It was the she-dog that had told them all that she was some part Butch, some part Grace Afton, some part Darek Afton, and some part Anna Gordon. The entity sat down in front of him and smiled at him with her human smile, showing him her human teeth. Her sad brown eyes were warm, inviting, reassuring to him. She was here with him, with all of them, and very soon things were going to be all right again.

Graham stretched out his hand to her and stroked the side of her face. He smiled back at her. He could feel it this time, his genuine smile. Then she crouched on her haunches in front of him, her eyes drifting up, somewhere above him. She looked like a bird about to take flight. She leaped toward him.

Then the lights went out.

Graham Gordon was gone.

***

Lee Gordon smiled when the consciousness of his limp-dick son went dark and disappeared from the body they'd shared. He was relieved. Overjoyed, even. The battle was won, and it was the climactic battle of the entire war. With Graham dead, he had full control over the body, and he could start making excuses for his bad behavior that morning as soon as the sheriff walked through the door. There was still the skinny man and the black girl to deal with. They'd met the black bitch, had talked to her. It was unlikely that he could convince them that the whole fight for control of Graham's body had been some kind of psychotic break brought on by his entrapment in the cellar. They could tell their side of the story, but who would the authorities really believe? Him, or a fantastic story cooked up by two television reporters who were in search of a spooky tale for their Halloween broadcast?

That was another problem, though, wasn't it? The old bat had sent his son some kind of film footage of the creature on that devil phone device that Lee was still carrying in the right front pocket of what were now his beige constable uniform pants. He could probably destroy that little device. What would he need with one of those things anyway? But the bitch reporter and her cuckold had both been pointing their own phone devices at him when he had finally emerged from the crawl space (on his own, thank you very much). Could he convince them to destroy their footage out of some kind of guilt or remorse for their failure to rescue him? That's assuming they truly believed he was Graham, of course. They might not. Could he confiscate them as constable? Claim they were some part of an investigation into the bodies that he, Graham, had discovered in the crawl space while he was clawing his way to freedom? That's one he'd have to think about but now was not the time. Now was the time to step forward, claim complete control of his new body, stall the sheriff, and silence the two nosey interlopers.

Lee felt the hunting knife drop from his phantom hand, lose its cohesion, and disappear into the Ether from which he had summoned it. Then he stepped forward. The real world in front of him swam in his vision, so he blinked what were once upon a time his son's eyes to clear it. His view came into sharp focus just in time for him to see the fur-covered, angry face of the dog creature closing down on him from somewhere in mid-air. At first it resembled Grace Afton then, in rapid succession, it transformed: first it was his dead wife Anna's face, then it was Darek Afton, then a face he thought might be the stripper from Bombshell's. There was a brief transition after the stripper into something that looked like an English bulldog. Then, just before it hit him, there was this body's own face glaring at him: the face of Graham Gordon.

The front paws of the black dog were stretched out in front of it, as if it were some kind of super dog flying to the rescue. Strange tendrils of bright yellow light were tethered to each of its legs. One of those beams connected to the camera the skinny man had set up. Two others connected directly to the black girl and the skinny man. The beam that connected to the black girl was attached to the hand in which she held her phone. The beam that was attached to the skinny man appeared to be connected to his hip. Another beam connected from the creature to the right front pocket of Lee's beige uniform pants. All of these beams were pulsing, as if they were drawing some kind of power from the sources to which they were connected. A final beam shot out of the back of the creature's head. It blew out one of the front windows of the old house and connected to something outside that Lee could not see.

Lee had time to utter a single startled gasp before he felt those paws land directly in the center of his brand new chest. The force knocked him backward. There was time to see the world panning down in front of him. The skinny man and the black reporter woman were staring at him with wide eyes and open mouths. Then their faces were gone, and he was staring at the old and yellowed ceiling of the main living area of his house. Then that, too, was gone, and his vision was filled with a pattern of gray cinder block as he plummeted backward and headlong into the cellar below.

He tried to scramble back inside the stream of consciousness he had shared with his son for a time, to protect himself from the pain of the impact and whatever injuries the physical body might incur, but he found that he could not. Now that there was only a single consciousness occupying Graham's physical body, there was no one behind him that he could shove forward. By grabbing the reigns of Graham's body after dispatching with his consciousness, he had trapped himself in that body. As long as it was alive, he would feel its pain and suffer the consequences of whatever he did.

The impact when he hit the hardened earth of the cellar floor was both bloody and brutal. Lee Gordon smashed into the floor head-first, completely missing any of the remaining standing structure of the cellar stairs on his flight down. He felt the anvil hardness of the floor as it caved in the top of his skull, exploding fragments of bone shrapnel that lodged themselves in the soft flesh of his brain. The angle of his fall along with gravity's tug at his flailing legs snapped his neck, causing the back of his head to touch his shoulder blades as the rest of his son's—*his*—body crashed to the floor. He caught a brief glimpse of the light of outdoors in the distance, through the secret crawl space door. That vision was then replaced by darkness and a horrible *pop* sound as his head rolled onto a rusted old nail that was protruding from one of the broken treads of the cellar stairs that lay on the floor beneath him. It punctured his right eyeball and became stuck there. He could feel the gel within his eye oozing out of the socket and onto his cheek.

Lee tried to scream. He tried to cry. He tried to call for help: from the black girl, from her cuckold, from the old bat, from the sheriff, from his long dead and gone mother who might be the only person in the world to have ever loved him, from anyone. He was no longer able to make a sound.

When the dust settled, Lee found that he was still at least partially sighted in his left eye. He could not move his head to look around himself, but he was able to perceive two sad human eyes staring back at him from just outside the hole in the wall that led into the crawl space. The dog with the constantly transforming face was seated there, staring at him, watching him leave the world. It seemed to be getting taller as he looked at it. Then there were two of it, or maybe three. Shadows of figures began to pour out of the creature's back, head, and chest. They rose to varied heights, but they all appeared to have a vaguely human shape that became more so as the shadows first transitioned to black mists, and then to swirling masses of matter that eventually congealed into entities. There were six of them in all, including the dog, which appeared to now be just a dog. It was an English bulldog—a black one, in fact—just like Graham's pet Butch who had pissed all over Lee's hardwood floors. It sat there with its tongue lolling out and a stupid dog grin on its face, just as it always had in life.

To the left of the mutt, with her hand gently scratching it behind the ears, knelt the figure of Lee's dead wife and Graham's mother Anna Gordon. He felt a surge of his former love for her when the recognition dawned on him. He tried to speak to her, but could not grab air and could no longer work the muscles in his mouth. She did not acknowledge him except to stare at his one remaining eye. She stared without any kind of hint of satisfaction over the circumstances that had befallen him, but also without affection and without pity.

Beside his dead wife stood the large-breasted blonde woman from Bombshell's, the one who had spurned his advances in her off-duty hours and whom he'd had to kill for her slight. She looked satisfied enough for both herself and his wife. She glared at him with what he used to call a "shit-eating grin" spread across the lower half of her face and a "gotcha" look in her eyes. It was the kind of disrespectful look he would have killed her for if he hadn't already killed her in decades prior.

Next to the stripper stood the stoic figure of Grace Afton. She was holding hands with Darek, her dead husband and Lee's former carbon plant coworker that he had murdered and left propped against the obelisk in the middle of Lost Hollow's town square. Grace looked sad, just as she had while she'd been the face of the dog. Darek somehow managed to look angry, ecstatic, and vengeful all at the same time. With his free hand, he flipped the bird at what was about to be Lee Gordon's second body to have died as a result of tumbling into the cellar of his own house. The gesture enraged Lee, but no one would have been able to tell because he could no longer manage facial expressions. The body he had stolen from his son was paralyzed, entirely without willful muscle stimulation and motor control.

At the farthest end of the spectral lineup stood the ghost of his son, Graham Gordon, the boy whose consciousness he had only moments before sliced apart with an Ethereal hunting knife and vanquished, banishing him from what had once been his own body. He wondered if that had been his mistake. Would the dog thing have leaped at him and pushed him over if it were possible that his son was still alive somewhere inside there? Lee didn't think so. He thought it was because the dog thing somehow knew that Graham was no longer inside the body that had leaped at him. Had Graham been inside the dog thing at the end? He supposed it didn't matter now. It had sure as hell looked that way. His dead son stared at his own soon-to-be empty shell with what appeared to be some combination of wonder and regret. There was loneliness there, too. Lee wondered if it was the same loneliness that was suddenly welling up inside him now as he was about to once again become ripped from the flesh. It was the loneliness he had felt over all those years as he wandered bodiless among the rooms and corridors of this old house, no one to talk to, no one with whom to share the experience. For the past twenty-four hours, he had at least been able to think at his son, and his son had been able to think back at him. Now there was a disconnect. Nothing. There was just a pair of eyes watching him die.

The world dimmed. The heart that beat in the chest of the man Lee Gordon had hoped to become thumped loudly one last time and was still. Before the last of the synapses in his brain fired and went out, Lee watched the dog, Butch, leap into the hole in the cinder block wall and disappear in the crawl space beyond. He was followed immediately by Anna, and her by the large-breasted woman from Bombshell's, who Lee thought was a nice package even in death. Grace and Darek Afton climbed into the crawl space together, Darek with one arm around her waist as they did. Then, finally, it was Graham's turn. He hesitated, seemed about to approach the dying body on the floor in front of him, but then changed his mind and climbed into the crawl space instead. He glanced back once before he faded from view. He looked like he was crying.

All alone on the floor of the cellar that had hidden his alcohol abuse, his murders, and his terrified beyond all rational thought young son those many years ago, Lee Gordon passed from earthly darkness and into the eternal void.

CHAPTER TWENTY-TWO

Thereʼs was a loud crash just out of sight. A cloud of dust rose from the maw of the cellar door into the lights thrown at it from Staff's video setup. Then there was silence. Staff stared at the empty door frame for a minute, blinked, and then looked at Afia, who also gaped incredulously at the empty space left by the scene of Graham and Lee Gordon's fall. Where Graham Gordon's body had previously stood there was now only the blackness of the cellar beyond. With no one to call out to, no one to plead with to stop the nonsense and come away from the edge of the abyss, there seemed to be nothing left to say.

In the end, it had not been Graham who had taken his own life, anyway. As Staff and Afia had stood there pleading with him, the little black dog creature that was actually one part dog and at least three parts human had leaped into the light from the shadows just behind them. She had bound like a deer jumping a fence at the side of the road on a cold morning in early winter. She had bound as if her hind legs were made of springs. She had hit Graham Gordon in the dead center of his chest and sent him plummeting into the cellar. Staff had seen him fall, tumbling over headlong in the process. Grace Afton and the rest of the dog creature had vanished into thin air after the hit, just as if she'd never actually been there.

"Should we check on him?" Afia asked, finally. She directed the question at Staff but did not look away from the cellar door, as if she expected the thick fingers of the man who'd just fallen to his death to crook themselves over the frame at any moment.

"No, I think you'd better let us do that," said a voice from somewhere behind them. It startled them both.

Staff glanced around to discover a tall, stout man with a thick salt-and-pepper mustache that swept his upper lip. On his hip was a shiny black holster and on his chest was an even more brilliant Hollow County Sheriff's Department badge. The man poked his head out the front door of the house and shouted "Come on, boys," at which point two EMTs carrying an extension ladder and medical bags started in. One of them sported rolled-up sleeves and a smear of grime across his forehead.

"I'm going to need you two to get this shit out of our way," the mustachioed man added, indicating the lights and news camera. "You're not to film anything we do, understand? That'd be a HIPAA violation for sure. This is private property."

Staff wasn't so sure, but after nodding approval from Afia, he began to tear down the camera anyway as the EMTs scurried past him, towing the extension ladder that he had dropped in the front yard. "He can leave the lights up if he wants to be helpful," the one with the dirt-streaked forehead said over his shoulder. "There aren't any on down there, and this switch on the wall inside the door doesn't seem to do anything."

The sheriff grimaced as if he hated to have to ask for any favors from those mainstream media liberal socialist elites at Channel 6 News, which was not a Fox News affiliate. He took off his hat, mopped his brow with his forearm, and then replaced it, grinning patronizingly at Staff. "Well?" he said. "Do you mind leaving the lights up then so our boys can see what they're doing down there?"

Staff folded his arms. "Not my call," he said, and tilted his head at Afia, making sure the sheriff knew that she was indeed the boss of this story. A part of him, in fact, regretted the frustration and anger that had led him to set all this up without Afia's input and say-so. Another part of him was glad he had because, at long last, they had all the pieces of a story for the evening news. It wasn't precisely what they'd been out to get—a Halloween fluff piece—but it was most definitely news.

The sheriff sighed, annoyed, and looked at Afia. There was recognition in his eyes. "We'd like to keep the lights on, Miss Afton," he said, "so the boys can see what they're doing when they bring him out. They'll have to use flash-lights while they're down there, and that's a lot to handle when you're trying to save a life."

"Be my guest, sheriff," she replied. "We'll wait outside until you're done. I'd also like to talk with you about all this before we leave. This and a few other things from a few years ago. You know, for the story?"

He nodded. "Yeah. I'm going to have some questions for you, too. You know, for the police report? You'll need to come down to the station for that, though. So just hold your horses on that leaving bit." He formed air quotes around the word "leaving." He started to turn his back to her, then stopped and grinned. "How was the foster care system, by the way? Looks like you took my advice and did better than your daddy, eh?"

Afia did not answer him.

The two EMTs lowered the extension ladder into the pit and climbed down, the second man waiting for the all clear from the first before he made the descent. Staff took the opportunity to move the LED light rigs closer to the cellar door, allowing more light to pour into the darkness beyond. From somewhere below, he heard a voice say, "Dear God." Then there were the hurried sounds of medical bags being opened and tools being extracted.

"Abe?" a masculine voice called out from the darkness of the cellar. "Abe, you might want to get down here and bring your lamp. We've got a situation."

The sheriff, looking caught off guard, strolled to the mouth of the cellar door and peered down, blocking much of the light that Staff had just shined on the situation. "That you, Ben? Thought you were checking out that crawl space the Blankenship woman told us about."

"Yeah," the voice called back. It was a young sounding masculine voice, and quavery with either nerves or excitement. "I am. It goes straight through to a big old hole in the cellar wall here. There are bones in there, Abe. Human bones. Old ones, from the look of it. I've counted at least two skulls and what looks like the fingers of a hand so far. It's a tight fit in there, though. I'm going to need some help."

Abe, the sheriff, shook his head. "Fat fucker needs to stop with the carb-heavy lunches," he muttered. Then he grabbed the radio mic from his shoulder and pressed the Talk button. "Jer, it's Abe. We're going to need the coroner out here on the double."

"Jesus, Chief, did he off himself?" came the reply after a burst of static.

One of the EMTs overheard the question and shouted up from beyond the cellar's darkness. "Mr. Gordon is dead, sheriff. There's nothing we can do for him now."

"Stupid weakling shit," Wickham muttered. "Never was anything like his dad." He pressed the button on his mic. "Looks that way. But we've got a bigger problem than that. There's more than one body. You call the coroner and then get Hoff to help you tape off the scene. I want the whole perimeter, front yard and all. No one else besides the coroner gets in, you got me?"

"Got it, chief."

"And tell the Blankenship woman not to go anywhere. We're going to need to talk to her, too."

"Yes, sir. Understood. Over and out."

Staff looked around at Afia, who motioned for him to follow her outside. From the front porch, they could see sheriff's deputies dutifully unspooling crime scene tape. They were, indeed, enclosing the entire perimeter of the old house, including the area of dead-end road in which

Graham Gordon's Tacoma and the Channel 6 News S-10 were parked. Just outside the tape sat two Hollow County Sheriff's Department patrol cars and something that looked a lot like the *Ghostbusters* car that Jeremy Beard had described to them that morning. Behind the wheel of that vehicle sat Beard himself, looking on the scene in amazement.

"Hey!" Staff called. "Hey! You're blocking us in!"

"Sheriff's orders," a deputy who sounded like he was probably the "Jer" that Abe the sheriff had been communicating with over the radio called back. "Also procedure. No one new gets in and no one who was here when whatever this was happened gets out."

"Great," Staff said and looked at Afia. "What the hell are we supposed to do now?"

She shrugged. "File our story with the station, I guess. We have our equipment. No one's said anything about gagging us just because we're on this side of the tape." A tear, from either mourning or exhaustion, crept from the corner of her eye, the underside of which had swollen significantly from where Lee Gordon had dealt his blow to that side of her face.

"You want to have the EMTs look at that?" Staff asked. He was examining the plump contusion that had formed on her cheek.

"Magic of makeup," she replied. "I'll be fine. Besides, it's not the first time people will have seen television reporters who have become part of the story. Remember how all those cable news guys looked on 9/11? Some of them were literally covered in ashes and dust."

Staff nodded. "Yeah. Are you going to be able to do this knowing that your mother was one of Gordon's victims? Her bones might be in that crawl space."

Afia pursed her lips together. "I'll be fine, I think. I haven't processed all this yet. All my life, I had assumed my mother had run out on us. That's what my father said, anyway. I guess he was protecting me. Now that I know that my suspicions about Lee Gordon were right all this time and that my mother was also a victim...well, I don't really know what I'm feeling right now. Part of me is relieved to know that I was right about that nasty old man. Another part of me is sad that my own father wasn't honest with me about what he must have known had happened to my mother. Then another part of me is just glad to see the beginning of some closure." She turned to face him. "I mourned both of my parents years ago when I was still a child. I'll always miss them, and I'll always wish things hadn't happened the way that they happened. But I also have it within my power as a journalist to be part of the force that finally brings *them* some closure, if not exactly justice. I need to do my part."

Staff nodded. He understood.

A hand fell on his shoulder just then. He turned to face its owner. Patsy Blankenship had somehow made her way onto the front porch without either of them noticing she was there. Her enormous eyes were wet with tears behind those Coke-bottle glasses. Mascara had run from her lower lids and pooled in smeary black puddles where her glasses frames met her cheeks. Across her wrinkled forehead was a purplish, painful looking lump where her own iPhone had struck her during their first experience with the black dog that turned out to not be a dog at all.

"This isn't what I wanted," she said. "I'm sorry you two had to deal with all this and have nothing to show for it."

"'Had to' would be the operative word there," Staff replied. "Based on what we know now, I think we might have been meant to be here. Well, Afia anyway.

"Besides, we do have a story to report. It's just not the Halloween fluff that we were sent here to get. It's supernatural enough, though. All three of us got video of the black bi—uh, the spirit creature, didn't we? I mean, it's right here on our phones." He plucked his iPhone from the hip of his cargo shorts as evidence.

"That's what I mean, though," Patsy said. "Remember how Mr. Beard told us that all the evidence on his phone disappeared? Well, I tried to show the video I took of the dog to both the sheriff and Mr. Beard when we pulled in here. When I went looking for it, nothing was there. Well, not nothing. There was video of us tracking her across the front of the house and around the corner, but the dog creature herself wasn't in the shot. There's just nothing there, even though we all saw it with our own eyes."

Staff and Afia simultaneously opened their Apple Photos app and examined the video that they had recorded of the creature that morning. They looked at their screens, at each other, and then back at their screens in disbelief. Patsy was right. Just like what happened with the video that Jeremy Beard had recorded through the rear window of the Gordon house, their videos were stored, but the creature herself was not in them. It was as if they had all been pretending to record a beast, maybe to have it inserted in post-production CGI, except that there was not even a green-clad place-holder creature in the shot. Instead, they watched image after image of dead grass, wood siding, and portions of cinder block wall that served as a foundation scroll by on their screens.

"Now what?" Staff asked Afia.

"What do we have on the Channel 6 camera?"

Staff hefted the device and jogged with it to the S-10. He connected it to a playback device there. All three survivors of the Gordon place watched that morning's recordings unfold for a second time.

There was Graham Gordon, standing at the precipice of the cellar, convinced that plummeting to this death was the only way to stop the madness. Previous to that, there was nothing but an open cellar door with lights trained on it. Staff allowed the video to play up through the moment when he and Afia had seen the black dog leap from the shadows and shove the man into the cellar, but there was no dog in the shot. There was only a sudden look of shock that spread across Graham Gordon's face, followed by his tipping over backward into the cellar. The last frame of him showed the grooved soles of his Wolverine work boots as they disappeared into the darkness below the door.

Afia, who had been watching the playback over Staff's shoulder, sniffled. "Well," she said, "we still have a news story. We have everything Graham told us before he died. We're going to have to rely on law enforcement and foren-sics to prove what he said about his father and the bones in

the crawl space, but the truth will come out. The truth will
come out. It always does. The only thing we've really lost
here is the most unbelievable part of the story, the supernatural part. So maybe that's for the best."

She turned to face both Staff and Patsy, clasping each of
them by a hand. "Let's make a pact here, while we're alone.
We do not discuss what we can't prove about what happened
here today. Staff, you and I will collect our footage of the
constable and report on that. To our viewers, it will look like
the ravings of a mind that had snapped after being trapped
in the cellar overnight, but that won't diminish the physical
evidence that it turned up in the crawl space."

Patsy piped up then. "What about Mr. Beard? What
about the sheriff? I told them about some of this while I
was showing them the video."

"But there was nothing on the video, right?" Staff said.
"So maybe you were just a little too excited about your ghost
tours business, eh? You made a few mountains out of mole-
hills over it. No one could blame you for that."

"Patsy, I'll want you on-camera, too," Afia continued.
"We're going to need you to fill in some of the backstories
that we don't have now because we don't have my mother's
words on video. I can fill in the stuff from my childhood,
but I'll need you to explain who Graham Gordon is and
make the connections from him to the house and why he
was out here in the first place."

The older woman looked as if she might be about to pro-
test. Staff interjected before she could. "Afia, what if we
promise Patsy to go out to the old cemetery on the other
side of town for our Halloween special?" He turned to

Patsy. "We'll do the Halloween special story to give Lost Hollow some positive attention if you'll help us with this. It's an important story, and if we don't get it straight from you, the other stations and outlets will get only the sheriff's department's version from police reports. I don't need to tell you that rural sheriffs don't make for the best PR people."

That seemed to convince her.

"All right," she said. "But you promise?" She looked pleadingly from Staff to Afia. Afia glanced at Staff, not without a little admonishment, then smiled and nodded.

"Sure, we'll see what we can do."

"Great!" Staff exclaimed. He disconnected the playback device, heaved the Channel 6 News camera onto his right shoulder, and looked at Afia. "It's settled, then. Where do you want to set up our shot?"

***

By the time Afia, Staff, and Patsy Blankenship shot their segments for the story about the tragic death of Lost Hollow's newly elected constable Graham Gordon, the Hollow County medical examiner had arrived with a minimal forensics team. A second—and now unnecessary—ambulance had arrived as well. Jeremy Beard, on the other hand, had been shown off the property. Staff thought he had looked none too pleased about being ushered away, but at least he'd have a story to tell his cosplayer friends.

The M.E. was overseeing the extraction of human bones from the crawl space as well as the body of Graham from the floor of the cellar of the old Gordon place. Afia filed the first part of her story about Graham with Channel 6, ensuring that they would break the news, and also teasing that more information from officials would be reported as it became available. Before nightfall, the area of dead-end street outside the sheriff's department's crime scene tape would be filled with lights, cameras, on-air reporters, and vans from the station's regional competitors. All of them would vie for the most exclusive access and information, but none of them would ever get as close to the story as Afia Afton and her cameraman Joe "Staff" Stafford.

The two women and the cameraman had moved away from the front porch of the old house and were leaning against the side of the Channel 6 News S-10, awaiting their interviews with the officials now in charge of the scene as well as their individual "interviews" that would take place down at the station later that night. By the time the sheriff himself reappeared from within the bowels of the old Gordon place, the Saturday autumn sunshine was casting long shadows of late afternoon across the front yard. The phantom fingers of trees that had already become barren of their leaves clawed at the clumps of dead grass that lined the driveway. Light breezes tickled their branches, making them appear to be moving of their own accord.

Now and then, there was a creaking sound from somewhere above them. Looking around, Staff surmised that it was coming from the hinges of the dome of an old security light that was stationed at the edge of the driveway. The dome had at some point become unfastened and was dangling from its arm on top of the pole. It swung there at the mercy of gusts of autumn wind.

Eventually, the sun sank below the tree line of the woods behind the house, darkening the front yard and all who remained on it. Soon after, the swinging askew security light flickered on in the dusk.

ACKNOWLEDGMENTS

No author's work is created entirely in a vacuum. For *The Gordon Place*, I owe a debt of gratitude to a number of unique and talented individuals, including all of the following:

- David Karner of ScareScapes for his suggestion several years ago that I attempt a novel.
- Brynda Baker, Emily Ramsey, and David P. Kolb for serving as volunteer beta readers and providing invaluable feedback on an early draft of this story. The results of their individual feedback is present throughout.
- Starr, Nia, and Jesse of Quiethouse Editing for their beta reading services. Without their input, this story would have been a significantly different experience.
- Paula Rozelle Hanback for once again designing an epic cover for my use in this book. Paula has so far designed covers for all my books.

ALSO BY ISAAC THORNE

ROAD KILLS is a collection of short tales of dark horror from the mind of Isaac Thorne. These stories are all connected to travel, to the road. It is always lurking there, just waiting for you to come out for a drive or a walk or a jog.

However you next confront it, the road is already there, plotting.

And waiting.

For you.

Available at paperback and ebook retailers everywhere.

ABOUT THE AUTHOR

Isaac Thorne is a nice man who has, over the course of his life, developed a modest ability to spin a good yarn. Really. He promises. You can find him on Twitter @isaacrthorne or on Facebook at facebook.com/isaacrthorne. Just don't push him down a flight of stairs.

In addition to writing horror, Isaac reviews horror movies for TNHorror.com and TheHorrorcist.com. He is also the host of audio narration shows *Thorne's Theater of Terror* and *Classic Cuts* on SCRM Radio, which is a 24/7/365 internet radio station available online at scrmradio.com.

THANK YOU

Isaac Thorne and Lost Hollow Books appreciate the time you've devoted to this novel. If you like what you've read, please consider reviewing the book on Goodreads or wherever you review books. Ratings and reviews help books like these become discovered by other readers like you.

9 781938 271458